D0104693

THE
OTHER
SHOE

THE OTHER SHOE

Matt Pavelich

COUNTERPOINT
BERKELEY

This is a work of fiction. Names, characters, places, and incidents are the product of the author's imagination or are used fictitiously. Any resemblance to actual persons, living or dead, is entirely coincidental.

Library of Congress Cataloging-in-Publication Data is available.

ISBN: 978-1-58243-795-8

Cover design by Silverander Communications
Interior design by meganjonesdesign.com

Printed in the United States of America

COUNTERPOINT
1919 Fifth Street
Berkeley, CA 94710
www.counterpointpress.com

Distributed by Publishers Group West

10 9 8 7 6 5 4 3 2 1

To Nick and Riley, and to George Withrow

Whoso removeth stones shall be hurt therewith; and he that cleaveth wood shall be endangered thereby.

ECCLESIASTES 10:9

Proceed then, my Lords, with that sentence which the law directs—I am prepared to hear it. I trust I am prepared to meet its execution. I shall go, I think, with a light heart before a higher tribunal, a tribunal where a judge of infinite goodness, as well as of infinite justice, will preside, and where, my Lords, many, many of the judgments of this world will be reversed.

—THOMAS FRANCIS MEAGHER, IN HIS *SPEECH FROM THE DOCK*

prologue

C ALVIN TEAGUE WALKED out of Red Plain at four thirty one August afternoon carrying an old Boy Scout backpack to which he had strapped a flannel sleeping bag. Grasshoppers rattled in the weeds, and the tar of Highway 200 was soft underfoot. Too shy and too well brought up to hitchhike, he marched through an indifferently farmed mountain valley with his back turned to oncoming traffic to discourage the offer of a ride. Sweat rolled down his neck. He had no hat for his freckled head, and he hadn't thought to bring any water.

For some miles he continued to smell cut alfalfa, but as he walked he never actually saw this harvest. Pastel homes had been trucked in and flung around the landscape to subsist on ten-acre plots in gardens of tired machinery; some of them were also beauty salons or secondhand stores or shops for small engine repair. Concrete figurines of Mother Goose and Snow White were offered for sale on someone's tiny lawn where a hand-lettered sign said,

U PAINT OR WE PAINT
ALWAYS YOU'RE CHOICE

He passed a herd of squat black cows, several grain fields plowed under. From the shade of a fading barn, a barnyard dog shot out to bark and bare teeth at him. Teague retreated through the far borrow ditch. Drenched in a new, clammy sweat, and extremely alert, he went

1

on, and when he came to an astonished cat lying flattened on the road he raised his eyes for relief—for the larger vista. Even the mountains had been molested. Square tracts had been cut into the mantling forests; in the clear-cuts, gray undergrowth was revealed, and gray shale and gray dirt. The clear-cuts looked, in fact, like vast incrustations of mange. The people who lived on this land were corrupting a great beauty, and Teague, raised on judgment and forgiveness, could not help but dislike them for it. Time and again cars bearing local license plates politely slowed for him; time and again, also politely, he waved them on.

His legs, unaccustomed to much sun at all, soon hinted pink, and he ducked into a culvert to change back into his long pants. In the pipe he smelled wet loam and moss, and he supposed this was it, some of the adventure he'd vaguely intended. On the strength of this notion he went on, his own man now, and he achieved a pleasing, ground-eating lope that brought him by late afternoon to the mouth of a long canyon at the valley's western end. Here the highway and a railroad track converged to run close along the north bank of a river on either side of which slabs of rock reared thousands of feet up out of the scree, the earth's massively broken crust.

In the canyon he smelled creosote, road tar, a field of mint, alfalfa still, and even the rocks, which seemed to breathe some cautionary odor. He walked under and then into the sun for hours, storing the day for use against all those impending beige days, all the plodding days and years that lay just ahead of him. He must be certain to remember exactly how far he'd walked, how tired he'd been, remember how once, one endless day of his twenty-fourth year, he'd exceeded himself out in a wild place where nature held him in benign contempt. So Teague was proud of himself, proud even of his raging thirst until he realized that the answer to it had been with him all day, that he'd been walking beside the river, more or less, for about as long as he'd been walking. Adventurer? Not really.

He crossed the railroad tracks and climbed a high mesh fence; he caught his pants leg on its top strand and fell to the other side to lie for a long moment on his back, on the railroad's vicious red roadbed rock. He crossed a field that caked his socks with burs. The river at this point was a solemn green thing sliding by like muscle under flesh, and there were no easy approaches to it. Hips working like a skier's, Teague slid down a steep gravel bank, his shoes filling intolerably with sand and small pebbles. He was standing one-legged on the little bit of beach and had removed a shoe and was brushing at his foot when he lost his balance; the naked foot escaped his grasp to rest very briefly on a round, slick stone in the river. Then he was sitting in the river, chest into the current and cooling rapidly.

The water didn't bear him away at first, but he couldn't stand. Each time he scrambled and fell back he landed a little farther into the current with his mouth a little nearer to going under. Then he was flailing, his butt bumping backward on the rocks, so Teague, not quite gone to panic yet, slipped off his backpack, and away it went—with the weight of that wet sleeping bag, and his shoe, and, as he would soon learn, everything. Sliding downstream and sinking out of sight. He rose only to fall back again, hard and deep. Then, breathing river, he finally managed to collect his feet under himself and stand. He could only just stand at first. The current was to his thighs and powerful, but then, with much the same caution with which he'd taken his very first steps, he took the few steps to the treacherous little beach and climbed the crumbling bank.

He lay down in knapweed, a new misery. Thirsty. Worse, much worse than before. The turban he'd made of his T-shirt was still wrapped round his head. So thirsty, but with every searing breath he was freshly resolved not to try the river again. Limping a bit for want of the shoe, he made his way back to the road. He thought he was between fifteen and twenty miles from Red Plain and about that

3

far from the next town on Highway 200, a town whose name he had already forgotten. He'd somehow retained his road map, of all things, but it was useless, fuzzy and illegible when he peeled its leaves apart. He knew only that he was at some far edge of a far state. He stood at the side of the road in his wet shoe, and his crotch was wet and chafed, somehow, even as he stood stock-still. Usually no one's fool, Teague hoped and expected that this would serve as the worst moment of his life. Nose blistering, lips pale, he was filled with all the old doubts and many new ones. He'd confirmed himself now as a little hometown fellow, fit to run a small circuit through thoroughly expected events, to live a prudent life. Why had he ever made himself available to all these accidents? He recalled his mother mentioning that as a toddler he'd suffered night terrors, and he remembered them, the feel of them at least, because they were all he'd known that might compare with being so much alone. He prayed, but not for deliverance, as he wasn't sure he deserved it. More sunset. It seemed stalled. As much as he feared the coming dark, he liked the long and lengthening shadows even less.

From the direction of Red Plain an engine labored toward him, the first familiar sound since he'd been standing by the road. A truck came out from the pines to the east of him and onto the open flat, a ponderous load of cordwood cinched to its bed. A chainsaw and a gas can and a mongrel rode on top of the load. Teague raised his arms like a referee signaling a touchdown. He felt foolish about the gesture, the extent of his problem. The truck came on—behind the wheel, under a black baseball cap, a pretty mouth rounded in an "O" of decent concern. Someone female. The truck slowed, accelerated again, passing him, then stopped a hundred yards down the road. Weaving half on and half off the pavement, it rapidly backed toward him, the big load rocking laterally, and if Teague had been healthier then, or more capably concerned for his survival, he'd have been running well before it finally, abruptly stopped, its bumper not ten feet from his knee. A bumper bent by previous misuse, a mottled dog grinning down at him. The driver leaned out. "Hey," she said. It was a statement, a question, whatever he wanted it to be. She seemed friendly.

She stepped out of her truck and came back to him. Teague's throat was parchment and he could not trust himself to speak. She closed the small distance between them, a woman, a girl, a person of about his own age, whatever that made her. Wide suspenders framed her breasts and she wore boots that made her throw her legs in a rolling gait. Some kind of logger's getup. Over her right shoulder lay a thickly plaited chestnut braid, but she walked like a bully at the county fair. Two-cycle gas, sawdust, beer—he smelled her drawing near. "Hey," she said again. Gently, so gently. Her hands were larger and rougher than his own, but for all that she conformed to some very latent and very odd idea of femininity he'd been carrying around with him, never knowing or so much as suspecting his own secret tastes. Accustomed to the company of plainer, softer women, Teague could think of nothing to say to the one now regarding him like a found lamb.

"You okay, honey?"

Teague's instincts, such as they were, were never of much use to him, but he was ready to trust the belief he'd instantly formed—more than that, he meant to rely on it—that the girl was the soul of kindness.

"I saw you earlier," she said. "Earlier in the day. You were a little ways down the road. What happened to all that stuff you had? That pack, and where's your other shoe?"

He'd wet his tongue enough to ask for, "Water?"

"Don't have any. Except in the radiator, which has probably got some antifreeze in it. Got beer, though."

"I'm a pharmacist," he declared. "Or I will be. And alcohol, if you're already dehydrated, alcohol . . . "

"It's Miller High Life," she said, "champagne of bottled beer. You better have some."

His education and former resolve fell away from him, useless. Teague reached for his wallet. He'd left it in his cutoffs, and his cutoffs were in the pack, and the pack—"I couldn't pay you anything, I lost all my money in the river. I'm really getting to be in a bad spot."

"Pay me? What kinda person you think I am?"

He'd never seen anything like her, eyes as beautiful as Easter eggs, and sweetly and cautiously glancing off Teague as if he were someone of interest. In the cab of her truck she pulled two sweating bottles from her cooler, twisted their caps off. She toasted him, and the report of that faint collision traveled well up Teague's arm. This girl was the biggest surprise he was ever likely to encounter.

"Where you coming from?"

"Courville, Iowa." How fondly he said it. How fondly he meant it. Home. "And Iowa City, too. School, you know."

"So, whadda they say? In Iowa?"

"Say? About . . . ?"

"'Cheers'? Or 'Here's to Mabel'? Or what?"

"Oh. 'To good health'?"

"Sure. You could use some."

The beer tasted, he thought, like superior bread, and felt like quicksilver at the back of his throat. He tried to savor it, but his thirst wouldn't let him. He drained the bottle in three long pulls, burped in rapture into his soft fist. "Excuse me. But that is quite the . . . Are you Mabel, then?"

"Am I . . . ? Oh, no. That was just an example. Of something they might say."

"Well, you'll think this is kind of funny," Calvin Teague admitted, "but I took a vow. When I was thirteen, I was at church camp, and I told Pastor Stensvold I'd never touch a drop. Of alcohol. And I haven't either. Until now. You wouldn't believe the grief I sometimes took at school. Even the real Christian guys in the house, everybody, they all loved this stuff. Now I see why. But, anyway, I wasn't too good at baseball or camp crafts, so I just took that vow. I was sort of caught up in the spirit."

"What that preacher don't know can't hurt him."

"No," he said. "They say at home, what my folks always say, anyway, is 'Ignorance is not bliss.' So I think I'll have to tell him, if I can still find him. I think if you make a vow, and then break it, you have to tell the person."

There was wonder in the girl's eyes. "You are a straight shooter," she said. "I like that. Or I think I do."

His hands felt as if they were floating above his lap.

"I've never met a pharmacist," she said. "Except for the ones in the drugstores, when they hand you your pills."

"If I've passed my boards," said Teague, gaudy in his honesty now. "And then when I'm certified, then I'll be, you know . . . "

"Certified. Wow. I've never met anybody from Iowa either. Where'd you say you were goin'?"

"I wanted to see the ocean."

"The ocean?" she asked. "The Pacific? Well, I couldn't get you that far, but I could sure feed you." Her wrist was hooked over the steering wheel, and as she drove off with him, some of her braid worked free and issued like vapor from behind her ear. Everything he noticed about her was new to him, and extravagant, and sweet. It occurred to him that if she was tender at all it must be because she thought him an idiot. Calvin Teague, the third generation of Teague Drugs in Courville and Handy, Iowa. He expected eventually to live in a brick residence on Mill Pond Lane and to serve on the school board and the boards of the better local charities, and he thought he'd probably marry the deeply loyal Janice Hartnett who stood to inherit Hartnett

Seed; his ordered and placid life had rarely needed explaining. He was unfailingly pleasant and obvious and, really, there was not much to be explained. But, oh, to somehow convince this girl what a capable fellow he was, despite present evidence to the contrary, in spite of how she'd found him.

"You know," he said, "I had it all planned out. Everything. I checked all the fluid levels and belts and the spare tire and everything before I left home. It was going along fine, too. Until this morning. I stopped to take a picture of an eagle, I think it was, a real big bird—oh man, the camera's gone, too—but anyway, when I got back in to go, the K car wouldn't start. So there I was, middle of nowhere, about a mile the other side of that Pair O' Dice bar, so I walked up there and must've had three cups of coffee before the tow truck finally came out from Red Plain."

"K car? That's a Plymouth, isn't it? One of those old Plymouths?"

"Or a Chrysler or something. But mine's been very, or mostly, it's held up really well so far. I've made zero major repairs to it. Until now. Then in Red Plain, I find out it's the wiring harness. A fuse failed and the whole thing burnt out. They said it might be as long as a week before they can get another one because of the age of the car, which is not so old, or so I thought, but he said there's so few of these left on the road they're like antiques already—you should've seen the rubber on those wires."

"I bet you went to Larry's Conoco, didn't you?"

"They were the ones who sent out the truck. They were the only ones in the phone book with towing service. But they did finally come along and get me, so I was very glad about that."

"And I bet you talked to Larry." She seemed dumbfounded at his haplessness.

He had been captive in Red Plain to a man with a prominent Adam's apple, a grave manner, and his name stitched on his shirt:

Larry. It had never occurred to him to disbelieve the serious mechanic. Now if, along with everything else, he'd been swindled, he didn't want to know about it. It seemed he was an oaf in nature, lost in the lay of the land, and also, possibly, a poor judge of character. "I only had a week and a half to make this whole trip," he told the girl, "so I thought I'd just set out kind of hiking."

"To see what you could see."

"Exactly." She understood him after all.

"But you're still quite a ways from the coast. Especially without your shoe."

"Well, I wasn't, I didn't intend to . . . As I said, I'm in kind of a spot."

She hummed a tune having to do, he thought, with a faithful dog, something numbing from kindergarten or Bible school, barely audible over her ratcheting engine. She turned off the highway and onto a dirt road threading first through cottonwood and birch, and then into an endless stand of ragged pine that crowded the road so closely as to form a corridor. A girl in huge boots. He never would have imagined.

"Sorry," she said. It did not seem to him that she was yelling, though she was. "Scraped the muffler off last week. Kinda got high centered. It's pretty loud if you're not used to it."

Less anxious about love than anyone he knew, he had always expected that it would come to him, eventually, in some stately way befitting his patience. A comfortable, durable love. He leaned out his window to clear his head; the air was turpentine. His sober self floated near, there in the gummy ether with Janice and his mother, and they were all disappointed in him. He was another man entirely than the boy he'd been this morning, but he knew that if he said so the girl would think he was getting carried away. As he happened to be.

"You married?" she wondered as if from far away. "Got a girlfriend or anything?"

He felt much as he had while sitting in the river; the girl had asked a simple question, she'd want a simple answer. "No," he said.

"Any kids?"

"Kids?" Calvin Teague could not remotely see himself as a family man, not yet, but this girl seemed to think it feasible. Girls. Women. They were to him the furthest, strangest end of biochemistry. This girl, at least, did not seem deliberately to confuse. He liked her very much. She made a second turn and they began to mount a road that had in some recent season been a streambed, the surface was still channeled and the truck wallowed over it like a boat. "Forest Service always wants to close this road," she said. "But so far they can't. 'Cause it's our access."

"You sure have a lot of privacy." He did not ask how much. Could she be alone here?

"Yeah," she said, "I've always lived somewhere off in the woods. Always will, probably."

"That's good."

"Oh? Why's that? Good?"

"It's sort of everybody's dream," he said, though it was not particularly his own. "Living off by yourself, you know, like Walden Pond."

"Never heard of him."

"Make your own rules, only responsible for yourself. That'd be pretty ideal for a lot of people."

"Oh, that," she said. "I think it's been way overrated."

They came to a small clearing where an antique bulldozer stood mired at the end of its ugly work, the end of the road, an end of civilization. The girl's dog flung itself from the top of the load, and Teague flinched as it flew past his window. The dog's legs buckled on landing, but it bounced up and pranced to meet three penned goats, and these, in their own odd, stiff friendliness, pressed themselves to the edge of their enclosure in greeting. "Ethel, Jean, and Jenny," said the girl. "You just hate to get too attached to the little buggers, 'cause they don't survive real good up here—that's why we don't have a billy at the moment—but they get to be pets anyway. And then, the minute you're a little bit sweet on 'em, then along comes a cat and chews 'em up for you. Those cougars got long memories, too; they'll come fifty miles outta their way once they've had a nice snack on Fitchet Creek. Cats, coyotes, we even lost one of these little guys to a hailstorm."

He followed the girl toward the trailer that must be her home. There was a considerable garden enclosed by chicken wire strung on tall poles; he recognized staked tomatoes and feeble stalks of corn. There was a pile of cordwood on a pitch of high ground, better situated than the trailer and about as big. "Fifteen cord," she said, "give or take. And I've already sold quite a bit right off the truck, too." She said she dealt almost exclusively in larch and that a truckload of it was worth an awful lot of money these days. "I'm dumb as a post most ways, but I do know where to find the premium firewood. Keeps me in beer and Cheerios all year long." Her residence, parked in mud, was thirty-two feet long, ten feet wide, and sheathed in quilted aluminum. The ModernAire wore pot metal winglets as its crest, and it was flanked by a number of large wooden boxes. "Laying coops," said the girl. Also attached to the trailer was a sleeping porch built of graying plywood and green netting; the girl led him into it and offered him the use of a lawn chair, and when he settled on it she stood above him, her fist on her hip. "You hungry? You like venison?" He so adored the color and pace and inflection of her voice that his pleasure in it often cost him the thread of what she was actually saying. It didn't matter. And if his legs ached for having walked so many miles on asphalt, that was also of no account. He was soaring; least of all was he hungry.

"I should probably try and call my folks," he said, "see if they'll wire me some money."

"You're miles from the nearest phone, honey." As if he were a child wanting comfort and direction. "Why don't I just feed you? Myself, I've been dreamin' since noon about some fried spuds and a little bite of backstrap."

The girl went inside the trailer and shortly, through the open door, he heard ironware resound dully on a burner. "We run most of our appliances off propane, the rest off the generator. When you hear that motor kick in every so often, that's the generator keepin' the meat and whatnot froze. People don't know how good they got it, just to hook up to the power line." She began to hum again, and he heard her chop something, then oil spitting, and soon enough the odor of frying onions called up a general memory of boyhood. "This guy's quite lean," she told him. "I took him outta season, poached him, you know. You don't mind eatin' illegal?"

He had never, not even legitimately, shot a deer, though he'd been on several expeditions for that purpose. He recalled himself walking through thickets in the narrow ravines that drain upstate grain fields—clumsy and loud, his borrowed shotgun rigged for plugs and sleeping like a babe in arms.

"I was out fishin'," she said, "and there was this little spike buck, and he kept hangin' down by the creek; I drownded a couple three worms, and there he still was, so I walk up to the truck for my .243, and when I get back down to the creek, he's still standin' there, not even browsin' anymore, just standin' there like he's been waitin' for me. So I shot him. Heart shot. Felt like I 'bout had to."

He could no longer see her through the door; the girl did not have to move very far within the trailer to disappear in it. He tracked the sound of her boots on an insubstantial floor, heard her performing small tasks, heard a wood partition slide open at the far end of the trailer, which was not so far from him. She quietly lay down a scolding in terms he couldn't make out. Her voice. No answer. Her voice again, a long pause, no answer. Talking to herself. Terribly, terribly lonely. He hoped so. Taking herself privately to task. But why? A cat, he thought, she must have a naughty cat, maybe a captive forest rodent living back there.

His thoughts veered wretchedly then toward Janice. His Janice, more or less, lodged in his imagination wearing a peach pantsuit. She stood behind some endless paper-covered serving table, offering food and pleasantries and subsisting nicely on her sense of duty, in her fog of old-fogey perfume. Because she was a nice person. A very nice person. Janice, who deserved better than his slim enthusiasm for her. Guilt rose up and sloshed back to the floor of Teague's being, all muffled. He felt very well. Drunk, perhaps. Unafraid, and yet acutely aware that he'd got himself pretty far into the wilderness.

"We," she had said. She'd said it several times. Or "our." "Our road," "our appliances." There was a battered old sports car parked in the clearing. There were jeans hung on a line, two very different sizes. He told himself that it couldn't matter whether they were or weren't alone—acts of civil kindness, that was all—and though he was in love with her, he was in love so preposterously he wasn't about to reveal it. He craned to see her and saw more of the inside of the trailer—black pots, an enameled kettle, blond cabinets. He hated to see her so meagerly provisioned, but then it must be thin living that settled the girl so wonderfully within herself; she was, he believed, of some slightly better species. He smelled the onions caramelizing. This girl, it seemed to him, could make a home anywhere. Be a home. She'd claimed the very word and slipped it off its mooring.

She appeared at the door. "How 'bout another beer?"

"I've had enough. For me."

"Yeah, I forgot you're kind of a teetotaler. I know you're still thirsty, though."

Moving quietly now—she'd removed her boots to walk around barefoot—she brought him out a tall glass of tea. "Sun tea," she said. "You put the bags in a glass jug and let the sun color it up. You get a real nice do this way, maybe it's more natural. You like?"

He liked the curvature of her jaw, the way her neck swelled from her shoulders. And her eyes, of course, though their particulars, color and so on, were not so clear. Dusk had finally, fully given over. Before he said another word, he thought, he should really ask if they were alone. The girl wouldn't be frightened or offended. No, the girl, bless her heart, would hear any question he might care to ask in exactly the spirit he intended it. But what, exactly, did he intend? What did he want to know? Do you live by yourself? Are you alone? Are we alone? His intentions had always been so plain, his motives and his curiosity so easily managed. What could she ever be to him?

"It's good," he said, raising his glass. "My mom makes it this way, too. I've always preferred it this way."

She fed him a meal swimming in grease and salt, and powerfully savory. The venison, his first, was as dense as calf's liver and tasted like the decaying floor of the forest. They sat knee to knee on lawn furniture, their plates balanced in their laps, and they ate without much comment. He was entirely sober again, beginning to see how the beer had never been all that responsible for his glow. The girl sopped primitive gravy with bread. He did the same.

"What was that song you were humming before? In the truck? That was so familiar."

"I don't even recall," she said. "They kinda spill outta me. I remember every tune I've ever heard, to hum it, but usually not the words. Hardly ever the names of 'em. Strange, huh?"

"No, I don't think so. I'm not too musical myself. Not at all, really. You should be grateful for whatever little gift you've got that way. I mean, they kicked me out of the church choir, if you can believe that. Tin ear."

"That was mean. You're big on that church thing, aren't you?"

"My family is," said Teague. "No. I guess I am, too. Or at least I try to be."

"Around here, seems like it's mainly assholes that pack them churches every Sunday. Aw, that's not quite it either. But you know what I mean."

"Maybe. But I have to say, the majority of the people in our church are really nice. It was the same in Iowa City. I'm a Congregationalist."

"I probably don't know what I'm talkin' about. I'm kinda goin' off what I know about my family. They're kind of assholes. The deal with churches—I just don't like people lookin' down on me, but you probably never had to put up with that. You must think I'm pretty bad, the way I talk?"

"You've been very nice to me," he said. "Very Christian, I might say."

"I've got somebody you really oughta have a little chat with, 'cause with your education you could sure tell 'em—some of these people, you know, they give out them pills like candy. Real expensive candy. I never saw a pill cure anybody of anything, except maybe aspirin fix a headache."

"Deeply Christian," Teague emphasized. "I'm humbled." Her mention of someone else had brought him up short. He was not interested in her future, or his future, or anything or anyone outside this very moment.

"You're what?" she said, "'humbled,' did you say? I never had that effect on anybody before. You're a lotta firsts for me. That what I said about my family—I don't want you to get the wrong impression or anything, or take it the wrong way. I really do love 'em. Most of 'em. Kind of. But religion-wise, you know, I'm nothing. Must be nice to be a believer, if you really do believe."

She had invaded the borders of his cosseted life, and he'd never be just as he had been before, but how, exactly, he'd changed was not yet clear. The girl undid her braid and ran her fingers through it, and it was a wave, nearly a cloak on her shoulders. Teague was forming a new faith.

"Love," she said, "is a very tricky deal."

"I've heard that. But for me it's been just Mom and Dad and the grandparents. My little sister. Pretty straightforward stuff."

"Some guys have a way of keeping things simple. I bet you're one of 'em."

"I was. Simple. But that might be a nice way of saying stupid. Because I think if I'd been paying attention, I would have known better. I would have known that things are not simple."

"No. I meant nice," she said. "You seem very nice."

"Oh, gee."

"Well, what's wrong with that?"

"Nothing. But it doesn't seem to count for much, either. Especially if you don't know any other way to be."

"I can't believe you don't have a girl."

"I do and I don't," he said at last. "I guess I should have mentioned it before."

"Oh."

Teague wallowed in. "I don't love her, is the thing. We're friends. Or just companions, you could even say."

"Do guys even need to be in love? I think that's way down the list of what they're looking for."

"I'd need it," he said. "I see that now. And with Janice—that's her name, Janice—we've been off in different schools, and we always see each other when we're home, summer and the holidays, but . . .

we don't date anybody else, at least I haven't . . . but . . . and we have a lot in common, you know, we're both going back to good jobs in Courville—she'll be teaching kindergarten—and she's a very admirable person, and sort of attractive, I think. Really, I'd always thought this whole 'love' idea was something people get too worked up about. I was wrong."

"You must be awful tired. You've had quite a day."

"No. I could go on quite a while longer. I like talking to you. A lot."

"I'm kinda bushed. Usually by this time of year the woods are closed. Fire danger. But it's been a rainy summer. Means a hard winter's on the way, probably. And, greedy me, I'm gettin' in all the wood I can. Hauled two loads today all by myself. Small ones, but still, 'bout wears you out."

He heard for the first time a sorrow or reluctance in her voice, something not to do with what she was presently saying. She leaned down to take up his plate and her face hovered near him a beat longer than necessary, within reach, he thought. His heart bumped, a menace, and as the girl went into the trailer with their dishes, he thought to offer her his help but found that he was mute again, just as he'd been in the moment they'd met. She worked at the sink briefly and then moved off to the back of the trailer, back to where she'd been angry before.

She hadn't put out the lamp in the trailer. She hadn't said good night. The moon had risen and slanted in at him through the green screen. There was a breeze in the trees, waxing and waning, and saying *Fooohl. Fooohoohl.* He strained to hear anything else, anything of her, but from where she'd gone there was only that silence, and it persisted so long and was so complete that it seemed to him it must be intentional. He'd have heard the water running if she'd brushed her teeth or washed her face, he'd have heard the bedsprings if she lay down— he was that close and that attentive—but instead he heard nothing at all. Nightfall had brought a penetrating cold, so Teague curled in on

17

himself, thinking God must have sent him a miserable night so that he might remember himself, his entire sense of himself, and quit wanting what was not his to want. He threw his arm over his eyes and could only too easily imagine how silly, how pathetic he must look.

"You asleep?"

The girl had floated to the door. Her whisper brought him well up off the lawn chair.

"Sorry," she said. She stood in the doorway, blankets draped over one arm, towels over the other. "Didn't mean to scare you or wake you up or anything."

"I was just lying here, thinking, I . . . Kind of thinking over the day."

The girl didn't move. She didn't speak, though she seemed to want to.

"I was thinking about you, mostly."

She wore a long T-shirt for her nightgown. It bore the ghostly imprint of a frolicking unicorn and was so threadbare he could see through it; there was a remarkably detailed shadow between her legs.

"I'm just filthy," she said. "How 'bout you?"

Teague yawned, or faked a yawn to keep from panting.

"You one of those morning shower people? I like to take my shower at night. Hate to go to bed dirty. All sticky and . . . " She laid the blankets at his feet. "Come on."

He followed her out of the sleeping porch and over a short wooden walk to a shed; she cast a flashlight on the shed, and a fifty-gallon drum was mounted on its roof; a garden hose fed into that. "If you fill this thing in the morning, by night the water's nice and warm. Specially on a day like this one was. Some people'll go to quite a lotta trouble for a warm shower."

"That's very clever," he said in a voice he'd never heard before.

"Oh, yeah. One of his . . . " The girl put the towels and the shining flashlight on a rock near the door of the shed. "Wasn't my idea. Come on, I'll show you how to work it." She drew the T-shirt up over her head and laid it on the towels. Fully revealed she was unearthly, suffused with the same interior light as the moon. Teague's legs threatened to give way beneath him. His eyes strained as the girl entered the gloom of the shed. "All you do," she said, "is pull on this deal." She seized a sort of lanyard and there was a trickling sound. She swept water over her face. "Come on," she said. "There's room for two, and only so much water."

Then she demanded it. "Come on."

He stepped into the shed, partly under the fall of the water.

"Well, you'll have to take your . . . you'll get your things all wet again."

He would need at least a moment more to overcome a lifetime of modesty. This was a thought far too complex for his present powers of expression. His clothes began to cling to him.

"You goof. Well, if you're . . . Here, soap me up, okay?" She put a bar of soap in his hands, turned her back to him, reached behind her to find his hands again, drew them up and around and placed them on her breasts. The roar of his own breathing. The water had found a particular course down the inside of his right pant leg, and he was slightly aware of its tickling. The girl sighed enormously, and her head drifted back until it touched his nose, and he moved the soap lower, circled her navel with it. She pressed back at him, and their breathing was everything until, from just behind him, there came another voice, a third voice, a yelp of fear or pain.

DECEPTIONS
NOT
HER OWN

·1·

SHE SAT IN a steel chair, her arms folded before her on a steel table, her head heavy and adhesive on her arms, and none of a half-dozen nightmares woke her. Her dreams were full of a pestilent cloud that chased her through a cave of wildly uncertain footing, then along the big ditch down by her folks' house; she ran barefoot before it, never quite fast enough to escape and never quite caught. Thus, she slept, but Karen Brusett had never stopped to rinse the soap from her chest and belly, and it itched terribly now, and it was that itch that eventually prodded her awake.

A writing tablet lay at the far end of the table, a pen upon that. The video camera was still aimed at her but was finally blind; the red light had died. Thank goodness for small favors. She wiped drool from her chin. They'd brought her down a cement stairwell, walked her for what seemed hundreds of yards through a concrete maze; she knew herself to be in a deeply interior room of the basement of the county jail. Fiberglass meal trays lay stacked on metal shelving, and there was a large collection of homemade and jail-made weapons and various restraints. Sepia light oozed from wire cages in the ceiling. She drew herself up from her chair and found that she was crabbed like an old woman, that every muscle in her treacherous body had foreshortened overnight. This was not the good stiffness to be had from hard work. Staring back at the camera, her vanity intact and more perverse than ever, she imagined herself the new Mrs. Brusett, saw herself waking into the world as she had ruined it, the very image of her own selfish heedlessness, lips thick and flaccid and dry, eyes like poached eggs.

At least she'd told them nothing.

Over their body armor they'd worn uniforms of an ugly, glossy brown fabric, and they'd tried to act like they were her sneaky new friends, and through the night the deputies and the detective and finally the sheriff himself had all made quite a point of reminding her that she could go, that she could leave whenever she wanted, and really, if she didn't intend to help them, she might just as well take off. What? Did they really think she liked breathing these fragrances they must buy by the ounce and wear by the pint? And go where? In the middle of the night with no way home? To Fitchet Creek? Did they think their coffee was so delicious, or that she'd been so fascinated by their silly, numeric way of talking to each other? She did not know what she could afford to say, or how she could say anything without further hurting someone, and she was not going to be of much use to the authorities, or herself, or anyone else, but she had sat with the poor officers through the shank of the night, and none of them could bring themselves to leave, and all she gave them for their company and kindliness was the shoddy refrain she'd framed in the first few minutes of the interrogation, before the camera had been arranged: "It's a terrible thing, I know it is, and I am so, so sorry. But, please, I just wouldn't know what to tell you, and please, please, please, no lawyers." Soon their smiles were brittle and vacant, their questions rare and further and further from the point, and she sat with them, with nowhere else to go, almost basking in their disgust until she went to sleep. Sleep, if you could call it that.

What was hers to say? She had gone well out of her way to avoid learning that poor boy's name. She knew that Henry, for reasons Henry had yet to mention, had hit the boy with his cane, which broke, and which she instantly, convulsively, broke in three more pieces and sent down the creek. It had been a stick, then Henry had used it for his cane, then as a club, and now it was sticks again, caught in a thicket or washed all the way to the river and indistinguishable from hundreds of thousands of other sticks. But they had never for an instant considered trying to dispose of the boy, and that, of course, was the problem, this dead boy she'd think of as dead for as long as she lived, and surely there would be hell to pay; but what was hers to say about it? Nothing.

She had driven in dread down to Buck and Mimi's, the Knuths big-eyed at their darkened door—here's the neighbor wanting to call cops—and Karen had called the dispatcher and hinted broadly at their trouble, told its exact location, and then she'd gone back up the mountain to wait with Henry, squatting on her heels like a farmer in his field, but turned a little away from the boy and from Henry, who was also sitting on the ground so as to cradle the boy's head in his lap, and while they were waiting for the others to come she might have asked her husband, "Why? Why, Henry, did you have to hit that poor guy so hard? Why'd you hit him at all?" Or she might have said, "He never meant to hurt me. Did you know that?" But she hadn't asked for explanations, hadn't offered any, and so there were none, and they found, she and her dear, gentle husband, that they dared not speak at all. There in the dark, waiting, she'd known already that she was never to have the luxury of confession, and that she was far from done with doing wrong.

She needed to pee. The door to the hallway, steel of course, had no latch on her side, but only a hole for a huge and complex key she did not possess, and another hole for a window looking onto a near prospect of more cinderblock. Someone's odd impulse had made the door powder blue. She banged it with the meat of her hand and it clanged like an empty holding tank. "Hello?" A fan blew distantly in the ductwork. She turned her back to the door and began to kick at it with her heel, and in kicking she attained a calm, eased the pressure in her bladder, and she was still kicking at the door when it opened. "Oh . . . " She stumbled backward into the hall and nearly into her liberator, who looked to be a cowboy dressed for a wedding with his white shirt and blue jeans and thick brown hands. "Thank you," she said. The man was of her father's age, or her husband's, but he had a readier smile. He used this on her. Rather than reading his eyes she considered his boots, and these were slightly encrusted with dung. He seemed authentic. "I didn't mean to raise such a fuss," she said. "Well, I guess I did, but I couldn't get anybody to come. I really needed to use the restroom. They said I could leave, but when I tried to I . . . I'm still okay to leave?"

"That's what I came to see about." The man's glasses had been repaired at the bridge with a glob of solder; his hair, iron and oak, was just long enough to stand in disarray. "You should never have been behind a locked door. I'm sorry about this, Karen."

She knew him? From last night? Did she know him? No.

"I really didn't mind," she said. "I was just sleeping, and I can sleep about anywhere if I'm really tired."

"It's an evidence locker, or it's supposed to be, but they use it for a break room and every other damn thing."

"They just wanted to talk to me," she said, "which I can understand." The officers had been, all in all and in their creepy way, gentlemen, and she felt she should be a little apologetic on their behalf.

"Go through there." The man lifted his chin toward another blue door at the far end of the corridor. "There's a short flight of stairs, puts you in the lobby. There's a lady's room. It's breakfast upstairs. You want some eggs? Sausage? Coffee?"

"That's nice of you to offer, but no thanks." Karen turned from the man and went off to a freedom she didn't much want.

Outside, she stood on the buckled sidewalk between the jail and the courthouse. There was no bus line here, no taxi, and she knew not a soul on earth whom she'd think of calling just now to ask for help. There were animals at home, waiting to be fed. There was Henry. Henry—she would have to go back into the sheriff's office and ask, back into the jailhouse to ask for any news of him, because her husband might by now be a mess.

A green pickup, Forest Service surplus, pulled into the parking lot and stopped just across the sidewalk from her. The man from the basement was behind the wheel with his arm slung over the door and his sleeve rolled almost to his elbow, nursing a toothpick that gave his lip a still more skeptical fold. "I'm headed up your way, you want a lift?" His engine rattled a homebuilt stock rack, galvanized pipe to which he'd lashed a shovel and a pitchfork and a kind of bunting made of bundled orange baling twine. "It's no trouble."

"I should wait for my husband."

"Henry's long gone. Didn't they tell you? He left last night. Guess they offered him a ride, but he wouldn't take it. They even offered to put him up in that new cheapo motel out by the old post office, but he didn't want that either."

Her husband on the highway—slow, slow, and none too distinct in the dark. "So he took out walkin'? He's got one leg three inches shorter than the other—it's kinda bent in, got arthritis all through it. He's stubborn, and he'll try, but usually he don't walk that much. He can't."

"I guess he managed it last night, though. Climb in, don't worry about that stuff." The man swept a pile of documents from the passenger's seat and onto a floorboard already furnished with a coil of rope and a horse-and-a-half motor leaking oil onto some Sunday's glossy ads for lingerie. He offered her a baggy of withered ears; her gorge rose in her throat. "Turkish apricots," he said. Firmly she showed him her palm, not "no" but "hell no," and her throat flexed again. "I get 'em at the health food store when I'm in Missoula or Sandpoint, them and wheat germ. They'll go through you like a dose of salts." He shook her hand, and, without ever releasing it, he backed away from the curb.

"Who'd you say you were?"

"I didn't. I'm Hoot Meyers."

"Oh. You're the whatta-you-call-him, huh?"

"The county attorney."

"Yeah? Shit. Sorry, but you know, shit. I mean, really."

His name had blossomed in gold every four years for as long as she could remember. The same gold-on-maroon signs at every important junction of Highway 200, instructing travelers to reelect Hoot Meyers, Independent, for County Attorney. Justice himself, if you believed the *River Register*, called to comment on everybody's troubles. A big shot. His name came up when people were going to jail, and she'd never heard it spoken fondly.

"And here I thought you were just tryin' to be neighborly." Karen had found a brassy tone she liked but knew she'd never sustain; she regretted her life very much, the secretive life to come. Not that she'd ever been too relaxed in public.

"Lost a filling," said the county attorney. "Had a filling about the size of a Subaru fall out of my tooth last night; Loosma told me he'd get me in this morning, get me kinda comfortable."

"On Sunday? It's Sunday, isn't it?"

"Dr. Loosma's a good man with that novocaine needle, too, so I'm headed to Red Plain. You're right along the way."

"Not exactly." As a criminal, she felt, she'd already become a quicker, keener judge of character, almost animal in her acuity, and she'd got the criminal's tendency toward outrage at any deception not her own. A lumber train clacked and rattled by, a half-million two-by-fours headed west; the county attorney's truck rolled east down Main Street. She smelled bacon and burnt coffee. After years of her husband's high regard for her, Karen Brusett had finally come to believe that even such as she might be cherished, that she might be somehow adequate in this world; but now she foresaw a future of lying. They passed a gaggle of geese in City Park and out onto the highway, through the empty log yards of the Caradine and United mills. This town was her town, so far as she had any, but beyond her education here, and now groceries and licenses and medications, she had never discovered any deeper design in it nor the slightest bit of charm, and it appeared ramshackle and shabby even though she had little to compare it with. Leaving it always lifted her spirits.

She rested her head on the passenger's side window, and the county attorney's truck, a disgraceful vehicle for a man with a steady job, sent every bit of roughness up from the road and through the chassis and rattled her skull on the glass, and though she tried to nap, the prospect of sleep was terrifying. Her neck kinked. She sat up and opened her eyes.

"You all right?"

"Am I all right? I mean—what? Why couldn't they let us ride down in our own truck last night? Was there any reason we had to ride with those police guys? You know, they never really said we were under arrest, in fact they kept sayin' we weren't—but I think we were anyway. Kind of." Complaint seemed the thing to do, but she was not accustomed to despise the tone of her own voice.

"They probably had other things on their minds besides your transportation arrangements. We got some sloppy deputies, and they're always the first ones to a crime scene. Makes 'em feel important. Then they go ahead and screw things up."

"Yeah. I meant to ask you, though, do you . . . do you know me?" He'd be one to know the dirt on everyone.

"Ruth Hemphill? Remember her? Gal from Social Services, she brought you by my office one day. Been a while, you would've been about twelve, thirteen, around in there."

"Eleven," said Karen Brusett. "I was eleven. Oh. Oh, man, how could I forget that? But I don't remember you exactly. I mean, did you look the same?"

"I don't think I'd acquired these bifocals yet. You weren't there for long, pretty nervous if I recall, and it was only a couple minutes a long time ago. Not very much happened."

"I wouldn't tell you anything. You had that lady there, she had her little thingy, that little box."

"I used to have Nelda tape those deals with my ten-dollar tape recorder. Do it myself, but I sometimes get sidetracked and forget to mess with the buttons like I should. People get shy in front of a microphone. You shouldn't consider what happened with you all that unusual."

"All that trouble so she could get my every word, and then I wouldn't say. Mrs. Hemphill was so pissed off at me. That was the only time I heard her use any cuss words. Aw, but, man, now does all that have to come up again? You can't believe how much I hate it that you know that stuff about me. I'd forgot all about that." She'd forgotten nothing of the strangeness of those years.

"Ruth was a very diligent woman," said the county attorney. "Still is, I suppose."

"She scared me, you wanna know the truth. I don't think she meant to, but she just did. She could be way worse than whatever it was she was mad about."

"She's got the flower shop now."

"Flowers," said Karen, "I could buy from her. I bet she's nice in there."

Mornings of late had been long and gingery, and summer was ending before it had ever properly started. The river was low and the cottonwoods standing out on the sandbars stood in mist. A phrase of "The Entertainer" sounded, as if from a tiny, tinny calliope, in the shoe box in the seat just between them; the county attorney took up his cell phone. "Used to be there were a few canyons where they still couldn't get me on this thing; now, seems like they can get me any-where." He thumbed the phone open and said into it, "Meyers." There was droning in his hand, with points of emphasis. "Maybe," he said in a way that seemed to mean "no." Then he said, "Well, the first thing is, we've gotta get the autopsy back. And I should really know who he is—was. There's gotta be some police work done, and it better be better police work than what's been done so far. Or I've got nothing. Right now I've got a body, and that's about it . . . And who would I charge? And for what?"

The humming in his hand resumed, now in level and measured tones.

"Yeah, all in due course, in due course," he said, "but right now it's Sunday, and I got a tooth killing me, and I been needing to do some welding, and, yeah . . . that's right. Sure, that'll be fine. Oh, and if I were you, Frosty, I'd leave that buffet alone; they've poisoned quite a few citizens with that buffet of theirs." The county attorney silenced his phone and returned it to the shoe box where it rode rattling among .22 shorts and pennies and small silver. "They call this progress? You got satellites overhead of you now like so many mosquitoes, and the bastards can get you anywhere you happen to be. I do not call this progress." He turned to her, took his eyes from the road to do it. "The boy's brain swelled, and that was all she wrote, or so says Farinelli. You may have met him, he's the emergency room doc. We'll wait and see what the medical examiner thinks, but I don't expect any real dif-ferent conclusions."

"I can't imagine what you must think of me."

"You're all right," said the county attorney. "That business when you were a girl I'm sure you did what you thought was right. What you had to do. That's all I ask of anybody anymore."

"What I *did*," said Mrs. Brusett, "what I finally *did* was marry Henry. So, sorry, but you'll see it's the same as last time, I won't be sayin' anything. I just, I just can't imagine, and I'm not too impressed with myself, either. But there it is."

"You're all right," he said again.

"My folks had that satellite dish, and we must've got about a hundred channels—in all those crime shows they say to shut up when you're in trouble with the law. Or if you think you might be. Those guys last night, I bet they read me my rights ten times. They keep sayin' I don't have to tell 'em anything, and I don't have to tell 'em anything, and I really don't have to tell 'em anything if I don't want, but then they kind of lean on you to say something anyway. They want you to 'help' 'em. Is that fair if they do that? Is that a right thing? I'm a . . . ? I'm a what, a suspect?"

"Kid's dead, and his blood's all over Henry's coveralls? That'll raise some concerns. Neither one of you has a thing to say about it, so that does make people curious."

"Cops?"

"Yeah, cops."

"You," she said.

"Not me," said the county attorney. "I really don't care to know. I can stand a little mystery now and then."

"You must think I'm one of these real, real crappy people."

"What I think," he said, "is that you've got the right idea. And you should stick to it. Just stay quiet."

"That's your advice?"

"That's my advice." He expected it would be taken.

"So you're on my side now? How did that happen?"

"I'm on your side, and I'm on Henry's side, and I'd appreciate it if you'd tell him that for me. Make *sure* you tell him that, all right? I'm letting you know, and I'm letting Henry know that this shouldn't turn out too bad for you. Especially if you can keep to yourselves about it."

"So if we're suspects—we're suspects, huh?—but, if we're suspects, aren't you the other guy, the guy on the other side? Our enemy, kind of? Shouldn't it be somebody else telling us what to do?"

"Usually, yeah. But—how to put it?—I'm gonna give you, both of you, *all* the benefit of the doubt. You see?"

"What are we suspected of? Exactly?"

"What do you think?"

"I don't get what you're telling me, then."

"Keep a lid on it," he said. "You're both already inclined that way, so maybe this doesn't have to be too bad. If you can keep to yourselves with it. Whatever it is. And, no matter what I do, it'll be best for you guys to just keep quiet. In fact, it might be a good idea if you never mentioned this conversation we're having right now. Except to Henry, of course."

"You know Henry, too?"

"Man and boy I've known him. We were in that Belknap school together, that one-roomer Mrs. Callahan used to run. When I got my Rambler in the eighth grade I'd take him to school sometimes. School in town. That was before his folks lost their place down below us."

"So, what're you sayin'—you know he's a good guy?"

"Right. He was when I knew him."

"But a suspect?"

"Yeah, a suspect. I can't do anything about that. It's quite a long way from being a suspect, though, to being indicted, and it's a long way from that to being convicted of anything. Lotta things can happen along the way. Henry's always been one of the good ones, far as I know, and that's my happy little understanding, and I don't care to know anything different at this late date. I believe you're all right, too, a good person. You and Henry are both good people—or good enough—so I'd like to leave well enough alone. If you see what I'm saying?"

"No. But I do know that if I did say anything, I wouldn't know what to say. Let me off up at this turnout, would you?"

"Whatsit, five, six miles still to your place from here?"

"Maybe just three," she said. "But I really do need to stretch my legs."

The county attorney let her off on the highway, and Mrs. Brusett crossed it and set off up the road into Spurgin Gulch, her flip-flops sucking and slapping at her heels. Within a mile blisters had raised between her toes, so she kicked off her thongs and went on on grimy feet. Why couldn't everyone just behave? Why couldn't she? Why must every moment be lived in the bottom of her gut? She searched herself for forgiveness, just any forgiveness for anyone, but she'd still found none when she turned up a track that cut the kinnikinnick and wild strawberry and bear grass of a north-facing slope, and through a channel in a stand of dog's hair pine, tall and dense, she climbed the shady road home.

·2·

GLUM AS A girl, she had stood outside her family's happiness, betrayed by it, a tolerated guest at the many thousand ceremonies by which the Dents were forever appreciating themselves as plain but honest folk. It was this. More than anything else, it was this constant bragging on their honest ways that had made Karen so often despise them, because they lied slyly in their silences. Never a word passed between them, for instance, about the too obvious fact that Galahad Dent could scarcely stand to look at his daughter. His eyes might touch upon everything and everybody in a room, but when they came to Karen they went over, past, or through. He would look at her only so often and for only so long as was absolutely necessary, and then as if she were a stain.

How to speak of this? She never did, and so Karen was left to wonder; her earliest memory was of wondering, "What have I done?"

The Dents lived at the north end of Fisher Meadow in a trailer house at the end of two long ranks of Lombardy poplars. There were no neighbors. When Karen had lived there with her parents and her brothers, she had lived as much as possible out of doors, though she had no particular taste for solitude or, in those days, for so much unrelieved nature. She recalled marking time alone, breathing visibly off in some stubbled field or up a brushy slope. Her girlhood was bound on one side by life in the cold or among the pestering gnats, and on the other by her impatience for the daily fraudulence of what should have been her home.

For many years the hinge of Karen's week had been Wednesday, because it happened that her mother got fed up at some point with the Good Shepherd and quit the church in favor of a Wednesday-night bowling league, and because her father would stand at the kitchen window watching Mother, as he called her, leave, and he watched her like a lost boy during the whole time it took her to disappear up the lane, and every Wednesday he fussed at the expense and trouble of her night out, and every time as she went out of view he conceded that Mother had earned and needed her nights of freedom from them. Then, usually, he would make potato soup for supper. This was soggy onion and potato, adrift in greasy milk. He served it merely warm.

"Go ahead and pepper the hell out of it," Galahad Dent would tell his children, and the twins, wads of Wonder bread in their little fists, would fall to that soup like kittens to cream, for the boys loved everything, and their cheeks would ripen like pie cherries. Leave it to the boys to delight and prosper so in a meal that Karen could on no account bring herself to swallow, though Galahad would from time to time force her to try it again. "Who," he'd ask her, as if she were someone he'd recently met, "who do you think you are? You can't eat what's made for you? Go ahead and be as stubborn as you want, but this is it. This is all the supper you'll get."

Karen could hold that soup in her mouth for a very long time. The stuff would pulse in her throat, and she'd gag and gag, but she had never given her father the satisfaction of seeing her puke. She held it until he was forced to relent and let her spit it into the kitchen sink, and then she was left with the vile aftertaste in her mouth. During these contests of will, a hatred vibrated her father's voice so that even the twins were uneasy at hearing it, so Galahad would take them into the living room and wrestle with them, a pair of mewling, farting, relentless teddy bears, while Karen would clean up the supper dishes. He'd play with her brothers. He'd bathe them and put them to bed. He'd tell them—she could hear it from just down the hall—that he loved them. And then, sometimes, Galahad would put his head inside her door to say "good night." Never more than that. In long, habitual hopefulness she would stand by her bed to await these visits, but then she'd be just enough startled when he came that she couldn't find a way to answer, though she wished to somehow make a conversation of it. Once he had come all the way into her room, and he stood there for a while pretending fascination for the poster on her wall, a poster she had already outgrown but would never take down, a princess with a sparkling wand who was also, as it happened, a pig. Her father had stared at this until he began to tremble, and then he had surrendered a single, unprecedented tear, and when it reached his chin he told her, "Get in bed."

"I'm . . . my jeans are kind of . . . well, they're dirty."

"Get in that bed," he said. "And pull the covers up."

After that he didn't come to her door. Wednesday nights her father would put the boys down with a little story, and he'd go to the living room, and sigh, and turn on the television. Karen would sleep then, lulled by muffled laugh tracks and with her dreams buoyed up by the fact that tomorrow, while tomorrow might be many things, would not be Wednesday.

One day she was taken along with the other girls of her fifth-grade class to visit the office of the school health nurse. There the girls were given a short lecture on touching. Some of it was good, they were told, and some of it was bad. Emily Schact asked for clarification. Resigned to answer, responsible for some answer anyway, the health nurse inhaled deeply and her great bosom heaved. "It depends," she said. There was a silent thirty seconds before Emily asked, "Depends on what?"

"Like I said before," said the health nurse, "didn't I already tell you this? It depends on who touches you. And where they touch you." The health nurse illustrated her point with a drawing that was supposed to represent a girl's body but looked more to Karen like one of the weatherman's clouds, and it was for her purposes less illustrative. The health nurse pointed to it from halfway across the room, and one of the fifth-grade girls began to cry, several others to laugh. A second session was held the following week, and this time the health nurse had been joined by a county social worker to ask the girls individually, one by one and in promised confidence, particular questions about their experience of touching. Karen, thinking she was defending an indifferent father, told them that Galahad touched her all the time. Where? "Everywhere," she said. Regular affection, she meant, affection in every room of the house. Touching. The health nurse and the social worker became grave and told Karen she could share with them anything she might need to say; they told her how important it was that she tell them everything. Their lips puckered in anticipation of hearing it. Karen thought that they must have seen through, and hated, her puny invention about being loved. "No," she said. "This is that nice kind. Very nice. Probably the best, okay? Can we just leave it at that?"

Karen was not accustomed to very much of anyone's attention, not yet accustomed to the necessity of having to cover her tracks, and she suffered the interviews that followed—talks with the health nurse and with Mrs. Hemphill, the social worker, and eventually, very secretively, with her mother—in deep confusion. Karen soon lost track of the facts such as they were, lost or misremembered those things she'd told them or failed to tell them previously, and by the time she was taken to the county attorney's office she'd decided to stay quiet, to act as if she'd lost the power of speech altogether. Someone had mentioned their purpose. They wanted to find out if she was safe in her home, safe in the company of her father. Safe? Safety, as far as Karen knew, lay in looking both ways before crossing any busy road. The truth, they said. They just wanted the truth. The only reliable truth lay crouched in her heart, composed of nothing like words, and was nothing anyone, despite what they told her, would really want to hear.

She remembered that when she'd left the county attorney's office that day, Mrs. Hemphill had huffed, "Well that really cuts it. We can't do anything for you. Can we, Karen?" Karen had never imagined that anyone could, and had never asked for anyone's help. She apologized, however, if only because that was what seemed to happen every time she opened her mouth.

Jean quit bowling after that, though she was carrying a 143 average in league play, and soon she had joined another church. She got busy at her sewing machine and made them all Sunday clothes so that they could attend services with her. Jean and Galahad and the twins were newly baptized, properly baptized at last, and the boys learned to speak in tongues, which they considered hilarious. Karen could never repent of her sins to the pastor's complete satisfaction, and so she was weekly admitted to the Chapel of the Lamb but never gained admission to the church, not as a member. Both Pastor Hurlburt and Jean would frequently remind her of how they suffered, of how fearful they were for her as she stood in darkness, outside the church, stubbornly denying herself its warmth and light. But all this dreamy talk of dying or not-dying, and of big swings in the temperature and in people's fortunes? A God so mean and grudging he'd require gratitude of men with holes in their filthy socks? She wanted no part of him. Having not found grace, Karen continued to haunt her family's twilight, and she entered a trackless adolescence where even the thrumming of her powerful good health sometimes made her anxious.

Jean's new religion required the doing of good works, so Pastor Hurlburt offered them a succession of rootless men who could benefit by exposure to the loving warmth of the Dents' home and a decent

Sunday supper. As Jean liked to cook, and as Galahad was willing to transform the floor plan of the trailer to accommodate a long table, and as his willingness extended even to going out and gathering up those selected strays who lacked transportation, most Sunday evenings in the Dent household now began to savor of Thanksgiving at the mission—good, aromatic food, bad hygiene, and, of course, our Heavenly Father to be beseeched and thanked for this and that. Not all their guests were bums or bums in the making, though, and it was at these Sunday suppers that Karen first encountered Henry Brusett.

Mr. Brusett was the only one of their guests to bring gifts for the household; it was safe to assume on Monday morning that the teapot left without explanation on the counter or the wildflowers tied to the screen door had been his offering. Among Sunday's smelly pilgrims, few found the wherewithal even to say thanks, and even Mr. Brusett, who was so very appreciative, would never hazard to say more than that. He had come up in hippie times and must have been one, for he still wore his hair long, tied in back and center-parted, and it was streaked with gray so that his scalp suggested a skunk's back. But he was not so glossy as a skunk, and not nearly so self-possessed. His right leg didn't carry him so much as it had to be carried, and to be lifted and thrown forward in every troubling step, and Mr. Brusett was so unwilling to give offense that in company, to be safe, he ceased to acknowledge his own existence.

Karen saw—could she be the only one?—that Mr. Brusett was embarrassed by the needy whining the Dents shared in prayer. "Lord, please help Slim endure those frostbit fingers, and let Tony find a way back to the loving arms of his Lucinda, for we fear you, Lord Jesus, and from you all things can be given, and to you all thanks is due." Mr. Brusett, looking away, looking at his feet. A man who spoke only as much as necessary to be polite, he was otherwise a blank slate, and each time he came, Karen imagined some new history for him. As his

Sunday appearances became more important to her, Karen grew more and more certain that her parents would soon drive Mr. Brusett away with their loony devotions, with their Let-us-all-join-together-nows, their constant Let-us-now-bow-our-heads. Ordinarily, only very hungry men could stomach much of her folks' blustery ministry, for the Dents' preaching was the kind that incites sidelong looks. Galahad worked for the county road department, but he liked to think he was more than that. He owned his own home. He was fully insured. He had a nice wife and a nicer fishing boat, and he'd seen his salvation. It pleased him to lord it over the woebegone, and share his gooey rapture with them, and Pastor Hurlburt called Galahad Dent his great soldier in Christ. Her father, beaming in his certainty of life eternal, would say, "Christ died, boys, died on Calvary for my sins, and he'll die for you, too, if you let him. He'd be glad to. Christ is Lord."

And, worse, there was Karen's mother, Jean. A mother who, out of sheer, sweet, unwavering incomprehension, had formed the habit of treating people like pets and conferring on them personalities having almost nothing to do with anything to be found in their actual characters. Jean would insist on everyone's general decency, and that anyone who came through their door became honorary kin, and she called Mr. Brusett "Uncle Henry." Every time Jean said something of that sort, Mr. Brusett's head would bob slightly, not in agreement, but another distinction, another little gesture that only Karen seemed to understand. He certainly never agreed to be taken in, but even so, and even though he kept no other company that anyone knew of, Mr. Brusett was their guest more Sundays than not for several years. That was the same set of years, as it happened, when Jean had taken to calling her daughter "Dad."

And so Karen would try to meet Mr. Brusett at the door, and when everyone came to the table she'd try to sit across from him or to either side of him, somewhere within the scent of the astringent soap he used. His knuckles were large and egg-shaped and uneven; she saw that his hands, when not concealed between his legs or under the table, would often clutch at something not there. They were alike, she and Mr. Brusett; they'd made ghosts of themselves and learned how to go unseen. Only in his presence did she ever feel less than completely alone.

On a Sunday also memorable because she'd been mentioned in church for having graduated junior high, there came a new visitor to the dinner gathering, a fat man infatuated with his own name who talked rapidly and exclusively of Ned and Ned's doings. Ned wore a yellow mesh cap streaked with some of the same greases it advertised. His hair and beard were cinder black and had been cropped to various lengths with clumsy shearing. In a half hour among them he had claimed to be the very best at some worthy thing which, unfortunately, he was not at liberty to describe or even name, and he claimed descent from Algonquins and presented the tips of his fingers as proof of it, and he told them he knew, more or less, what most of them were thinking. He said he didn't mind. Mad in some barely governable way, Ned, it seemed, had known Mr. Brusett in years past, and he asked him about a woman named Juanita. Mr. Brusett said that Juanita was probably in Alberton with her new husband. What about Dave, then? Mr. Brusett, his voice an eggshell cracking, said that Dave was in jail, he thought. In the joint, actually. Deer Lodge. And Denny? Mr. Brusett shrugged with such finality that even the blithering Ned knew to let him alone. But Mr. Brusett was to spend no more Sundays at the Dents'. After that, Sundays were Ned's, Ned who was not long in becoming, for Jean's purposes, "Uncle Ned," and the man, fascinated not only by his name, but by any name anyone might care to give him, would sometimes huff it like a toy train, "Uncle Ned. Uncle Ned. Uncle Ned. Uncle Ned."

A summer passed. Karen entered high school without a friend in the world.

With just these few years ahead of her in which to become some kind of woman, she knew she could probably use a pal, and Karen thought that it was immature of her to not have one yet, but pep band and the like filled her with revulsion, and she knew that she must be revolting in her own turn, and the very situations in which friends were typically made were the times and places she could not abide, not when given any choice. There was always sufficient reason to not belong. Volleyball was out of the question because of the yelling involved, the yipping the girls did in that echo vault of a gym, and Karen wouldn't think of basketball, knowing she was too clumsy for it, and her folks said their long Lent prohibited her running track. Karen did not join the glee club. She didn't raise a sow to show in the 4-H barn at the fair. She was reliable in her studies, responsible about her homework, and invariably graded "Not Disruptive" in classroom deportment, but teachers did not call on her to answer. Karen knew she somehow willed this result. As a freshman she adopted the dress and swagger of the lumberjacks she'd found a generation back in family photo albums: Grandpa and Great-Grandpa on Jean's side, standing rakish always on some freshly butchered sidehill. They held tools capable of such work, peaveys and pikes and two-man chain saws, big machines with malice for all and built to give no quarter, and these men seemed in every shot to be entirely satisfied. In their honor, or in honor of their contentment, she wore her denim pants spiked or cuffed, and she wore suspenders, and long underwear, and wool flannel, and the heaviest boots a girl could buy in her size, and it all proved itself again and again to be imprudent wear for the well-heated classroom, but she wore it anyway.

"All that girl wants," Jean said of her, "is to be left alone. And I've got no kick with that. I'd rather have that than have one of these boy-crazy little brats on my hands—now that'd be a rodeo. One of these ones that's always got their belly buttons hanging out? You just know that can't be chaste—not in thought and deed."

In her high school's bleak hierarchy, Karen, when she was thought of at all, was thought to be a lesbian and coveted by no one, no one willing to announce themselves. Of too little consequence even to be persecuted, she ate her lunch in an exclusive and especially ugly corner of the cafeteria with her hair tied in the tightest knot she could form with it. Her hair, she knew, could be like field-ripened grain, but she kept it in a knot on her neck. Her whole range of expression consisted of tilting the slash she made of her lips, sometimes to the left, sometimes to the right, and behind this blank display she'd be crowning herself High Priestess of the Half-Moon. Her imagination flourished, but it was only to preoccupy and gave no real satisfaction. She wanted something, anything, that was entirely hers and that might be touched. She wondered if she was ever to learn anything of love. The girls at school, those girls she could approach near enough to overhear, talked of loving each other, they talked of loving Brad and Wesley and Tim Flowers and Louie Natrone, they loved their moms and dads, and even sometimes their siblings, "soooo much," and they loved colts and cats, rain in the spring, pretty blouses, and they draped "love" on every scrap of pleasure or longing that blew by them, and even if they were mistaken, even if they were working it way too hard, love, or their constant mention of it, seemed to keep them at a level of enthusiasm Karen could not sustain.

She was not very interested in anyone of her acquaintance, and so, by default, by protracted accident, she fell a little in love with herself. She conquered the last of her girlish bashfulness about mirrors in less than half of one mild May upon discovering in them that she was good at any angle, in any light, but, as she had no prior reputation for beauty, it was hard at first to credit what she so furtively saw in the glass. She looked harder, longer, and still she liked what she saw, liked herself too much, probably, but at least now she had a better use for the extensive privacy that had always been her only privilege. In private, she let her hair down, and, as it wasn't customary there, she was fully aware of its whispering friction on her shoulders.

Her face was taut as an apple, square but not mannishly so, and her color ran from bronze to khaki depending on the current warmth of her blood. Her skin was clear. Her breasts were successful, she thought, or should have been—ready little monuments to reproduction. She had a golden brow, a kitten nose. With high school came more excursions, and Karen found herself more often among strangers, shopping with Jean in other towns, swept up in field trips or field trials or whatever she was being forced to attend that day, and as she passed among strangers now she saw that she caused sudden, deep interest in them. The boys. The men. Everyone, really. And it was so very strange that in these strange places she'd got such power when at home and in those places where she was most familiar, where she had been so ordinary for so long, Karen was still nothing special. Her blooming passed unremarked and largely unnoticed there.

Jean's notion of her daughter, a notion she published to anyone unable to avoid her on the subject, was that her Karen was the guileless fawn, a creature so delicate of spirit she needed more than anything else to be left alone. "She's out there talkin' to the ravens, and that's how she likes it. Girl's half-wild herself. All she wants, all you ever got to give that Dad is a little toast and plenty of breathing room." Of course Karen was not at all the feral nymph her mother wanted, the innocent chipmunk. She was just a girl too often alone, and like any such girl, she was bitter about it. Too often alone, too often cold, and she spent far too much time in that tiny tract of personal wilderness that could be lit by her parents' yellow yard lights. After nightfall, she did not explore. She would stand out by the henhouse listening to the sage dialogue of nesting, dreaming hens, and wondering still, "What have I done?" She was ashamed of herself without knowing why.

"Remember," Jean would say. "Remember, remember, remember, 'cause these are the good years, Dad. These years here might be the best ones you'll ever get. Remember."

But, for a very long while, nothing memorable occurred. Karen was a freshman, then a sophomore, reduced to playing chess with pimpled and humped Tana Holt. The girls said, "It just flies by, doesn't it?" They'd say, "We have so much *fun*." Karen could detect little momentum, but she did become a junior. For weeks on end she'd get by on the utterance of a few dozen words. She brought her lunch in a sack to avoid standing in line for hot meals. She rode the bus sitting right behind the driver. She read *Black Beauty* twelve times. On Friday nights, Jean let her make popcorn and a powdered fruit drink. Karen endured like a weed in drought, having learned nothing useful so far but how to wait. She did what each day required of her.

· 3 ·

A T FIRST, MRS. Ashcraft gave her a choice: Karen could ride on the class float, or she could go to detention with the noodle-heads. She might want to try wasting time in company with Keith and Hans Boethcher and Mr. McFeely and his son, the slavering Gabe; she might like to see how much she'd enjoy scraping fossilized gum for a couple hours off the undersides of desks and heat registers. But then Mrs. Ashcraft reconsidered, and she said that, no, there was no choice—this was homecoming. Karen was to report immediately to the rec room and have her face painted. "I'll be there in five minutes, too, so you'd better not try sneaking off to chem lab or the sick room or somewhere. You can show your support like everyone else, Miss Dent. Loosen up for once." Karen admired silliness very much but could never join in it, for she had no personal dignity to spare, and she wanted no part of anyone's parade, not even to watch. There would be flags and cars and silly ways of walking; there would, she expected, be some horn honking.

The school was nearly empty. A locker slammed in another part of the building and echoed for seconds down the halls. Tennis shoes slapped linoleum, and Karen heard two shrilling boys as they ran together into, and then explosively through, the eastern exit. The big door echoed in the following silence, where it seemed at least that no one had been hurt. She read a butcher paper scroll rolled out along a ceiling, a thing she'd read many dozen times before—HAWK'S EGGSELL—WE RHAWK AND ROLL!!!—and she took very short and very slow steps but reached the rec room in under a minute, and there she joined a short line of waiting girls, and there the vice president of the Hawk Chics, Darlene Mews, gave her a sponge heavy with paint. "Blue, okay? Everywhere there's skin showing, make it blue. You have to do it by feel at first, 'cause Yvette needs to use the mirror. Jannie Fay puts your finishing touches on you when you get to her. Okay?" Darlene spoke to her as if she were an exchange student or a special-needs student, and though she was herself notoriously stupid, Darlene, as a cheerleader, had to wear only a decal on her cheek, and a little eyeliner, and the lavender ribbons that coiled so prettily in her hair.

The girls in line ahead of Karen had already daubed themselves with this paint, which was in truth nearer black than blue, and it had made some of them almost unrecognizable, and their faces flexed to work against flesh suddenly, interestingly inelastic. Though at first touch it burned, and though it smelled to her of mold, Karen wet her whole face with it, and it almost instantly dried, leaching oil and sweat from her skin. The mix became a desiccated crust, and she looked and felt like the end of a mud puddle.

Her head still hurt when Jannie Fay Palmer filled the hollows of her eyes with orange and wrote SPIRIT in orange on her forehead. Mrs. Ashcraft completed her look by giving her an inflated inner tube to wear as a sort of belt. "Now run," said Mrs. Ashcraft. "Run. If you move it you should still be able to catch up; they're leaving from down by the bus barn."

The juniors had been assembled and were milling near an old overturned section of wooden bleachers. Mold and moss clung to its feet. As soon as Karen joined them there, Dennis Frame drifted to her edge of the crowd. He began to hitch his Levis very high so that his squashed privates were raised to press at his lower abdomen and bulge in relief behind the denim. He narrated the move each time, "*Pres-to Change-oh. Wheeee.*" Karen was, except for Dennis Frame, the only person on earth who found this funny, and no matter how awful she happened to be feeling, no matter what company they were in, he would seek her out to give some performance like this, and she would laugh for him, and then everyone would continue to think them creepy, which she supposed they were, and so Karen turned her back on Dennis Frame and went to stand among a little clutch of religious girls where she knew he would not follow her.

Dingy Bergson was holding forth to the gingham crowd, and she knew her audience, "Teen Renewal, *that's* the program. That's where I met him, and now we get to see each other every Thursday. Justin's so responsible. He's putting a motor in one of his dad's old cars. Or he wants to. If he could find the right size. I think he was way too godly to need high school. Do these boys here know one psalm by heart? No, not one of them does. And he's mine, you might say, and it's because of Teen Renewal."

At last the word was passed to load up. The junior float this year was nothing more than a flatbed truck, and mounting it, Karen happened to see in a rearview mirror that the paint had caused her face to swell in lumps, and the whites of her eyes were pink, shot with electric veins, and she would, of course, be hideously allergic to something that was for everyone else just fun. Ugly, she rode at the front of the truck, to get it over with, being seen this way, and when the parade turned down Main Street and into a wind predicting early winter, the additional sting of it made her eyes boil up in tears she dared not wipe away. Underclassmen led afoot, marching in loose order and throwing penny candy to spectators and to places where spectators should have been. The band followed in a bus, desecrating "Dixie," "The Battle Hymn of the Republic," and "Sugar, Sugar," every tune broken on the same thready pulse, and the whole band blared in vain against

Elston Cannon's more persuasive drumming. Elston, a free agent, a sort of thief, staggered to carry a bass drum he'd taken from the music room, and he stroked it with the heaviest mallets to be found there, a three-beat phrase, inexhaustible, *Boom Boom Boom*. And they shouted "Let's go Hawks!" over and over, and in undertones the wits were whispering "We're no good, we're no good," for the Hawks had yet to win a game that season, and the drumming, the whispering, the perfectly genuine hatred for people they knew only slightly if at all, kids with similarly dismal prospects whose only fault lay in matriculating at the next hick high school down the state highway— all of it was born instantly away in that wind which also burned the cheerleaders' knees the color of strawberry ice cream. Elston's drum sounded inside and outside Karen's beating skull, and it carried down to push at her stomach as she rode along, stretched low and wretched over the cab.

As the parade came abreast the Buck Snort Saloon, Karen saw Henry Brusett in the parking lot of Paulson's Dollar Store, a business that had been dead for as long as she had any memory of it. Mr. Brusett was turned away from the passing noise, stroking at a metal casing with a wire brush, and she recognized him by the top of his head, knew his pickup. He sat on its tailgate, surrounded by a dozen pieces of chain saw, and when he took up one of them, a part no bigger than a pea, and when he held it near his eye and compressed his lips in concentration, she realized how much she had been missing him, if not precisely why, and before she could think better of it, Karen made her way to the edge of the flatbed, sat on it, and pushed off. She felt the inner tube catch behind her, and this pitched her forward so that she landed on the balls of her feet and the heels of her hands, which she sacrificed to the asphalt to save her face from the pavement, and she bounced up bleeding, glancing back at Mr. Pingre, the junior class adviser, who had chosen to pretend he hadn't noticed her leaving.

Neither stealth nor speed was possible for a painted girl in an inner tube, but she ran as best she could, bent at the waist, and she took cover behind a beer truck and waited there until its driver came out of the Buck Snort with a keg on a dolly and a very puzzled look at seeing her there, crouched near his truck. He nodded to her. Karen nodded back and went on. The parade had advanced another block by then, and she felt free to move away from it as she liked. She crossed the street to Mr. Brusett, and as she approached him, Mr. Brusett looked just to her left, then just to her right, and then, as she closed on him, he became transfixed by her stomach. The inner tube. Karen raised a bloody palm. "Hi," she said. "It's me. Remember me?" She hoped he'd recognize her voice.

"You in some kind of trouble?"

"I'm Karen. Jean's girl. Karen Dent?"

"You okay?"

Karen considered the heels of her hands. Black pebbles were embedded in them and they were leaking blood and some other fluid, something clear and viscous. "I'm fine. You wouldn't believe how often that happens to me. I just go down. Skin myself up. Graceful, I'm not." She could think of nothing else to say, no reason that might make any sense to him, or to her, for her being there. The air around him smelled of solvent.

"It's homecoming," she said.

"So I figured. We used to have that, too."

"They make you, oh . . . you know, do stuff. Did you even know who I was?"

"Yep." Mr. Brusett fitted steel rings onto a piston.

"I didn't know if you could tell," she said at last.

"Sure." With the tip of his tongue visible between his lips, Mr. Brusett slid the piston into its sleeve in the little engine block. He secured it to a wrist pin.

"I also didn't know if you'd remember my name. I wasn't sure you ever even knew it. They never call me that at the house, so . . . I didn't know. It's been a long time since you quit coming out."

Mr. Brusett caressed the saw's teeth with a small round file.

"I wish you would've kept coming," she said. "Those other ones drive me crazy, the ones my dad rounds up. We had one of 'em wet his pants last Sunday."

"It's quite the crowd they gather out there."

"So, why don't you? Come?"

"Oh, I get kinda busy. What're you? You the queen?"

"What?"

"Of homecoming," he specified.

"Are you kidding? Me?"

"I thought that might be why you were in that getup."

"This is not," she said, "what the queen wears."

"No, I guess it wouldn't be. But you're not . . . I saw you kind of . . . you're sure you're not in trouble?"

"Would you help me out if I was?"

Mr. Brusett filed at the saw, every stroke a sigh. Shifting foot to foot, Karen watched him. Her stomach had settled but her head still hurt. Mr. Brusett blew at the file and a shimmering rode on his breath, tempered steel made stardust. She could hear the pounding and horns honking down at the baseball field where the school was rallying.

"Is this what you do? You fix saws? I never really knew what you did. You didn't talk about that. But I guess you never said anything about anything." He had been her speculation. He'd been, mostly, whatever she wanted or needed him to be at the moment, and it occurred to Karen that it might be better to leave things that way. To truly know someone, she suspected, could be hard on a friendship.

"I ran into Sandy Dean in the hardware section of the drugstore, and he wanted to know if I can get a saw going for him. Told him I'd take a look at it. All it actually needed was cleaning. Which he probably knew." Mr. Brusett's voice was like an old toy, something enduring but fitful in its operation; this was so much more than he'd ever said before.

"This paint is killing me."

Mr. Brusett screwed the spark plug back into the machine.

"They probably shouldn't use this kind of paint on people's bodies," Karen said. "Least not their faces. This stuff is bad. You know how to get it off?"

"Gasoline'll take about anything off, but that'd be awful. Maybe just soap and water? You tried that?"

Mr. Tanner, the principal, came trolling up Main Street in his Ford, probably only going back to school, but there was some chance that he was looking for her, so Karen put Mr. Brusett's truck between herself and the street and ducked down beside the front fender. She did not believe Mr. Tanner had seen her. The rest of the student body and faculty followed along, headed back to fourth period, and through the ten minutes it took them to straggle past, Karen squatted by Mr. Brusett's truck, hidden, she hoped. In this posture her nose was not far off the inner tube, which smelled overwhelmingly of rubber and of the benzene compound used to patch it. She heard Mr. Brusett's tailgate slam; he came around to where she was crouched. "They're outta sight now. They've all gone around the corner."

Karen, having stiffened in the knees, stood in stages. She stepped out of the inner tube. "You want this? It's school property, and it's got this harness thing on it, but . . . What a day this has been."

"What kind of help you need? They had you crying, didn't they?"

"Crying? Oh no, that's just, like I say, it's just this paint."

"You're not in any trouble?"

"I might be in a little bit now. I think I'll get an unexcused absence out of it. Kind of a hooky thing. I'll miss the bus home, too. Never did that before. But the main thing, I gotta get this paint off my face. This is the worst stuff they ever invented."

Mr. Brusett drove her to Cale's Gas and Pawn, and in its powder room there was a cold-water tap, and she pumped granular soap from a plastic onion mounted to the wall. There was a towel dispenser and its stiff, filthy loop of toweling, so she tried wiping herself with toilet paper, and when that clotted and shred, Karen wet soap by the handful to make two supple grinding stones which she used to rasp at herself, cold water running off her wrists and all down her best Pendleton shirt, which was now irretrievably, she supposed, streaked with the blue of her school colors. The paint yielded in layers, the last of them nearly fused with her skin, and she scrubbed and scrubbed to achieve at last the complexion of a tie-dyed T-shirt. Her eyes felt better, but her face burned now, and she was wet and cold.

Mr. Brusett gave her a chocolate bar when she came out to him where he waited at the tire rack. "Tell you what," she said, "that's my last parade, and I don't care what I have to do to get around it. It's not a very . . . not civilized, I'd say."

"I never cared for 'em."

"I gotta ask you one more favor. Could I borrow a quarter to call my mom? Is it a quarter to call? Aren't you supposed to leave people money when you use their phones? Even, like, gas stations?"

"I can run you home."

"Oh, thanks. But you did enough already."

"That's all right."

"You don't wanna drive way out there just for that."

"After all the favors your people have done me?" he said. "Sure I could."

"She's gonna be so mad. Or maybe she will, or maybe she won't, I don't know. I've always made it home on the bus, like I'm supposed to. I guess it was kind of an emergency, though, and I could tell her that."

"Your mom? What if I let you off at the head of the lane? Maybe she wouldn't know the difference. Far as she'd know, you came home like every other time."

"You're way too nice," Karen said. "I don't think that would work, though, 'cause it's a couple more hours until the bus would get out there. I guess I could just wait in the weeds a while, but I'm already kinda cold."

"Oh, I think we can kill a couple hours," he said. "About all I ever do is kill time."

He turned his heater to high and set a fan to ticking and whirling behind it, and they drove out to Badger Bridge Road where, without waiting to be paid for it or even thanked, he left the saw he'd repaired at someone's hunter-orange door, on a porch full of funked equipment and arching cats. The same road brought them, a little farther along, to a switchback that they mounted steadily, though it was steep, and they'd soon reached an elevation upon which snow had fallen all the previous night, but a dry snow that achieved no great depth. Mr. Brusett stopped and got out of the truck and walked some hundreds of yards up the road, and he shot a grouse. The bird's head lolled from his fist as he walked back to her with it. He was a long time coming because he stopped like a dog to ponder every little disturbance on the ground. When he finally reached her he apologized. "I got an elk tag when the season opens, and I really like elk, too, but if I don't get one right close to the road, I don't get one. So I have to do a lot more scouting than most guys. There's a little herd that travels through here sometimes. Took a nice bull right up around the bend there, a couple years ago. Had him loaded in half an hour. All I had to do was winch him off the mountain with a come-along. You'd rather be lucky than good, but it sure don't hurt to keep looking all the time, especially when you got a chance to see a fresh sign."

"That's all right," she said. "I didn't mind waiting. This is a real good spot for me." He'd left her on a ridge from which she could see into all the valleys that had contained her life, could see that part of Fisher Meadow where two faint lines joined to form the corner where, she knew, the Dents' mailbox stood, and she liked the world reduced this way: train line, power line, the Clark Fork and Flathead rivers, gray rivers, lines on a map, vines in a dead garden. She considered the huddled homes below and enjoyed the truly effortless sympathy to be had for creatures so insignificant as to live in them; Karen found that at this altitude, she was even somewhat tolerant of herself. She liked to cut new snow. She told Mr. Brusett, "My dad got a pheasant once. But he must've got too close, 'cause he kinda blew it up. He brought this thing home, it was about half bird and half BB shot, and Mom just laughed at him, which kind of hurt his feelings."

"Grouse are stupid," said Mr. Brusett, "and some are *really* stupid. I've knocked 'em over with sticks while they were looking at me. Species like that, I don't see how you could call 'em a game bird, and I also don't see how they survive, but they do, and they're everywhere. And you can eat 'em. Pretty dark meat, and gamy, but if you don't need variety, and if you didn't need a few vitamins, you could probably live off of just grouse."

"Sounds like a awful lot of feathers and guts to me," she said. "They must really breed like rabbits, huh?"

Her bird was the magpie, she told him. She stalked them with a wrist rocket. She said she'd flung an awful lot of shots at them and never hit one; everywhere you went, there's another magpie standing just out of range, or standing on a window ledge, an inch from a big, expensive window—they did not make targets of themselves, and if they were as elegant a bird as the sky could ever offer, still they never pretended to be anything but scavengers, and something irresistible in her told her to drive them off. "But I never do connect," she said. "I don't even wing 'em or anything, 'cause I'm right-handed and left-eyed, that's what I think it is. It's that and my ammunition. Can't always afford marbles or think to buy 'em when I'm in a store, and I absolutely cannot make a rock fly straight. Almost any rock's gonna wobble or hook or go way catawampus when you shoot it."

"Well," said Mr. Brusett, "I got something you should try." He stopped again, this time to let her fire his little pistol, and she used a box of cartridges to chase shattering pinecones down the road. Mr. Brusett said that he had quite a few more bullets for it, and he'd give them to her, give her the bullets and the gun, too, because she'd sure get better use of it than he ever could. She was a natural. Though it was so, and though she wanted as much more shooting as she could get, Karen said, "No." She said that he was trying to be way too kind. "*Too nice?*" she said. "I wouldn't know how to deal with that." But Karen stood to be persuaded; she did love the accomplishment of hitting, with that little catch in the breath, hitting exactly where she aimed. With the pistol would come that black holster, too, and she could certainly see that strapped to her thigh. But then she happened to think that in her short acquaintance of the gun, she'd learned to make it deadly but not how to make it safe.

"And who needs another tragedy?" she said. "You're always hearing about people gettin' shot. I can't believe how many people seem to get shot, and a lot of 'em for not too good a reason." Still, she wanted it. "No," she said, "that'd be way too much." But she wanted her little sweetheart, with its bark and its bite, she wanted that pistol pretty keenly now.

· 4 ·

FROM THEIR FIRST afternoon together Henry Brusett said that
he knew he'd eventually bore her, but in the beginning she saw
no end to him. Though he warned her early on that he'd been
named a mental defective by the Social Security Administration, they
both thought him competent enough to teach her how to shoot, to
hunt and fish, how to run a saw in slash and in heavy timber. He would
not, he said, show her his way of doing things; he would show her the
right way, and in his company she finally learned to read the country
she'd so poorly inhabited thus far, for Mr. Brusett knew what wanted
direct sun and what wanted shade; he knew what lived in standing
water and which birds ate voles and which birds ate berries and seed;
he could find weasel, ferret, and ringtail pheasant if he wanted them;
and viscerally he contained the knowledge of the day, sometimes the
hour, when trees would fruit, when flowers would bloom; and when
all these things that he knew bubbled up in him, apparently because
she was near, they would smile at each other. "Listen to me," he'd say.
"I just go on and on, don't I?"

"I like to hear that stuff. If I didn't, why would I be here?"

He told her she'd tire of it, he was sure, but as long as she'd be his
legs for him, he'd be happy to point things out to her. He had only to get
himself a little way off the road before he started finding and describing to her new threads in the tapestry of his practical understanding.

With an eye to harvest, he showed her that an alder thicket was an almanac, and for Mr. Brusett the grass and the weeds lay this way or that way not randomly but for some reason, and the wind never merely blew, but blew from a certain direction, at a certain velocity, carrying a specific, telling scent. He was a barometer, never surprised by any weather. For Mr. Brusett, all things, saving Mr. Brusett himself, served perfectly some purpose, and through him Karen was introduced to a reassuring order. "There'll be a mayfly hatch tonight, and if you got a fly-casting rig at sundown, you'll have good fishing. About anywhere along the river or the lower parts of the creeks. There I go again, the endless expert, huh? But it's true, watch and see."

Karen's solitude out of doors, after she'd spent some time with Mr. Brusett, was a larger, more sovereign place; there was more in it to see and to think about, and though he'd furnished her with many new resources for being alone, she now preferred passing time in his company. She had never before been so useful to anyone, never nearly so necessary.

"I was married over twenty years to the same woman," Henry once told her, "and I didn't know her good enough, really, just to pass the time of day. Same thing with my boys. Same thing with everybody." He said that the state had once tried to patch him back together, back when he'd gotten bunged up, but they'd found that he was a little crazy, too, and so at that point everyone threw in the towel, and they put him on full disability, and now he was one of those drains on society that a working man always hated. They told him he suffered a form of high anxiety, a severe case of something to do with other people. "But see?" he said. "When I'm around you I get to talkin' like the old gals down at the beauty parlor. Which I kind of like. When I'm around you."

Henry was to give her at different times the small pistol, a Buck knife, and six years of *Reader's Digest*s, and she learned to avoid looking for very long at or commenting favorably on anything he owned for fear that he'd make an instant, irrevocable gift of it. Henry's was a sometimes terrible gratitude. He did her the favor of seeing her, though, of attending so closely to her existence as to know her shifting essence, to confirm it, and for this favor she was every bit as glad of his company as he was of hers, but she never would convince him of it.

The Dents saw her apprenticeship with the puzzling Mr. Brusett as a very fine thing, and they were pleased with the occasional fish that came of it, and venison and duck, and at finding red fir split and rucked high and deep on their porch. When Karen brought home her .243 Savage, her first gainful wage and first substantial property, Jean offered thanks in prayer: "Lord God," she said, "thank you for this rifle, and for the blessing of showing our girl a way to get by." Karen knew that the Dents liked to see her put to good use, but Karen knew that what especially pleased them was having her so frequently off somewhere with Mr. Brusett and not, therefore, lurking around the property, in and out of sight. They liked her better at a distance, and they always had.

As graduation approached, Karen had only one certainty regarding her future, and that was that she'd lived with the Dents as long as she could. Her folks were hinting often and broadly that they felt the same. She received as a senior many pamphlets that offered ways to go about putting herself on the road to success, or suggesting programs that would allow her to seize opportunities "NOW." There were loans available. Her mother became very excited for a time at the hope of Karen becoming a dental hygienist; in just eighteen months she could be earning a good living and have her independence, too. Or, Jean suggested, what about becoming a certified care attendant? That was a goal that could be reached in six weeks, and the enfeebled and slightly disabled were, according to the literature, to be found in every city and town across America. A licensed CCA could work anywhere. But

Karen didn't think she'd have the patience or compassion for those careers. She wasn't drawn to secretarial work, didn't think she'd like bookkeeping. She was too shy, she thought, to be in the armed services or to be a waitress. She was not lazy, or so she hoped; she simply couldn't think of how, in very practical terms, she was to begin life apart from her family.

In April a reporter from the *River Register* came to collect copies of graduation pictures. The reporter told the seniors that the graduation issue was the *Register*'s number one printing all year, that an extra four hundred copies would run, every one of them crammed with sheets and sheets of coupons for the meat department at IGA. The reporter provided forms on which they were to write out their full names, their parents' names, how long they'd been in district schools, and, in twenty-five words or less, what they intended to do next. "Karen Ellen Dent," she wrote, and "Jean Dent," and "Galahad Dent," and "13 yrs," and, rather than admitting that she'd been too stupid to imagine any future at all, she wrote, "I have a job helping my friend and that is where I would like to maybe live with him." Her picture and aspirations were published countywide the following week, and the day following that, she stood at Henry Brusett's door with her father, who had brought the .243 to the meeting also, and not with the intention of returning it.

"Brusett," said Galahad, "what have you been up to?"

Henry, in his long johns and a chenille bathrobe, had tried to invite them into his strange old trailer, and when that failed he stood on his metal stoop, blinking. His boots were on, unlaced.

Galahad walked up close, face to face with Henry, the rifle loaded and armed and its sling wrapped round his forearm. Her father was in a mood. Though he was often angry and always stupid, Karen could not recall seeing him quite so beside himself as this. He'd drawn the sling so taut over his arm that his hand lay bloodless along the rifle stock. His lips had bled salt. Such a fit, such an upset over his daughter's virtue, which was at any rate intact, and which was in all events a technicality. How did Galahad think her virtue was in any way his to protect? Now she meant life or death to him? Now? Her father seemed to adore the thought that he'd been so betrayed and so wounded that he was free to wander off into a glory of self-pity where, probably, anything he might do should be excused. Karen could not imagine where his judgment might take him next; she only knew that she didn't want to be afraid. Her father would enjoy her fear, and why would she ever want to allow him that pleasure? His throat had constricted, and when he spoke, sincerity and a spray of spittle were evident, and he wheezed like the dented tin teapot unable to contain a head of steam. "Mister," he said, "I think you're down to just one thing you can decently do here. You better marry this girl in the eyes of my Savior."

Henry made a visor of his palm and blinked steadily at them from beneath it as if they were at the far end of a field. There were welts on his cheeks from heavy sleeping; he'd had no recent acquaintance with the light of day. This, Karen thought, must be one of those blue periods he'd mentioned by way of explaining the times, the months, when he didn't come around. He'd told her he was prone to burrow in, but this was the first she'd seen of him in hibernation. He was smaller for it. The twist and stiffness in his body were more pronounced. He looked at them, and there was something mechanical in his regard. "Karen? Did I . . . is there something I don't know about?"

"Don't play stupid, Brusett. You know what this is." Galahad had decided that he might after all be, in the right circumstance, a hard man. If sufficiently wronged, he might even become a hero. Either way, it appeared he was working himself up to some kind of drama with the rifle.

"This is a misunderstanding," Karen said. "I told him. I told him and told him and told him, he's got it wrong."

"Yeah," said Henry. "But what? What'd he get wrong?"

"I told the paper guy I might come up here to live. That's all it was. And now I think, well, I *know*, he's got some misunderstanding out of it. Dad. Dad. I told you. Come on. Please."

"The paper?" said Henry. "The *news*paper?"

"You could say it slipped out."

"What slipped? I think I gotta have a few more details."

"And where did she come by that idea, Brusett? The two of you up here? Don't that make a cozy arrangement for you?"

"I don't recall that it was ever discussed."

"I explained that, too," said Karen. "I told him it was my own idea. *Just* my idea. And I told him that. And it wasn't even an idea, hardly. Just something I said at the moment."

"She could stay here if she wants," said Henry. "But where?"

"Right," said Galahad. "Where? If she got the idea she should come here, then you must've put it there, and if she's coming here, even if she's just been here before with you, that calls for a ceremony in my mind. The ring, the ceremony, the blessing—you better get ready for the whole shitaree . . . I mean the sacrament or whatever it's supposed to be. See how mad this has got me?"

"What're you gonna do, Mr. Dent? Shoot me?"

"You'll do the right thing, Brusett."

"How could you wish that on your own daughter? Damn. Look at me, would you? You want this for her? What the hell?"

"What do you mean?" said Karen. "What do you mean, 'Look at you'?"

Henry drew his robe closed. "Let's everybody settle down. First thing, why don't you switch that safety on? Were you gonna shoot me, or what?"

"I think you better say you'll do the right thing."

"Put the gun down."

64

"All it was," said Karen, "I told the newspaper I worked for you. Not even for you—I told 'em I worked for some*body*. I told the paper I might come up here to live. But I wasn't even thinking. I hadn't thought it through, I just said it."

"Seems to me," said Galahad, "that neither one of you has been thinking too much. But you better start now."

"Something got by me here," Henry said. "I must be missing something."

"Yeah. A proposal of marriage. You want her livin' here, that's what it'll take."

"He never asked me to live anywhere," Karen repeated. "Or do anything, or . . . "

"So," said Galahad, "he didn't even have to ask. Does that make it any better?"

"Hold up," said Henry. "I think if you keep talkin' like that, then maybe you will have to shoot somebody. 'Cause you're pissin' me off. How you can talk about your own girl this way—poor-mouth her? She's a good girl, and you oughtta know that. What's wrong with you? Fuck you. Shoot me."

"Think I wouldn't?"

"I think I don't care. Shoot or put it up; don't embarrass yourself. Ah, but it's too late, Dent. Shoot. Go on and shoot me."

"Wait," said Karen.

Galahad sent a round into one of the tires under Henry's trailer, which popped, and they all flinched and then stood there looking from one to the other. Galahad leveled the .243 at Henry's chest, and Henry said once again, "Fuck you."

"He doesn't even use that word around me," Karen told her father. "Now, see what you're doin'? Stop it. You're crazy. You are crazy, and I don't like you, and I wanted to live anywhere but where you are. Stop it. Henry doesn't even talk that way."

"Shoot," said Henry. "Don't stand there shakin', shoot me."

"Henry," she said, "would you please shut up? Please?"

"I don't like what he said. This is a good girl, she's your own daughter, and I don't see how you missed it, or didn't know. Why do I have to be the one to tell you she's a good girl? That's what's wrong here—me havin' to tell you."

"He's crazy, Henry. He can't see anything. He doesn't know anything." Her father's forefinger, she saw, was snug on the trigger, and the rifle's barrel ended just a foot from Henry Brusett's heart. "Look," she said, "if it makes you happy, I'll marry him. Why not?"

"You don't have to do one damn thing," said Henry.

"What if I wanted to? How do you know I wouldn't want to?"

"Karen," said Henry, "now, this is gettin' out of hand."

Galahad's lips were crusted white, his breathing shallow but loud. "I said I'd marry him."

"No," said Henry.

"I want to," she said.

A vein burst in Galahad's nose and splattered his sandy mustache.

"No, I really want to. Who else would I marry, anyway? Who'd suit me better than you would?"

"About anybody," said Henry. "Anybody, honey. Now, quit it, or you'll get me cryin'."

"Honey?" said Galahad Dent.

"He doesn't call me that. And he doesn't use bad language, either. Usually. Put down that gun. Come on. Please. Before anything can happen."

"I guess we could try and make a little sense here," said Henry. "But Mr. Dent, you have got no business . . . You got a wonderful girl, and you talk like this? You even hear yourself?"

Eyes twitching and raised to heaven, Galahad pleaded, "Master, let me know." He knelt and they waited an odd amount of time until he had his answer or was bored with waiting for it, and then Galahad finally unslung the .243 and laid it on the ground before him. He remained on one knee, too tired or too contrite to rise. A crow called to another crow off in the trees, and a gray squirrel capered out over open ground. Henry toed the rifle to point it away from everyone.

"The same thing still goes," said Karen. "I'd like to marry you. For me, not for him or what he thinks. I'd like to. For me. This is modern times, and I'm the whattayacallit. The age of consent. Anyway, I can propose to somebody, I think, like, legally. Sorry it had to be this way, but that's what I'm doin'. So, do you want to, Henry? Get married? To me, I mean?"

It took her three days to convince him, as she had convinced herself in a moment, that he was her only sufferable option. She asked him to call her, though she knew it meant his coming down off the mountain each time; she asked that he call every night at six, because they really did need to talk, and when they talked she told him that all she wanted in all the world was to be with someone who she could expect to be nice to her. Was that too much to ask? She said she would not be a problem, that she could cook a little and would learn to do better. She could be his legs for him all day every day, and just think what they might accomplish. She said she'd take up very little room because she intended to leave almost everything she had behind with the Dents. She'd bring her clothes and her woods gear and her own shampoo and toothbrush and that was all. She said she needed to go somewhere, anywhere, and she needed to go right now, and she had nowhere else to go, no one else that she could think to ask for any help. All she wanted was food, and all she absolutely needed was shelter under some roof other than the Dents'. Henry said he thought maybe he could buy a second trailer for her, but Karen said that it wasn't necessary, that she was talking about marriage. She was very surprised to find herself in agreement with her father on a point of such importance, but, truly, if they were going to live together, they might as well live together as man and wife; there were too many advantages in it to ignore. "Actually," she said, "I think it's a great idea. I mean, don't you?"

"Oh, I'd like it fine, and I wish that was the only thing we had to consider, whether I liked it or not. Problem is—it's ridiculous. Because you could do, you *should* do a lot better for yourself. I just can't tell you how flattered I am, but no."

"I don't know that. I don't know that at all. In fact, I doubt it very much. You're as good as they come, Henry. Good as I've ever seen, anyway. And, as far as ridiculous goes—everything is ridiculous. Believe me, I'm ready right now."

One Friday in May, Karen rode with Henry over Thompson Pass, just the two of them, and though by then the road had been open several weeks already, there were still stretches of it where snow lay drifted and plowed into ten-foot berms on either side, and they traveled in those places through a crystal canyon, under a faultless sky. The twenty-fifth of May. At the top of the pass, somewhere along the state line, Henry mentioned a trailhead, buried now, but that trail, he promised, led to a lesser trail, and that trail, about three miles along, came to the biggest huckleberry patch he'd ever seen, a place rarely without a bear in it. He'd show her sometime. They descended into Idaho and drove over the Fourth of July Pass and on into Coeur d'Alene, and before eleven thirty that morning, Pacific Standard Time, they'd bought two plain white gold bands and been to the Kootenai County Courthouse for their license. At the Old Joinery, a pleasant receptionist told them that Justice Quinlevan had committed to unite three couples before them that day, and with that and with a lunch break for the staff, she wondered if they would be willing to come back at four forty-five?

Henry took Karen to Sterner's Family Restaurant for the endless pink lemonade it advertised and for its broasted chicken. They went to

Sears to look at generators and to buy a wheel for his wheelbarrow. He tried to buy her a jacket that was on sale, marked 60 percent off. "For a wedding present?" he thought.

"But it's supposed to be other people who give us presents, isn't it? Which I don't want anyway. I got my wedding present soon as we loaded my stuff in your truck. Soon as we drove outta that yard." Karen did not wish to seem ungrateful, but it was a girlish garment he was offering, its hood lined with a purple pelt, a thing otherwise white and puffy and not at all her taste. "Anyway," she said, "I won't hardly have any use for a jacket until it gets cold again. Next fall. I don't wear 'em any more than I have to. You'll be surprised by how little stuff I use."

Henry bought her instead five hundred rounds for her pistol and some neatsfoot oil for her holster.

Karen wondered how some women stood a wait of months and even years to marry, for it seemed to her that once an agreement was reached, an understanding, then the rest was urgent work. Before sunset, her name would no longer be Dent. At the restaurant, Henry asked her if she was sure, and she said yes. In Sears, he asked her again, and again she said yes. From Sears they walked the mall until they came to a snow cone stand. Karen had a coconut-lime, Henry a raspberry, and, his lips scarlet, he told her, "I wouldn't be a good catch even for a woman my own age. Even for an ugly one. As you say, I'd be nice to you and all, yeah, you could be sure of that. But you can back away from this any old time, and I'd sure understand it if you did. No hard feelings at all." Karen dismissed this with a face she'd already learned to make at him. Poor dear. Slow learner. Every struggling word made him more completely hers, and if he was trying to get out of it now, he was going about it the wrong way. They went to the bookstore and bought collections of crossword puzzles, and pinochle decks, and some spy novels, and then it was time to go back.

There were typed bulletins in the vestibule of the Old Joinery dating from February and June of 1967, and these had been preserved on onionskin, now a urine shade, on black velvet under glass:

Our own Lake Couer d'Alene one of seven most beautiful lakes in the World

No Solicitors

No Warrants—this Court does not do business but marriages

Marry in Haste Repent in Leisure

Stay Out of the Dominican Republic

There was a tally sheet of ceremonies performed by Justice Quinlevan each year since 1967, and no one of those years had seen fewer than eight hundred marriages. There were framed and signed portraits of Consuela Quinlevan, taken at intervals of decades, and in each of these she was deep at the same console, consumed in her Wurlitzer's swooping keyboards and pedals and stops. It was Mrs. Quinlevan who came to lead them into the Matrimonial Chamber—she explained that they had to call it that for tax reasons—but they only recognized her as Mrs. Quinlevan when she took her place at the familiar organ, for she had withered very much since the most recent of her photographs. When at last they met him, Justice Quinlevan was scarcely sturdier than his wife. He wore his wife's rouge. Another ancient couple was in attendance, seated along the wall under a placard that read WITNESSES—SUGGESTED GRATUITY—$10.00 PER SIGNEE. These were the birdlike Bernardos, she in crinoline, he in gabardine, and they spent their days waiting for moments like these when the betrothed arrived without bridesmaids or groomsmen. The Bernardos for their little fee would form the genuinely pleased and fully legal complement for a wedding party. They rose to do so. Mrs. Quinlevan's hands instantly ceased to tremble as she set them to "The Wedding March," which she played, verse and chorus, as if she'd only just perfected it, as if it were not a dirge, as if their progress to the altar was not a matter of a few stunted steps past ranks of empty folding chairs.

Mrs. Bernardo pressed a bouquet of cloth baby's breath into Karen's hands. Justice Quinlevan asked her a question that she could not understand, for he spoke torturously, as through a mouthful of scalding oatmeal. So he asked more simply, "Rheadhy?"

"Yes," she said. "Yes, please."

The justice's tongue, lips, and lungs were all at odds, and he was not only hard to understand but painful to hear and to see speaking. It seemed from the pace of his voice that he'd begun the ceremony, and that he was telling them a story, and Karen worried that when he got to her part, her time to recite, she would misunderstand him and fail to jump in. The justice said the word "obeedienth," the phrase "heavnen nun nirth," but finally, when it came to the matter of the rings, he made himself clear enough, and then he prompted them through some minimal vows, and then he invited Henry to "kidth the bohrdh." It seemed to Karen that the justice and all his staff were addicted to the optimism of this moment; Mr. Bernardo whispered, "Kiss her, sir." And Henry, regretfully if she was not mistaken, brushed her cheek with his lips. "Conlahnshuhns," said Justice Quinlevan. "MidsuhnMihz Ehnday Butsuhdt." Mrs. Quinlevan played them out the door with her powerful rendering of "Tiny Bubbles," and they didn't go arm in arm as Karen had expected, nor hand in hand; they walked out as they had walked in, side by side, and they could still hear the Wurlitzer skirling when Henry started the truck.

The twenty-fifth of May, she thought. From now on this would be their anniversary.

They went back the long way, the flat route home that leads to the bridge that crosses to Sandpoint, and along the shores of Lake Pend Oreille and through Hope and East Hope and then upriver and back into Montana, and they rode as if they'd driven this road many times before, as if they'd now said all they could say to each other, and they pretended that the new silence between them was comfortable. Still, this was so very much better than any trip she'd ever made as a Dent. Karen considered that if she had just seen one of the seven most beautiful lakes in the world, and if the scenery was at least equally good all the way home, then she must be a very lucky girl to live in such a lovely, large paradise. A lucky woman. She was entitled to think of herself as a woman now, and she thought that she might as well do that. Being a girl had certainly been no good.

· 5 ·

THE TRAILER ON Fitchet Creek had two bedrooms, one of them little more than a closet with no window and a sliding door for its entrance. This was the room Henry assigned himself when Karen moved in. When with crippling diffidence she tried to question the arrangement, he told her, "Women need more space." He apologized for the fact that in the larger bedroom, her room now, tiers of bookshelves were everywhere, but Karen said that they made it seem homey; they reminded her of a quilt she'd seen hanging in some fussy old woman's sitting room, and, she said, she'd probably have time for quite a bit of reading. He'd been a long while alone here—the books were organized by labeled sections: SEA STORIES, SPY STORIES, WESTERNS, MANUALS, RELIGION & PHILOSOPHY & HEALTH. The walls were of a honey-colored veneer, and Henry had contrived to make it smell of vanilla in the room where she was to sleep. She was to lie on and under goose down in her new bed, and so from the very start, he'd already given her an abundance of everything she'd asked of him, but he seemed to want nothing more than her presence in exchange, and so, though life with Henry was a remarkable improvement over anything she'd known before, the old question had yet to be answered. The terms of her marriage left her asking still, "What have I done?"

That she'd become Mrs. Brusett, she soon discovered, was a startling fact in many quarters. Principal Tanner agreed to print her diploma that way, but he did ask if she'd consider calling in sick or making just any excuse to skip the graduation ceremony. It was her decision, of course, and he couldn't keep her away, but did she think that it would be fair to the other seniors to create all that stir when her new name was announced onstage? Wouldn't that kind of take the wind out of it for the other kids? Mrs. Henry Brusett? Could she imagine him reading that out loud in front of people? Did she want to be such a big distraction or put her new husband through what would have to be a pretty embarrassing evening for him, too?

Karen didn't want any of these things, and so, a week early and with Mr. Tanner's tepid congratulations and his promise that her diploma would be in the mail, she was allowed to be done at school; Mr. Tanner said of her last few days of class, "Why bother?"

Henry had sent her to school that day in his old Triumph, which, as soon as he'd seen her in the driver's seat, he'd pronounced *her* Triumph, " . . . for what it's worth. It's the TR4, and they're worse than temperamental, but it happens to be runnin' strong right now, and you look good in it, so have a big time." The car made an outsized rumbling, and it rattled from a history of use on roads for which it was never designed, but as Karen drove out of the school parking lot, summarily dismissed from the last of her old life, her life to date, and chafing a bit at the injustice and the anticlimax of it, it felt fine to shake her hair out and run through the gears, which she was already doing with precision. With the money that had been earmarked for her cap and gown, she stopped at Pearson's Supply and bought three laying hens and a newly weaned kid, a goat with a puppy's disposition, and she had these crated, and she stacked and strapped the crates into the passenger's seat and set off with the top down and her new chickens flying in place beside her. She had in mind an endless summer.

On seeing how her menagerie pleased her, and how perhaps Fitchet Creek had been a little underpopulated while he'd been its sole tenant, Henry bought her more pullets later that week, and he bought her more goats, and because all these creatures would want feed and make fertilizer, Henry thought a garden should be made, and so early one morning the Brusetts went into a stand of lodgepole together, and by late that evening they'd decked enough poles to raise a deer fence around the new garden and to build some pens and a supplemental roof over the trailer. Henry said that during the previous year or two, a series of heavy snows had gradually crushed the trailer's roof out of shape, and so the ceiling had been leaking, but he hadn't been too bothered by it until now. He said he'd been overlooking a lot of things until she came along. He told her during their day in the lodgepoles he marveled at it, that he felt better than he had in a long, long time, and he kept saying this even as he stopped from time to time to breathe like a woman in labor and as his limp worsened until his simplest locomotion was acrobatic. "Fresh air and exercise," he told her, "used to be those were the last things I needed to remind myself about." Uneven ground was hard for him, or any kind of lifting, or to walk very far even on the level, but he said it was a price worth paying to get out sometimes. He said he'd been in real danger of turning useless before she showed up.

When he was feeling right, Henry liked to make things. He had a shop somewhere in the valley, on a piece of land behind the lot where he had lived with his first family. Karen imagined a space full of good light, bins filled with incomprehensible materials and tools. There, Henry could fashion from metal or wood or even from heavy fabric almost anything he thought to make, and whatever he made was for her: the pineapple carved in pine, the miniature windmill he set spinning on a stump, the spice rack. Karen once mentioned in passing her preference for eating and for sometimes sleeping out of doors, and so Henry had built the sleeping porch, built it in sections at his shop and then hauled these up the mountain and attached them to the trailer, to each other, and all at once one day there was the enclosed porch they'd use in all but the worst weather for their dining room.

Karen guiltily preferred those times when Henry wasn't feeling well because that was their time for talk and for the routines that were theirs, their experiments—serviceberry tea, the works of Charles Dickens, her embroidery. It was the first reliable intimacy she'd ever known. Their tuneless, easy little jokes were mother's milk to her, and in the beginning, and for a long time after that, Henry was horizon enough, and it was just as well because, as they discovered before they'd been together a month, anywhere they might go together as a couple—the grocery store, the post office, ten minutes at a gas pump—these were all to be stations in a hell of swiveling chins, and checked glances, and mean and tawdry giggling. Henry and Karen Brusett caused, especially among women, an unmistakable disgust wherever they went, either that or some weird glee, and Karen wondered if it would have been so if they were not timid, if they'd flaunted their arrangement. When together in any public place, they could not avoid constant, naked staring, and neither of them enjoyed being an abomination, though it was, if anything, better than being mistaken for daughter and father. In time, they began to make most of their trips away from Fitchet Creek alone. Their pleasure in each other was odd, they knew, and must necessarily also be private.

But they did often fish Flathead Lake that first summer. Out on the water they could be two people seen distantly on a boat, of no particular sex, or age, or relationship, and the mackinaw fishing was very good that year in the channel between Wild Horse and Cromwell islands. Also in that season their farmstead burst into production, and they were eating fresh eggs every morning and an eventually obscene abundance of zucchini and the fancy pods from a Chinese pea vine. They built the roof over the trailer and rolled out asphalt roofing over it, a redundant forest green. Cordwood accumulated on the rise, cabbage grew. Henry, with a new tan over his faded and ancient one, was looking better, too.

"Wouldn't it be great," she asked one day, "if the ground never froze? That would be a dream of mine."

"Yeah, but it does," said Henry, "up here it freezes hard, and long about February, we'll be like twins in somebody's belly. A person's only got so many secrets and tips, you know—you could run out of things to say. There's only so much. You probably better have a hobby."

"We'll talk," she said. "We just do, don't you think? Like we're makin' up for lost time?"

"Yeah," he said. "But there's only so much a person can say."

He saw the dust on every surface, the rust in every mechanism, and his resignation would at times wear on Karen until she noticed that her husband was too old for her. It was not as though she never noticed.

Hunting alone that fall, she filled both their deer tags. Henry said he was feeling a little used up, feeling like he'd better not try the woods again for a while, and he'd started spending many of his days doing some secretive thing at his shop. So she hunted alone, and she toured the National Bison Range in her Triumph, which she also drove to Missoula one Saturday to hear a droopy, famous folk singer. She drove well into cold weather with the top down, and every mile of it put her that much farther from high school and her time as Miss Dent. They could have their Jesus and their periodic tables—she had Henry and her little income and her luxuries, and so, she supposed, she could let bygones be bygones.

On their first Christmas together, Henry gave her a hammer dulcimer with a rosewood sound box and hammers worked in yew. "Those pegs," he said, "I had to buy. For those I had to send a bank draft all the way to Birmingham, England." He gave her a tuning fork as well.

"You made this, Henry? This is the most beautiful thing I ever saw in real life, but, honey, you know, don't you, I'm not one of these skillful people? You might've kinda wasted this on me."

"I've seen you shoot."

"Yeah, but I don't think that would have much to do with . . . "

"And I've heard you sing."

"It's just, I don't have a very complicated mind."

"Oh," he said, "it'll get that way."

He then showed her a deed naming Mrs. Henry Brusett a joint tenant on a 10.8-acre parcel in the Diamond Peak Ranger District—the accompanying map showed them surrounded on all sides by miles and miles titled to lumber companies or the federal government. "Joint tenant," Henry explained, "means that when I die, the property is automatically yours. It is anyway. It was yours as of last Thursday down at the clerk and recorder's. Joint and undivided."

"Henry."

"Makes for a hideaway. Or you could sell it, get something else, do something else if you wanted. Should be worth a little something with the improvements and everything."

"When you die? Henry, that's a topic I don't care for, okay? It's just gruesome, to get into that."

"Well, I don't have any plans that way. I mean, just in case."

"Please," she said. "We're practically still on our honeymoon."

There would be no honeymoon, for theirs was not that kind of marriage. Her portion was his kindness, and he could not be other than kind to her, and she found this very comfortable. But Fitchet Creek was, just as Henry had warned her, in the middle of a snowbelt, and in those months when the snow was deep, it was necessary to park the truck down on the main road, and eventually they rarely left the place at all, and their little residence became, just as Henry had said it would, close and steamy as a womb. In winter his bones attacked him, and he could endure the pain but do very little else while it was at its worst, and Karen, having found herself essentially alone again, learned in their first winter together to play all the tunes in a book called *Soldier's Joy*. In winters to come she learned to play them at tempos so hot her hammers blurred above the piano-wire strings.

· 6 ·

SHE HAD BRUISED her heel walking barefoot, and the last half mile home was an unbalanced agony, a window into her husband's life. The shower shed had been encircled with wide yellow tape, and she found Henry out on the sleeping porch, sitting on an overturned five-gallon drum and wearing only the fat man's jeans they'd given him at the jail. In five years of marriage, this was the first she'd seen of his naked torso, his naked feet, the first she'd seen of his many wounds. He wore a towel over his head and breathed vapors he made with a camp stove and water on the low boil in a saucepan. From out of his depletion he looked up at her, a bead of sweat at the tip of his nose. The flesh around his eyes was so swollen and discolored that she thought at first they'd beaten him. "You're home," he said gratefully.

"Does that tape around the shed mean we can't use the shower now?"

"I'll hook the propane up so you can get a hot shower inside."

"That's all right," she said. "I can do that. Can I see your back? Maybe I shouldn't ask, but can I?" There was damage on it he mentioned infrequently but lived with always, an injury with which she, too, had been living.

"You don't want to see that."

"But I do," she said. "You're my husband, and it's time I put my foot down and took a look at you." She went around behind him. A rope of raised tissue snaked down his shoulder, down and across his back, and into the waistband of his secondhand jeans; lesser scars, livid little starbursts, clustered all around it. "No wonder." She touched the rubbery mass where it passed between his shoulder blades, and he didn't shrink from her touch, and she thought it might be warmer than the flesh surrounding it. But she had small experience of his flesh, healthy or hurt. "They tell me that when you break your back, usually it gets the spinal cord, too. Which don't heal at all. I could've been baggage. Could've been dead. Very elastic spinal cord, they told me. Some guys get all the breaks. Honey, hand me that shirt, would you?"

"It's all right," she said. "It's hot in here. And where do you think they got this thing? You gotta wonder who came in wearing it. Let me get you one of your own, honey. I thought this would look worse. Well, no, it looks pretty bad. But you get over it almost right away. Seeing it. You think something like that scares me?"

"It's too ugly," he said. "Know how many times I've seen that thing myself? Too ugly for me, anyway. You've got to rig up some mirrors, and—I've seen it twice, which'll be plenty." He put the shirt on and sat again as he had been sitting before, as if he'd just been kidney-punched.

"They would've rode you home, Henry."

"You know how I am."

"Yeah, but to get yourself all crippled up over it—for you that was a dumb kinda walk to take. Looks like they let you wear your own boots, though. Mom'd call that a blessing."

"I think those people, those cops and everybody, they might be comin' back. If they got to lookin' around in the medicine cabinet, or my room, I could get into quite a little trouble. More trouble I don't need. Those authorities find a couple hundred sample packs, they know you must be some doctor's special little buddy. Couple guys writing the same prescriptions, they find all those bottles, and pretty soon quite a few people could be in trouble."

Regret was in everything this morning; she felt anemic under it. "I can't get used to thinking of us as criminals. Can you? Are we? We must be. If you stop and look at it, we were already breakin' quite a few laws. Just the way we been livin'. I been known to cut forty, fifty cords of firewood on one five-cord permit."

"Yeah, we're some real desperadoes, honey. Look, we've had the right principle—just stay out of sight. We let everybody alone, they let us alone. That works, as long as it's workin', but now we're somebody else's business. That won't be good. I feel very bad about what I did, but so what? That kid's still just as dead. So I don't know what happens now. I don't even know what should happen."

"You did what you thought . . . "

"I did what I did," he said.

"You think they're comin' back?"

"They said they might. One of those deputies did. He could've been woofing, but they might be comin' around. To investigate. Though I can't see where there'd be much left to look at."

"There wasn't much, was there? Just . . . That dang water heater burns so much propane, I really hate to go back to usin' it." Henry was sometimes no better company than a hundred-pound sack of potatoes. Henry and his old hurts, Henry and his new ones. "I didn't tell anyone," she said. "Not anything. Did you?"

"With all those people around? All of 'em lookin' right straight at me? I was lucky I didn't swallow my tongue. *Couldn't* say anything. They saw how much it bothered me, so then they make it a point to stare you down. How could we have got any farther out of everybody's way? We didn't go lookin' for trouble. Did we?"

"One thing we could do, we could just go ahead and tell somebody what happened. I think we'd only have to tell one person. That should be enough."

"What happened? What do you think happened?"

"Well, you thought, you must've thought . . . "

Henry's head swiveled in the negative.

"But you could still say that you thought—something."

"No," he said.

"You wouldn't have to lie. Everybody, and I mean *every*body has been tellin' me not to say anything. So I think that's probably right, don't you? If we just didn't say anything? At all?"

"Want me to get that water heater hooked up?"

"No," she said. "I can do it. It'll be nice to feel a little bit clean again."

But first there were her morning chores, for which, this morning, she was grateful. The goats were restive and hungry. The nanny Jenny, previously mute, had lately developed a tremulous, heartrending bleat, and she met Karen with this, and it sounded the whole time that Karen milked her. Two days earlier, Jenny had eaten a pair of black jeans that had blown off the clothesline and into her pen, and her milk was still gray with it. Nature. Karen weeded the garden with her short hoe. She picked and ate a tomato. She unloaded the truck and shored up a collapsing corner of the woodpile. She stacked some orphan tires. While the police and ambulance people had been there the night before, she'd known a ludicrous moment of embarrassment about how hillbilly they'd let the place become, the clutter and half-assed geegaws everywhere, and just plain garbage. So Karen went about clearing up, and picking up, and she established a burn pile and made a layer of order on the clearing, and only when she'd made it presentable did she happen to think that her sudden tidiness must surely seem suspicious in the eyes of any return visitor. Well, suspicion would be thick on the ground now, no matter what she might do or not do, and having seen Fitchet Creek through the eyes of strangers, she'd been ashamed. It was half past two in the afternoon, and she was not at all tired, or not in any useful way.

Karen, very ripe, decided that she must bathe at last, and she attached a propane canister to the small water heater that served their bathroom. When she'd lit the heater's pilot light, and as she waited for the water in the tank to warm, she saw that the shower stall had grown a film of mold during its time of disuse. She got a bucket, a brush, and some liquid bleach, and she stripped and went into the shower stall like an avenger, scrubbing. She began to cry. She cried, recovered, and cried again, all the while leaning into the scrub brush with both hands. Breathing caustic fumes, she nearly fainted, and so she finished the job with a milder solution, and then at last she cleaned herself, draining the hot water tank. She dressed and asked Henry if he was still not hungry. He said he was not, but she gave him peanut butter anyway, a smear of it on a slice of an early apple. He sat on his bucket, barefoot, and she saw how one of his big toes jogged in at a sensational angle.

"I've been a little shaky," she said. "What about you?"

"Me too."

"You scared? I am."

"Not yet," he said. "Not like I will be."

"All right, but . . . Henry, was it just your extra pills you threw away, or was it everything? 'Cause I, I don't think you can stop like that, all at once, because you been, well, you know. You been on it so hard for such a long time now. Much as I'd like it if you could, I don't think you should try and stop all at once that way. Try and do that with everything else that's going on right now? Too much. I don't think it's a good idea. You better try and come down easy, huh?"

"I was a man once," he said. "Good, bad, indifferent—I couldn't tell you, but I used to be some kind of man."

"I'm not sayin' anything," she said. "That's what I decided to do. They don't seem to know too much. They can't seem to figure it out, so I'm zippola. It's my right."

"Do you know what you pay for that right, honey? I'd just as soon you told 'em what happened. I really wish you would."

"You could," she said. "In fact, you're the only one who really, really knows. Why don't you?"

"I keep tellin' myself I was addled. Like it would make a difference."

"Oh. But it does."

"I've been poor me in my own mind, and now that's all I am. You get to feelin' sorry for yourself, and before you know it you're . . . it's like the old-timers used to say . . . you know, I'd be kind of offended if you did do anything to protect my sorry ass. Why get saddled with some story you have to go on repeating the rest of your life? It'd be beneath you."

"No," she said. "I stay quiet. That's what the guy said. You know a Hoot, a Hoot somebody-or-other?"

"Meyers?"

"He's that main law guy? And he told me to stay quiet. I caught a ride with him, and he said we'd be okay if we stayed quiet. Which I don't understand, but that's what he said, and he told me to be sure and tell you, and I think he kind of said he liked us, and so we'd be okay. But, does that sound like a trick to you, Henry? You know him, don't you?"

"No trick," said Henry.

"And you know him?"

"I used to. He's probably about the same as he was. Same person, more or less."

"Then . . . we're okay?"

"I doubt it. I'll have to pay for this one, I think."

"Henry. Don't be that way. They don't know who he is. I get the impression they can't do very much about it if they don't know who the person was that died."

"How can they not know who he was?"

"Maybe he lost his ID," she said. "In fact, let's just say that's what happened. He lost it."

"He *lost* it?"

"That's right," she said. "Lost it before he ever got here. Henry, look, a lot of things can happen when you just sleep all the time. You pull that Rumplestiltskin thing, or whatever, and stuff's going to happen while you're asleep. Not very much, but just sometimes when I'd been out cuttin' wood, and I had my wedding ring off, so I wouldn't get it caught, and I'd keep it off if I stopped in at the Bitterroot Room for a beer. That's all. Not much. I had a few ideas, that's all. But you were asleep and asleep and asleep. And then I, I just tried to wake you up—again—and I couldn't even get a peep out of you, and then, all of a sudden you're . . . I don't know. Imagine how you must feel."

"I'd like to get my head clear," said Henry, "but I can see already I might not make it. You say they don't know who he is?"

"Doesn't seem like it so far."

"That is the loneliest thing I ever heard of. Poof, and you're gone, and nobody who knew you is any the wiser."

"Yeah, but it's better for us, I'm pretty sure, if they don't know. So maybe we better not get sentimental about that."

"Honey, you do what you . . . but I'm asking you, if you could at least give him a name, then I'd like to give him that much back. Talk about the least you could do."

"Yeah, when you put it that way, I know. Man. Shit. All right. But you gotta help me, Henry, okay? You think you can?"

"Help you?"

"Find out his name."

"You didn't know it?"

"I know how to find out what it was," she said. "But it'll take some doing. I think we gotta break a few more laws, maybe, to get it."

"But—you didn't know his name?"

"Right. So now I guess everybody's ashamed. Okay?"

"Okay," he said.

"We gotta live with this," she said. "We just gotta find some way to live with it."

"There's days on end when I don't envy the young at all."

"Nah," she said, "enough of that, now. Let's just do what we gotta do."

They waited until dark before they drove down to Red Plain, where they fueled at Orsino's and where Karen did not invest her complimentary quarter in the keno or poker machines. She did buy a sparkling quart of malt liquor. She drove them past Larry's Conoco, looking in the lot for an honest little car with Iowa plates, and they saw it, and they went on to cross the bridge and park in a stand of failing cottonwood on the far sandbar, just off the road, down near the river. They watched the water spin wherever it met resistance under the moonlight. A full moon, of course, entirely unobscured and shining near daylight down on them and their mission. A lone drake strutted back and forth on the packed sand beach, searching perhaps for the flock that had already taken wing above him. Karen fretted in preparation.

"What if there's nothing in there?" she said. "'Cause, if there isn't, if I don't find something in there that says who he is, I won't know. I wouldn't know who he was except he came from Iowa. He said he was in school there, had a kind of a girlfriend; he was almost a professional man, too, a pharmacist. That's what I really wanted. I wanted him to talk to you. If you would've woke up, then I doubt . . . "

"His name," said Henry, "is all I want to know about him."

"Just a couple more swigs," she said, "and then we'll do it. I gotta try and calm down."

They made another pass down Main Street to reconnoiter and lay a plan. The young Iowan's car had been fitted between the tow truck and a school bus that was also awaiting parts or repair, and from the street a passerby would see the K car only from a certain angle and only briefly. Karen thought that if she could reach it without drawing any attention to herself, then the rest shouldn't be too hard. She decided to approach it on foot, down through an alley leading up to the rear of the lot. "Good thing we hunt," she said. "That's where an honest person can learn to be sneaky."

Henry said he'd wait for her with the motor running, wait across Main Street and across the tracks, behind the grain elevator.

Karen's pulse tripped along at a rate much faster than any she'd ever achieved as a hunter. She put her fingers in the door latch but said at the last moment, "There's no reason why you should have to be in on this, honey. Why don't we just call it off? For right now. I'll come back later by myself."

"Go," he said. "I'll be over there waiting for you. You don't need to take any big chances, but go."

The alley was narrow and bound on one side by old brick work, on the other by a tall hedge of lilac; moon shadow was available all along her way, and Karen kept to it but met in the dark with a limping dog, an exhausted old chocolate Lab that seemed to know they were both intruders there, and they stiffened and gave each other as wide a berth as the alley would permit, and Karen climbed over a chain-link fence, and, once onto Larry's lot, she immediately lost heart. She hid behind the school bus, her back pressed to it, and it was the most mercilessly solid thing she had ever touched, and this the hottest night ever recorded in Red Plain, Montana. Karen could not make herself be calm or very smart.

Think, she thought, and she thought that it was impossible to steal from the dead, and that it was honorable to name them as necessary, and Karen knew that what she was after should not be very jealously guarded. It was not reasonable to tremble so. *This is not wrong*, she thought. And she thought of her waiting husband, that he had been waiting a while now, and she thought of this and that, and then, when she knew that courage was never coming, she decided to go on without it, and she dropped to her knees and crawled around the nose of the bus. Still on her knees, and sweating like the heroine of a jungle movie, she tried both doors of her dead friend's practical, forlorn little car. They were both locked. In what should have been an inauspicious hour of an inauspicious Sunday night in late summer, it seemed that some-one's headlights were sweeping down Main Street every few seconds; the traffic seemed consistent with the end of a ball game or a popular person's funeral. Karen waited on all fours, and she wondered if she were to stand and look into those oncoming lights her eyes would reflect red in them like a cat's.

At last, Red Plain settled into a Sunday rhythm again, and Karen felt it safe to rise from her knees and pick through the bed of the wrecker until she'd found a length of pipe in it. The pipe would be her hammer. Karen swung from the hip. The shock of that first blow made a crystalline fabric of the driver's side window and traveled up into her wrists as voltage, and she dropped the pipe, and it rang off the car then bounced on the pavement, tolling like a cracked bell. She dropped to her haunches to squat and wait and listen, and when all she heard was the crickets in their incessant surprise, she found the pipe where it had rolled under the wrecker, and she rose with it once again and delivered two more blows to the window, swatting as best she could with her face turned from her target, and at last she punched a hole in the safety glass, and she reached through it and unlocked the door.

She threw herself into the front seat so that she lay face down across it, her face pressed to the square beads of glass she'd just blown out of the window. A light swept through the rear window and off the rearview mirror, and Karen lay on her greasy cheek, hoping she was only sweating. She did not wish to bleed here. She'd made so much noise.

It was dark inside the car, darker still in the glove box; working by feel she found in it a lead weight for a tire rim, and five American Legion poppies, and a pencil stub. He was the kind of boy, she thought, who would have had his insurance in order, his registration ready for display, and Karen Brusett lay there, not very disappointed, while another light passed through the car. One of these lights would be stopping. Wouldn't someone be coming for her? So much noise. Having terrified herself, she bolted, and, backing out of the car, she banged her head on the door frame. "God," she called, high and loud. "Damn." As she paused to absorb the pain, she happened to see the leatherette folder strapped to the driver's visor, and she snapped this free and crawled back around the car and the bus and vomited, and climbed the fence again and ran back into the dark side of the alley where she stopped to catch her breath. She put her hands to her knees and heard herself panting, and then the old chocolate Lab sidled out from behind a trash bin as if he'd been called to come, the happy and confident dog now, and he came and jumped up and planted his dusty forepaws on her hip. Her heavy friend.

"Scat, buddy. Scat."

Still winded, Karen ran. She went along the alley another two blocks, turned north, and circled back across Main Street with the dog frolicking in and out of her path and plunging along trying to herd her. Then the dog, in its decrepit playfulness, began to bay at the moon. Karen shifted into a breathless sprint. Even howling as it was, and lame and old, the dog was able to run with her, and it ran with her all the way back to the waiting truck.

"Go," she told Henry. "Go, go, go, let's go."

The chocolate Lab had risen to his hind legs to bid her farewell and bay. Where had it found the strength to do all this? "Shush," she said, far out of the beast's hearing. "Shush, boy. See that, Henry? That dog latched onto me. I think he thinks he's mine. I tell you—the stuff that's been happening to me lately. Could you hear all that racket I made gettin' in and out of that car?"

"You find anything? What's that?"

"I don't even know," she said. "I didn't stop to . . . Sorry I took so long. I kept freezin' up. No, don't turn. Let's just go straight on out of town. God *damn*. Now it's runnin' after us. You believe this? Go, Henry, let's not worry about that little speed limit too much."

"He won't run far."

"Yeah, but step on it," she said. "He's like a actual demon."

A BUCKLE,
SOME BONE

·7·

A WAITING A CALL, Hoot Meyers paged through a portfolio of fifteen pictures of a corpse on a gurney, a thing presently without history or anyone to lament it and only slightly more tragic than a dissected frog. There was fascination, a comfort—*this is not me*—in seeing a stranger so utterly dead. Rigor mortis had rolled the upper lip into a sneer revealing good teeth. A careful, recent haircut and a clerk's pudgy physique. During the last hours of his life the boy had been bruised on his calves, his butt, and his shoulder blades, and these injuries, in the opinion of the medical examiner, were sustained some hours before the fatal one. It seemed he'd had a hard last day. At the back of the boy's head, shot from several angles, was a window cut into the skull to reveal a blood-laced mass of chicken fat, still glistening, recently the seat of a soul. The coroner's report mentioned seminal discharge in the corpse's shorts, but naked in death the penis lay abject upon the shriveled scrotum, and only about the eyes, not merely closed but clamped shut, was there any semblance of will in it.

Meyers held a piddling modern notion of mortality, the sense that when he himself expired he would merge with the infinite. But to do what? And what had he made of his time as flesh and blood? The enduring accomplishment of his tenure in office was a maple tree that had grown up outside his window, and it was none of his doing. Once, these sunny summer mornings had been hellish affairs, the sun streaming straight in from the east or shredded by the county's tattered blinds, the old fluorescent fixture blinking and ticking in the resulting dark. Now the blinds were long since removed. Now the red leaves had risen up to provide a dappled shade on his corner of the courthouse, and in the serenity of such mornings he might briefly drift like the lily pad on a pond.

The phone rang in the outer office; from the tone of his secretary's first remarks he knew that she was speaking with her grown daughter concerning one of her grown son's many misadventures, their inexhaustible topic and bond.

"Nelda," he called around the corner. "Nelda, we need to keep that line free." Meyers operated on the cheap with one incoming phone line and one legal secretary.

"It's kind of a crisis, Hoot."

"No doubt. You've got five minutes, okay? You tell me this guy's gonna be calling, and you don't get a number so I can call him back if I need to, and then you tie up the phone all morning. We've got to do better than that."

"All morning? I'm sorry, but all morning?"

"Five minutes," he said. "Take five minutes. You can't get it fixed from here—whatever it is."

Nelda ignored him and said to her daughter, "Yes, he's forty, but that girl knows he's just a big kid. She should know that by now. And it was a hamster. A hamster, for Pete's sake. She knows how he is, but she just keeps blowing up over the slightest little thing. He needs to find a girlfriend who doesn't always see the worst in people."

Meyers closed his door against it.

He leaned on his knuckles to read the four short police reports spread across his desk; these bore smeared notations from previous readings, his leaking ballpoint. The briefest of them had been written by Sheriff Utterback, typed all in caps, and in it Utterback said he'd been summoned at approximately 0216 hours on August 22 to Law and Order, where he met with two persons of interest who were being questioned regarding a possible homicide. The sheriff had personally spoken with both Henry and Karen Brusett, and neither of them was willing to offer any information regarding the incident or the body they'd been found with. Neither individual was known to him from previous law enforcement contacts. It was the sheriff's impression that, considering the circumstances, they were both quite calm, especially Mr. Brusett. Utterback said that Henry Brusett appeared to be somewhat crippled and that he had left the complex in the middle of the night, refusing a ride home and all other offers of help or advice. The sheriff had directed his officers not to write any citations until the investigation had been completed.

The investigation did not promise of completion. Meyers's notations were smeared ink and question marks; everyone who'd touched this case so far had fobbed it off on someone else to try and understand. It was a funny, small set of facts, and what more would ever be discovered? What was left to know?

Deputies Lovell and Sisson had arrived on scene together because Lovell, known to his fellow officers as "Skippy," had torn the oil pan out of his cruiser responding in haste over bad road, and Sisson, who'd been ten minutes behind him, had picked him up along the way, and the deputies' reports described their arrival at the Brusett property in essentially the same way—Mr. and Mrs. Brusett were outside their mobile home, in the dark, sitting on the ground near an outbuilding that appeared to be some kind of bathhouse. Henry Brusett held the victim's head in his lap, and he had been smeared with blood. Lovell asked Mr. Brusett if he was hurt, and when Mr. Brusett did not respond, Lovell examined him, as best he could, as he sat there. Lovell had determined that all of the blood was the victim's and asked the Brusetts if there was anyone else nearby, anyone who might be cause for concern; Karen Brusett told them there was no one. She would not say if anyone else had been there earlier, but she did confirm that she'd been the party who'd called dispatch, and she provided the officers with her own and her husband's full names.

Then Lovell asked her about the identity of the deceased person, and she said she didn't know it, and she refused to say anything more except, when Sisson asked her if there was something wrong with her husband so that he couldn't talk, she said that there was nothing wrong with him, only that "I think he's a little bit too upset to say anything right now. It's been a lot to take in."

The deputies' reports described the deceased by his coloring, his condition, his approximate dimensions. They said his clothes were wet and that he was wearing just the one shoe. Sisson included a list of things they hadn't found—there was no vehicle found on the premises that was not registered to the Brusetts, no weapon had been discovered, there was nothing to indicate a struggle had taken place, nothing on or about the person of the deceased to say who he might have been. The investigation, as described by the deputies, ended with the arrival on scene of Detective Flaherty and the ambulance.

Detective Raymond Flaherty had been with the sheriff's department even longer than Hoot Meyers had been the county attorney, and he had achieved his present status entirely by longevity. As a deputy, Flaherty had been lazy and wary of any information that might disturb his equanimity, and he'd patrolled the inscrutable cedar forests west of the Taurine River avoiding all but about ten arrests a year. Since his promotion, though, Flaherty had proven to be an often able if still lazy investigator. Much of his report was cribbed directly from Sisson's, with the addition of one fresh observation—Flaherty noticed how thoroughly the dead man's naked foot had been abused, that it was scratched and bruised and covered in ruptured blisters. Flaherty said that as soon as he was satisfied that they wouldn't need medical attention, he'd asked Mr. Brusett to come in with him, and he'd arranged for Mrs. Brusett to ride with Deputy Lovell, and in this way the subjects of his investigation had been separated and transported directly to Law and Order.

Detective Flaherty's skill—his only professional enthusiasm—was sufficient in Conrad County to clear many cases. Flaherty made people confess themselves. When the detective succeeded in capturing these performances on videotape, Meyers often had all he needed to dictate terms, but watching the tapes again and again, as might be necessary with evidence, was not pleasant work. Flaherty was far from deserving his good opinion of himself, and his wormy methods were hard to see in operation. His report made mention of such interviews with the Brusetts, but said of them only that tapes and transcriptions were soon to follow for further review by the county attorney. In accordance with the sheriff's order, he'd written no charges.

Now, of the unknown traveler who had dropped into nowhere, from out of nowhere, and been found wet and weirdly wounded and dead, Hoot Meyers would be expected to make an official story, a case. Some sense must be made of this, however artificial. Often these days he was called upon to tell courts of law and tell the victims proliferating in this county like ants at a picnic that he no longer knew why people did the things they did, that purely pointless crime was often hard to solve. Motives unknown and unknowable. Facts insufficient. So it may be for his old friend Henry, a man whom Meyers had known as a simple and immaculately sane boy. What a nightmare. Poor Henry had got himself mixed up in yet another death by misadventure.

Unless Meyers was mistaken, however, and he was willing to be a little mistaken in this, the Brusetts were harmless. There was a body, which would be admissible as evidence, and Henry Brusett's silence, which was not, and it would be that silence that should be most suggestive and most damning in the affair, but it was nothing Meyers could use to convict him. Meyers thought that probably someone had done something out of sudden necessity up on Fitchet Creek, or out of character—and he was curious about it, but he would this once spare himself the search for the damning detail. He held about a pair of deuces for his hand, and he would stand pat. They were meek people, Henry and his woman. It was hard to imagine how in the course of their normal affairs they might ever again hurt anyone. Between the lines of these spare reports what was there to be read? A desolation. Meyers knew the lives that were led in the deep woods. The Brusetts were already confined there, and probably chastened, and all at no cost to the Department of Corrections. He'd passed on stronger cases than this, hadn't he? He'd been handed another muddle, and there were good and practical reasons to believe it might never be anything else.

His phone began to wink.

"County attorney. This is Meyers. Hello? Nelda, did you . . . ? Hello? I'm on the line here, Nelda, if . . . "

"Hello." A man's voice, reluctant.

"You'd be Mr. Teague. From Iowa?"

"Sorry, my wife's sort of distracting . . . Midge. Midge, just wait a second. Yes, well anyway, I'm, or we were . . . Midge, just wait a second, will you please?"

"Is this Mr. Teague? Teague, is it?"

"Yes, Mr. and Mrs. Wesley Teague, we were told to call you, I forgot about the time zones. So—your secretary told you? I called before, before you came in. I think she might have been a little annoyed with me. It was quite early there."

"Nelda lives at that desk, Mr. Teague, and she always likes talking to people. That's why I keep her around. She tells me you might have some information for us."

"No information. Oh no. No. I'm sure we don't know anything that might be of use to you. Or that anybody could want to know.

We're just, we don't know anything ourselves. I mean, what would we know? About? From here? You're in Montana? But we did have a few questions. We debated whether we should call you at all, but we are curious now."

Meyers, a father himself, knew exactly the species of curiosity that springs forth full-blown at the birth of a child to stalk a dad's head forever, the bull in the china shop, the greatest love of all, and all for a creature who, after you've only just taught it not to eat its own shit, is off somewhere, somewhere out of sight, making its own decisions. Though his trade was in bad news of every kind, Meyers had never delivered news as bad as this. "There's been an accident here."

"Oh, I doubt we'd know anything about that. My wife took the message, spoke to some young lady. Or it might have been a real young boy, she thinks. Didn't get her name, or his name. No, I guess she *wouldn't* give her name. But she did insist, this girl or whatever she was, she said we just had to call you, and she gave us this number and everything, and told us to ask about the boy from, what was it? 'Up on Bishop Creek'? What would that mean? *On* Bishop Creek? That's a place somewhere?"

"Do you think she might have said 'Fitchet Creek'?"

"Maybe. Midge? Midge? My wife won't come to the phone. This young woman, this young woman spoke very fast. She was hard to understand. There was something funny in the, maybe some static in the line. But, anyway, it happens our son is off on a trip right now. He was gone on a vacation, I guess you could call it. At first he was saying Austin, Texas, but then he changed his mind and said he was just going, and he left it at that, and he left." Teague's voice issued through a long, tinny tube, fear overmastering him. "He said the whole idea was to get away for a while, completely away. He wanted to go off and think. And you can't really discourage that sort of thing. That was fine

101

with us. Fine. So he's been . . . we didn't know how it was supposed to go. When children went off like that. Off on their own vacations. Should they be expected to call home? You'd like them to check in, but I suppose it gets to be too late in the day."

"Your son is how old, Mr. Teague?"

"Twenty-four last May. Getting on up there. They get so . . . they need a little bit of independence, so you just have to say . . . Well, there isn't much you can say. But Calvin is, believe me, he's just as reliable as they come. Almost too reliable, if you can believe that."

"You say the name was Calvin?"

"Yes. Calvin. Calvin *Winston* Teague," said the father. "But . . . do you . . . ?"

"You didn't know where he was going?"

"No."

"How he was going?"

"Oh, he was driving. He took his car, of course. He's a great one for those roadside monuments, points of interest."

"And you're calling from Iowa, wasn't it? Have I got that right? Mind if I put you on the speaker phone so I can take some notes?"

"Yes. I mean, I don't mind. Yes, Iowa."

"You don't know who called you? Who that was?"

"No," said Mr. Teague. "We don't know how she got our name, but we know she did, and that's a little funny, don't you think? That this young woman, or boy—this person—that they should have our names? How would they? Our telephone number? How would they get that? This person told my wife we were supposed to get in touch with you immediately. But we weren't sure. It sounded like a hoax. What kind of accident?"

The armored beast got up to pace Hoot Meyer's gut. "Fatal. We've got a body we can't identify."

"What, drowned? Because that wouldn't be Calvin. He had years and years of swimming lessons. I mean, that's the whole reason for maintaining a municipal swimming pool, to . . . "

"Drowned? Oh, Fitchet Creek. No, that's just where we found him. *Near* Fitchet Creek, would be more accurate, or off in that drainage somewhere."

"Found?"

"Did this woman, or this girl, say how she knew to call you?"

"No. I don't understand. Drainage? No, I don't think . . . Why would she be calling us? Do you think? Did she call you?"

"Sir, does your son have blond, dirty-blond hair? He'd be about five-nine, five-ten, a hundred and sixty-five pounds?"

"No. Calvin's one-seventy. At least. At least. Sometimes quite a bit heavier, I think. It's nothing, I think this might be a practical joke. Is that what they call them? Some of these kids don't always use the best sense. But we did think we should call when we're . . . what? Not knowing."

Meyers put best evidence into play. "Has your boy got a slight deformity of his left ear? Ear lobe is kind of withered, looks like a— say, a pale raspberry?"

There was scraping, a bump in the line. Wesley Teague said nothing then, but Meyers heard Mrs. Teague hovering near behind him, her sudden keening.

· 8 ·

T HIS WAS THEIR third call in an hour, and it was developing that Midge just could not bring herself to fly and that she wasn't about to let her husband go through something like that by himself, and so the Teagues had decided they would drive up to see about identifying the remains if that was all right with Meyers. Meyers told Mr. Teague to come as best he could, as soon as he could.

"I've got a pretty serious form of night blindness," Teague explained. "My license actually prohibits me from driving after dusk or before full dawn, so it's going to be a minimum of thirty hours, I think, and maybe forty-eight, maybe even a little more. Midge gets tired. So, would that be all right? If we took that long to get there?"

Always inclined to want the promptest answer, Hoot Meyers could not understand how anyone might let this, of all doubts, linger. Could the man be asking about the rate of his son's decay? He must know the boy was refrigerated. "That'll be fine. There's no practical reason to hurry."

"Couldn't you just tell us . . . something?"

"There are a lot of things I need to look at. They just delivered me some tapes—I'll show you what we've got when you get here."

"Tapes? Wasn't this an accident? Did someone? Tapes?"

"There were some interviews done. Some interviews with some of the people involved. With any luck, they'll be on tape, and maybe those'll tell me something."

"Involved? Involved how?"

"We don't know. That's why I want to watch these tapes now."

"Someone was involved, though?"

"Yes, but we don't know how much or in what way."

"We're thinking," said Mr. Teague, "that it's probably not even, that this has to be a—what? A mistake, really. We'll be leaving our daughter Luana right here by the home phone while we're gone. I wouldn't be surprised if she gets a call from you-know-who. So we're leaving her there, just in case."

Meyers was not given to wishful thinking and was always surprised at the force it could exert in others' lives.

"Could you at least tell us something?" Teague lapsed in and out of hopefulness. "What you *think* happened at least?"

"I've got bits and pieces, and they don't make much sense. Yet. When you get here I'll show you everything we've got. You'll draw your own conclusions." Meyers was not accustomed to dissemble or parse. The bluntest kind of honesty was the one luxury he'd bought himself with his small influence, but now with his integrity on leave he'd gone to the funhouse, bought a ticket, and was groping for the way out. "You want me to call you back when I've watched these things?"

"No," said Mr. Teague. "Please don't. We'll know everything soon enough."

Detective Flaherty's interview with Henry was flawlessly produced in accordance with the manual on police interrogations, with Henry sitting very near the camera and frontally lit so that his face filled much of the screen and was amplified until the slightest movement of his eyes might be tracked; his eyes moved only rarely and then only to roll a little upward. He blinked at long intervals. The detective's voice was the disembodied voice of the camera, and it sounded as if a microphone had been implanted in his very mouth, and he said that they were in the squad room of the Conrad County Law and Order Complex and that the time was zero zero thirty hours. The subject, he said, was Henry Brusett. "Now, Mr. Brusett, I'm giving you more rights than you actually got coming to you, because you are not under arrest. You understand that, don't you? We're just working our investigation here." Flaherty described for Henry the several civil liberties as if they came of his personal benevolence.

Henry's mouth worked as he waited this out—he was chewing the insides of his cheeks. Henry, though he was a little younger than Hoot Meyers, had gone gray even in the flesh and had got a blasted pair of eyes. He had turned still more scarce in the years since the trees had taken their revenge on him and butchered him in his boots, and there had been years on end when Meyers hadn't so much as glimpsed him, though they were living in the same county, trading in the same little towns all the while. Meyers knew, of course, always knew that Henry was probably somewhere nearby. They'd gotten old, apparently. Gotten old, never speaking to each other.

"Do you understand these rights I have read to you?"

Henry's face remained set, closed.

"Mr. Brusett, I have to ask you, 'cause it's important that I make sure—do you understand these rights I have read to you?"

"Yes, I do."

"Say your name for the audio, please."

"You just said it. It's Henry Brusett."

"We like to know we're saying it right. Middle name?"

"Don't have one."

"And how old are you, Mr. Brusett?"

"You know how old. I gave you my driver's license."

"That's right. Okay, so . . . do you think you'd need the services of a lawyer tonight?"

"No." Henry was seeing something not presently before his eyes.

"Oh, great. You know, you can certainly call one in any time you want, but right now that would have to be at your own expense. Because, until you're arrested—unless you're arrested—anyway, I'm glad you feel like you can talk to me."

"No." There were deep vertical seams in Henry's lips, places he'd shaved badly the last time he'd shaved.

"It's all right," said Flaherty. "I think I know how you must feel."

"No." His tongue swept his lips.

"Would you like some water?"

"No. Thanks."

"'Cause, it's not a problem. Pop. Coffee. We'd like to try and make you comfortable if we can. There's no reason for anyone to be uncomfortable here, Mr. Brusett, 'cause, personally, I don't really think anyone has done anything wrong. Of course, I don't know for sure. But I just have this idea that the man I'm talking to here is not the kind of man who does things wrong. Am I right?"

"No," said Henry.

"If there's something you need to tell me—feel free."

Henry pinched his nostrils as if to stifle a sneeze, but then, distracted, he held them so for several minutes.

"Whatever you need to tell me," Flaherty offered again.

Henry released his nose. "I better go."

"Sure, if you like. Any time. But can you wait just a second? I need to step into the other room. Just give me a couple minutes, all right? I'll be right back."

Flaherty could be heard leaving the room. Henry remained for a long while before the camera, and he waited almost completely still. He disappeared from the screen for a time, then returned to the frame in a black T-shirt. There were mumblings made too far from the microphone to be heard distinctly on tape; Henry's half of these exchanges was to nod. He did or said nothing else. Eventually a new, well-amplified voice was heard off camera, a new presence in the tape, and this announced itself as Sheriff Utterback, and it gave the time and date again, and wondered, "How we doing, Mr. Brusett?"

Henry didn't seem to know.

"Me and Detective Flaherty have just been chatting with your wife."

Henry sighed in disappointment and continued looking out upon the long view.

"She's told us everything we need to know. So, I guess we won't need your help after all. Course, after what she said, you might kinda want to give us your own version of what happened up there. You don't come out too good, Mr. Brusett, the way your wife tells it. She says you clobbered that guy, says she doesn't even know why. Kind of an odd story, if you ask me, but that's the one she's been telling us."

"She has?"

"She's young, probably scared out of her wits. But her version of this is the only one we've got to work with so far. We'd sure be happy to hear what you had to say about it, hear your side of it."

"If that's what she said, then why don't you arrest me?"

"There's always time for that. And it's just her word so far, and the way we found you, which, you'll have to admit, was kind of odd, and I mean *real* unusual. Right now, it's just mostly a matter of trying to make everything go together with what she's telling us. Put a case together, you know. But, Mr. Brusett, we always like to try and go with the truth if we can get it. I bet everybody involved would be a lot happier if the truth came out."

"What'd she tell you I did?"

"Well—she told us you killed the guy."

Henry made a grin as from spare parts. Never at any age had he been prone to this expression. "You think I don't know her any better than that?"

The sheriff seemed to understand that he'd been outflanked. "So, that's all you got to say to us? A thing as bad as this is, and that's all you can tell us about it? Does that seem right to you?"

"If I said anything at all, I said too much, and that's how I feel about it all the time, not just when I'm in trouble."

Meyers had been raised in and had lived by the same principle, but somehow less righteously than his old neighbor. The interview had been concluded without Flaherty, or the sheriff, or Henry himself having done Henry any harm.

Young Mrs. Brusett, however, had been at Law and Order all of that same night. It was Meyer's impression that there was very little guile in this Karen's intelligence, and though she'd assured him she'd given them nothing, he worried about remarks she might have thought incidental, the possibility of artless lies. She'd been hours among the cops and was just the kind of innocent who will wreak havoc with her own interests. Meyers saw to his relief that the transcript of her evening with the officers ran to just three pages. He read:

Q: This is Detective Philip Flaherty of the Conrad County Sheriff's Office. The time is 0110 hours, and I'm with Mrs. Karen Brusett, and Mrs. Brusett has signed the advice of rights form. Do you want a lawyer, young lady?

A: No.

Q: There is no reason to be nervous. I don't think you have done anything wrong, not yet.

Q: Do you want to get started?

Q: Why don't you just go ahead and tell me when you get ready. We can start any time you are ready.

Q: Do you know what obstructing justice is?

A: I have an idea.

Q: It's a crime.

A: I suppose it would be.

Q: It's a crime to try and cover up somebody else's crime.

A: That is fair. I see why they have that law.

Q: Want me to come back later? I will give you some time to think about that and then I will come back later.

A: Sure, if you want.

Q: This is Detective Phillip Flaherty and I am with Karen Brusett again, and the time is 0145 hours.

Q: How are you feeling, Mrs. Brusett?

A: Feeling?

Q: I think you have got a chance here to help us all out quite a bit.

A: I don't think so, sorry.

Q: Help yourself is what I'm thinking, Karen.

A: I am too dumb to do that, sir, but I do appreciate your concern. That is nice.

Q: At least I am having better luck with Henry.

A: That is fine because you know he is the one to talk to. If anybody can tell you, it would be him.

Q: Tell me what?

A: Whatever he has got to tell you.

Q: What does he have to tell me?

A: I thought you said he already told you? You were having luck with him, you said.

Q: Well, Karen, you don't have to help us if you don't want to. That is your decision, and you know what they say? They say you should let your conscience be your guide.

A: Okay.

0150 hours–0230 hours—subject statements made at different times to unknown person or persons:

Q: [Inaudible]

A: No, he is my cousin. He lives in St. Regis.

Q: [Inaudible]

A: Brookies? You gut those [inaudible] in aluminum foil [inaudible] a lot, a lot, lot of butter [inaudible] your fresh parsley [inaudible] had that sourdough working I don't know how long before it went bad. You do have to pay some attention to it.

A: Could you take these lights off me, please? They are really hot. You mean that thing has been on the whole time running? Oh no. I hope I didn't pick my nose or anything. That is so mean to do that to somebody.

A: [Inaudible] had to turn that thing on again because I am still not going to say anything and [inaudible] who wants to see that?

A: [Inaudible]

A: Yeah, I know, and like I say, I am sorry—real sorry—but I've got to take another little rest now if you don't mind.

A: Was I snoring? Sorry.

Hoot Meyers watched the interview tape to see if the girl's manner might be more incriminating than her words had been. She'd not been placed so near her camera as Henry, but she too had been ruthlessly lit, and in the beginning her head was in constant motion, her attention bouncing from one fascination to another, like a tourist's. Someone kept turning the camera off and back on, and because a judge might see this as suspicious editing, the tape could eventually be barred from use as evidence, but Meyers soon decided that there'd be nothing of legal consequence to see in it. The girl settled gradually into a trance, a plastic pen spinning almost constantly between her forefinger and thumb. Even in the ugly room, the ugly circumstance, the stark light, she remained a creature of awful grace, and this girl, her every intention to the contrary, would be the most dangerous thing in the woods.

·9·

B EFORE MEYERS COULD escape the courthouse on Monday morning, Commissioner Cornish had cornered him with an offer of free lunch at the Outlook, and before Meyers could take the first bite of his club sandwich, the commissioner had begun to pose hypotheticals about how a public official, an elected one, might safely cheat on his wife. Legally. Cornish seemed to remember reading something about some morals clauses somewhere. Was there such a thing? Who would they bind, and to what? The official's buckteeth were yellow and gray, and he wore a bolo tie, and he was far too proud of himself and nervous to be anything but the lothario in the clandestine fun he kept suggesting. The thought of this malformed fellow in bliss threatened Meyers's appetite. "Adultery?" he said, lifting his eyebrows, keeping his voice low, and investing the concept with dreadful majesty. The commissioner paled and excused himself from the table. Meyers finished his sandwich. He ordered and ate a caramel sundae, admiring from his alcove the misting falls below.

After lunch he met with the county sanitarian and Sam Baxter concerning Mr. Baxter's septic system, which was simply the overturned and buried body of a '57 Ford Crown Victoria. Baxter had come to inform them that he'd raised a dozen children, his own and some strays, on the garden patch that grew right above that septic, so he knew it had to be safe, and Baxter, a man no doubt decrepit from birth and who breathed grievance like spores, rocked side to side on his heels, his eye always on the door. Nobody, he said, would ever convince him there was anything wrong with that septic.

"Maybe not," Meyers told him, "but now it's come to my attention that you're breaking the law with this, so you know I can't let it slide. You need to get yourself one of those cast-concrete septic tanks, get yourself some real seep line, and some pea gravel. I'll grant you, everything does cost more these days, so I'll give you four weeks from tomorrow to have it done. If you don't, I'll get an injunction against you to where you can't even relieve yourself in your own toilet, and I'll get the judge to fine you a hundred and fifty dollars a day until you do come into compliance. We can go that way, if you want. You're poisoning that aquifer, Mr. Baxter. You'll have your written notice by tomorrow's mail."

"Who votes for you?" Baxter despaired. "What kinda people would vote for you?"

"Not many," said Meyers, "but I run unopposed."

At two there was a hearing for young Jesse Jones who should be sent, Meyers suggested, to juvenile detention in Troy, and the boy's mother, Mrs. Loretta Jones, hung at Meyer's elbow wafting some violet concoction over them and constantly interposing, " . . . no . . . oh, no, because he's really only . . . no, that's wrong." The public defender argued that it would be unnecessary, that it would be contrary to the relevant statute and unkind to lock this young man up, but in the end the magistrate ruled for the state, and as Jesse was being taken off, he shot a leer over his shoulder at his mother, a grin of crazy triumph intended also for the county attorney. Still, Loretta Jones pleaded, "Wait. Now—wait, I'm telling you, I already told you this bruise was an accident. Really. This thing was my fault. I was, I was mad at him, so I said what I . . . If you just have to lock somebody up, why wouldn't you lock me up? For lying? Wait. *Wait.*"

Then, before the public defender could get away to her office, Meyers caught up with her in an empty length of courthouse hallway to tell her, "I've decided what I can offer your salesman. The guy pleads to all six counts, max sentence on all counts, but to be served concurrent. I don't know if I'll ever get time to dictate it or get it written up, but that's what I'll offer."

"Which is still six months in jail. These were some nickel-and-dime misdemeanors. Six months? Hoo."

"Theft by fraud," said Meyers, "to me is the worst kind. Gullible people tend to be poor. Thirty, forty bucks, that's something to them. It's the idea of the thing, the sleaze of it that kind of gets me. Guy cheats old ladies on make-believe cosmetics?"

"You're telling *me* about poverty now?"

"Giselle, he did this when he was Richard Rennat in North Carolina and when he was Charles Tanner in Colorado and Utah, Casey What-was-it in Oregon. You get the idea. And you can see by his record that everybody just keeps punting him. Well, he's Nat Dinley here; we've got him by his Christian name, and we've got him dead to rights, and he's gonna do some time for once. I'll suspend half of it if you enter your plea before next Friday. After that I'll file it as a felony, common scheme, and we can talk about years, if it's a few months he's afraid of."

Meyers had the spare half hour then for some approximately urgent paperwork, but he used it instead to tighten the C-clamps that held his delaminating desk together, and, because he was already fading at three thirty-five, he thought to nap in his chair, but along came Mrs. Ingraham once again, still incensed about her missing dolls, and he told her, again, that they were gone, that unless someone put them up for sale on the Internet or tried to move them through one of the pawn shops he himself had contacted, unless that should happen, her dolls were gone. With her long jaw and linen jacket she was clearly money, and she would not be accustomed to disappointment; Mrs. Ingraham neither appreciated nor accepted his pessimism. What, she wanted to know, were the police for? How could they let things like this happen? Her hands were long and regal and flew to illustrate the several points she wished to raise with him.

"It's sad, ma'am, I know it is. But you can't stand guard over everything." Her collection had been featured in the *River Register*'s Society section, and Meyers had seen it there, as had, no doubt, the thief. From a well-appointed couch a cluster of stillborn horrors had yearned, arms outstretched. "Priceless," Mrs. Ingraham had claimed in the article, "almost literally priceless." Carlotta, the oldest of the collection, had been in Mrs. Ingraham's family for four generations, more than a hundred years. Her tiny slippers were modeled after a pair worn by a lady-in-waiting at the Sun King's court.

Mrs. Ingraham was new to Conrad County, but Meyers believed she'd been a woman of influence somewhere, that she'd be well equipped and well contented to be anyone's pain in the ass. Palsy or rage? It was exhausting to watch her shake, and so when Moon Pope, the brand inspector, called from up on Bailey Peak, his call came as a reprieve. One of Meyers's cows, it happened, was stuck in a ditch and would likely drown in it unless he, Meyers, got up there pretty quick to pull her out. Meyers made a great show of rushing away in concern. "Got an animal in trouble. Gotta go. Nelda has your number, right? Soon as we know anything else, we'll sure let you in on it."

Mrs. Ingraham continued telling him as he passed through the outer officer that something must be done, and she called to him even as he gained the hallway and was making his way at last to fresh air. Something must be done, she said, and he must be the one to do it.

· 10 ·

MEYERS MAINTAINED HIS hobbyist's herd of six cows and a randy bullock if only so there'd be something to kick at him from time to time, and so that he'd have calves to pull in February and to brand at Easter. There had never been any money in beef, not even in those years when he'd shipped his calf crop to Omaha by boxcar every fall, but Meyers could not tolerate the local country-side without at least a few animals in it to wear the U-Bar-U high on their right rump. In 1903, his grandfather Felix Meyers had bought, sight unseen, a cluster of mountain springs and the hundred acres in timber and meadow immediately surrounding them up on the sunny southern hip of Bailey Peak. Old Felix would learn too late that his ground had been graded in recent geologic times by the advance and retreat of many glaciers, that there was no depth of soil here, and that nearly all of that sweet, free water would percolate through his rocky dirt to be of little use to anything seeking to grow in it; the Meyers family had contrived by one means or another to remain land-poor ever since.

Just inside the gate was the sawmill where Felix had milled the planks, timbers, and boards to build a cavernous barn and the tall, narrow, and narrow-windowed farmhouse now listing on its crum-bling foundation out behind a shelterbelt of mountain ash and willow. Meyers called it the home place though no one had lived here these decades past, and if his chores brought him here several times a week, still it seemed new and necessary to him every time he saw it—a poor patch of ground sloping away to a good view so that a man might feel superior just for standing on it. Passing up the lane, Hoot Meyers looked to the door of the barn loft and to his father's lone contribution to the place, the rust-stippled hubcaps Dusty had nailed in fanwise display and the whirling wind chime of license plates he'd strung on baling wire, hung from a jutting spar, along with the usual block and tackle.

The springs issued from the highest corner of the tract to feed a stock tank and a ditch, and, always prolific, they had run at full pool all summer. Only the day before, Hoot Meyers had been up to close the headgate of the ditch so that the runoff wouldn't overwhelm his pond below, which was choking on green silt so late in a warm season. Now, just below the headgate, the ditch banks were gluey mud, and he found his best breeder cow there, thrashing as he approached her through the pussy willows. Not fifty feet from a brimming, galvanized stock tank, she had chosen to drink from the ditch, and she was stuck in it, her hips upslope and well above her head, and her forelegs were sunk to the hocks in mud, and her rear legs sunk past the knees. She'd been struggling for hours, her every movement sucking her deeper into the clay. She had been flinging her head, and the reeds all around were draped with her slobber. She could only fight in fits and starts now, and she was near collapse, nearly resigned to dying.

Meyers took his boots off and waded out into the ooze. He got in front of the animal so that he could press his shoulder up into her brisket, and, hoping she wouldn't start to throw her head again, he shoved. He shoved again, much harder but with no more effect, and the cow laid her great chin on his shoulder. He backed away. He went to his truck for his lariat, and from the ditch bank he roped her, but even as he was dallying off on his bumper, he knew that he might keep the cow up for a while this way, but that he'd never pull her out alive; the loop would strangle her if he were to pull it that hard. He lacked the rope to build a harness, and his gun rack was presently empty, but he did have his pocketknife, which happened just then to be sharp, and he considered this. Decency might eventually require him to slit her throat. Slit her throat and drag the meat out of the muck however he could, and no finicky concern then for the crushed windpipe or broken neck or legs. Just drag her out. But the mess of it. The hours of butchering to be done in the dirt; Meyers thought of the heavy dance he'd have to do with that poor, doomed creature in the mud, and he thought of the last several calves she'd thrown, voracious babies with something in their breeding that made them tender as veal.

He slid his boots back on and jogged back down to the old mill yard, and he was reminded of his age—his lope was no longer an efficient or comfortable gait even for going downhill. From the millworks he removed the long canvas belt that had driven the old mill's head saw, and he dragged the belt to the barn, which he entered. Spider webs soared through the shuttered light and into the gloom under the rafters, and from a clutter that was general and generations deep, he selected a singletree, a shovel, and, just in case he could not save the cow, a splitting maul. There was rope everywhere, but it had been nibbled by field mice and torn by pack rats and was unreliable. Meyers drove his tractor with its front-end loader back up to the cow.

In compound low, he walked the tractor up the dry side of the bank and nosed the bucket out toward her. If he pitched forward now, he'd have at least two things in the ditch, at least one of them, very likely, dead. He set his brake and switched the motor off. He removed his boots again and waded out to the cow with his armload, the long belt, and the singletree. He meant to get the belt under her belly and lift her, or at least bear enough of her weight so that she could scramble out. The apparatus would consist of the belt under the belly and twisted in loops to receive the singletree, and he'd tie the eye of the singletree to his rope, and the rope to the bucket hoist. And pull her up. Meyers stood wriggling his toes in the mud, trying to imagine just how he was to accomplish all this rigging with just one set of hands when, providentially, Deputy John Lovell came in through the gate and up the hill in a cream white Corvette. To Lovell's possible credit, he used the Corvette no more tenderly than he used the sheriff's million-mile cruisers. The car passed into a grassy stretch of lane where its tires disappeared, and it came on like the gliding predator, but loud, continuously knocking and scraping, and as he came nearer he brought with him the high wail of an emasculate saxophone which persisted even after he'd parked. Some kind of mood music, Meyers guessed.

Deputy Lovell carried most of his weight in his hips and thighs, but even with this low center of gravity he'd never be much good off pavement; afflicted with every kind of clumsiness, he climbed the bank.

"John," said Meyers. "I don't suppose you want to get dirty, do you?"

"Nelda sent me up here. Gave me directions. I got some news on that case. I maybe even solved it. Or part of it."

"You think so, huh? Which case we talking about?"

"The dead guy. That recentest dead guy? And the guy with the young wife. Brusett. So, I thought I better let you know, and I called Nelda, and Nelda said you could use some help up here. So I thought I'd come up."

"There's not an hour of the night or day when I don't need help. I got all kinds of messes you can stumble into, if you want. Long as you're okay with getting dirty."

"That's all right," said the deputy. It was more than all right with him. He desired action.

"You got your service weapon with you?"

"Always," said the deputy. "Keep it under the driver's seat."

"Okay, but let's try some other tricks first. If you really wanted to help, what I need you to do is untie that rope from the bumper, and take your end of it, and crawl out there on that bucket. Careful you don't kick any levers or anything, and watch out for that hydraulic fluid. You get that stuff on your clothes, then it's there for good, and I've even tried that powder they sell on TV. Doesn't get it out. Wouldn't want to piss your wife off."

"Not married," Lovell said. "I'd have to get a raise or a rich girl to do that."

"Now, right there, right there where your foot is, no the other one, that's exactly the set of knobs I don't want you kicking. That's right. Yeah, just shinny on out there. Nice of you to do this, by the way. Careful. Yeah, and look at this, I believe this belt's gonna reach all the way around. Yeah, just the way we want it to. This could work out, believe it or not. Look at this, we've got plenty of belt. We are set."

Lovell lost a handhold and fell sideways off the bucket and into the mud. He leaped up, slipped, and fell again.

"Take it easy, now," Meyers advised him. "This clay's slick when it's wet. But don't let that rope get away from you. I guess you'll have to try getting up there again; shouldn't be all that daredevil if you just remember to hang on."

Lovell climbed out and onto the bucket.

Meyers directed him: "Tie up to that crosspiece behind you there. Now don't tip outta there again, that's not getting us anywhere."

Meyers finished jury-rigging the belt and the singletree and the dangling rope, and he held the whole apparatus taut, standing on tiptoe in the muck, leaning on the cow's heaving ribs. "Now, what you need to do is get down there and start the loader and pull up on that bucket just enough that I don't have to hold this anymore. This'll get old very fast."

"I've never . . . I've never run one of those before."

"It's pretty easy. I'll talk you through it."

"I don't think," said Lovell, "that I want to take my first lesson with you standing almost right under it that way, Mr. Meyers. I'm usually up for anything, but not that. That could be bad."

"Okay, you might have a point." Meyers's junkyard hoist was heavy, and his shoulder cramped with holding it up. "All right, I said you might get dirty. Hop on down here, then—no, get your shoes off, first, you don't need to ruin those—come over here, and if you could just grab a hold of this outfit and pull it up tight, about like I got it, and hold it there until I can get the slack out with the bucket. Whole thing loses integrity, see, if you let any slack into the system."

Meyers started the tractor again and slowly fed power to the bucket, and when his rigging was taut he supplemented the rope in his lifting system with a length of chain, and then from the driver's seat he told Lovell, "You better back away from there now. I'm not too sure what this'll do when I throw some torque to it, and you wouldn't want to find yourself under a swinging cow."

As Lovell retreated, Meyers moved the control forward gingerly and throttled up the tractor, and the pressure of the belt rising under her chest pumped an unearthly bellow from the cow, and she began to struggle with new energy, with terror, but still she could not suck free, and Meyers slid the lever slowly forward and the bucket pulled and strained and the tractor had tipped slightly to bear its weight on its front tires, and the whole assembly was in equipoise, the motor howling, before the cow finally, explosively sprung free. She'd scrambled halfway up the bank when the canvas belt dragged her hind legs out from under her, and she fell and rolled once in the mud, and she shot up and over the bank, and in twenty seconds she was grazing with almost no recollection of what had just happened to her. Meyers throttled back. He switched the tractor off.

"Did it look to you," Lovell asked him, "like it broke its leg coming out? Or maybe broke its rib?"

"No, I don't think so."

"I could still shoot it for you, if you wanted."

"She's fine."

"You just hate," said Lovell, still standing in the ditch, "to see 'em suffer."

"Maybe you do, but I kinda like it. The sonsabitches. They bring it on themselves. That old girl never has had the sense God gave a goose. What a project she's been."

Meyers told Lovell that they could rinse the mud off themselves in the stock tank, said the easiest thing would be to bathe in it, clothes and all. "This thing completely flushes itself, every two, three days," he bragged, "it's all gravity-flow. So it doesn't matter if we muddy it up a little." He lay back into the big round tank like a skin diver off a boat, and he spread his arms and legs as if to make a snow angel. The water billowed brown around him. "I've got perfect teeth," he said, "and this is the stuff that did that for me—drinking it when I was a boy. All you really need is good spring water and organic prunes and plain beef. Maybe some bread and greens."

"I've got the same thing going with Mountain Dew," said Lovell. "That and Kraft Macaroni and Cheese. But anyway, I came to tell you I think I might have got a break in this case."

"You did, huh?"

"I'm off-duty, but it just kind of came to me when I was sitting on my couch. I thought you better know what I found out because, you know, you're probably the one guy who can do something about it. Thing was, I got called over to Red Plain yesterday to look into some vandalism that was done on Larry Manion's lot. He had a car there that'd been left to be serviced, and somebody busted a window out of it, and he's got to report it or he can't make an insurance claim if he needs to. So I ask Larry, I ask him, 'Who's this belong to?' and he tells me that's the other odd thing, said that the kid who owned the car just wandered off, and he hadn't seen him since. Wasn't sure he was coming back for it. Or maybe it was even him—the guy—who broke the window, but why would he do that? Come back and break his own window?"

"So what's your conclusion, John?"

"I think that might be our guy."

"You ask Larry what he looked like?"

"I told him what our guy looked like, our dead guy, and Larry said he sounded pretty much like the kid who owned the car, who hasn't come back yet, by the way. I checked with Larry again this morning."

"Manion didn't have any paperwork?"

"No. He said the kid left him a fifty-dollar bill for a sort of deposit and then he pulled some stuff out of his car, camping stuff maybe, and he took off. Afoot."

"So you ran the plates to see who the car belonged to?"

"Yep," Lovell was pleased that his thoroughness was appreciated. "It was a car out of Iowa."

"And it belonged to a Calvin Teague. Calvin *Winston* Teague."

"That's right," Lovell had already fallen a little behind; this always happened to him. He hated being the last to know.

"You didn't call his people, did you?" Meyers heaved himself up and out of the tank. "If you've got a billfold," he said, "you better remember to take that out of your pocket first. Days like this are exactly why I don't carry one anymore. I bet I've lost twenty wallets in my life."

"His people, you mean . . . ?"

"His parents, or wife, or whatever he might've had."

"Oh, I . . . But how would I . . . ?"

"Never mind," said Meyers. "They've been notified."

126

"Good." Lovell let himself fall back into the tank as he'd seen Meyers do, but he did not know, as Meyers knew, that the springs were the fruit of a deep and frigid cavern. Lovell's breath escaped him all at once, and, convinced he'd never retrieve it so long as he sat in this water, that his testicles might never again descend, he bolted out. Meyers loosed a rotten giggle, and the deputy shook himself like a dog.

"That's a little brisk," said Meyers, "isn't it?"

"Took me by surprise." Lovell, once again the butt of a slight betrayal, did not appreciate having to be the good sport about it. "So now," he said, "I guess you can go ahead and do some arrest warrants, huh? Now that we know who the guy is? I'm back on duty at six tomorrow, but I'd grab whoever you wanted me to grab as soon you could get the warrants done."

"You think we better mobilize the National Guard?"

"Well, okay," said Lovell, "I'm sure it's not that urgent the way you see it. But when there's an arrest, I want to be in on it. I really need that experience. I get drunk drivers. Them and wife beaters."

"You don't like wife beaters?"

"It's kinda tame, usually, by the time I get there, or it's got to where you don't know who you're supposed to restrain. You should hear the things people argue about, the reasons they give for hitting each other, stuff you can't even believe."

"I'd believe it," said Meyers. "So, who was it you were you wanting to arrest?"

"No," said Lovell. "It's whoever *you* want me to. You say the word."

"I just can't think of anybody right now, but if I do, you'll sure be the first to know. You should try not to get too excited on some of these things, all right? Your even keel, that's the way to go. Over the long haul, you know."

"They whacked that guy."

"Whacked him? Where do you get this, uh, outlook? 'Whacked'? The words you hear anymore."

"What else could've happened? They killed him."

"*They* did?"

"One of 'em did," said Lovell. "I think the old man."

"You mean the old, crippled guy? The guy who's got everything he can do just to stand up? Him?"

"Well," said Lovell, "somebody did. He's still a pretty stout man, if you look at him. Been kind of tweaked, but he's still strong enough, I'd say. And that girl's no weakling, either."

"All right, then," said Meyers. "Which one? You pick."

"Me? I'd say it was that Henry Brusett. He's the man of the family, so . . . "

"All right, and what's the charge?"

"Murder?"

"Henry Brusett murdered him?"

"Well, he sure could have," said Lovell. "Or she could have, too."

"Yeah, and in either case 'could have' doesn't cut it. I can just never impress that on you guys, can I? Do they teach *any* criminal law down there at that academy?" Meyers thought he might be more gracious to a kid who'd gone so far out of his way to lend a hand. "All right, here's the theory, the principle, we've got to work with: innocent-until-proven-guilty. I'll tell you right now, there's many and many a case like this where I don't have the goods to prove anybody guilty of any specific thing. So does that mean they're innocent? No. Not in the way you see it, not the way I might see it, but in the eyes of the law . . . This is not a rare occurrence in the law, John, and if you just can't take it, if the, you know, the weird result is more than you can stomach, then you might want to consider another line of work."

"This is all I ever wanted to do."

"You do it however you can do it. You come at it sideways, come at it backward. You do as much as you can, see what I'm saying?"

"No," said Lovell.

"I am the guy who agreed to shovel out the barn," said Meyers, "so that's job security, but in the course of my day, my usual day, I never, *ever* make anybody happy."

Lovell dipped his legs, one at a time, into the tank and agitated them, and scrubbed barehanded at his pants legs until they were clean enough to reenter the Corvette. "Somebody," he said, after long conjecture, "did something up there."

Meyers lost his patience. "Somebody's always doing something wrong. But, look, we've got all these hardheads who always lived here, and now you also have the whole lunatic fringe of the United States moving in, all these people trying to hide out from the law or the dusky races or whatever, them and the military people retiring here, and down on the east end you've got your Indians, Native Americans that is, and it's been my observation lately that just about everyone is pissed off just about all the time, and so you've got this bunch of assholes running around, armed to their grimy fucking teeth—and that is the one and only principle they can all agree on, their right to bear arms—bunch of yahoos just aching to plug away at each other, and they're gonna play high minded and show everybody what a set of stones they've got with their gun. So the thing is, we get a good supply of cases. You'll be in on plenty of cases, John, and on most of those you'll have all the evidence you could ever want or need. I believe ballistics is their specialty down at the state crime lab."

"What about this case, though?" Lovell's face was, and would always be, a child's face, fleshy, florid, and unlined, and he yearned for the lurid things so that he might solve the problem of evil, at least on the local level. He did not suspect of himself that he was a member of that sullen crowd Meyers had just described to him.

"What about it?"

"Well," said Lovell, "it just seems like something should be done."

"Why does everybody always want to *do* something? A real high percentage of the time about all you can really do is bear witness and wonder 'What the hell?' I tell 'em, I tell 'em all the time, over and over again: There's nothing I or anyone else can do. I tell 'em, 'I don't know' and 'I don't know' and 'I don't know,' till I get pretty damn sick of saying it, but that's all there is left to say. I can only get so creative in the way that I handle these things. Do you see what I'm getting at?"

"No, I still don't." Lovell stood at his side, mistreated and conscientious, and he faced, as Meyers did, straight into the sun, and he held his shirt away from his chest to get some circulation behind it. Meyers could think of nothing more to say to him and began to wish that he'd leave.

Instead, Lovell asked, "Whatever became of your boy Bob? Jump-shot Bob.

"Robert?" asked Meyers. "Santa Barbara, been down there for years."

"California? Why's everybody have to go to California all the time? But I bet he makes a killing down there, doesn't he? Probably rich, isn't he?"

"Does pretty good. Throws pots."

"Throws . . . ? Oh. Why?"

"Likes it."

"Are they gardening ones, or for cooking, or what are they for?"

"It's art. Does it by hand. They don't do anything but look good, which is more than enough in California. He gets more from one of those pots than I ever got for a cow. Lives in a tent, got himself a sort of a sultan's tent set up down there in the eucalyptus and madrona, and you can see the ocean from where he's at. You can smell it. Oh, he's got women, money, got a bulldog named Buster. No, Robert's the first Meyers in quite a while that didn't get himself tied to this sorry-ass country. So he did okay."

"You don't like it here?" Lovell marveled.

"I must, 'cause I never even thought of leaving. But it wasn't for him."

"You just never know, do you?"

"No," said Meyers. "You don't."

When at last the deputy thought himself clean and dry enough to leave, Meyers set about restoring things to their usual places. He cleaned the long industrial belt and determined it was no worse for wear, and he guided it back onto the equipment it had once turned, onto the spools and rollers as if it might once again be called upon to spin the thirty-inch blade into a rusty blur. Meyers returned the single-tree and the maul and the shovel to the barn. He parked the tractor and sat slumped in its seat. His exertions sometimes caught him unawares these days; having slept very little these last few nights he was almost dangerously tired, but he hadn't finished picking up after himself.

Once he'd hoped to grow timothy here, or just any richer mix of grass, and to that end Meyers meant to run a spring-tooth harrow over it, but the lower meadow was too rocky even for that rough tool, and so he set out to clear the bigger stones, and Meyers would pick rock over the course of many years only to find each spring that a new crop of it had come out of the dirt for him, and in time he would build a wall with it to transect the whole property, with fancy stiles and a fancy gate. It served its purpose and did no harm.

Meyers parked his truck in the barn.

He cut a square out of an old canvas tarp and walked up to the place in the wall where, in 1978, he and Henry Brusett had commenced its construction. From here the thing had spread in either direction like a vine, and Meyers's dedication to it had been a rare constant, as near to religion as he could come. He was thick through the shoulders and back for it, his fingers so thick he could barely type with them. Here lay his shame, obscured if not subdued; here lay Mike Callahan, the bottom piece of the whole structure. Though his every instinct balked at removing stone from this wall, Meyers began to lift it away. He worked his way down through the courses, and he had lifted tons of it away and was beginning to entertain the most macabre doubts when at last Callahan's shinbone was revealed. Mike had been wearing jeans. Cotton. Nothing left of them. What had been cotton or flesh was gone, but Meyers collected on the tarpaulin most of the many small bones from Callahan's feet, and, of course the larger bones, his legs and pelvis, and the rotten twist of leather that had been his belt, and a brass buckle, a flaring sun. Meyers took away ribs, and spine, and so many joints of his fingers as hadn't somehow been washed away. These were very like gravel now. Teeth rattled out of Mike Callahan's childish skull as Meyers picked it up. He gathered the rubber parts of Mike's tennis shoes and a Ban-Lon shirt that hadn't faded a shade since the day the boy had died in it.

Altogether, it made a small pile under the folded tarp. Darkness fell while Meyers rebuilt the wall, and then in darkness, with flights of pinwheels skidding across his eyes, he carried Callahan back down to his truck, and he drove down to the valley and into town. He went to the reservoir and stole someone's rowboat to go out with the remains, enshrouded with a hydraulic jack for their aid and comfort in the underworld, and over what Meyers thought to be the deepest deep in the reservoir there was a burial at sea. No invocation, not even a splash.

Alone again, he rowed back to shore.

· 11 ·

I N HIS SECOND year of law school, while Hoot Meyers was home
for the Christmas break, he happened to be watching through the
kitchen window when his father's final heart attack draped him
over the top rail of the pole corral. Dusty had spent the last moments
of a charmed life walking out to moon at his new colt, sugared coffee in one hand, cigarette in the other. As a Lutheran elder said at his
funeral, he would now be missed by anyone who'd ever known him.
Dusty was beloved because he'd been content. He'd played the same
Gibson dreadnought all his life, and, as beer and bait and tackle are
easy enough to acquire, he'd never needed to strive very much or con-
tend for much, and he was well known and universally liked. As was
often remarked, Hoot Meyers was not in many ways his father's son; it
had been lineage and love with them, but they were not alike.

So he sold the colt to help cover the bill from the funeral home,
and there was a party he did not attend, a wake without the body but
with a free lunch, and then the funeral, and then Hoot Meyers went
back to Missoula and a mandatory semester of tax and commercial
law, a brutal study that felt to him like expiation for some failing of his
own heart. He also pulled the occasional shift tending bar at George's
Indonesian Lounge, and two or three mornings every week he'd drive
home to observe the ongoing collapse of the Meyers' estates, which
had become, he soon discovered, encumbered by tax liens. Dusty had

let it go to weeds, and Dusty, strangely adamant about it, would not lend his consent to any other use of the family's lands while he was alive. "Let it alone," he'd say, as if there were something pristine and fine about their scattered properties, the many hearty crops of knap-weed and milk thistle where even mule deer wouldn't bed. "Just let it alone; your Grandpa Felix had me roped into that deal long enough. You start messin' with it even a little bit, then pretty soon that's all you ever do, and you're not a dollar ahead for it, either. They pay me just so they can let their cows out on those fields. Run somebody else's cows—run 'em in, run 'em out, that's what I like—easiest way I ever heard of to turn a buck."

The Meyers holdings, during Dusty's reign over them, had been so neglected as to be unfit even for poor pasture, and now the widower's son could not escape a certain joy at the absence of his father's interference. It was not very flattering to find that on becoming an orphan his strongest impulse was to dirty his fingernails in his inheritance. One Sunday just before midterm exams, a day he should have spent in his carrel at the law library, Hoot Meyers found himself instead driving his one-ton truck through early-morning fog on Highway 200. The ground, having thawed, was breathing, and he wanted to be on the mountain at dawn, and he did not wish to suffer anymore the misery of considering capital gains, and like-kind exchange, and third-party complainants, and so he thought to be on Bailey Peak all day, doing something.

A set of headlights appeared and blinked off again, somewhere down the highway. Meyers slowed. Again the headlights appeared and blinked off. They seemed no closer. Finally his own headlights brought up a shape in the eastbound lane which proved to be Mike Callahan's Volkswagen, parked on the shoulder. Callahan, with no jacket and apparently no idea of the cold, sat on a front wheel well with his palms pressed together and his hands and arms forming an arabesque above him. Henry Brusett was in the driver's seat, his leather sombrero pulled low. Meyers slowed and slowed, wanting to slide by. He stopped at last, and with many reservations he called across the road to them, "What are you guys up to?"

Callahan's hair was cut to cheek length in a Buster Brown that pinched his narrow face and twitched with his every movement so that he seemed possessed of ridiculous, uncontainable energy—this style had never been fashionable. "We almost made it," he said, in awe of himself.

"Made it where?"

"Back," said Mike Callahan.

Henry Brusett rolled his window down. "Transmission," he said.

"You can't get it in any gear?"

"We had it in third," said Henry, "for about the last thirty miles. Just about burnt 'er up. Then even third went out, and here we sit."

"Well, I'd give you a ride," said Meyers, "but I'm going up the hill, up the mountain."

"Up the mountain?" challenged Callahan. "Sermon on the Mount?"

"Yeah. My place. Thought I'd try and get a little something done today."

"You got a place?" Callahan mugged incomprehension.

"What's wrong with him, Henry?"

"He called and asked me to come and pick him up. He was stuck in Spokane. So I did. I brought his car over to get him, which was maybe not a good idea."

Meyers was only a few years older than Callahan and Brusett, but he'd been that many years older during their early boyhood, and so they continued to look upon him as their elder.

"Henry Brusett," crowed Callahan, "is one of the best people I've ever met. You ask him for a favor, and he doesn't ask you 'Why?' Or 'How much?' Or 'How many?' Or 'How long?' 'I'll be right there,' that's what he tells you. And he is. Right there. A right-there person, that's how I'd describe him."

Callahan had failed for once to overstate. Henry Brusett was generous to a deep fault. For Henry's sake, Meyers thought, he'd better offer them a way off the road. "Like I say, I'm headed up the mountain, but you're welcome to ride along."

"Where?" Callahan's head flipped as if to track the flight of a roman candle.

"So here you are," Meyers assessed, "you're sitting by the side of the road, fucked up as you can possibly be, and I bet you're holding, too, aren't you?"

"Well, Lord High," said Callahan.

"Acid," said Henry Brusett.

"On you?"

"On Mike." Henry's moustache had in those days involved half his face; he was solemn behind it. "Or he did have some of it. They were in his jeans, but he just had 'em loose in his pocket, and every time he went after some change or something, a few fell out. And I didn't—you know I just said, 'Good riddance.' Don't know if there's any left. It's just little bits of paper. He's been takin' it for days, I think."

"Mike?" Meyers inquired.

"I'm not deaf. I can hear better than you can. Just call me Angel of the Morning."

"We're getting you out of here," said Meyers. "You've got no business being anywhere near the beaten path right now."

"I am not," said Callahan, "paying anybody to tow this car. But they could have it. You could have it if you want. No. Henry, you're the one. I now declare: This is your car."

"Go ahead," Meyers suggested, "hand him that pink slip and a pen, if he wants to sign it over to you, Henry. Be a blessing to motorists everywhere."

Mike Callahan's mother, the sainted Naomi, had been the only teacher any of them had known during their first six years of schooling, and as well as her gentle guidance had worked with all her other students, it had been insufficient to the rearing of her son, and the boy had just never mustered the strength of character or imagination to think well of himself. Since high school Mike had tried and quit a community college, go-cart racing, fine wines, archery, six jobs, and one marriage, and though he was fairly new to hallucinogens, he thought that here at last he'd found his abiding passion. "Usually," he told them, "usually you're just the nucleus, the . . . *pro*ton, and you're just sitting there. Drop acid and you get to be the electron for a while. I mean, *spiihn*."

This, Meyers thought, was the first interesting thing he'd ever heard Callahan say. "Come on," he said, "let's go." He was not much concerned with the fate of Mike Callahan, but he didn't want anything too out of the way to befall Mrs. Callahan's son.

Callahan stood, crouched, and stood again in a surfer's stance, his legs thrust fore and aft, his hands and elbows cocked to balance him. "Eeewh, I don't know if I can get inside that truck. I mean, fit. Look at me." A new impulse made him rock up onto the balls of his feet and remain poised on them, the ugly ballerina.

"Get your ass over here, and let's get down the road before anybody else comes along and sees you this way. Come on, Henry. You blistered, too?"

"Straight," said Henry Brusett. "I don't think I'd care for it."

They brought into the cab the smell of bundled air fresheners and, as an undertone, the smell of Henry Brusett's cowhide jacket. Callahan sat in the middle with an expression usually associated with private time, of shocked gratitude, and he quivered at the pleasure of being in his skin. "You know the way you've been led to believe, how the world is so heavy? *Wrong*." Meyers posted up through the International's gears, and all through their whining progress to overdrive, Callahan declaimed so as to be heard over it, "You can touch the hand of God, and it only costs you three dollars and fifty cents. And, Ireland? We're way better. Way better. Way better. Try saying that. That makes your mouth feel great."

Callahan, under the best of circumstances and at the very height of his coherence, was never going to say anything useful, but there'd been a kaleidoscope lurking in him, and now he was not so easy to ignore. Meyers was somewhat jealous that so much lightness and facility had come to this callow boy so easily. Hoot Meyers knew only how to make sense, and it was always laborious. "Tell you what," he said, "with a couple extra hands, I might move some rock. You guys want to make some money today, long as you need to get yourselves out of the public eye? I could pay you a little, but you'd really be earning it."

"I should ride in back," said Callahan. "Know how dogs ride, with their tongues hanging out?"

"If you were a dog," said Meyers, "I'd let you. Now, try and jack down a little."

They arrived at the home place that morning with the rising sun, and Callahan stood on a stump to embrace it, and he invited it to advance and see them and make them warm.

Meyers drove the truck along the lower perimeter of the property, and Callahan and Brusett walked alongside, loading rock onto the flatbed. Later, whenever he thought of this day, Meyers would always remember that neither of them had ever asked him why he might wish to do something so pointless as to move rocks from one part of his field to another part of it; they simply agreed to help him and never did think to ask after the purpose of what must have seemed, at least to Henry, a futile exercise. The boys, with no other options before them, had been along for the ride, and Meyers had been, as usual, responsible for all that happened.

The work was hard and clumsy, but Callahan, frolicking like a puppy off its leash, moved right along with it, and he said the sky remained stable, that the ground often whirled when he looked down. "But not sick, it's not like the drunk-whirlies—Not-At-All. I *will* say, I've never been *less* sick. In my whole life. Wow. Woohw. Every little breeze blows right through my whattayacallum? My intestines. I am so clea-ean."

Henry, invincible in those days, a thirty-gallon barrel of a boy, walked along on the other side of the truck at a pace that would allow him to do whatever he was asked to do for as long as he was asked to do it.

Eventually Meyers, out of fairness to his little crew, and seeking to make them more efficient, thought he should abandon the brutality of having them lift the rock up and onto the flatbed, and so he fashioned a stone boat by pulling the hood off the resident wreck of an Oldsmobile, and by blowing holes in its nose with his .06 so that he might hook a chain to it, and with a clevis pin he attached the chain to the draw bar of a tractor, and with that they were off and running. Callahan and Brusett ran along behind and tossed rock into the loud hollow of the upturned car hood, and they described skid trails in the mud and gradually made a mound of rock on the upslope. Only when Meyers himself got thirsty—and this would be another source of shame in his recollection—did he think to offer the others a chance to drink. He'd worked them that morning like Egyptians. "Hop on," he told them at last, and they boarded the stone boat, sitting side to side, and he slid them to the truck, where he got the pack of Fig Newtons he'd brought for his lunch, and then he dragged them on to the stock tank, and they drank like camels from the pipe that fed it, and Meyers tried to distribute his cookies as a snack.

"Not for me," said Callahan. "The only reason I even drink is so it'll rain."

Henry Brusett took one as a courtesy and he put it in his mouth and bit it. "People eat these things on purpose?"

"You have to chew it a little. What's wrong with that?"

"Well, it's glop, is what it is. Hadn't you noticed it's quite a bit like shit? Now I'm thirsty all over again, and what about all these seeds? Man, you should warn people first, before you give these things out to 'em. I mean, thanks and everything, but . . . hoo."

With infinite care, with hands already stiffening from that morning's portion of work, Callahan turned out his hip pocket to catch some pennies and a nickel and a complex wad of lint, and some lavender scraps of paper about as large as his smallest fingernail, imprinted with tiny rainbows. "Three," he said victoriously. "That's a lot. Of this. They said it was Sandoz, and I think they were right. I probably better take 'em before these get lost, too."

"Nah," said Meyers. "Now, you don't need any more. How long you been without sleep?"

"It's all I need," Callahan declaimed. "Your problem is you think you've gotta sleep to dream. But there's dreams everywhere, if you know how to grab 'em."

"Now you're sounding like the Navy recruiter, Mike. My luck, I'd catch a nightmare."

"No. No. Look. This is it. I'd be happy to share. Somebody's gonna take it because it's a sin to waste. Be like the, like the, I don't know. The Host? Along those lines."

"Neither one of us slept much last night," said Brusett. "And I am startin' to wear down."

"You think that's a problem?" Callahan was exasperated. They were simpletons, cowards. "Give me some men who are stout-hearted men. *Please.*"

Meyers and Henry Brusett had known each other nearly all their lives, but never very well, and now they looked from one to the other— for permission, for a better idea, for a wiser head to prevail.

"Well, I've see him work like I bet he never did before," Meyers said. "So there's that to be said for it. But what's in his head? Would you want that? Can you get hooked on this, Mike? What am I asking him for? He could get hooked on milk."

"I'm right here, Hoot. Quit talking like I'm not here. Because I am. Quit that. I am right *here*."

"Sure you are."

"Hoot, what are you tryin' to . . . do?"

"Forget it," said Meyers. "Okay. Give me one. I'll try one."

"You?" wondered Henry Brusett. "You're a college graduate, aren't you, Hoot? Kind of a goody two-shoes? If you didn't get in a fight once in a while . . . "

"Can't even do that anymore. Littlest little thing and I wind up on probation, and, mind you, I'm the only one who got hit on that occasion. So let's just say it is a fool who hires out as his own attorney; you could also say Dean Sullivan was not too pleased with me, and I'm on probation with him, too. I've got to stay completely away from that kind of trouble now, 'cause they already think I'm the wrong orangutan down there at the school of law. Does this stuff ever put you on the fight, Mike?"

"It's love," said Callahan, pressing a dose into Meyers's palm.

"Is that what it is?" Meyers was a legend of hard sobriety. "Then it's probably wasted on me." He threw it into his mouth. "You just swallow it?"

"Leave it under your tongue," coached Callahan.

Henry Brusett said that no piece of paper could be worse than the cookie he'd already tried. "So, I guess I'll take one, too. Maybe I better, if you guys are."

Meyers's higher education had occurred in Missoula, a northern Babylon, and he had grown well accustomed to the reek of one incense and another, but he'd taken small advantage of the consolations of his age. The risks he took were not for pleasure, and he did not ordinarily aspire to happiness or enlightenment, but this morning he was tired of himself. A flake of paper in his mouth, not so significant there, not so flavorful as gum. Meyers didn't expect to achieve anything like Callahan's condition with it. He thought Callahan had probably taken too much, because that is what Callahan would always do, and Callahan was a right foil for any placebo or misconception or joke, a boy of far more imagination than intelligence and with no resistance to any passing fancy. Mounted once more on the driver's seat of the tractor, Meyers surveyed himself pretty steadily for any sign of change, and after what seemed a long while of feeling nothing out of the ordinary, he was reclaimed by the monotony of driving at four miles an hour. Let those escape who might escape, but it seemed he was stuck in a mind with plodding methods, and he'd written the experiment off as a bust and his spirit as an unapproachable one, when, and somewhat suddenly, he was overtaken by a new appreciation for the warmth, the lovely, pulsing sludge of his blood within him. An ember glowed on either shoulder, and in the space of several minutes, he was purged of every last reason to dislike himself. The boys skipped and giggled behind him, rough-looking sprites; the brim of Henry Brusett's sombrero rode up and down, the wings of a thick brown bird in flight.

They gave over entirely to play then, and they took turns riding the stone boat like a sled, sitting on it at first, and then standing and being pulled at a high rate over remnant drifts of snow, pulled across wide and slushy ponds where snow had only just melted, and as acrobats and nymphs they rode, and they fell without being hurt, were soaked to the bone without being cold. Their histories released all claims against them, and they laughed continuously, a laughter at no one's expense, and they ran without becoming winded.

Meyers was never to remember just how or why it had come into his head to climb the mountain, and he could never specifically remember leaving Callahan behind. But they had. They'd been wild to climb, he and Henry, and with no forethought or ceremony they started up.

The climbing was very hard almost from the start; they were into thick timber as soon as they'd left Meyers's high meadow, and in the forest shade, the snow remained in many places waist deep. They walked without benefit of road or trail, and reckoned that they were headed in the right direction so long as they were going generally upward. The trees obscured their track behind them so that they could not tell if they were advancing straight or meandering. Birds and chipmunks disturbed by their coming raised a chatter, and Meyers heard it as threat, as invitation, as choir, and as telegraphic code. Upon snow that he knew to be undisturbed, he now saw living Mayan friezes crawl, flowers budding and blooming as from a heavenly soil.

"You feel like Ulysses, Henry?"

"No, I don't think so. But I can feel my heart pumping in my ass. That's not too bad."

"You look around and you think, 'Nobody's ever been here before. No man.'"

"They probably have," said Henry. "Somebody else has been everywhere you go. They've been everywhere."

"Well, sure they have," said Meyers. "But it doesn't *feel* that way. Here. *Feels* like we're the first ones."

"I don't have a clue what you're sayin', Hoot. And, if you want to know, I usually don't. Why do you say those things?"

"What do I say?"

"You know," said Henry Brusett.

They walked for five hours without another word between them, and never more than ten yards apart. With his marvelous eyes, Meyers sowed spring before him in the forest, and the forest promised in return a big but very coy answer; a shattering understanding of the universe advanced just ahead of him through the trees, and Meyers could not believe that, having had his whiff of this, he would ever entirely or happily return to the old confusions. Implication ran riot in him, accelerating until he could only just manage the cataract of his thoughts by clinging to the one very simple and sustainable idea, and he climbed. There were more and more reasons to climb.

"If we don't get up to where we can see something," he said at last, "I'm lost. You know where we are?"

"Cabinet Mountains," said Henry.

"And if I asked you the time, you'd tell me it was the twentieth century?"

"We kind of know," said Henry. "But, don't you get it? Here's what I've found out: You just *kinda* know. Anything."

"I've never been lost before. This'll take some getting used to."

"That's what it's tryin' to tell us," said Henry. "It says, 'Relax.' Says, 'Wait and see.'"

"Relax? How I'd like to. Nothing on this earth *relaxes* me."

"That," said Henry Brusett. "*That* I understand."

The crest, when they reached it, was sunk in trees and offered no view at all, but they had attained a ridge, and along that ridge lay a logging road quite familiar to him. The road became his new constant, though he knew that following it meant very many miles of gradual switchback descent. It offered, at least, that much certainty, and as they descended through the waning day, and as the drug began losing strength, Meyers felt himself dipped in nostalgia—he'd come to consider this hike the last episode of his youth, the last thing he could ever afford to do for the pure hell of it. Blithely still, he endured his blistered feet and the ache that had clamped itself around his back during his struggles in the snow, and he felt an affection for Henry Brusett that seemed to come of nothing more than the fact that he was there by his side, making the same walk.

"Did you hear I was getting married?" Henry asked.

"No."

"You're invited to come."

"I'll be there."

"You know Juanita Swan? It's her."

"Juanita?" He recalled a slim young thing at a pancake supper, just pretty enough to be full of herself. "Has she got that, I guess you'd call it 'red' hair?"

"Wild Abandon Red, yeah. She's gotta keep touching up her roots, so there's always a bottle of it in the bathroom."

"So you've been living together, huh?"

Henry was proud to admit it.

"You like that?"

"I'm used to it," said Henry. "No, that's not accurate. I should just say I like her, 'cause I do."

"That's Sam and Elena's youngest girl?"

"Sam," said Henry, as if he'd just stumbled upon him in the trees. "Oh, caahhh. I hope he never finds out about this. He would not understand. He would really, really not understand. I'm supposed to go saw logs for Sam pretty soon."

"How would he find out?"

"Well, if I didn't get straight again, if I just stayed high."

"We're okay," Meyers said, "I'm coming down from it already."

"Me, too. But I've still got a long, long way left to go. You believe this stuff? My brain's been rewired. Who knows how we'll think from here on out?"

"We're all right, Henry."

"Yeah, I think so. I wasn't too sure there for awhile. That was gettin' to be too much. I stayed fairly calm, though, didn't I? I sure tried to."

"We're fine," Meyers said again. "I'm surprised it lets you down as easy as it does. I still feel pretty damn good, in fact. A lot better than usual. I get myself in a tub, I'll feel great."

"My cheeks are tired," Henry noted. "Usually you wouldn't smile that much. Those muscles just don't get used that much. Even so, this is no way to be, is it? Not for an old married man. And that's what I'll be. Soon. Real soon, if she doesn't get her period. She wants to be a June bride. Who wouldn't?"

"This is one little story, Henry, that we don't necessarily need to tell on ourselves—Our Big Adventure with LSD. Callahan, I don't know. You can never know what Mike'll say, but whatever he says, no one necessarily believes him."

"You've always been an old man in the way you think. You think ahead, you think behind—that is a lot of work in your mind, lot more than I'd want to do. But I guess somebody has to keep track of things."

"Old man," Meyers complained. "My mother used to call me that. My own mother."

"I don't think Juanita would be very happy to hear about this, either."

"She won't," said Meyers. "I don't see where she'd have to. You did all right for yourself, bud, and a little thing like this shouldn't screw it up. Should it? Altered states, they call 'em. We had our little go, and now I'm good. You? You think you'll need to do this anymore?"

"No," Henry said. "Way I see it, I've gotta be a family man now. That's what I want to be."

"And I," said Meyers, "have got to get my ground in some kind of shape. So I've got that, and you've got your Juanita—boy, did you ever get the better end of that deal. There's absolutely nothing better than a pretty girl in my opinion. Congratulations."

146

"Also, she makes the best french toast I ever tasted."

They came into view of Meyers's land lying far below them, and the road went round a bend and into more trees, and they lost sight of the home place again for another mile and a half, so they walked on, and when it rolled into view again they were all but upon the meadow. "Look at Mike," said Meyers. "Stretched out on the back of that flat-bed like it was a Sealy Posturepedic. He must've finally worn himself out."

He was not, at first, very convincingly dead.

Meyers called to him as they came, called him Sleeping Beauty and Creeping Doody and Lawrence Welk, but Callahan didn't stir. He seemed a little off-color, but they were still hallucinating mildly. Meyers pushed at Callahan's shoulder and it yielded. "Dream guy, wake up." Then he knew, and he touched the hollow of Callahan's throat, and Callahan's flesh was cool and still. He slid the boy's eyelids back and there was no recognition or hope in them, and Callahan's hands, when Meyers took them up, were fish-belly white and cold.

Henry, having never touched him, reached the same conclusion. "No," he said. "Not that. That cannot be. That just can't."

Hoot Meyers walked circuits around the truck while Henry wept for a young friend, dead, so far as they could tell, of bad luck.

"I told myself this morning, 'You better drive on by.' I knew this could not go right."

"Mike," said Henry Brusett. "Mike."

"So what do you think we better do, Henry?"

"Do? Well, we take him somewhere, we tell somebody. You should know, Hoot. If anybody'd know what to do. Shouldn't we try and bring him around?"

"He's cold. Cold. The place to take him would be the hospital. We'd take him to the hospital, and they'd tell us what we already know."

"Was it an overdose?"

"I bet he got just got too chilly. He must've quit moving, sat down to space out, and it probably didn't take long at all. It never did get very warm today. He'd been wet, no jacket, cold all day. Bet he sat down and keeled over. So, you say you want to take him to the hospital? That's where they'd start with the questions."

"I'd like to know, for sure, how he died," said Henry. "I think his mother would, too."

"All right, then. And you want to answer those questions? You think you'll be in shape to be answering questions in an hour or two? Or less. What would we tell 'em?"

"What'll they want to know?"

"Listen to me. What we've got in our blood right now is a felony."

"In our blood?"

"They'd autopsy Mike. They'd find it in him, I think. And—they'd probably want to know why we let him lay out cold until he died, too. There's another felony, maybe, that could be a bad one. They stack up quick, once you get started. We're way on the wrong side of this. What'll we tell 'em? Tell 'em we were only trying to help him out?"

Callahan's body had an endearing quality, like an infant in deep sleep.

Meyers pressed. "So, what do you want to do?"

"Crawl under a rock."

"There's some good features to that plan."

In under an hour they had shifted their day's work so that Callahan lay under many ton of stone, where he should always remain now that they'd committed themselves to add insult to injury and crush him so terribly. He would lie here for as long as they were ashamed of themselves, and that, as they had supposed from the moment Meyers had rolled the first rock onto Mike Callahan's chest, must be forever.

· 12 ·

HE GRADUATED, MOVED home, and rented a cupboard of an office above the old bank. Immediately enmeshed in several divorces, Hoot Meyers bought the annotated fifth edition of *Professional Ethics for Attorneys*, which told him over the course of its two thousand pages that his loyalties belonged to whoever paid him first. It was a mercenary code, nothing he didn't already know, and the book was never to describe to his satisfaction just how he might honorably do the work he'd taken on. He'd become an instrument of the precise revenge that festers out of betrayed loves; he'd enlisted profitably in wars the combatants rarely wanted to end. As soon as he hung out his shingle the clients came to his office, righteous with old anger and new stratagems, and they were often disappointed at how little he shared in their outrage.

Do you know how many loads of laundry that man did the entire time we were married? One. Ruined my best summer blouse. Now he wants the damned washing machine?

Marital assets. Hoot Meyers charged his clients in six-minute increments to hear each new installment of their sad sagas, and he bore witness to that second, terrible intimacy where confidences are turned for use as weapons, and children become bewildered pawns. For someone new to the profession, he was making very good money, but it soon became clear to Hoot Meyers that so long as he was a paladin in family court, the hairs in his nostrils would smell a little singed, and there'd be very few places or events he might attend in Conrad County without encountering someone who despised him, frequently with good cause. He tried not to reflect too much on the majesty of the law. He had very often to remind himself that all he'd wanted from the profession was a drought-proof crop, a cash cow, and it seemed he'd have that. Who was he, after all, to take exception to anyone's evasions? He made his living. He repaired equipment a generation out of use, and piece by piece he began to reclaim his grandfather's ground. He bought some red heifers.

Then one Friday night, an Independence Day, En Smith, longtime county attorney, stuffed with flank steak and angel's food cake and flush with bourbon and Seven-Up, ended his term of office at sixty-five miles an hour, asleep at the wheel of his Brougham. He left an office in such disarray that a number of local attorneys declined the commissioners' offer to replace him pro tem, but when the commissioners narrowed the field at last to young Hoot Meyers, he claimed the office at once, and he found that he made a ferocious prosecutor, a useful and resourceful hypocrite. He gained convictions. He stood for election and was elected, and in the security of his victory, he married Claudia Donabli, a determined little beauty with charcoal eyes, a supervisor of nurses, and eventually he'd be a father who bought his son a mare and a set of the *World Book Encyclopedia*. His properties were ever more populated by festive, thick little cows, and as his operation grew, he sometimes thought that it was all better than he deserved, better even than he'd intended.

It was shortly after his first election that Naomi Callahan made, unnecessarily, an appointment to come in to see him, and he was relieved when she came that she hadn't been wasted by grief as he'd almost expected. She still resembled a hale Mamie Eisenhower. An old woman all her life, with the prissy posture that comes of wearing a girdle, she took his hand when he offered it and she grasped it in both of hers, and one soft talon traveled a bit up his arm and gripped him there, and she beamed bravely at him, too delighted at first even to speak.

"Well, look at you, Hoot Meyers."

Meyers could not agree to look at himself. He offered her one of the creaking chairs he'd inherited from En Smith, wood that needed to be glued again in its joints, and she sat across from him with her huge purse by her side. Meyers had, as her student, made just such a purse himself and long, long ago given it to his mother, who had called it her hamper; it was a rude design of woven reeds that tended to fray after any use at all; Mrs. Callahan was forever sending her charges home with another artifact—she was strong on arts and crafts. And geography. Now her hands lay knotted in her lap, a little prayerful, and she seemed to think they'd made quite a success of him. "Just look at you," she demanded. She sat among tawny stacks of first-series *Pacific Reporters*, books Meyers had just then been moving out of his office, and while these towers were no taller than the seat of her chair, she seemed small among them and surreal. She sighed, and the prow of her bosom rose and sank, that haven for so long to so many tiny heads— she'd been especially kind to her younger students. What could you say to such a woman? To Mike's mother? Poor Mrs. Callahan. He'd avoided her for quite a long time now, no easy thing in the county seat.

"I am so, so pleased for you," she said, "and what you've made of yourself, and I can also say I'm pleased for the community, too, because we've needed a young man in here. Some real energy is needed right now in this office. So much more is going on these days."

"There'll be a lot," Meyers said, "a lot to do." He would never in her company be more than a tongue-tied ten-year-old.

"But you, young man, are just the fellow to do it. You always have been. You're young, but I think the people know you're the kind of person who gets things done." She did not cease to smile. Never. Meyers remembered the rhythm of this now, and how she would circle around in her own good time to her question, to making some velvet demand of him. "Mr. Smith," she observed, "poor old thing. Bless him. En. But he had gotten to the point that he wasn't really equal to the job anymore. He did so well, for so long, but the drinking, that catches up with a person after a time. Sooner or later. The temperance people had a good point, really."

Hoot Meyers had argued a number of cases against En Smith, and the man's lawyering, if nothing else, had never been besotted. "From what I can see, he was pretty darned efficient. I don't know what else he was, but you can look through the files and see he kept right on cranking the pleadings out."

"I'm sure," said Mrs. Callahan. "I'm sure he was doing the very best he could. But—Mike. It's Mike, you know. For me. That's what I'm always thinking about. It's years now, Hoot; it's getting to be years, and right from the beginning almost nothing was done about it, and I get the feeling they want me to believe that he just vanished off the face of the earth, because no one has ever seemed too concerned to find out what might have happened to him. I, I can't get anyone to really look into it. Not until now. But, Hoot, I happen to know what kind of young man you are. You're thorough, you're tough, and per- sistent—I mean, as a child . . . if anyone can find out for me, you can. I waited until you were elected. I waited until you had the mandate of the people. But now it's time. I think I can let you be my hope. Will you be my hope?"

No. No one's hope, least of all Naomi Callahan's. "I'll look into it," he said, and he gave her a lawyer's tiny, calibrated promise. "I'll do what I can for you."

"It will help so much, I think, if someone who knew him is doing the looking."

"I knew him, but by the time he . . . I didn't know him all that well anymore."

"You weren't exactly moving in the same circles."

"No."

"But you knew him. You knew him when he was our little Mikey, and I think you know exactly what I'm talking about—sure, he could be kind of impulsive, but such a good heart. Basically so trusting, and he was a good boy, and I'd like to get some of these rumors stopped." Here, at last, her voice rose.

"I hadn't heard those."

"Hoot."

"You'd be very surprised at how little gossip I hear. This job takes me pretty well out of that loop."

"I need to know what happened to my child. If I . . . He was my only child, you know."

"I'll see if anything was missed or overlooked the first time around."

Meyers, as he thought of it, would be nearly as interested as Mrs. Callahan to revisit the investigation. No findings had ever been published, but he was an official now with the means and reason to know—had he been implicated? Had Henry? Were innocents harassed? Meyers warned Mrs. Callahan—and he saw her eyes go into soft focus to discount it—that the passage of this much time would have to mean that the trail, if there was one, if there had ever been one, would be cold. Cold. What a choice of words. He could, and very often did recollect exactly the sensation of touching her Mikey's drooping hand.

Conrad County's missing persons files, fifty years' worth of them, were kept in a mildewed banker's box in the basement of the courthouse. Only eighteen incidents had been recorded in all that time, and all but two of those had been cleared within a day or two of the first report—hungry, sheepish hunters making their happy way home or found hunched over Ritz Crackers and tins of potted meat, the picnicker who'd spent a night outside, not a hundred yards from a busy Forest Service road, a woman who'd reportedly given herself up for dead. In the unresolved folder there were just two files. The thicker of these concerned the case of Bella James, who'd last been seen gurgling and learning to roll over on a blanket near her drowsing mother. The Elisis municipal park? Meyers could picture no such location, but this had been June of 1952.

And there was, of course, the less tragic but equally complete mystery of Michael Patrick Callahan.

Notes handwritten in pencil indicated that there'd been a search of Mike's Volkswagen for evidence of foul play, and that no such evidence was found. The mechanical condition of the car was advanced as the best explanation of how it happened to be parked along the road. A vial of fifty crosstops was found humming under the driver's seat, an empty Annie Green Springs bottle on the floorboard.

The file also offered a small sheet of stationery with floral borders and lined along one side with Mrs. Callahan's flowing, Palmer Method script, a list of names, of associations:

John Scatcavage, friend

Marshall Howlett, friend/co-worker

Bella Fondren, waitress/acquaintance

Henry Brusett, friend

Lee Warren, business owner/employer

Jim Callahan, biological father (probably Omaha, Nebraska)

Herbert Valens, grandfather

Cap Warren, Darren Orth, "Goodge" Nicholson, friends or acquaintances

There were check marks in red ink beside just two of these names—
Henry Brusett's and Lee Warren's, and a third scrap of paper in the
file, this one torn from a wire binder and with jottings on it in yet
another hand, another shade of ink:

*Warren—boss   MC misses a lot of shifts   sometimes goofy
at work   always scatterbrained   maybe in with some bad
company   not sure   probably last to see him   Thursday
19th later in the evening*

*Brusett—HB has been working out of town   Callahan
pretty good friend of his but hadn't seen him lately   no bad
company   will call if hears anything*

With that the official inquiry, at least as contained in the file, was
finished, and Mrs. Callahan was right—no one had been very curious
about the fate of her boy. But the only promising lead had been followed. Someone had talked to Henry, and Henry must have had to
tell that questioning someone that he did not know what had become
of his friend. It was not in Henry Brusett to lie easily or well, but it
seemed he'd lied well enough.

Meyers sent letters to some of the people named on Mrs. Callahan's
list who had not been interviewed before. For reply he received a baf-
fled call from Goodge Nicholson, an outraged one from the grandfather Valens. Neither of them, of course, could offer any insight, any
new information. "New information" was the phrase that occurred
four times, always in the negative, in the letter Meyers then wrote Mrs.
Callahan. The letter also contained his final promise to her—he'd keep
the investigation open.

When he next saw her she lay among banked candles, still very
ruddy in that creamy light, done in by pancreatitis. She had died in the
deep of the winter when Father Yelich finally finished sealing off the
drafts in the Catholic church, and Meyers, a late arrival to the funeral,

stood bowed at the back of the choir loft, under the arching ceiling, and generations of her students and their parents and their children had come to sweat in dark clothing, and mourners stood outside in the cold, and the censers, with their addition, made the air near the rafters so close and cloying that it penetrated Meyers's clothes and lay like syrup against his skin. There were tulips handmade of construction paper and heaped round the bier; her dreamily illustrated *One Thousand and One Nights* was propped against the casket, a book she'd read to them scores of times through the years.

She'd asked for a Latin mass, and with the several eulogies that were said, and the heat and stench, it all went on too long for the largely Protestant crowd. But all were agreed, even the irreligious Meyers, that justice demanded for Mrs. Callahan, either for her sufferings or for her good works, a berth in her own particular heaven. All the formalities should be observed. From high above, Meyers saw that she'd been laid out in the pale gray blazer she'd worn to conduct her holiday concerts, and he knew the bright smudge on its lapel to be a brass lark. Mrs. Callahan had also asked that each of her former students in attendance that day should pass by her casket and leave her a note, even if it was nothing more than a name, but thoughts and wishes were encouraged, too, and pencils and sheets of her own vibrant stationery were provided for the purpose. Meyers joined in the slow moving rank, and when he reached her, he saw that the mortician had made her strange and stern. Meyers had written her to say:

I am sorry. Maybe we can all rest in peace now.

He dropped the note unsigned.

The reception afterward was hosted by the Ladies Auxiliary at the steak house that had sprung up just down the road from the old school. The school had been maintained since Naomi Callahan's retirement as a sort of museum, but it was too small to seat them all, and so the

Ladies had provided for some vans to shuttle back and forth between the school and the banquet room of the steak house. This day was also by way of a reunion. The school district was dissolving, and the school itself had been sold. Next spring the teacherage was to be torn down and the schoolhouse to be renovated for use as a realtor's office. The new owners had given every assurance that the bell—of course!— would continue to hang in the belfry, but the sense among those visiting the school that day was of another good thing passing. Meyers was careless enough to board a van upon which Mrs. Henry Brusett then shooed her family, Henry and their two boys, one writhing article for either lap, aliens with moon faces smeared in blue frosting. There were two more women along who looked to be too near to Mrs. Callahan's age to have been her students. Their driver, the apologetic chair of the school board, another of the endless Orths, seemed to think he should narrate their short trip, and as a tour guide he told them that Mrs. Callahan had for thirty-two years single-handedly run one of the last one-room schools operating in the continental United States. He said that during several of these years she'd received no pay at all. One of the Brusett boys began to cry and kick in his mother's lap and the van suddenly smelled sweetly of baby shit.

The Belknap school had the look of a country church, a brave, often luminously white little outpost at the corner of two county roads, set among malnourished apple trees. On the grounds a tall set of swings had been built of welded pipe and set in concrete footings, along with a similarly made teeter-totter and a hoop and a backboard upon a pole. The ruts and hollows under this equipment were filled with ice. Inside, the school was very much as Mrs. Callahan and her last class had left it, very much as it had always been, that one immortal room with its sink and stove and refrigerator, the smell of white glue, the recessed stage always awaiting their next performance, and the cloak closet, the clock, the globe, the piano, the library, steam radiators along the walls, desks of indestructible tiger-striped oak that had been cast off from an even earlier school, and that were now, as particularly venerable, particularly prized antiques, more valuable than the building. Looking for certain inscriptions in pocketknife and pencil lead, former students moved among them, tenderly stooping to touch the wood.

At the foot of the stage, to either side of it, were china cabinets now belonging to Mrs. Callahan's estate. She'd used them as showcases for framed pictures of each year's student body. Meyers was studying these when Orth of the school board came up to explain that it had been decided that the small balance remaining in the district's general fund would be used to publish a volume containing the class pictures, year by year. Would he be interested in helping them name as many of the pictured students as possible? They were looking for people from different eras who would know names, especially family names.

Meyers said that he could of his own knowledge identify nearly all of them. He pondered this haunting fact. From across the room, not very far at all from the perspective of a grown man, he watched Mrs. Brusett settle her spreading ass on the piano stool. A woman who would never recover from making her children, she pulled the older of these once again onto her lap, and was mesmerized by his strong, discordant pounding on the keyboard. Henry stood nearby with the other, younger boy in his arms, the little one whose face did not move and whose body never ceased moving. A steam pipe happened at that moment to bang like a shot; it banged again, upsetting the boy in Juanita Brusett's lap; the pianist began to swing stiff-armed back at his mother's head. Juanita, for her part, rained slaps on her son's thighs. Henry held the other child and looked away. Meyers found himself approaching them.

"So now we know," he told Henry, "why it didn't warm up too much in here. Air in those pipes. You want to help me bleed 'em?"

There were a succession of valves in the line leading out of the boiler and to the radiators, and when the boiler had been silent for a while, it was necessary to sequentially let the air out of the lines before steam would decently translate to the radiators above. It was a job for two, and any boy who'd ever reached the fourth grade here had been instructed in the art, the partnership, of bleeding the lines.

Henry offered the child in his arms to his wife, but his wife said, "Nooh, no," and waved him off, and so Henry, his odd baby still on his hip, followed Meyers down the ladder into the cellar. The child was not alarmed, not interested, and its fixed face was yellow under the cellar's sickly light, and its hair was a shock of corn silk.

At each of the valves in the line, there hung a crescent wrench on a string. Meyers reached deep into a crawl space to open the last of these valves; the smell of pack rat was profound where he'd placed his head. Henry, working one-armed, opened the valve nearest the boiler; a hiss issued from either vent. Meyers stood on tiptoe to reach—as boys they'd used a footstool for the purpose—and, stuck in his balletic pose, he faced Henry's son, who stared at him with an infant's frankness, an ancient's recognition. "I think you can twist yours off now, Henry. I'll leave this one open till it really spits at me."

Henry put his child on the floor, and he pointed to the concrete between its splayed legs and said, "Stay. You stay put, Davey." He never looked away from the little one as he opened the firebox and threw in several tamarack blocks. The little one never looked away from Meyers, not even when his father scooped him off the floor again.

"It beats me," Meyers observed, "how she kept this outfit down here from coming to somebody's attention. I can think of a couple, three agencies that would've closed her down right then and there if they had any idea about this boiler being here. This boiler was brought over on the *Mayflower*."

"Newfangled. She hated that, didn't she? Anything newfangled. Remember how she made you use both sides of your paper? She was the original environmentalist and about the only one I ever liked." Henry's baby struggled to free himself again from his father's arms, but in its sallow face there was no evidence of struggle, not even when the child used it to batter his father's chest. Henry set him on the floor again.

"My wife's pregnant," Meyers said, "so I guess I'll be a dad myself here in a couple months." Would Henry regard this as good news? Henry wasn't saying. "Henry," Meyers went on, "I've been wanting to thank you. I saw that they came and talked to you back when Mike disappeared. Somebody came around and asked you about Mike, didn't they?"

"Did you notice? Not one person has mentioned him today. You'd think somebody would say something about him, too, since he was about the biggest thing she had. Him, not this school. He was by far the biggest thing in her life. You think people just got used to not talking about him?"

"I hate to say it, but I don't think he ever exactly springs to anybody's mind. Mikey didn't leave much of a hole in the world."

"Yeah, but there wasn't that much wrong with him, and he was my friend, too. I haven't had many. But I kept my mouth shut anyway. Didn't I?"

"And that's what I wanted to tell you, wanted to tell you how much I appreciate that. You really had a lot less to lose—if we . . . I know you wanted to do what was right, and instead I let you get caught up in the worse thing I ever did. You didn't have to be, Henry."

"I went along with it easy enough. We were out of our minds, or I know I was—I don't take so much as an Alka-Seltzer anymore. After that."

"I only ever talked to her that one time," said Meyers. "After. But that was enough. It came into my mind, not every day but pretty damned often that I should tell her, and every time I decided against it. So here I am at a good woman's funeral, kind of relieved about it. What a specimen. Well." Meyers flinched and reared back. "There. There, that's nothing but steam. I think we finally got it purged. At least she's done wondering now."

Henry stooped to keep his baby from crawling onto the boiler. "We never did have that wedding," he confessed. "Remember, I said you'd be invited? We just never had one. Kids came along, and we never had time for it. I guess we're married, anyway. Common law." Henry had then given his hair and beard to do what they liked, prophet-in-the-wilderness style, and he'd been given this horrid family.

"I know Mike was your friend," said Meyers. "I didn't mean to make light of that."

"This one," Henry said of the child, "they make up a new test for him every few weeks, and it's a thousand bucks here, a thousand bucks there. He's just a strange, strange boy, Davey is, which is about all these tests have told us. They don't quite say why. It's too much for Juanita, so I have to hire sitters for him when I'm off in the woods, and I'm off in the woods all the time so I can pay for everything. One thing leads to another." He picked the child off the floor again; its grubby body went rigid in his arms, and it turned to stare once more at Hoot Meyers. The baby's mouth hung slack, but there was intelligence enough in its eyes.

LET ME GO?

· 13 ·

HENRY BRUSETT HADN'T lasted long without his medicine. The walk back home from jail had hurt him, and he couldn't make the pain subside at all, so within a few days he gave in and scuttled around to different druggists in different towns to get his many prescriptions refilled. He traveled his two-hundred-mile circuit for Lortab, and Lorezapam, and Percodan, and Percocet, and pills with names unknown to him, and pills to help him tolerate other pills, and then home again to that buoyant wait for nothing. One of the pills, or some combination of them, commended him in his weakness, so he took them all to be sure of the effect, but no matter what he took, he could not subdue the new alertness in him that had come of killing that boy, and not all the knockout drops ever concocted could make him sleep through the first few hours of dawn. These were, he suspected, precious days.

He would sit by his wife's bed to listen to her breathe and mumble, to watch as gray light crept through an oval window and slowly sketched her where she lay. It was how they had been conjugal, but now when she woke and saw him there beside her she would weep— so, so unequal, she said, to all that blessed love. Rather than see her cry, Henry Brusett began to spend the early hours in the garden, often on hands and knees, on soil damp with dew and radiantly painful in all his joints. He liked to eat a carrot straight from the ground. He liked how, in the midst of any apocalypse but winter, there was always weeding to be done. Day followed day. Karen went out to pick huckleberries and came home with a quart jar well filled, and they made their fingers, lips, and guts an inky purple.

She'd begun to speak of a time when her husband would be healthier, and of how they might live in a place where he could more easily get around. "Somewhere with, like, sidewalks, and where I could get a decent job. Regular money. I'm sure we could do that if we put our minds to it—live in society. Like everybody else. I mean—*they* all do. Maybe we should try it now." Why not, she wondered, give the goats away and make gumbo of the chickens, and just kind of try for once living among other people? They both knew, however, that his wife was as much society as Henry Brusett would ever willingly tolerate. After a week had passed and still the police hadn't returned, she was made so bold as to ask him, "Do you think you might have any sperm I could possibly use? 'Cause I'd sure like to have a baby while we're still . . . I'd like to have a baby is all. You know. It's what you're supposed to do. I say we get off all these bad habits and get on to something better."

She'd taken to playing the tune about someone's daughter far away, the rolling river, and Henry Brusett, her constant audience, heard her devise a dozen variations on the theme, and from his comfy, fuzzy hell he was determined to listen so long as she was inclined to stroke the strings. *Shenandoah.* This was a most satisfactory world, but a small one, and he expected to fall or be pushed off it at any time.

A visit one morning by Deputy Lovell ended the suspense. "Mr. Brusett," said the plump young lawman, "I am Deputy John Lovell of the Conrad County Sheriff's Department. Henry Brusett, I meant to say—you are Henry Brusett. Anyway, I've got a warrant for your arrest."

"All right. Can you let me get dressed? You caught me right in the middle of a bath."

"Could you go for a cup of coffee?" Karen asked the deputy. "Or are you in a big hurry?"

"The charge," said Lovell, "is deliberate homicide on Calvin Teague, so that means it's pretty serious." Deputy Lovell made rapid mention of Henry Brusett's many rights. "Do you understand these rights I have said to you?"

Henry held a knot of towel at his waist, his gourd of a belly rolled out in a furry, rude display. "Yeah," he said, "but can I get dressed?"

The deputy searched the pockets of the prisoner's jeans, and when he found them empty, he watched Henry put them on, and then a sweatshirt, and then his boots. Lovell took him out and shackled him close, his wrists and elbows secured to the belly chain, his strides hobbled to six inches—all this though no one imagined that Henry Brusett had the will or the capacity to run. Karen followed along at his side, arms tight across her chest and mouthing a long message, not one word of which he understood from the gyrations of her lips. But he made a quick dip of his chin as if he did understand, and then, just as he was being tucked into the back of Lovell's cruiser, she asked him aloud, "How long you think you'll be?"

"Longer than I can go without my scrips, honey. My cousin Tubby's a jailer, so . . . Oh, and you might want to pick that corn tomorrow. Tomorrow's the day."

Lovell, driving away, examined him fairly constantly over his shoulder, tight-lipped and tense about it, and Henry Brusett found that, though he was a murderer, he did not care for the deputy's pissant disapproval. He found once again that the presence of another human being filled his veins with hissing apprehension. Of all the horrors then marching through his head, the worst and most repetitive of them was the thought of the crowded life he was now likely to join. The deputy wanted small talk. "You get any fishin' done this summer? I see you had some tackle up on your porch."

Sere forest. August drought, the first of Indian summer.

"Judge wants to see you right away. A case like this, everyone likes to do the exact right thing. Make sure, you know. You want perfect procedure every step of the way, 'cause you're lookin' to get a real high conviction rate on your homicides."

Henry Brusett's pulse surged against the drugs; he never had any secure notion of what to say, and rarely had there been much refuge in saying nothing.

"But who knows?" the deputy speculated. "Things might not be as bad as they look right now. Look on the bright . . . Well, you never know how things'll turn out. We got quite the legal system. You ever pray?"

Henry looked away.

When they reached the highway, Deputy Lovell, stung a little by Henry's unsociable ways, hit his lights and siren, and they made ninety miles an hour getting to Law and Order, and when they reached it, Lovell hustled Henry straight into a holding cell, and he said, "They'll book you after. So just sit tight, all right? Good luck, I guess."

The room was small and hard. His breathing echoed bluntly under the noises bouncing through the jail. There was a bench along the wall, and cinched as he was, the most comfortable thing he could do was sit on it and stare at his knees. From some other cell laughter burst now and again from a cheap television. Riveted walls, all within arm's reach, a drain in the floor, the itch of old disinfectants in his nose, grain alcohol chief among them. This was not temporary; this was also not undeserved, but he had no reason to believe he could stand it. He wanted to tell them he was guilty and then to say no more.

In a near room a load of laundry ran through a washer, and then a dryer, and the machines could be felt pulsing in their turn through the floor. A meal was served in the jail, but Henry wasn't fed, not that he wished to be—only evil could come of anything he might trust to his stomach. The rhythms of the television and other barely audible events marked the passage of time, and at times a banging developed somewhere nearby. He had the comforting sense he'd been forgotten, misplaced, and when at last the cell door swung open, regret rushed in on a draft of fresher air. A pleasant young woman in riot gear and a ball cap awaited him in the hall. "Mr. Brusett." She smiled and held fast to the black baton on her belt. She stood with her legs well braced. "Everything all right?"

He was greasy with fear. "Sorry, I sure never meant to smell this bad."

"You're a rose compared to some of 'em."

"Does Tubby still work here? Tubby Ginnings?"

"He's been night shift," she said. "Sorry you had to wait so long. They were gettin' everybody rounded up. Lotta times it's just me and the accused guy at these things, these initials. So, see, you're kind of a big deal now." The girl's eyes and mouth were too small for her face and somewhat misaligned. Thrust up by a Kevlar vest, her arms rode out and away from her torso like a wrestler's. "Well, let's get this done, Mr. Brusett. See what they want to do with you next."

The office of Aaron Mendenhal, justice of the peace, was filled like any other in the courthouse with houseplants and mementos from the home lives of bureaucrats, in this case a broken oar mounted on a wall, a bicycle wheel, and there were photographs of many Mendenhals, ranked by generation. The judge was robed and so ugly that it was hard to see any connection between him and the happy subjects of his family pictures. Henry Brusett could find no way to look past the spray of blackheads, the cratered nose, and even briefly into the man's eyes. The judge spoke of the state of Montana as if it were someone else in that already-crowded room, someone unhappy, and he spoke of proceedings in another court, orders signed by another judge, and Henry Brusett stood as tall as he could make himself just before the desk on a patch of linoleum worn gray by worried feet. There were three of them behind him—the dumpling jailer, still winded from their climb to the third floor, and Hoot Meyers, and a sharp-chinned woman with a smashed mouth who wore a dark, heavy suit.

All eyes on Henry Brusett, everyone inhaling his stench, and the judge had more information to offer than Henry could possibly take in, but he perfectly understood him to say, "A term of imprisonment of not less than ten, nor more than a hundred years."

Henry Brusett happened then to think of his son, Davey, who might very well still be in prison himself. Deer Lodge, he thought, must be the scene of many family reunions. "All right," he said. "Let's get it over with."

"Not now," said the judge. "Not here. Your case is bound over to district court. But I'm appointing Ms. Meany to represent you, and after you've had a chance to talk to her, I'll set your bail."

"That's all right, Judge," said Hoot Meyers from behind. "The state will recommend a ten-thousand-dollar bail, with whatever release orders the court sees fit to impose."

"On a deliberate homicide, Mr. Meyers? Seriously?"

"Seriously. He's not going anywhere."

The woman came forward then, Henry Brusett's attorney, and she made to shake his hand until she saw how near his groin it was strapped. "Giselle," she told him. "I'm Giselle, okay?" And to no one in particular she said, "Does he have to be trussed up like this? Is this necessary?"

"I don't even have the keys with me." The jailer made as if to search her belt for any sign of them. "The keys to this exact set of restraints. So I guess he's kind of stuck with 'em until we can get him back to the jail."

"April," the judge directed, for that was apparently the jailer's name, "take Ms. Meany and her client back to the jury room and wait outside the door. It's fine, there's only one door to it, and he's welcome to try the window if he wants. It's a long fall. They have to have their privacy."

"I'm ready to just cooperate, if I could." Henry Brusett's pain took the shape of his several injuries, and, oddly, of a tree—a large trunk with many branches. "There's no reason to drag this out." He felt his attorney's hand clutch his elbow, found himself being directed by April the jailer and Ms. Meany out of the office, down the hall, through the big courtroom with its rows of pews and its smell of carpet shampoo, and the lawyer showed him into the jury room, a stifling thing with one long table, many chairs, and a single window that occupied nearly all its west wall. April called to them through the door, "I'm supposed to be off work in twenty-six minutes, so kinda step it up in there, would you please?"

The lawyer drew him into a far corner of the room before she asked if she might call him Henry. As a killer, he had noticed, he seemed to command a new level of courtesy. There was in this room a library of leather-bound ledgers dating from Prohibition, an incomplete but vast history of Conrad County's transgressors. Toiling dust. Henry Brusett, still in his chains. Ms. Meany positioned him so that he couldn't back away, and she told him, "They don't have much of a case, Henry. If they can't come up with a lot more than what the county attorney had in his affidavit, then I don't, I can't see how they'd get a conviction. They have to prove this charge now, and I don't think they can do it."

"Is that what they think?"

"Who knows?" Ms. Meany's eyes were direct and of a yellow cast. "But it does seem like kind of a bluff to me. What they're charging you with right now."

"I'd like to get it over with." He feared the woman meant to believe in him.

"You're upset. You've been through some upsetting things, and it's not a good time for you to be making any important decisions. Anyway, Judge Mendenhal can't hear your plea. You can't do that until your arraignment in district court when Judge Samara comes to town, and I doubt if that's what we'll do even then—enter any kind of plea just yet. This won't be simple, Henry. It's just not a simple thing, and there's nothing anyone can do to make it that way. But we can get you through it."

"A fact," he said, "is still kind of a fact. For me. I am really, really sorry about the way I smell. You don't have to stand so close."

"They do not have a good case. That's the point I want to emphasize, and that's a point I want you to consider before you make any important decisions, before you talk to anyone. Even me, Henry. About anything. Right now you shouldn't do much more than pass the time of day, and even then you'd better stick to weather chat. We'll talk eventually. You and I. Pretty soon. We'll decide what details we want to get into—but later, all right? For now we'll just concern ourselves with getting you out of jail."

"They'd let me out?"

His lawyer knew from papers already filed by the prosecution that he had a wife, and that, the lawyer said, meant he had ties to the community—a good thing. Did he have other warrants outstanding? No. A criminal history? None. Any troubles with his neighbors—restraining orders, public squabbles going on? No, no neighbors. Did he have a job? He was ashamed to say he didn't. How much could he scrape together to pay a bondsman? Maybe six hundred dollars, the bare remains of his life's savings.

"Well," she said, "you're practically a knight in shining armor, Henry. And Meyers seems to think you're okay. And it's such a skimpy little case—I think we can get you out of here. Today, maybe."

"And I'd go home? They'd just let me go?" He had not expected to have his freedom any time soon, but from the moment its star rose in the east he was transfixed.

"Sure. Well, maybe. You've got a lot of factors going for you." Ms. Meany was a small woman lugging an insupportable will around, and she flung this at him, pressed him into a corner with it. Perhaps she wanted him at a disadvantage, or maybe she hadn't noticed how he shrank from her, or maybe she didn't know how to back away—she stood between Henry and all the rest of the room. "Promise me, no rash decisions. And no talking to anybody. Please? Can you do that for me?"

"What happens if they let me out, and I hightail it?"

"You wouldn't do that." She was innocent only in her faith in him. "But if you did, they'd catch you and drag you back here. They'd probably hit you with a bill for the transport, too, and you'd wind up paying for a lot of gas and overtime. Then you'd be absolutely stuck in jail until your case was finished. But you wouldn't try and run, would you? There wouldn't be any point in running. Right?"

"Well, if you can get me out, that'd be real good. I can just about see myself stuck on a wall in that jail. It's loud in there. Maybe louder than I can take."

So she took him back before the judge, and Ms. Meany spoke of his reliability; his lawyer went on at length about his absolute lack of any criminal record, his physical condition and its challenges, and she asked that her client be released on his own recognizance; the county attorney did not oppose her request. The judge, however, set bond at fifty thousand dollars, saying, "They've got you accused of doing something pretty bad here, Mr. Brusett, and I can't see just sending you home on the promise that you wouldn't do it again. It's public safety I have to think about, as I'm sure you can appreciate."

April the jailer hied Henry back to jail as fast as she could make him mince down the stairs in his shackles, and Ms. Meany kept pace alongside, explaining, "What-an-asshole—well, anyway, do you own any vehicles worth five thousand? Five thousand to a bondsman, and you can get out of here. But the five thousand would be gone—or, you wouldn't have anything worth fifty thousand or so? Do a property bond? You'd have to own it free and clear. In fact, that would probably be the only way. I just don't see why he couldn't set a reasonable bond, take in *all* the factors. But, do you have anything?"

"Maybe the place," said Henry, "our land."

"Okay. We'll have to have a title search done before you can put that up. Maybe an appraisal."

"How long does that take?"

"It can take weeks. It's a real low priority for those folks down at the title company. They've never sat in jail, so it's hard for them to understand how it might be a little urgent."

"Weeks, huh?"

"We might get Judge Samara to lower the bond at arraignment, but I doubt it. I'll think of something, maybe—and would you please get those chains off him now? I'll be seeing you pretty soon, Henry. We'll be talking soon, all right?"

The Conrad County Law and Order Complex was built as a bunker and did not appear very large from outside, but inside there were dozens of enclosures, each room specific to some small purpose. April the jailer left him in one of these to change into his orange jumper, and when Henry emerged from it, she was gone. His cousin had come on shift. "Of anybody," said Tubby Ginnings, "you're the last guy I ever thought I'd see in here. Nobody's heard a peep out of you for . . . ever, just about, and now look. Geez, Henry. You ever had your fingerprints done? It makes kind of a mess, but we gotta do it." He was ideal to his calling, Tubby—night shift at the county jail—thirty years old and already thinking nightly of that adequate pension.

"Has Karen come around? She bring some prescriptions by?"

"She did, but the sheriff has to authorize those, tell us we can give 'em to you."

"Is he here?"

"You kidding? He goes home to take his little nap at lunch, and usually he don't come back."

"You can see my name right there on the bottles. They're prescriptions. Can you call him? There's a couple of those I can't do without. Pain pills."

"Sure," said Tubby. "I'll try. Now, when you get back there, there's a guy named Leonard, and he's on his way to Washington, or Mississippi, or our pen, or somewhere—eventually. There's a bunch of places that want that guy. You know that three-strikes thing? Well, he must have about three dozen. At least he'll never see the light of day, but right now he's waiting on an appeal—or his lawyers are—and for some reason that makes him my customer. He tries to be kind of a badass in there. Sometimes."

"There's no empty cells?" Henry Brusett needed a shower.

"It's not a Super 8."

"How about that holding cell? That first cell they had me in? That'd work fine for me."

"We could actually get in trouble if we left you in there too long. That's isolation. The holding cell? Whattaya? Relax, nobody'll hurt you in here. I run a pretty nice jail, cuz. Just keep an eye out for that Leonard, and you should be fine. Most guys prefer the barracks cell. It's gin rummy to a zillion points in there, and that's where the TV is."

"No," said Henry involuntarily.

"Come on," said Tubby. "It's not that bad. Here, you get two blankets—one of these can go away if you get in some trouble, not that I'd think you would—and your towel, itty-bitty bar of your own personal soap, your slippers—and, believe me, I wash these real good. I go through a gallon of Clorox a month, man. You're not a smoker, are you? We give 'em one smoke a day, but it's a lot more treat than the non-smokers ever get. One smoke a day, no exercise, and three squares. We had a woman once, a welfare cheat, she did thirty days and gained about thirty pounds. Boy, was her old man pissed when she came out. It's starch that does it to 'em. But that'd be about the worst that could happen to you. Blow up a little bit and get fat. You'll see."

"There's gotta be someplace you can put me by myself. What do you have to do to get into solitary? What would I have to do to go in there?"

"Solitary? Noooh. Come on, it ain't Alcatraz, either. What we do have is a woman, and a lunatic, and a juvenile, so that's three cells right there. All that leaves us is the barracks. You'll be okay. They're good guys, most of 'em. They're just doin' time."

"See about those prescriptions, would you, please? Just . . . please, and now you've seen me beg, Tubby, and I'll probably keep beggin', too, till you get me that stuff. I'd rather not be a nuisance if I don't have to be."

"When did this happen to you? When'd you get this way? You were highly regarded, cuz; I remember it well—highly regarded in your day. Bull of the woods, weren't you?"

The bunks were ranked all along one wall and positioned against it so that those prisoners who owned lower bunks could make personal cubicles of them with their extra blankets, and Henry Brusett staked himself to such a homestead within ten seconds of entering the barracks cell. The other prisoners were asleep or pretending to be, and, working quietly, he used both of his blankets and his towel in the building of a soft-walled crypt, and he lay in it, on his plastic mattress, and there was nothing left to do but sweat in his manufactured dark. He did not think it likely that Tubby would trouble himself or his boss to secure a weak man's comfort, but Henry waited with the big ache growing, and he listened very hard for his cousin's return, and as he waited and as the evening progressed, the barracks cell came to life again, and he lay on a mattress an inch thick, and he listened, his knees traveling slowly up toward his chest.

· 14 ·

W HEN GISELLE MEANY went out as a newly minted Juris Doctor to look for work as an attorney, she found herself forced in every interview to admit that, though she'd graduated summa cum laude, she also came with a ten-year-old daughter in tow, and she was raising the girl alone and intended to raise her properly. Because Sheila had seen little enough of her mother during law school, her mom could not now conscientiously commit to work more than fifty hours a week. She tried to stress, though, how strongly she felt that she could meet all her obligations—to everyone—that she was intensely organized and, if anything, almost too responsible. She had managed against all odds to be a very diligent and very exacting law student, and she expected she would make the same kind of lawyer. Her intellect and a sample of her expertise were on display in a recent law review, where she'd written *The Interplay of Federal and Montana State Taxation Provisions Governing Like-Kind Exchange in Real Estate Transactions*, the whole point of which was to demonstrate that she was capable of learning boring but useful things and learning them well.

But there came a sticking point in every interview, a place where team play was mentioned, and where would-be employers in silk ties began to rhapsodize about the local supply of young, fee-generating associates just then aching to live every waking moment in the offices and at the service of an established law firm. Giselle was informed that this kind of dedication, rigorous though it may be at first, was how futures were built in the trade, and she was advised to think of all the child care options that became available to women with improved incomes, and so, before she'd ever managed to fight her way completely into the profession, she had already conceived a certain loathing for it, already begun to understand that as a vocation, the law might partake a little of her learning and good heart, but mostly it would want her time, and all of it.

Quite plain and chronically unlucky, she was barely making rent. Student loans were falling due. She had meticulously researched and written and circulated on ivory bond a hundred letters of introduction, been to a dozen interviews for firm handshakes and a good deal of looking squarely and earnestly into incurious eyes, but to date she'd received for offers only the memo from the office manager at Corwin and Mizner, a firm where she'd interned, and where, it seemed, one of the partners had wondered if she'd like to come in for some occasional light typing.

These were the dismal months when her daughter's doctor recommended that Sheila be given a stronger, more expensive inhalant to use, a time of no insurance. They were living in a studio apartment on a shag carpet then thirty years in continuous service, a thing that had absorbed the gross spillage of a hundred prior tenants and that wanted vacuuming twice a day. Giselle went six days a week to Ari's Little Athens, where she wore a smock and a floppy chef's hat and stood eight and ten hours at a time slicing spiced lamb from the spit. Ari was Syrian. He paid her under the table. She came home from these shifts and, even after her shower and a change of clothes, wore the scent of rendered fat and rosemary. They were eating surplus and hijacked Greek food at that time, and cheap noodles, and they were not especially healthy. They owned a hula hoop from the Goodwill, and a Candy Land game that they kept for sentimental reasons though they both secretly hated it, and the radio, which they fought over, and they subsisted on a few exquisitely observed rituals: Friday nights were for bubble baths, Sunday mornings for cocoa over a their scattered *Missoulian*.

From this buck-fifty bonanza, Giselle extracted advice to the lovelorn and tips on how to play certain hands of contract bridge and how to do gratifying things to a garden. With Sheila deep in the funny papers, mom would read through announcements of births and weddings, read the obituaries and the gossip magazine with its lists of all-Americans, and finally, when she'd given herself a headache anyway, she'd turn to the paper's help-wanted ads, a place where, browsing under the Professionals heading, she was always made to feel the trespasser. Week after week, the state and the tribes and various law firms and debt collectors were seeking attorneys under this heading, but never new ones. There seemed to be no need of fresh blood in the legal industry, and the unmistakable implication of the want ads was that she was not wanted.

Finally a Sunday came, though, when a place called Conrad County was soliciting bids for its public defender contract. Applicants were only specifically required to hold a license to practice law in the state of Montana, and so her bid for the position was in the mail that Monday morning, equal parts a figure she'd pulled out of thin air and language she'd lifted from the ad itself. Giselle agreed, for what would prove to be a disastrously paltry sum, to stand for the calendar year as counsel within the county for all indigent persons accused of felonies and jailable misdemeanors or who faced probation and parole violations, and she would be indigent counsel as well in juvenile court and in some social services matters, as per appointment, and she would hold regular office hours in the county seat. She'd done none of these things before, but this was no time for the irksome detail, and Giselle thought the terms of her offer might be desperate enough to succeed.

She found Conrad County on her road map. It had the profile of a bent leg with river systems for its bones, and it lay almost contiguous in places with the northern border of the county where she'd lived for the last fifteen years, yet she didn't know it by name. Conrad County? There were so many counties and their names were of no significance unless you lived in them, but she did recognize the names of some of the towns—there were three of them—and at some indefinable time, and for reasons she couldn't now remember, she'd passed through them, and of the towns and of the roads between them she'd retained an impression of remoteness, of shade-tree industries and oiled gravel; she remembered deer bounding across yellow road signs. There must have been people, too, along the way, but she could not particularly recall any—there had been several long bridges, a dam she thought, and those deep and darkly timbered valleys. Perhaps the human presence was negligible there.

When she learned she'd won the contract, it came, somehow, as no surprise, and the flush of success lasted just half an hour before subsiding into a more familiar sense that she'd fallen into something else unwholesome, and this was the mood that persisted while they were moving and as the Toyota kept breaking down under the strain of being overloaded. Giselle went still deeper in debt to buy a desk and rent an office and rent them a cottage in the woods where Sheila, for the first three months, might be found weeping two and three times a day. Giselle Meany bought the Montana Code Annotated and some shelves to hold it, and she did her best to completely absorb Titles 45, 46, and 61. She painted their bedrooms, for they had bedrooms now. She screwed a hook outside Sheila's window and hung from it a hummingbird feeder, and it became her daughter's duty, as the birds regularly emptied the thing, to recharge it with Karo syrup.

And then one day she was the public defender. Giselle took possession of a filing cabinet full of cases, many of them still active. Her recent predecessors in this job, and there were a startling number of them, did not on paper seem to have been very interested in the work; she opened files in the hope of deconstructing them, of learning from them how to mount a defense, but counsel for the defense was a rare and tepid presence in these records, and there was little but professional contempt to be learned from them. So, without a mentor, and without any real example or precedent, she waded in, the throbbing razor of her ignorance always right at her throat, and she was suddenly in constant conference with people of astounding depravity, clients who knew far more law, or claimed to, than she could ever conceive of learning. In her first week's work she was presented with a burglary and an arson, and two fragile, raging alcoholics for clients. Giselle Meany finally understood that she'd thrust herself into the gravest affairs, and she was terrified all the time, and she'd managed her own circumstance so ineptly that she couldn't pay herself quite as well as Ari the ersatz Greek had paid her. She was working all those hours she had hoped to avoid, and all for an income so bad that she might have had food stamps if she'd applied for them. She remained a somewhat superfluous mother.

But a table was set for each of them in the life of the community, and they settled in. Sheila acquired Viktoria, a peculiar, angular girl, for her regular baby sitter, and Viktoria, as it happened, was an athlete, so Sheila became one, too, an agile, tireless prodigy, her asthma an unpleasant memory once she'd breathed greatly of the mountain air. With her mother at work, there was nothing much to prevent the girl from dribbling a basketball endlessly in the kitchen, and in time, other athletes learned of her, and she was always wanted for one game or another, and she fell into friendships with fellow soccer players and softball players and the like, an energetic group of giggling pals. Her mom, meanwhile, became addicted to caffeine and adrenalin.

It wasn't ennobling work Giselle Meany had got, but it was pure in its way. As she lacked the right to rank her clients with respect to their just deserts, she argued full force for all of them, all of the time, and in the county's courts and various offices, she gained a reputation as a meddlesome fool, a heart worn on a sleeve and bleeding inexhaustibly, without discretion—so be it. She was paid bottom dollar, and her clients were, by and large, bottom feeders, quick to whine and lie—and so be it. In the absence of any other satisfaction or incentive, she learned to serve the shining principle. Giselle Meany had decided it must be her lonely lot to just be everyone's champion.

So, year by year, she negotiated slightly better contracts, and in time she began to buy the cottage in the woods.

Six years into it now, and too stingy and too stubborn to buy professional wear appropriate to so short a season as Montana's summer, she waited on a muggy morning in the county attorney's outer office in one of the three suits she wore in rotation throughout the year, a garment that felt in such weather like chain mail over a hair shirt. Breathing her personal miasma of lanolin and bargain brand deodorant, she frequently let slip the word "bullshit." There was always something better to do with her time than wait, but she was a professional supplicant and spent a good deal of time waiting. "Nelda," she said, "what's he doing in there? Should I just come back later?"

"He's got the commissioner on the phone." Nelda included Giselle in her league of long-suffering women, gals who met at random to express doubt about the doings of men folk.

"Which one?"

"Oh, it's that Mr. Rudolph," said Nelda, "or Commissioner Chatty Kathy, as I call him."

When Meyers finally did call Giselle into his office, he greeted her there with an open tin of Dr. Platko's Health Mints.

"How many times do I have to tell you I hate those things? It's like chewing Drano." They were bracketed by whirling floor fans, and she had not the option of speaking softly if she wished to be understood. They did business always in his office, never hers, and she resented this several times every week. "I wanted to get started on this Brusett thing. I think we'd better work something out now, don't you? Don't you think it's time to be just a little bit reasonable? Deliberate homicide? What a mess now. This is a lot of extra work, and there's Mr. Brusett sitting in jail, which looks like it could just about kill him off. You've just barely—just *barely*—got probable cause, Hoot."

"Take a look at what I do have, and you tell me—what am I supposed to charge in this thing? What other charge fits? It's this or let it go completely, which I am not inclined to do."

"You can't prove it."

"You want to talk to the kid's parents for me? Tell 'em what a weak case I've got?"

"You could tell 'em what I just said. You could have told 'em you didn't have enough to convict. Which is only the truth. I mean, this is a 'mere presence' case. It's well-settled law, you can't convict a guy of being in the wrong place at the wrong time."

"With a corpse in his lap. The man's blood all over him."

"Okay. Probable cause. But that's it, and you know it. I think we've really got to do something now. Something smart."

When she had first met the county attorney she'd mistaken him, with his brick red complexion, for a drunk, another lawyer too fond of his cocktail, but there was a pale boundary at his temples. It was weathering, a farmer's tan he wore, and she would learn in due course that he was the canny baron here, beholden in this fiefdom to no one. The practice of law, as she'd known it, had consisted almost entirely of shadowboxing with him. Of the men in her life—tormentors, lovers, friends—it was Hoot Meyers, constant opponent, defining other, who'd been most like a husband. He'd won eleven of the twelve cases they'd tried before Conrad County juries, and this hard history bordered their every conversation.

"What do you propose?" he asked her.

"I don't know. Motion to dismiss? You could do that."

"Why? What's my basis? Tell the judge I was just kidding? Never mind. Sorry, Your Honor, I kind of lost interest. Look, I've got this fund drive going on for the hospital, and this-that-and-the-other-thing going on, so if you can give me any reason at all I'll be happy to ask for dismissal. But it would be up to you to find me that reason. Wouldn't it?"

"You can't prove it," she said, an image of bloody, matted hair in her mind's eye. "How's that for a reason? How about you can't prove murder here? For a reason?"

"That remains to be seen."

"It remains, that's the problem. What are we gonna do? You know as well as I do that that guy doesn't belong in jail."

"All right. Personally, I think Henry Brusett's one of the nice ones, and personally I don't think he's likely to harm a hair on anybody's head. Not without a real good reason. But, see, that's just my opinion. If you look at this thing objectively, it's a little harder to come to that same conclusion. Looks like he must've done something or other up there."

"Something or other? You know, this is just not like you. That man does not belong in jail, and you know it."

"No? Who does?"

Giselle Meany had decided early on, and despite her client's murmuring to the contrary, that there was no violence in Henry Brusett. Having formed that companionable hope, she was not about to abandon it any time soon. There were lunar phases in her career when her need to touch upon actual innocence was so great that she would sometimes cobble it together out of the most unpromising parts, and then believe and believe. Eventually someone had to be innocent, if only to satisfy the law of averages. "He's just an old sweetheart," she said. "Not to mention a cripple."

"Henry'll tough it out," Meyers assured her. "He's been through a lot worse than this, and he'll be all right."

It seemed to her that Meyers knew every living soul in Conrad County, frequently knew their whole genealogy and how they were likely to behave in a given situation. He graded people, like any livestock, much in terms of their breeding, and often quite accurately.

"I can't think of any other way to say it, so I'll say it again—you've got him in there on a charge you can't prove, and that's wrong."

"Okay," he said. "Then let me hear it from him. That I'm wrong. And why I'm wrong."

"He's so . . . If I let him say anything at all right now, that'd be malpractice. Mal-something. I think he's probably trying to protect his wife."

"Why's that?"

"I don't know, but at least I don't reduce my theories to writing, and flop 'em in front of a judge, and have some poor guy thrown in jail."

"You've got the means to fix that." Meyers propped his boots on the ruined quarter of his desk. "Here's the keys to the jailhouse: He can plead to whatever he did. He can make something up, for all I care. You can make something up for him, and who'd know the difference? Tell me some tale that's got a plausible defense in it. Tell me the kid fell down. Something. If this isn't what I've called it, just have Henry tell me so. I'll do about anything for him that I can, but what I can't do is back off altogether and pretend that nothing happened and nobody's dead. If I bailed on every shitty case I saw . . . I know it's thin, so I'll be real flexible, but I won't just pitch it. I can't. Henry knows that, too."

"Henry knows? How do you know what Henry knows or doesn't know? At this point? The guy is too far gone. In some ways."

"I hope not," said the county attorney.

"I suppose he's another friend of yours?"

He knew most of her clients of old. The county attorney had surprised her at times with an easy sympathy for them. But the county attorney was privileged to decide when and where his sympathy was due. Giselle Meany's own compassion, too long overtaxed, had become a creaky mechanism, just another set of rules to trouble a girl when she should be sleeping.

"You want this taken care of? Go down and talk to your client. Give him a way out."

"Hoot, what are you . . . ? What are you trying to do here? This is getting a little strange, if you ask me."

"Have him tell me what I want to hear, and we can get this out of our way—business as usual—let's have that sad story and be done with it."

"Jeezus, Hoot. Buck up. Did you really think everyone can always afford the truth? They don't even know it half the time."

· 15 ·

THE TELEVISION WAS turned off, the talking died away by stages, and then, finally, when the toilet was no longer being flushed, Henry Brusett thought he might come out of his shelter. His own bowels had been demanding release for some hours, but as this was only one of several agonies, and not the most pressing of them, he thought he could stand it if it meant avoiding the other prisoners. When at last there was nothing to be heard in the cell but his own gurgling gut, he risked to lift the blanket and was met with the tired light from a bulb that was never extinguished and with a stranger's steady, hooded stare. There was a plate steel picnic table within a few feet of Henry Brusett's bunk, and the man was sprawled along one of its benches with his back to the opposite wall of the cell. A big animal, comfortable in its lair, the man was amused by and expected Henry Brusett's alarm at seeing him there. A trail of tattoo question marks ran down his cheek as tears. "Can I fluff up your pillow, prisoner?"

Now what? Henry Brusett couldn't fully straighten out of the S he'd made of himself on his bunk, and so he duckwalked to the back of the cell where a partial cinder-block wall was raised, the official concession to modesty upon which a flaccid two-foot penis had been inscribed. He opened his jumper and slid it to his knees. A black paste flowed from him the moment he sat down, a pudding acrid as burnt metal, and he tried calmly to wonder if there would ever be an end to the ways he found to disgust himself. FUCK YOU WENDY was scrawled on the wall, and THIS BUDS 4 U YO, and ARE WE HAVING FUN YET? When he flushed the toilet something more poured from him, something that smelled, at least, as if it had once been organic. Henry Brusett could not recall having eaten enough to account for so much waste. He flushed the toilet again, but the bowl hadn't emptied before he was forced to turn and embrace it, the chalice he'd just befouled, and his eyes bulged, and he puked all that was left in him, and then he puked to no good purpose, and after several twisting minutes of this he was very tired, and he rested with the stainless steel bowl for his cool pillow.

Then he felt himself rising away from it, hoisted from the head by his hair and from the waist of his half-mast jump suit, and this was not the passage he had wanted, that smooth ascent from the mortal coil; this would be his fellow prisoner's doing, the work of the man at the picnic table—Leonard, he'd supposed—for whom two hundred pounds must be a doll's weight. Maybe a squalid little death had come—which might do. Toes dragging, nose running, Henry Brusett did not even try to look around behind. He was flung into his bunk. "Don't you die, you fucking Lazarus. I'll abuse you if you die in here. County time is hard enough as it is without that. They tell us you're in here for murder, but you don't seem to carry yourself like that much of a man. Get a grip."

It was the best advice he'd had, but a goal already out of reach. Henry Brusett wasn't equal for now even to the rebuilding of his enclosure, the reclaiming of his battened dark, and so he made a shell of himself again, but with eyes for Leonard, Leonard who had decided Henry was a kindred, a sufficiently lost spirit, and so he made like a friend to fill the wee hours with reminiscence and with four-square observations from his life as a detainee.

"I specifically *do not* like dead people. That's where I draw the line, because they're, well, they're too icky for me, and it's probably a good thing I'm squeamish that way, probably accounts for how I got to have a few glorious years on the outside. No bodies. After the reformatory, I had seven years there when I wasn't even on parole, and a Firebird with many extra horsepower, girlfriends, and none of this institutional-grade meat. Aw, it's pussy I miss. Pussy I grieve. No bodies, though, that's such a simple little rule of thumb. You can do quite a bit of mayhem before you ever catch any serious time—unless you leave a body—and that's where you made your mistake, Geronimo. But even if you're, you know, spotless in the mortality department, eventually they'll get around to calling you a sociopath, and you start to hear a lot of this raving about the good of society, and the next thing you know, you're just completely screwed. Sociopath? Isn't everyone? It's just a question of who's got the courage of his convictions. They say I may be eligible for parole if I can just exhibit fifty, sixty years of good behavior. I'm even wanted in Mexico, *cabrón*. There's a little country brothel down in Chiapas where you pay by the week and the girls have big, soft eyes, and the buying power of the peso is just unequaled, and I even ruined that for myself, so you might accurately say that I *am* incorrigible. But Conrad County? Con? Rad? County? I have never killed anyone. Weenies and green beans, night after night? For entertainment it's this one channel and the pamphlets the church ladies bring down. I've learned fifteen ways to get to heaven, sinner, but I've also read that King James Bible several times—every joint's got a Bible—and what they say is in it, ain't in it. Hope for mankind? Shit, that fucker's plague and pestilence front to back—and dirty dealings—isn't the gist of it they crucified our Lord? So for entertainment? Goddamn you stink, skunky—let's see, what do we do? You box these assholes' ears. Some of these guys come in here picking their teeth, I swear to

God, with a straw. So I like to make 'em shit their pants. What else is there to do? Think it's anywhere near six? They turn on the television for *The Morning Show*. April and her remote control—whattaya want to bet I get my hands on her some day? Yeah, but it's your county thing here, your steady string of drunks, and every last one of these local doozies comes in here oozing Old Thundermug, just *bleeding* it out their pores. Them or meth junkies, who smell even worse. Right now we've got a shoplifter, chronic shoplifter, and a guy sitting out some fines. Murder, huh? That's actually pretty good. We'll double-team 'em, pardner. We'll just scare 'em to death. You ever feel like you were at the top of the food chain? When Tweedledee and Tweedledum wake up, we'll have some fun with 'em. They just de-*mand* to be hurt."

Henry finally managed to ask, "How do you get a shower?"

"Every five days they take us down to the shower room, whether you need it or not. Take you down one by one. You get about five minutes. Oh, it's the Bastille, Pierre, for all practical purposes. You want to try and find a rat to tame or something. I wrote to Denny Rehberg about our conditions, but believe it or not, the good congressman hasn't got back to me. So, anyway, best you can do is drag over to that sink and use it like a fuckin' birdbath, and some of these drunks can't be bothered, so then it falls to me and I scrub 'em down, and they come out very rosy, too. You play euchre? I'll teach you a game they call Calypso. That's just about an endless pastime."

"Can you sleep in here? Doesn't seem like you sleep too much."

"Sleep? That's not how I cope. In point of fact, I *don't* cope. They serve a decent breakfast, and that's the highlight of your day. I've been here twenty-one months, and night is day, day is night, and they tell me I've set a modern record for consecutive time in this bunghole. You thought they'd try to break you, but no, now you see, that's too much trouble. They just throw you away is all they have to do. Throw you away, and leave you to your own devices. Let you break yourself. Ask me if I care. Fuck it. Bring it on. Life is good, or so I'm told."

He went on without pause, and in time, Leonard's voice was joined by others, some of them long dead, and all the early ones were agreed—tough it out, they said—for that was the faith of Henry Brusett's fathers and the practice of the women of his line. Wait for it to be better, they said, it's all you can do, and for nearly all his existence, Henry Brusett had been as tough as any, more uncomplaining than most, but now he was someone else; arthritis made his old hurts new every day, and he knew he'd not quietly outlast it as he was supposed to do; no amount of patience or fortitude was to be rewarded. There was only the medicine now, and if it was ever long out of his blood then he began to be sick in every stitch of himself, sick, in part, just for lack of the medicine, sick so that his large muscles clenched, and his small muscles twitched, and his stomach ground away with or without anything in it, and he could feel his nerves misfiring, feel them weary of delivering the same old message. Without the drugs he could only wait for exhaustion to knock him out, and that was always much too long in coming. He'd been built for endurance, not understanding. It seemed he was regulated by a timing belt and that it was slipping.

· 16 ·

BUSY HANDS SEEMED the most reliable way to blur the fact that she didn't miss him very much. Karen Brusett had made Cream of Wheat for breakfast. Feeling stout, she went out to turn the heap in the compost bin; Henry had shown her this marvel of sweet rot, this way of making chocolate soil, but once again she noted how her husband was not quite the sum of his parts or of her remembrance. For all his presence here he was very much gone, and an absence of rather small consequence in her leaky heart. She fed and watered the chickens, fed and watered the goats. She milked. She hammered some Cape Breton reels she'd sent away for, and she read her horoscope in last week's paper, and all of it seemed a little luxurious. And poor Henry, locked up. Once, she had dreaded to be alone; now she relished it, and she was rewarding her husband very shamefully for how he'd helped her to this independence. In all the world she owed only Henry, knew only Henry, really, but there had been such a long sadness with his dwindling away, and she was tired of it. Still, she meant to do better by him.

Having once encountered Katherine Hepburn at the city library, coltish on the cover of an old *Life*, Karen Brusett had come to own a pair of high-waisted khaki slacks and several demure blouses and a string of fake pearls. This is what she sometimes wore to town, what she now wore when she expected to encounter other women there, or if she wished to be taken seriously. The townspeople seemed to think her somewhat unclean in her usual mode of dress, and often they'd been right enough. She lived a little dirty, but now she had also taught herself how to apply lipstick, and how to do the essentials of a manicure with a pocket knife, and so she cleaned and groomed, and she put on her maidenly pumps and the perfume she'd got for their second anniversary, and she was driving in to see about her husband when a recurrent exhaust leak sprung once again from under the Triumph. A gray, fuel-rich vapor leaked through the floorboard at the shifter, and Karen leaned out past her windshield and into an onrush of clear air that scoured her eyes. Her hair, gathered in a bun, burst into capering strands, and wasn't she just the saucy gal racing to hop the mail plane to St. Paul? And still not cured of daydreaming.

She arrived at the jail smelling of gasoline. The building was bermed and squat and appeared to have weathered a dirty sandstorm. She rang a buzzer three times to ask into it. Eventually a voice like tin roofing flipping in the wind told her to state her name and business. "I am Karen Brusett, or *Mrs.* Brusett, I should say. I'm here to see him. My husband, who's in there, I believe."

"It's not visiting day."

"I need to see somebody. To find out if he's okay."

"He's okay."

"Because he's got some problems," she said.

"I'm sure he does. He's okay." The crummy speaker popped between every word.

"Does he get his, uh . . . he has some medications he needs. Does he get those? The ones I brought down before?"

"How should I know?"

"Could you check? It's real, real important. Could you just let me in the lobby there? It says, 'Press buzzer for entry.' And I did that."

The monitor spit another burst of static and went dead. She saw a camera leering from under the eave, and suddenly she could not think what to do with her hands to seem natural. She felt she'd waited a long while before she rang the buzzer again. Required again to state her name and business, she said, "It's me. I'm the same person."

"Step to the microphone, please, and state your name and business."

She said again that she was Karen Brusett, but now it was beginning to feel like a fabrication. She said again that she had come to see about her husband. "I need to find out if he's getting his medicine."

"We'll look into it."

"Who are you?" She asked the grated wall.

"Visiting hours are on Tuesday and Thursday—for authorized visitors—if he puts you on his list and you're approved. Two thirty to five, and it's first come, first served for the visiting room." The crackling in the monitor died again. Karen Brusett turned to the camera and raised her palms to it in surrender. She fingered the clasp of her necklace. She paced a bit to think, and then she went into the courthouse and stopped at the treasurer's office to ask a large woman with a jeweled poodle broach where a person should go to see about trouble.

"What kind of trouble, dear?"

"Bad."

"Oh. Well, not here. We wouldn't handle that kind of thing. License plates is what we're—have you tried the police?"

"They won't let me in."

"Won't . . . are you a *victim*?" The clerk wore reading glasses on a tether and was, Karen saw, afraid of her.

"Me? No, I *wish*. It's—my husband's in . . . some trouble. Actually, they took him to jail, and I need to find out some details."

The treasurer's clerk sent her to the clerk of court's office, and from there she was sent to Justice Mendenhal's office, and the secretary there sent her to see the public defender. "She's down at the other end of Main Street. Over the Photo Express. You know where the Ford garage used to be? It's past that."

Karen Brusett decided to walk. She did not wish to smell like a mechanic when she met with this lawyer, and so she thought to give herself a good airing, and she walked the six blocks of the town's business district, a main street strung out along the river, storefronts facing a sidehill and railroad tracks, and she passed Gifts N' Things, Luigi Tang's Chinese Garden, Elk Tooth Surveying, the Buck Snort Bar and Casino. A number of shops were refaced with barn wood and were offering garbage for sale as antiques: an embossed bread pan, a threadbare teddy bear, socket sets. Much of this town had been raised in a spasm of affluence a hundred years earlier, built up of chalky brick and brooding failure, and it would have looked, she imagined, spent from its very beginning, but someone had opened a bakery now, and there were lemon tarts in its window, and Mrs. Brusett told herself that these would be her treat for later, when she was finished, and she walked on to where Main Street suddenly became Highway 200 again. An iron stair hung on the side of the Riddle Building, and, clanging, she mounted it to a door that led to gray and serpentine halls. With the direction of several hand-drawn arrows, she made her way to the lawyer's office. Karen Brusett was only aware of any confidence when she felt it leaking away. She thought of the bakery again, thought she'd better reward herself first, but here was a door with an opaque pane in it, and in gilt upon that was the name and title of Giselle B. Meany Esq., and behind it a powerful child was crying. Karen went in.

There was a woman in pink sweat pants, a dirty shirt, and the crying child on her hip; the woman examined her for a moment, and, having reached no conclusion, she called over a set of dividers to the other half of the room, "Giselle. Giselle. Somebody here to see you."

A certificate on the wall established G.B. Meany as a member of the Montana Bar Association. The Bill of Rights was written out in phony script on a phony scroll, and next to that hung the Tulip of the Month calendar, its days X-ed away to mid-October.

"What is it?" the receptionist asked over her brat's bawling. "What can we do for you? I'm Brenda, by the way."

"My husband got arrested, and I'd like to find out what's going on. They just kind of dragged him away."

"Oh, he must be that . . . Giselle . . . I know how that is. Gi-*selle* . . . She gets so distracted." Brenda's burden began to kick at her as if he wished to gallop; she jogged him hard on her hip. "*No. Cody. Giselle!* I have got to get him to his grandma's. Oh, you're that, Karen. My sister went to school with you. You're not what she . . . Oh. Oh, wow. So you're here about that Brusett guy? *Cody.* Whew, I hope that kind of works out okay, but, here's hoping, huh?"

The lawyer came round the divider then. "Shure," she said through the pencil clenched in her teeth, "take awff. But pleathe . . . " She took pencil in hand, " . . . could you take that bottle with you? That milk starts to smell so sour after a while."

"It's *formula*." Brenda left with her awful offspring, and they were well down the hall before there was much quiet in their wake.

The lawyer dully watched the door. "Welfare to work. A real good program, I think. I think she'll eventually be quite the, uh, it's actually a very good program. You're Henry's? What did you say?"

"That kid still takes a bottle, huh? Man, he's kind of big for that, isn't he? I'm his wife. Henry's."

"Oh." A pebble dropped in a pond. "Good. Great. Because we do need to talk, and I sent you a letter, but I'm glad you came in, because we do have a lot to talk about. I'm always surprised at how many people around here don't have any kind of phone. I just thought everyone had a phone."

"No phone, and about all we ever get in the mail is our book of the month. But, now that I've showed up, I sure hope you can fill me in a little bit, because nobody else has."

The lawyer, intending to smile, grimaced. "Let me turn the phone off, turn the ringer off so that's not—you can't have very much peace with it on. In fact, why don't I just lock the door?" Ms. Meany turned a dead bolt and led Karen Brusett back to where clutter burst into profusion behind the dividers: law books and binders splayed everywhere on their backs, on make-do shelving. A computer breathed, its cursor blinking on a field of fine print.

The lawyer, right down to business, folded her hands before her on her desk. "Where shall we start?"

"He's in jail, I guess? I know he hasn't come home."

"Right."

"That's not gonna work. I don't think he can be in there very long."

"No, I don't think so either, so I'll be needing a legal description of the land. Your land."

"A what?" This and Karen Brusett's few minutes with the county attorney were her whole experience of lawyers—they were strange and indirect.

"It's a way they describe property," said Ms. Meany. "You'll find it on a deed, a mortgage, something like that."

"But what about Henry, though?"

"You're using the land as collateral, you could say, to get him out."

"Oh. But I don't even know what that is . . . oh, like for a loan?"

"Yes. Security."

"Collateral? Well, there's an ugly word if I ever heard one." The room's one window, a tall, narrow window in a deep casement, overlooked the playground across the street, a small plot all in the shade of a linden tree, and with a swing and a hobby horse mounted on a spring. Karen Brusett noticed these amenities every time she came to town. She'd never seen anyone use them.

"I'm sorry," said the lawyer, "I didn't get your name. Your first name."

"It's Karen."

"I'm Giselle."

"Okay. Look, you know I've been kinda stuck up in the woods, and this right here is one of the reasons why. When I do come to town anymore, seems like I can only understand about half of what people say. I never got very educated. Also, we don't have a TV up there. So I'm what you'd call outta the loop, but it only really hits me when I come to town and people start tryin' to talk to me. If you want me to understand you, you might have to break it down pretty simple. Sorry. But if you tell me what to do, I'll do it. You'd never know it to hear Henry say, but he's one of the better people there is. That I know of."

"I know he is. That's my idea of him, too."

"Can you help him out, you think?"

"I'll try. I should be able to. First thing we need to do is get him out of jail."

"They won't even let me in to see him."

"They have a policy about visiting." The lawyer seemed to hold it in contempt. She had a very misshapen mouth, and should by all rights have had a lisp. "See, if they follow a certain policy, then they don't have to exercise any independent judgment, give it any thought, and that's always the popular option for cops. No thinking. They will let you visit, though, at the regular times. Just don't expect anybody to bend one of their little rules, even if it's reasonable to bend it. They won't."

"Henry needs to take some prescriptions he has. I brought 'em down there, but I don't know if he's getting those like he should."

"I can see about that. As soon as we're done here, in fact, I'll go down and see about it. What are they? These prescriptions?"

"Oh, it's a whole shelf of 'em. It's for his back. His back hurts a lot. And his hip, his legs, that bunged-up foot he's got. His head hurts. Then he's got this thing where he's always afraid a little bit—and if he gets around people, except for me, I guess—it just does him in. He takes some stuff for that, too. Anxiety. If he doesn't take it, it gets pretty rough for him. Real rough. He used to do without every so often, without the pills. But not anymore. He can't for very long."

"He's too sick for jail," agreed the lawyer. "I may need you to testify to that next week. Would you do that for me? For Henry? We need to take a run at getting him out without paying any money for it, or tangling up your property, or waiting for a title search. But I think, just in case, we'd better keep on pushing to finish that title search."

"Ah," said Karen Brusett, "I don't think it would even do any good if you said that a lot slower. I just want him out of jail. Sure, I'd testify to it. Whatever you said."

"This must be pretty hard for you."

"He's a great guy, and I'm not too bad myself. Well, maybe I am. Bad. It's me if it's anybody."

"We need to lay some ground rules before we get into certain things."

"I thought that was in baseball or something. You call it a ground rule?"

"You should understand a couple of things. Important things—I am Henry's lawyer."

"I knew that. They already told me that at the courthouse."

"Yes. But what it means is, when I talk to Henry, what he says to me is confidential, and I can't breathe a word of it to anybody. But you're not my client. I don't have that same relationship with you."

"I'm a young person, and I been just kind of a brush monkey, so . . . there is quite a bit of fairly usual stuff that I don't understand, that you'd have to explain to me."

The lawyer pulled her glasses off, and there were two blue dents at the top of her nose; with her eyes no longer magnified, she was not as imposing. "It's not my job to protect you. If you say something that hurts you and helps Henry, then that's how I'll use it. Understand?"

"Sure. That's all I wanted to hear. What if I said he didn't do it? Would that get him out of there?"

"Just that? His wife saying he didn't do anything? What do you think, Karen?"

"What if there was a . . . a misunderstanding?" Here was a good and useful term.

The lawyer became ominous. "This is where you might want to be a little careful. You could hurt more than help if you're not careful. Henry, I mean. Hurt his situation. As I told him, they don't really have enough evidence—right now—to prove he did anything criminal."

"Then why's he in there?"

"Because he's in there. Let's put it that way. I agree, he shouldn't be, but I don't have the final say on that—the judge does. They *think* he did something. Which, which isn't supposed to be enough—they are a long, long way from proving anything at all. I think they may be trying to squeeze one of you to talk."

"They?"

"The county attorney, Flaherty, Utterback."

"Oh? What do you think of that guy? That Meyers?"

"At the moment, I don't know. He's usually pretty good at his job. Or he's very good at it, which can be kind of a problem when you're facing charges here. But even a guy like that has to have some kind of case to work with."

"You trust him?"

"I don't know if that even enters into it. But I suppose I do; he's fairly trustworthy, I think."

"You don't think he might be a liar?"

"Anyone *might* be," said the lawyer. "About everyone *is*, eventually."

"Wow. That's probably true, and I guess you'd know. But where's that leave you? If that's the way you believe?"

"Leaves you with the law. But we're getting off into generalities. What I'd like to talk about is this case. The point I'm trying to make is—what they know so far is enough to raise quite a few suspicions, sure, but not enough to prove anything, and it's almost certainly best for Henry if we keep it that way."

"Then I gotta ask—again—why's he in jail?"

"Because he is. You started to tell me, though, that he didn't hurt that young man. Did I understand you correctly?"

"Absolutely."

"So, does that mean you know how he did get hurt? Killed, I mean—just for the sake of accuracy."

"Not exactly."

"Can you see how that doesn't work? That probably wouldn't do him any good at all, if that's your position."

"My position," mused Karen Brusett. "I never had one of those before."

"Maybe you just found him? The two of you found him?"

"Yeah. Yeah, exactly. We just . . . that's all, we just found him."

"Karen."

"All right. It was me."

"What was? You?"

"I hit him. That guy. I was the one."

"Why?"

"Why? Why'd I hit him? Oh, well, I was scared?"

"Because?"

"Do we have to get into all that? All I want is to get Henry out of that jail. Believe me, he doesn't belong there."

"Henry was the one they found the blood on. You can see how that might complicate things—as far as what you're saying? What you're trying to tell me. You'd probably have to get real specific if you wanted anyone to believe you on that."

"Maybe. Yeah, I can see that. What should I say, then?"

"Tell me, why were you scared?"

"You hate to talk bad about somebody who's dead. Disrespect 'em. That seems wrong."

The lawyer stood and went to her window and looked out of it. She had a narrow back, thick calves encased in disastrous pantyhose, and she seemed sunk in permanent sorrow. "Have you ever heard that phrase, 'The truth, the whole truth, and nothing but the truth?'"

"Truth, truth, truth. That's another thing they hit you with when you come to town. 'What's the truth?' But they always act like they already know."

"I'm just trying to tell you what you'd have to do if you want to be of any help to Henry. If you think you have something to say that would help him, that's fine, but you'll have to come out with everything. Are you willing to do that? And not leave anything out? If you're willing to go that far—*and* if you've got something to say that you're absolutely sure will help Henry—then great, I'm all for it. I'd say let's get started on something right away, do an affidavit, maybe we'd even get the court reporter up here and do a deposition. But unless you're ready to cough up the whole hair ball, then the less said, the better. Probably." The lawyer kneaded the tip of her nose. "Except for the fact that he's in jail, his position isn't all that bad right now. I'd like it if nothing came along to mess that up."

"I never told 'em a thing," Karen said.

The lawyer warned her that the law would return to her in one form or another, that someone would be questioning her again, and that when they did, they might try to be a little threatening about it. "So you might be hearing terms like 'obstructing justice' and 'perjury,' things like that, but never mind all that. Just always remember—you don't have to tell anyone anything. No one can force you to incriminate yourself, and it's basically up to you to decide what might or might not be incriminating. So—do you see what I'm saying? You don't have to say anything—to anyone—ever. It's always your decision, of course, about what you'll tell them. But it is *entirely* up to you."

"I'd kinda made up my mind about that already. Keep my mouth shut. Even if it was gonna backfire a little bit. I mean, I should actually be the one in trouble if anybody is."

"It's up to you to protect yourself, Karen. I think you have a good idea how to do that."

"We been so far out of everybody's way, it just, if I wasn't . . . what? Sociable. But, isn't there a thing about how you can't testify against your husband? Or you don't have to, if you don't want? Isn't there something like that?"

"That's not much of a privilege anymore. You can't testify as to anything he might say to you in the course of your marriage. But that's it. Big deal. Never mind that, though—as long as you keep your wits about you, and as long as it's in your best interest to do so, you can just stay quiet. And that's about the last legal advice you'll get from me. It has to be."

Karen Brusett's first impulse, and the counsel of every lawyer she'd heard on the subject, had left her perched on the tiny, loathsome platform of her rights, to which she might be confined for quite a long time. She felt the drain of this new silence, felt truth set running fugitive in her once again. Why was she forever being asked to describe something she'd never clearly seen? They only ever wanted the truth out of you. "So what's he been tellin' you?" she asked the lawyer. "What's Henry been sayin' about this?"

"I haven't had a chance to talk to him at any length." Ms. Meany carefully returned her glasses to her face. She was ashamed. "No, in all honesty I, well, I wasn't sure exactly how I wanted to approach him at first. He seemed to be very distressed in a way. Agitated. He was trying to say some things that would've made it harder to—technically harder—to defend him. Sorry, I'm, I know I'm rambling. I'll be seeing him pretty soon. Maybe later today. It should be pretty soon, at least."

"I can see you maybe kinda figured out what he's like. And I bet you'll do what's best for him, too."

"I'll do the best I can," the lawyer specified.

"The main thing would be those pills. If he's not been getting those pills, then it's been, oh, more than fifty, sixty hours now, so he'd be in hard shape. He's just a good guy, and I think you saw it in him, so I'm glad. Henry's done less wrong stuff than you can even believe. And I will do *anything* for him, okay? You just say the word. Whatever you think might work, I'll give it a go."

"Just get me your deed—or a copy of it. That's about all I can think of for now. That, and stay in touch." The lawyer kept glancing toward her computer screen. She had other problems.

A scrim of cloud had gathered and sunk low upon the valley while Karen Brusett had been in with the lawyer, and it was unseasonably cool in the town, and the town smelled of the river, and the river smelled of fish. She had wanted to do, or even to identify, the noble thing. It would be nice for once to set things right, but all she'd been given to do was the easy job of finding a paper, and she knew just where it was—in Henry's fireproof box, under the foot of his bed. She would get the paper, and then there'd be the waiting, and she'd wait as long as necessary, and she wasn't sure when or how the waiting would end, but she knew there'd be no atonement in it, only boredom and fear, and she did not expect to feel any better during the foreseeable future.

There were rose gold pastries in the baker's window, new there, and Karen believed these might well be warm. She'd promised herself, hadn't she? She turned in, and the door tipped a bell; she crossed a checkerboard floor, large squares of clean and modern linoleum, and the shop smelled of butter, powdered sugar, and coffee. It was good to be the girl who yielded to temptation. A young man in a long green apron came out from the kitchen and pretended to flinch at seeing her there, startled by the big, pleasant revelation. "I know you," he proclaimed. "You were a freshman. I was a senior. You had your own style back then. Quite the style, I remember. Look at this. You, you are . . . okay, just give me one second."

"Karen," she said. "It's Karen. That's all right. I didn't know your name, either. I didn't know anybody's name, hardly. It was just high school."

"Long time no see. I'll bet you didn't have the slightest idea who I was, did you? Bet you thought you'd never seen me before."

"Sure I did. I mean, you changed, but. What's that on that tray?"

"That," he crooned, "is baklava. Honey, and phyllo, and butter, and walnuts is how I do it. It's addictive. I've made myself sick on it sometimes."

"Ooh, give me one of those. Yeah, I will say, it took me a second. It wasn't the best idea you ever had, to dye your hair that way, hack it all up like you got it. That's sort of a disgrace."

There'd been some breathtaking moments in that year he'd mentioned, their common year of high school—she'd managed to walk close behind him nearly every day between second and third periods, walk behind him the full length of the school's longest hall, and he'd been thick-shouldered, and blond ringlets lay round his bull neck, and he was sometimes a long while making the trek from English to industrial arts. "Greg," she said. "I guess I actually do remember it. You were Greg. Still are, I guess."

The postered wall featured bicyclists in a Bavarian setting, a fly fisherman. There was an open invitation to join the Valley Scrapbookers Club. She tried to make it clear that there was a great deal in this room, apart from the boy in the green apron, for her to look at. "Could I get a mug of that house blend, too? That smells so great."

She sat in a wrought-iron chair, before a glass table, and Greg served her. "Isn't that about the best thing you ever tasted? You should come back Tuesday. On Tuesday afternoons I do spanakopita. Or Wednesday for my strawberry blintzes." He said he'd been gone, gone to the Tri-Cities area, but now his mother wasn't doing very well. So he was back for a while, and he was trying to do something at least a little creative while he was here, and business was building little by little because he made damned good bread. Greg was not so manly and fine a boy as he'd been before he'd made a statement of himself, but he seemed very glad to see her.

"Me," said Karen, "I never did get around to goin' anywhere. I'll bet that was pretty nice, wasn't it? To get outta here?"

DO
OR
DO NOT
SAY

· 17 ·

H<small>E WAS A</small> long while bringing his cousin into focus as a human being, much less a relative, much less a helping hand. It was Tubby. Tubby, pestering, pestering, "Come on, you're scarin' me, Henry. Come on and come to, would you? Come on and sit up. I got those pills you wanted. Should've heard the hell your lawyer raised. It was human-rights this and human-rights that—sorry, I just forgot about it. Here, sit up. I have to watch you take these. Here's some water. You actually don't look very good, do you? How you feel?"

"Fine," said Henry Brusett, which was not true.

"From now on you'll get some of these with breakfast, or right after, and some more after supper. I mean, you get 'em all day long, man. We're not exactly set up for a hospital, you know. This makes a whole new set of chores for me, 'cause of what type drugs you take— whatsit? Really heavy duty, huh? So every single time you take 'em, I have to watch. Three times a day. Me. Just me—this asshole over here scared April off, and now they can't seem to get anybody else hired because of some budget thingus, and so it's just me and old Fess and his goddamn asthma, and that's your regular jail staff now. Yeah, you think that's funny, do you, Leonard? Me workin' a hundred hours a week? Oh, you'll be seein' a lot of me, and they'll probably move a deputy in here, too, do some jail shifts, and that poor guy, he'll be pissed off right from the start, won't he? Go ahead and laugh, but . . .

you sure you're all right, Henry? Man. Had yourself hid away in this little cubby hole of yours, and we didn't know. But you'll be okay now. Won't you?"

Henry Brusett took a capsule and three bitter pills and eight ounces of water.

"You'll be all right," Tubby said, "if you start eating something. We've got old Germaine back in the kitchen again, and she's not too bad a cook, either, so you better get up and eat when I bring it. Keep your strength up. Keep that asshole from getting any extra cake."

"Good cook?" Leonard could not let this pass. "She boils hot dogs. And what would your idea of *bad* food be? We get the sweepings off the slaughterhouse floor—in my opinion that woman, that Germaine of yours, must be a miserable, miserable human being."

"One square of cake for you, Leonard. That's all anybody in here is entitled to."

"Waste not, want not." The big inmate leaned down and past Tubby, who cringed a bit, and he looked in upon Henry Brusett where he lay, and he offered him another strain of advice. "If I were you, old-timer, I'd go ahead and fast. Why not, considering the alternative? Why not do a Bobby Sands? *That* was an outlaw. Brits couldn't hold him, could they?"

Having let Leonard get in behind and above him, Tubby was crouched at the edge of Henry Brusett's bunk with no ready defense and no line of retreat. He sought a lighter, friendlier tone. "You mean that lounge-type guy? You mean that old singer they used to have? Was that the Bobby?"

Wide awake now, Henry Brusett closed himself in again behind his blankets to wait to feel better, and he lay for a while supine, and then he lay by turns on either side, and then face down, and then he sat up for a time, not all the way up as the bunk above him wouldn't permit it, but with his arms angled behind him like the legs of a deck chair. Pain management. He wished to be more alone in this. Deeply and conscientiously he breathed himself in—in and out slowly through the nose, until his nostrils were chapped with it, and still he felt as if he'd been gripped at his shoulders and feet, that vast hands were twisting him, and at times he'd catch himself groaning, and then his good leg also cramped, and his hamstring seized so hard and suddenly as to jerk him off his steel rack and hold him arched up and away from it for a long, long moment. Finally the muscle unbound, and he lay back. Eventually, some of the pills took hold.

There was Leonard's voice and two others beyond the blanket, a small society of inmates gathered at the picnic table, just feet from his head. The younger voices, dog's-belly voices, spoke of things from the television, of actresses and other personalities and of how they should properly be used. One of them went on for a time with his opinion of the expensive brands of toilet paper advertised so heavily at that time of day. These prisoners seemed not to have guessed that they were stupid, and so they kept offering bad jokes and juvenile boasting, and all of it in the dangerous hope of somehow pleasing Leonard. Leonard suffered them to say very little, but these muffled, vacant youth were too dull ever to be entirely discouraged.

"I can't believe," said Leonard, "that you'd brag about shooting a helpless animal. You sick, sissy little prick. What are you—humming now? There'll be no humming, goddamn you. Unbelievable. The company I keep. That old hipster in there, he's got the ticket, blitzed out of his mind on some fine pharmaceuticals, opioids I'll bet, and look at me. Shit, do I not suffer? Priscilla, you better quit crimping that fucking hole card; I happen to know that's a jack or a queen. Who's suffered more than I have? I've got pain. I've got people in here humming, cornpone willies, it is just completely beyond the pale, and next I suppose somebody breaks out a harmonica—but do they ever bring me anything for *my* pain? They'd never dream of it."

When at last Henry Brusett's jaw unclenched, he forced himself up and out of his gray sanctuary and to the sink. He made himself naked before the other prisoners, and they appraised him as meat gone bad while he bathed. He scrubbed himself entirely, washed out the wash-cloth, and scrubbed himself again. If a man had to mortify himself, then he may as well be thorough. He knelt before the sink to get his head under the faucet, and even the city's chlorinated water was an improve-ment over how he'd smelled before—on no account was he quite so ashamed of himself as he was ashamed of how he'd come to smell.

"That," Leonard told the others, "is your classic whore's bath. *That* is a guy they just can't disturb. I mean, what could they possibly do to him? Look at him. What'd you get blown up, or what? Glad to see you getting clean; that was my one and only gripe with you, but now you're remarkably clean."

Henry Brusett also washed his jump suit in the cup-sized sink, and he wrung it out and put it on again, and he sat on the concrete floor to wait for it to dry.

"A *gentleman*," Leonard instructed the others. "Finally a serious man in here on a serious charge, and how can you even hold your heads up in the presence of a gentleman? Sir, I never asked your name. What do you like to be called?"

With no hope now of being ignored, Henry Brusett surrendered his name to them.

"Why don't you come up here and sit with us?"

"I'm fine."

"See? See that? Says he's fine. Somebody made hamburger outta that guy, but there he sits on a concrete floor, telling us he's just fine. Take notes, you pussies, and you might learn to conduct yourselves with a little dignity." Leonard dropped to the floor and, with his hands formed in a triangle directly beneath his heart, and breathing like an engine, he did 160 correct push-ups.

Henry Brusett knew that to lie down again just now would be intolerable, and he saw that he'd need a certain ration of light each day, even if it was only this light, even if it meant being in this company. When lunch came, he made himself go to the picnic table for macaroni in margarine and oily coffee that proved savory and bracing. Now the octagonal pill was working, the one he took against the possibility of social encounters, and, as a simple courtesy, he sat with his fellow inmates. They watched *Tony's Bitterroot Kitchen*, a guest chef describing the easy, practical, and charming peasant cuisine of the Loire.

"Look at her chop," said a petty thief who'd been four days without his chew and who was forever sucking at his nicotine-starved gums. "What are those she's workin' on?"

"Vegetables," said Leonard. "Kale? Kohlrabi, for Christ's sake? How can you not know? You live on the outside where the things, where they actually grow. How can you possibly *not* know? But I imagine you're a Doritos man out there, aren't you?"

"I like chicken strips," said the thief, "and I'm just one day away from having some, too. Chicken strips, and cheese strips, and Dr Pepper. Rent a movie. Get a blow job. I am never, never, ever, *e-e-ver* goin' back in jail." The thief, Sydney as he called himself, was thin and round-backed and had a beard just sufficient to deepen the hollows of his cheeks. Aswim in his orange jersey, he sat at Leonard's side, within easy reach, but he could not refrain the regular mention of his sentence nearly served. "One day and a wake-up," he would say."

The other young man, who'd once referred to himself as Jamie, was half-finished paying the justice court its eight hundred dollars, and at fifty dollars a day, he had more than a week left to sit. He'd had no better offers. Bloodlessly he wondered, "You ever had scampi? That's what we had. Scampi. That time we went to Wenatchee? We had some wine, too, some wine that was supposed to go with it. Go with fish, kinda. My Uncle Arch paid for everything. I mean, what a nice guy. He said he might get me something out in the orchards. Not picking or anything, but you know, some white-guy job."

"I fuckin' hate seafood," said Sydney the thief. "Hate the way that shit wiggles."

"Everything wiggles," said Leonard. "Everything wiggles when it dies, prisoner. Do you want to take the whole animal kingdom out of your diet?"

When he was alone, Henry Brusett was prone to wonder how he'd become so mortally shy, but among these inmates it was no mystery. Each of them sustained an atmosphere around him of humid warmth in which it seemed fungus must surely grow, and he might reflect as often as he liked that he was by far the worst of them, and still he felt defiled by their company. They were too many. They were too close. While the early news was on, Tubby delivered them yet another lad fallen low, and the new convict, with an expectant tilt of the head and an apparently expensive haircut, joined them at the picnic table. He introduced himself as Nat, said he'd been out on bail but he was checking in to do his ninety days, and suddenly, wetly, he wept.

"That's right, luscious," said Leonard. "Let it all out. Have yourself a good cry. But you better know—that beat-to-shit old hippie you're sitting next to there, he's our murderer in here, and he doesn't go for a lot of nonsense. *Gnat*—parents can be so cruel. 'Bug,' maybe, 'Skeeter'—but *Gnat*?"

"That lawyer was of no earthly use to me," Nat sniffed. "She was no good at all. Plead guilty? What kind of advice is that? I might as well just plead guilty? Why? So they can throw me in here?"

"You pleaded?" Leonard was concerned for him. "You *pleaded out*? How many counts?"

"Six. But six misdemeanors. I mean, these were just misdemeanors. Your so-called 'property crimes' at that. They always tell you,

'Just cooperate.' That's what your public defenders say. But really—
you should really *never* cooperate."

On television there was a blond girl in a department store, followed by an older woman at a desk, followed by ads for adult diapers
and corn chips. There was a short film about a girl whose leg had
been reattached, but not very successfully. Tubby brought tepid turkey
loaf under a lime green gravy, and from the moment this meal made
its appearance on the steel picnic table, it was clear to everyone that
Leonard would avenge himself on someone for it.

"This is just more of that waste product," said Sydney. "They
keep feeding us this waste product." And to the newcomer, "I am
almost done with this shit. This time tomorrow, I'll be playin' keno
and drinkin' Schlitz."

"Couldn't they just warm it up a little?" wondered Jamie, who had
got the jailhouse habit of posing the futile question. "How do they get
it so cold and stiff like this?"

"Aw, dear lord," Nat said, contemplating his starvation. "What
are you supposed to eat in here? I thought you guys looked a little
skinny. I've got food allergies. I've got sciatica. This won't be a good
fit for me."

"You'll learn to love it," Leonard said. "We sure like having you
here."

"No," said Nat, his downy cheeks abloom, "I know you're kidding. And I know probably no one really *likes* it in here—very much—
but it's just not for me. The thing, mine . . . it was a mistake, a couple
mistakes and that's my so-called *crime*. Because I really was going to
get, well, every one of those ladies was supposed to get her cosmetics.
That's what I actually planned to do. Get those ordered. I could still
do it, too."

Leonard leaned to their new associate and looked him up and
down.

"Cosmetics," said the newcomer. "Timeshares. Supplementary insurance. In business you try to stay flexible. I may be young, but I'm a businessman with a heart of gold, but then that's what always bites me in the, you know, the hind part. Some little bookkeeping problem. If I could just get out of here, I could always generate whatever I needed to make those ladies happy again. I'm an entrepreneur, I'm a businessman, so wouldn't it be better for everyone if they'd just let me do business? I could be out there paying taxes."

"But we like you in here."

"Yeah. I know you're kidding with that, Mr., uh . . . ?"

"That's Leonard to you. We're now on a first-name basis, Mildred."

Steadily subduing his gag reflex, Henry Brusett broke the skin that had formed on his supper, and he ate it.

· 18 ·

WITH A LONG, thick torso on short, bowed legs, he looked like an ape, and he'd been born to pack a saw through the woods. Henry Brusett felled trees from the Selkirks to the Big Horns, and with his Husqvarnas throwing snowy sawdust, he'd dropped timber enough to raise a city, made money for everyone who'd ever used him, and he'd dragged the ModernAire many thousands of miles to go sawing logs. All those timber sales and all that devastation and income had made him a good reputation in the woods. He was the homely kid who came early and stayed late, and who ran hot all day. He'd been a natural disaster for hire, and in those years he'd lunched on sardines and saltines and measured himself in board feet, and for a very long time he was the high, wide, and handsome Henry Brusett, to be found on some eminent ridge a long way from home.

As a young man he had hoped, like anyone else, for a loving family, and he had thought that a draft of new kin might be the answer to a burrowing loneliness, thought that because he'd selected them, because they were more or less cut from his same cloth, that he might have some hope of reaching understanding with such people. Only too late did it occur to him that he should have founded such a family on a happier wife. Juanita did not for any reason smile in his presence, not even after he'd invested so much in her teeth. The woman seemed to eat as patiently and continuously as a cow. She bore them children, and the boys were her boys, creatures in her image, mean, sneaky, and unsatisfied—but she didn't like them. No one liked the boys, least of all the many professionals who'd tried to diagnose them. As none of his family was salvageable, Henry Brusett bought them a good house with a dry basement in an otherwise empty neighborhood, and he made sure to call them on the third Friday of every month at seven in the evening, and if they were home to take those calls, they would ask him for money. They were welcome to his money. When they had it all, as was frequently the case, it was a relief to tell them so. Out of stubbornness he loved them.

Henry Brusett got for his work, for himself, only the barbarous joy and vigor to be had from it. The world as he knew it was laid out so that a man might never carry his saw on the flat but must somehow move always uphill or downhill with it, and always through brush, but it was just this activity that had made him nimble and had built him a heart like a minor sun and a chest to house it, and when the other boys on the job stopped to share a bowl or snort a line off a Forest Service map, Henry Brusett never did, for he liked nothing so well as unfettered work and felt himself the athlete in competition with God, very lucky to be praised and compensated for his compulsion. He knew mornings when the wait for first light was almost unbearable, down in the smell of mossy dew, nothing particularly to think of until he could see to crank up his saw and start cutting.

He did not wear a hard hat, but he wore large rubber cups over his ears to protect them against tinnitus. He wore a sort of leather apron or chaps and considered himself, accurately, to be careful enough; he thought as young men do, that he'd be the one to go through untouched, and he never imagined himself as anyone other than the pristine, quick sawyer, and this confidence, which began and ended with physical bravery, had been well rewarded for many healthy years. But one night he caught a ride off the mountain with Billy Jackson, and a brake line on Billy's Kenworth ruptured as they were coming down out of Garden Creek, and Billy managed just one downshift before his clutch was also useless, and then they were runaway, and with loaded log bunks bouncing along behind, they slammed around a switchback and onto a long straightaway to gather more speed—how serene the memory of sunflower stalks gliding past—but then the approach of that next sharp turn. Billy Jackson jumped and broke his shoulder and his arm. Henry Brusett smashed a kneecap landing, and mangled two toes in a good boot. Rocks in either case, both men had found rocks in the weeds beside the road.

There was no question then of waiting to heal very much, for Henry had no place to wait. His sons were already long in the tooth as dropouts by that time, and they ate from boxes they carried from room to room. They rarely left the house, but when they did, they would return smirking with the fruits of their operations; they stole a potato chip rack from a sandwich shop; they stole scrap iron and copper, burst tires; Davey stole a sack lunch out of someone's car just to throw it away and then laugh telling the story. Each of them watched a separate television all day, and his family came together only to squabble or to steal, and at home Henry Brusett enjoyed the esteem and favor of a lug wrench left in an easy chair. He was back at work when work still meant a bloody boot at every break. This made for protracted healing.

Never again would he be well balanced on his legs; he had learned to favor the injured limb and couldn't entirely unlearn the habit, and he was very much slower. He was awkward now, but he hired out to Monk River Lumber as a master sawyer to do thinning and selective cutting. His job was no longer a matter of reducing a patch of acres to stump and slash, but of harmlessly dropping trees among other standing trees, and he enjoyed the precision, the craft of it. The company valued his skill enough to leave him alone. He had the use of a fine company truck to cruise their timber and the understanding that he would never be assigned to work with any crew. The company sent him checks and form letters that spoke of valued resources and implied to Henry Brusett that he and the trees he felled were being mentioned in the same hushed breath as Monk River's property. But Monk River's checks were large and regular.

He did not attempt home again, though he continued paying bills addressed to that location. Juanita told him that Davey had enlisted in the army, that Davey was in training, that Davey was discharged, and then in every subsequent call she said that there was still no word from their younger son. And Denny, she informed him, who was supposed to have an IQ of 126, had got himself put in a group home, a particular group home, in fact, that allowed smoking. Henry Brusett was to see no savings with the boys gone from the house. Juanita told him every time they spoke that her stomach was not good, and this regularly resulted in astounding expenses. She had tried everything for that touchy gut except to forgo her twenty cups of coffee a day. Henry Brusett, thinking he'd signed on for some of it, would call, and in all the years, the decades of calling, Juanita never once asked after his whereabouts, his well-being, his doings. He was to Juanita only another ear, and it might have been any ear, in which to pour her troubles. Still, he called her at decent intervals to hear his share of it.

Henry would see some benefit of that first wreck. Overnight he was in middle age, a time of life to which it seemed he'd be well suited. Moving slower, he found he paid better attention, witnessed a somewhat richer parade of events. Poor circulation in his blunted foot made it prone to chill and even frostbite, and in winter he could no longer work long hours out of doors. So, in those Octobers following his first accident, he would set up on the outskirts of some new town with his lathe, his collection of planes, drills, and routers. He started with making Quaker chairs. There would be seasons of shaping rocking horses, of making gleaming cedar chests, and he was heartened by the discovery of this higher intelligence in his hands. But Henry Brusett was also discovering around that time that he was beginning to fall away from his species, that in virtually anyone's company he was suddenly aware of all his shortcomings and miserably unhappy with himself. To do a bit of commerce, he thought, should be a healthy thing, and so he had forced himself to do business and to take an occasional hand of pinochle or cribbage, and wherever he went he tried to have his morning egg at a diner with a regular trade, to meet people. Pointedly timid, he was fortunate in his encounters. He met with very much kindness but would have preferred to do without it. In all seasons he was his work, and he was at ease only in solitary labor, and there were times still, sometimes on the side of a mountain with a newly sharpened chain, when, with the thing snarling in his grip, he'd have his potent thrill again.

Early one May he was sent to clear an old roadway in Jimminy Gulch. The road had been dozed to briefly serve a logging site a generation earlier; closed and in disuse since that time, the track was now overlain with deadfall, set upon by volunteer growth, and it was obscure enough in its contours that company surveyors had gone ahead to redefine it on the mountainside with blue tape strewn like Hansel and Gretel's bread crumbs. Henry Brusett, the patient, hourly employee, was just as happy to advance not at all as to clear a hundred yards a day. Impertinent little pine had grown up in the road, and many of these were tall already, if scrawny, and all were fairly gleaming with a pitch that dulled and gummed his saws by noon each day. He would smell of these peculiar trees, of this particular pitch for as long as he worked Jimminy Gulch. Eventually the job, the road, took him up onto a slope overlooking a high desert valley of buff grass and sage, and here the sky was infinite and backlit. Here, day by day, the sky was cloudless.

At the road's end, a landing had been made; a turnaround for log trucks had been pushed well into the mountain and was still circumscribed by a scabby wall of gravel, raw and unreclaimed. In making this wound the Cat had undercut a ninety-foot bull pine so completely that the best part of its root system groped out into thin air. Standing on nearly nothing, the tree stood, nonetheless, erect. Half-dead and in piebald bark, it had become tenement to beetles, squirrels, and jays. In an older calamity it had been split by lightning or some-how broken so that it had grown a forked crown. There were green needles, though, at the top of either crown. Under the suspended root ball, a tuft of red fur remained of the fox who had birthed and suckled her kit here. But the tree stood uncertainly above ground that the com-pany intended once more for road, and so, with the arrival of Henry Brusett, its time had finally come.

He climbed the embankment and saw that, short of building a scaffold to it, there would be no way to notch the downslope side of the tree, so he got uphill of it, and he set about dropping it with one oblique cut down through the trunk. The wood was sounder than he'd expected, and his chain duller than he'd thought, and he wore through rather than cutting it; he made and breathed a powdery sawdust. When at last the tree did begin to tip, its immense leverage pulled at the roots remaining in the bank, and all in a moment the ground beneath Henry Brusett's feet was liquid, flowing downslope, and he was backstroking upon it, trying to check his fall, and his idling saw bounced by him, and then from above came the crack of one of those crowns breaking free, and he looked up to see that the broken part would not be follow-ing the graceful swoon of the tree, but the snag would tumble straight down at him. Without time even to hope for the best, he turned from it, heard pine needles gathering pace, and it hit him.

The snag did him a world of harm, but it never did knock him out. It was clear from the beginning that the tree was to spare him nothing. With vertebrae fractured and exposed, with a broken femur and his lacerated kidney bleeding in and out of him, he had walked a half mile and had driven thirty more to finally pass out in St. Joseph's parking lot, near the emergency entrance. He'd been in the news for it, a human interest story, an impossibly lofty example of the local grit, but Henry Brusett made an embarrassed hero, for he was aware of no courage in himself. Then as now, and for as long as he might be given to live, he was only trying to feel a little better. He was obedience to pain, nothing more.

In the hospital he inhabited a twitchy, narcotic dream that gave over to agony every four hours as his shot wore off. He lived shot to shot. He lived, at first, on a diet of ice chips, as he was in surgery on successive mornings being reinforced with steel pins. Even in that first week, when he lay suspended in a harness face down above his bed with the gash in his back periodically aflame, the nurses would come round and approve his luck. To survive such a horrible accident? To have feeling in his extremities? He was very lucky, they told him, that he hadn't severed his spinal cord with all his shenanigans. Nurse Buchanan went so far as to say that he was a miracle, but Henry Brusett was a citizen of the scientific age, and he only wanted his shot.

Juanita never did visit him, though she must have known where he was; he was still in the hospital when he received some papers asking for his signature to consent to a divorce he wouldn't have thought necessary. They'd never formally married, so the formality now of becoming unmarried seemed a bit evil. In a separate note, the only one she'd ever written him—he didn't even know her hand—Juanita explained that she needed to sell some things to start her new life in Alberton with someone named Ted. She needed to sell the house on Blackbird Lane. She needed clear title. She knew he'd understand. She wished him the best of luck in all his future plans and urged him to get well soon. Henry Brusett, still half-encased in casting and gauze and gluey disinfectant, signed her paper. Why not? Juanita was the lesson he wished he'd never learned, and he was cheaply rid of her at any price. How odd to feel any disappointment at all. He was left with what Juanita hadn't wanted or what he hadn't known they owned, and ordinarily he had his wits about him, and that, he'd supposed, might be enough.

As soon as he was able, he parked the ModernAire on a piece of ground where he'd once meant to have a hunting blind and a warming hut. With a settlement from workers' compensation, he drilled a well there, and then he moved to Fitchet Creek where he hoped he might privately heal. It was touch and go. He'd become the concern of bureaucracies, Social Security and Woodman Accident and Life with its sunny agent, Kline Interhoffen, and for a time they kept trundling him off to specialists; eventually, though, when all available experts had agreed that nothing useful might be rebuilt from what was left of Henry Brusett, he was made a pensioner and mostly left alone. Mr. Interhoffen assured him that, as Woodman's client in perpetuity now, he would never have to be uncomfortable. Prescription drugs, regardless of type or amount, were 100 percent covered under Henry's plan, and there were some very sophisticated therapies these days for dealing with, really, any discomforts people might have. Mr. Interhoffen asked only that he tell his family and tell his friends that Woodman really does pay up. Kline Interhoffen asked that he spread the word, as a satisfied client: If you're covered under Woodman, you should never have to suffer. "In this day and age? There's absolutely no point in it. But you have to have coverage, and that's why I like my job so much."

Soon enough, Henry Brusett had made the acquaintance of a clutch of doctors who shared Mr. Interhoffen's progressive humanity, and, drugged, he went on, mending slowly, ever incompletely. The view from the ModernAire suggested he'd outlived his race—from his door he saw trees and sky and clutter of his own making, and all of it too close at hand. He'd been extinguished without being killed.

·19·

TUBBY SAID THAT the public defender did not seem to have a very good way with some of her clients, and she had been attacked three times in this very jail, so now there was a policy requiring her to be monitored when she met with them here, since there was only one working surveillance camera in the whole jail, the one in the holding cell. The policy was in place for the lawyer's own protection, but she'd still gone to court to try and get it changed, and the judge had denied the motion, and so it was the holding cell where they'd talk.

"That's just so you know, cuz—somebody's watching you the whole time you're in there, or they're supposed to be, and it's not that anybody thinks you'd do anything really . . . it's not that anybody thinks you're any weirder than anybody else, but just be careful, okay? No sudden moves. She spooks pretty easy, and you can't hardly blame her. That one guy split her lip dang near up into her nose, and for a gal, you know—woo—that really did not improve her looks. She's been a little jumpy ever since." He pushed a thick brass key into a blue door. "Usually, they'll have a plea bargain cooked up, some take-it-or-leave-it thing for you." Tubby liked civility in his workplace, and he spoke well of almost everyone there. "Maybe she can explain it to you. She tries hard, you'll see."

Just a few days previous Henry Brusett had passed hours in this closet of a room, but it was no longer familiar to him. The lawyer was in it. She sat on the bench among stacks of documents she'd made, and she was writing on a legal pad in her lap, and she was, as he'd remembered her, unafraid of him. She shook his hand, and when he felt her measuring him through his grip, he tried politely to slip free.

"How've you been feeling, Henry?"

"Fine."

"You're getting your meds, I take it. Makes quite a difference for you, doesn't it?"

"It's to where I need 'em anymore," he said. "Which is, I know it puts everybody to extra trouble."

"Sit," she said, and she nodded at the small bare patch she'd left on the bunk beside her.

"I couldn't read anything in this light," he apologized. "Not without my cheaters. Do you mind if I stand?"

"I want you as comfortable as you can be." She was mild and practical. Probably kind.

Henry Brusett pressed his spine to the wall and knitted his hands to keep them occupied and still. His fused neck kept his eyes up, his gaze aimed at the top of the lawyer's head, which was divided by a wide part. She wore a child's dime-store barrettes.

"It's just another day or two," she said, "at most. Can you hang on that long? One way or another, I think we're close to getting you out of here. When you see the judge, we'll ask for an OR again, and what I'd like to do is have you talk a bit—or testify—about your health. I'll have you explain your medical condition, and why it's not a real good idea to have you in here. Why you're not a flight risk. I'm sorry I didn't get here earlier—we do have so much to talk about, but I thought, well, I thought we'd better wait until you were stabilized on your meds again. Before we talked."

"Don't worry about that."

"No, I really should have been in, but I kept thinking I'd get you out of here, and then we wouldn't have to . . . they can't hear us, by the way. They can see us on the monitor, theoretically, but they can't hear us. This makes me, and I mean this *instantly* makes me claustrophobic. Every single time I come in here. How anyone stands this I . . . but we really do need to talk because for once it seems like there may be quite a bit I can do for you. I think we may actually have the upper hand—unless I'm missing something. These people aren't really the kind to hide the ball, so I don't think . . . I wanted you to have a chance to get more—what? Collected, I guess." Her voice hurried on like a tire sent rolling down a hill. "I'm sorry. I should have been in a lot earlier, and I am sorry, but I have been working on getting you out of here. I really have, and by hook or by crook we should be pretty close to getting you back home. I hope."

She seemed to think he was anxious to start learning the specifics of his fate, and from her guilty tone he could tell that she was just as happy to be talking to his chest. He was all but standing on her and very impressed to see that she could write one thing while saying another. Henry Brusett had trouble enough expressing even a single stream of thought. "Thanks," he said. "For that. But I hope you didn't waste too much time on it—or, what I mean to say—don't bother. You can just forget about that bail." He knew of a valley in British Columbia that the Mounties were said to ignore. He could go state to state, province to province, and only rarely touch pavement in his travels, but he knew he'd make a sluggish fugitive. "I set foot out of here, and I'm gone. I know that. I've got a good idea how that'd end up, too."

"Henry, it doesn't need to be that way. This may not be as bad as you're thinking. It may not be nearly that bad. You'll have to trust me."

"There's a real good chance I'd run," he said. "I don't have the cash or the legs for it, but I think I might still try and scoot if they gave me the chance." More than anything else, he wished to be absent, and it was pleasant to think of himself wild-eyed and aloof in some woods—young again, whole again for being hunted.

"All right," said the lawyer, "let's talk about our long-term goal, then. Let's just concentrate on getting you out of here once and for all. Which is quite realistic, I'm thinking."

Goal. His lawyer was not a true believer in her own optimism, and Henry Brusett suspected it entirely. She had talked a better game, so far, than she'd played. He did not wish to owe her any gratitude, or to have anyone on or at his side. "What do they want me to do?"

"That's just exactly my point. This is exactly what I'm trying to tell you. I don't think they're in any shape to tell you what to do. It may not seem like it, but you're sort of in a position to dictate terms here. In a way."

He had never dictated anything to anyone and was now almost too weary to speak at all. Never had he been so tired. "How do you go about just admitting that you . . . "

"Whoa," she said. "Let me talk first, okay? Then you can get off your chest whatever you think you need to get off your chest." She held her fingers splayed and to the side of her face. "You'd better not pick an option until you know what your options are. Doesn't that make sense? Let me talk first. And then, then maybe you'll have a better idea of what you want to say. Or if you want to say anything at all."

"I already know the honorable way," he told her. "I know the honorable way to go, but I'm not sure I'm up for it. This is bad in here. There's too many of us, and they never do turn the lights off. But you want to do the right thing, if you can."

"The right thing? I guarantee you, Henry, it's not exactly a universal impulse, and I'm no expert myself, so I'll leave that to you and your conscience, which, since you actually seem to have one—that could be complicated. There's a few different ways this can go, all right?

Tomorrow, we've got your arraignment in the district court, and the judge is going to ask you at some point, 'Guilty or not guilty?' What we need to decide is how you want to answer him."

The lawyer made a chart with bold headings on her notepad, and as she jotted notes into the columns, notes Henry Brusett could not decipher, she was saying, "So what happens if you were to just tell 'em you're guilty? Say you came into court and just spit it out, 'I'm guilty,' well then the judge keeps asking questions, or he'd have me walk you through some questions, because he has to be sure you really did, deliberately, intentionally kill somebody—or this specific somebody—and he wants to hear you say so on the record. He'd want to hear it in sufficient detail. Once you've satisfied him on those points, the elements, then he enters a judgment of guilt, and then he can do about anything he wants to do with you. The state owns you then. You'd belong to the Department of Corrections for a long, long time. And those people, they're boobs, Henry. They've got their 'programs,' and their 'facilities,' and so on and so on, and it's all just a cash cow for incompetents. They've never made anyone a better man, as far as I know. That would also be up to you. Personally, I think the few people I've ever seen fixed in any way—rehabilitated—it's always been a do-it-yourself project. You can't hire it done, you can't have it forced down your throat."

"Is it true you can still get hung in Montana?"

Her chin rocked back and in, and she instantly calculated, "No. Well—yes, technically. But this is not a death penalty case. They'd have to do a bunch of different things to make it one, and they haven't. Oh, no, this isn't even close to a death penalty kind of thing. So we can take that right off the table."

"Yeah? I thought I might finally get all the kinks pulled out of me. What happens if I say I'm not guilty?"

"I ask the court to set it for jury trial. Which is, in my estimation, the best way to go right now."

"That would be a lot of trouble."

"I'm not saying we'd necessarily go to trial. We'd ask for one. In fact, that's fairly standard at this stage of things. This is where all those rights you keep hearing about really start to matter a little bit. What we do is use those to try and get you some reasonable result. Or, I should say, the best result available."

"Reasonable? You think we can get there from where we're at?"

"Again, I'll leave that up to you, Mr. Brusett. It wouldn't be easy, I didn't say that." The lawyer seemed a tough little gal, and only trying to help.

"Don't leave anything up to me. If you do, we're off to a bad start. Everything that's been left in my hands is, well, you can see."

"I'm very confident. I am very, very sure you'll make a good decision. But I want you to make a smart one, too."

There was some strange tension in his cheeks; he was smiling. He remembered that he was to give her no cause for alarm, and he said, "You ever been over to Playfair in Spokane? You strike me as somebody who might like to get a bet down on a horse."

"If—" she said. "Say you actually did kill that guy. And you meant to. Then that means you're guilty, of course, but it doesn't mean you have to say so. Also, there would be several scenarios where you would *not* be guilty. If you just got messed up while you were trying to help him. Say there was an accident, or somebody else—say you came along after he was hurt. You tried to help. Or what if you did do something? You hurt him? Killed him? That's not necessarily murder, either, not if it was an accident, or if you thought you had to protect yourself. If you meant to protect yourself or even to protect someone else. That's a defense to murder. Problem is, if you raise that particular defense, then you might have to prove it. Prove you really needed to do it, then you wind up talking about how and why you killed somebody, which is always a dicey topic to get started on. Who knows how someone else, somebody who's looking at the incident long after the fact and a long way from the heat of the moment, who knows how they'd see it? Fear can be hard to explain."

"I'm sure it is," he said. "Anyway, who cares what I'm scared of?"

In another quarter of the jail, Tubby's highest falsetto suddenly sounded above a deep, industrial banging, "Get your fucking hands off me . . . I will, I swear . . . get . . . get . . . I swear to God . . . I . . . said . . . get *off*."

"Please, please, please . . . oh . . . *pleeease*."

More banging, which ceased, and then the distant television, as ever, droning into every metal crevice of the jail. Some laughter, live laughter from the cell.

"Nat," said the lawyer, having recognized the lesser voice. "I'll bet he's a pain to be with back here, isn't he? I hope he's not constantly getting into more trouble because a guy like that can generate more work than you'd ever . . . Look, Henry, unless you let me do something about this bond, you'll be in here until we get this taken care of, and things do tend to drag on sometimes in the system. There are times, and this could be one of those, when delay can work to our advantage. The longer it goes, I think, the better off you are. Look, there's some loony people, there really are. I see some unbelievable folks. There's people, and I have to admit it—even though they're my clients and it's usually my job to prevent it if I can—some people I just can't wait to see safely locked up again. One thing I know is—you're not one of those guys. Okay? Sometimes I just have to believe that about somebody. I know this poor kid is dead, and I'm pretty sure it's quite a tragedy, too. But it's not anything you can fix now. It's my whole idea that you don't fix one tragedy with another—that makes no sense to me—and what I'm telling you is the poor kid's dead but not one single officer of the law or of the court, including me, knows how he got that way. As I see it, unless that changes, unless there's more to this than meets the eye—or unless somebody chimes in with some new evidence—you should walk away from this thing eventually. Just pretty much walk away. I don't see a conviction. You'll do what you need to do, but I think there is a way past this if you choose to take it. Which wouldn't be the worst thing that ever happened." Now she was also talking to herself, he thought, trying to convince herself of something.

"What's a guy supposed to say, anyway?"

"Tomorrow, if you follow my advice, we'll enter a 'not guilty' and ask for you to be let out of jail pending trial. And, by the way, if we don't get you out, would you please see Karen when she comes in for visiting hours? It's kind of mean to keep her away, don't you think? She just needs to see you with her own eyes, and I don't think that's too much to ask. As long as they're not trying to prevent it, there's no reason at all why you shouldn't see her. She's come around to ask me about it several times, and I don't know what to tell her."

"You think I do?"

"You don't have to say anything if you don't want to. She only needs to see that you're all right."

"I think she'll take your word for it, won't she? Let her know I'm okay, would you? I'm sure there's things incubating back here. Nobody should be exposed to this stuff if they don't have to be."

"All right." The lawyer had him sign two papers, which she read to him but which he could not force himself to hear. She collected all the rest of her documents, bundle by bundle, and she laid them in her briefcase. They'd served little purpose here. "It doesn't seem like we're necessarily getting anywhere at the moment. So let me just say what *I* want to happen. I'd like it if you took my advice and you let me enter a 'not guilty' for you tomorrow. They've got the burden of production, burden of proof, all of that. That's right where we're at as far as I'm concerned, and what I'd like to do—for now—is go ahead and put the state to its burdens."

"I know you would," he said. "Let me sleep on it."

Back at the barracks cell Henry Brusett learned that the banging they'd heard during the lawyer's visit had come from Nat reaching through the bars to latch onto the back of Tubby's belt. There were several versions of the episode, but in all of them, Nat's arms were through the bars, and his fingers were well hooked into the jailer's belt, and he'd hung on too hopefully while Tubby dragged him again and again face-first into the bars.

"*Blam, blam,*" as Jamie eagerly described it. "It was just *blam, blam, blam,* and I said, 'Woooh,' and after a while I don't think he could've let go of that belt if he wanted to. Which he probably did. Want to. Sure glad it wasn't me. Could you even let go, man? Should've seen it, your face was just really bouncing off them bars."

"'*Oh, please, please,*'" Leonard mimicked and mocked. "'*Let me out. Oh, Tubby, let me out.*' Like Tubby can just take it on himself to let you out of here. He's a flunky. What's he supposed to do with you, put you out in the exercise yard they don't even have? He supposed to go and tell the judge you asked for a pass to attend the fair? What the fuck? If you tried that in any other joint, prisoner, they'd break you up. Break your arms at least if you got hold of somebody through the bars that way. '*Oh, let me gooh, oh, let me go.*' Don't you know that's disgusting? Tubby should've used his baton on you. You're too lucky."

"Lucky? He wrote me up for disorderly conduct."

"He should have," said Leonard. "There are some kinds of behavior you just can't allow, not even in here. That whining of yours, for instance."

Nat sulked all of that day, flinching whenever he forgot, and drew breath over his freshly chipped teeth, his large and glossy underlip. His brow, also enlarged, suggested more intelligence than he really owned, and it was not until supper that he was finally struck with the starkest thought yet. "Another charge? Oh, noooh. Now I see

what they're . . . You know what? They'll probably try and use that
to revoke my other ninety days. Suspended time, suspended time, it
always, it sounds so good when they're handing it out—but one way
or another, you always serve it, don't you, you wind up serving every
last day, and it's always about the almighty dollar. Isn't it? Isn't it?
Money, or something. No, no, no, no. No. If that county attorney has
his way, I'll probably be in here for six, six *months?*"

"Do you know," Leonard asked them generally, "why anyone
bothers with iceberg lettuce? This is not food. These things that *look*
like food, or they *look* like tools, or toys, or weapons, or whatever
when they're in the store, but then you buy these things, and you find
out they're useless. They don't work, they fall apart. It's shoddiness,
it's whorishness, it's modern life, that's all, and it chaps my ass. I like
to think that if I was a craftsman, I'd be a *craftsman*. If I was a farmer,
I'd grow fucking food."

Nat, the hard old soul, the fawnlet, winced once more and wept
again, just as he wept at the release of every fellow prisoner, a very
regular event in a county jail. He had developed the tic of stroking his
lank forelock several thousand times a day with the heel of his hand.
"They just keep piling it on. I have never *hurt* anyone. I'm a *kind person.*" He trembled over his noodle dish. There were flecks of boiled
egg on it, and it was nothing he'd ever eat. "I'm *not, I am not.*" He
was becoming sallow. His eyes had begun to move, jailhouse fashion,
primarily side to side. "Who ever thought I was so . . . really? Yaaahw,
ugh. Gaahd."

"The essential minerals," said Leonard, "are in the air you breathe.
Even bad air. So that's how you do your time, you shut up and you
keep breathing, and, Tallulah, you can even skip the breathing for all I
care. As long as you shut up."

They'd been given something pink—not lemonade—to drink.
Germaine's casserole that evening was of ingredients she'd rendered

gray, and this lay on their trays undisturbed. They ate their quivering slivers of canned peach, which only reminded them they were hungry. They watched a show with a handsome vampire. There was a crime drama with several aggressive women in it. Leonard watered himself at the sink, drinking out of his cupped hands, and on his way back to the picnic table he whirled in passing, neatly, precisely, and he kicked Nat high on the outside of his thigh, kicked him hard enough that Nat grunted, and pressed his cheek to the table top, and grunted again as if to defecate.

As the evening wore on they tried to play whist, but no one was confident of the rules. The cards, soggy with overuse, prompted the invention of a game in which each player was given three greasy face cards to skim at the floor drain, with scoring as in horseshoes. Attractive people mumbled from the television; Leonard insisted the volume be kept low. Leonard kept reciting a pessimistic line from a poem about the best minds of his generation. Nat, calmer now, somehow dreamy and sentimental for having been kicked, described the superior courtesy of the South and how he longed to return to it. Jamie, who lacked nearly any pigment of hair or flesh or personality, mentioned with the usual approval another of his uncles. "You know him? He's fairly well known. Clive? Clive Bakken? He used to have the tire shop?" Jamie was a secondary figure even in his own stories. Leonard assigned him to sit on the floor by the drain and retrieve each round of pitched cards, and Jamie was happy as a pup to do it.

Nightfall, for their purposes, came at eleven o'clock, when Tubby came around to click the television off and deliver the day's best dose of Lorezapam. Henry Brusett took the drug and set himself up behind his blankets again, gratefully out of sight, and while awaiting chemical transport, he heard Jamie as he settled into the bunk at his feet and commenced hours of soprano snoring. Beyond the blanket, Leonard was talking as if he might talk all night, and Nat murmured with counterfeit interest at Leonard's tale of an affair with the astrologer Medea Miller, whose phony nose he'd had to bend. She wore the head scarf, he said, and the loopy earrings, but he'd been the one to make her look so authentically gypsy. All credit to Medea for her genius in spotting a mark and for setting up such a steady and easy grift, but her moon was in the money box and her greedy goddamned hand was in the seventh house, or whatever, and she'd eventually miscalculated and tried to chisel Leonard. But maybe she couldn't help herself.

As the second veil spread over Henry Brusett, the somewhat soundproof curtain of his nighttime dose, he fell back through his pet and shopworn recollections of his wife. She was the music springing from a near room. She brought him the consolations of sliced tomatoes or tea, and when she sang, she sang of the soft sigh of the weary, and on a cold day she would keep the stove stoked and the ModernAire smelling of bread and pine. As always when Henry Brusett escaped in this direction, he thought of times and places when she'd said she loved him—out on the water with the lake licking their plastic hull, on the muddy road at the base of Baldy, once over a supper of trout and cantaloupe. "I'd heard about it," she'd say, "but I still didn't know really what to expect. So I was kinda relieved to find out who'd be the one—that you'd be."

He knew, even as she was saying such things, even as his chest boiled for hearing them, that he should correct her. He should in fairness try to let her know how much remained for her to learn, and that she could never learn it so long as she was with him. For some safety she imagined she had with him, she'd given over an especially lush youth, and there was nothing equivalent or right about this obligation, but Henry Brusett had never found the strength to stop it. He couldn't bring himself to ask her to leave, and he couldn't make himself be mean to her, and he'd fumbled along appreciative, unable to show her a way off the tiny, barren continent of their marriage. Instead, he'd become drowsing Henry, the coward who slept and slept and hoped to emerge from his diligent stupor one day to find that his wife had come to her senses and left him. One day she must leave him, and this had been for him the backbeat of their whole time together.

Henry Brusett knew there'd never be a full accounting because that would require that he tell his little story. He would have liked to claim that he did not remember, but ten minutes of bad night had become the endpoint and burial ground of his every reverie, and he remembered it incessantly. He had smelled half-burnt kerosene in his sleep; its fumes had accumulated as an oily slick in his sinuses, and he sat up in seemingly combustible air and in his own dismal odor, a rancid presence refreshed with every disturbance of the blanket or his coveralls. How long had he been down? A long time. The clock in Karen's room counted out each second with two clipped knocks, and Henry Brusett did not even bother to look for her there. She was not in the bathroom, but her jeans and suspenders had been shucked to the floor, and one stiff sock stood alist beside them. The cane was in his hands, must have been in his hands while he slept. The lamp guttered on the counter in the kitchen, and one side of its chimney was sooted velvet black. Crystals were set racing in Henry Brusett's blood; he didn't know why he was terrified. He went outside. The cane, *tonk, tonk* in the sleeping porch, *thog, thog* on the ground. He went out under stars so abundant they appeared to have frayed and torn the firmament. The cane, *donk, donk* on the boardwalk. When he arrived, he should have come as no surprise.

But he'd never looked in on her in the shower shed before, had he? It was become almost his life's work to respect her privacy.

And he hadn't called out as he was coming, there was no *Are you there?* His eyes adjusted poorly to starlight. A small beam on the towels, on the rock—he might have stopped to pick the flashlight up, to see better.

A back not hers, an unfamiliar shirt, running water.

Before he'd selected any particular reason to strike, the cane was in motion, a stave obedient to misbegotten instinct, and while the blow was in transit Henry Brusett lived a life compressed, a life, like most, filled in its latter stages with regret. He felt and heard the cane snap, an undertone of thumped melon, and no outcry.

He dropped the broken cane as the boy took one step back.

The boy collapsed.

And there was Henry Brusett with open arms, waiting to catch him.

·20·

"THE JUDGE," she said, "is almost ready for us. I understand he likes to do these in chambers. It's a little more intimate that way." The subject of the hearing was a baby girl named, thus far, Baby Rita, the child wrapped in her adoptive mother's arms and so new to the world as to still be writhing in it; Baby Rita lifted her wobbling head and included Giselle Meany in a look of all-embracing disbelief.

"See how strong? Oooh." The radiant Mrs. Olds was a latecomer to motherhood, and she had a happy disposition for a client. "See how curious?" Mr. Olds hovered at his wife's shoulder, looking on through thick glasses and trying hard to share the thrill. This studious man would have noticed how the baby commanded all attention, and perhaps he had already guessed a crushing future in his wife's devotion to it.

"She's one week old today," said Mrs. Olds. "So, in a way, this is sort of a birthday, too. Can you get over how tiny . . . how perfect? They say we have to be really, really careful of heat and heat rash. But they say that air-conditioning can be hard on them, too, the little ones, so we'll have to figure something out. Really, though, the weather is getting cooler now, so that should help. You want to have everything perfect for her, if you can. Good ventilation and everything."

Giselle Meany's own maternal impulses had only ever been sufficient to their purposes, and seemed slight in the face of such joy and addled concern. "You'll do fine. My Sheila, even when she was that size or so, she always seemed to tolerate about every kind of weather better than I did. She still does. They're rugged little things, they really are." Giselle Meany didn't usually think of her carelessly beautiful daughter during work hours.

The court reporter, a chubby, silent woman who traveled with the judge and did many small chores for him, stepped out into the hall to beckon them into chambers, a room cluttered with cardboard boxes bound in duct tape and coated in dust, a room that was aired just twice a month when District Judge Carbon Samara deigned to hold law and motion day in a county seat he despised. He was, in his robed and saturnine person, as imposing as his chambers were disgraceful. A blister of a human being with a polished skull and a friendly way with these potential voters, he pumped the Olds' hands and wondered if they were getting enough sleep, or was the little one dictating otherwise? Mrs. Olds said the greatest pleasure she'd ever known was to nap with the baby on her chest, and the judge made his appreciative face, and at this Giselle Meany very nearly snorted.

Judge Samara then settled behind his desk and glanced at the papers she'd filed. "Giselle, is this the first adoption you've handled?"

"As you know, Your Honor, I've had to concentrate my practice on criminal . . . "

"Is this the first adoption you've handled?"

"Yes."

"Presumably the first petition for adoption you've written."

"Yes."

New mom's smile had a fixed quality; her eyes swung between the judge and her incompetent lawyer.

"You consulted the statutory requirements for such a petition, counselor?"

"I did, Your Honor." The judge would mince and preen. Giselle would, needs be, genuflect.

"What about the child's assets, then? The child's assets are supposed to be set forth."

"It's this child, Your Honor."

"Yes, I'd taken judicial notice, believe it or not."

"She's a week old. She has no property."

"Then that is what the petition should say. Leaving that item blank in the petition is not the same as specifying that the child is without assets. Is it?"

"No, Your Honor. May I simply aver for the record that the child is without assets?"

"Do you think that's good enough?"

"Your Honor, these folks have traveled from the other end of the county with this . . . "

"Oh, I'll sign your order, Giselle, but you'd better have an amended petition to me by Friday. And I mean *to* me, not in the mail."

The judge, as if he'd originated the whole idea, signed the baby into the Olds' legal custody, and there was more shaking of hands, and Mr. Olds said thanks so much, and Mrs. Olds blew kisses around the judge's chambers, and as the small party trailed back out into the hall Mrs. Olds gushed, "Oh, Daddy," and she rose up on her toes to press her miraculous bundle an inch nearer heaven. Giselle Meany, who had served pro bono just to reach this nice moment, found that she was a little stony within the celebration, and she thought, too late, that maybe mom would be too much mother for this poor unsuspecting little spawn of unprotected love.

All that morning, until just moments before she was to appear in the adoption, Giselle had been trying to get in to see Henry Brusett; she'd been three times to the jail, and each time balked by a wheezing

old jailer who'd been too overwhelmed by breakfast and other matters to ever bring the meeting about, and now, at a quarter to ten, she
was minutes away from arraignment, still without knowing her client's
mind. She excused herself from the Olds family to wait at the top of
the staircase where they'd be bringing Henry up from the jail, but the
court reporter tracked her down again and shyly led her back to the
judge's chambers where Judge Samara and Meyers were talking boy
talk, property law, and something about natural gas.

"Giselle," said the judge, collegial now, "you've got to get these
pleadings right, and I've got to call you on it when you don't."

"Yes, Your Honor."

"It happens that there are wealthy babies. It is not unknown. Some
of them probably far wealthier than we could ever dream of being. I'm
sure you can appreciate that."

"The judge," said Meyers, "has called us in to talk about the
arraignment."

"Not *about* it," the judge corrected. "I don't want to hear much
of anything from either counsel without Giselle's client present. But
there are a couple of pieces of information, just procedural things, that
I think you should know. The bail is going to remain as is, Giselle; go
ahead and make your motion for the record, if you feel you need to,
but the bond is already pretty liberal, I think—*very* liberal—considering the charge."

"You may change your mind, Your Honor, when you've seen him."

"No," said Carbon Samara, "I won't. Now, if you two can find
any way to untangle this, then God speed, and I can tell you that the
court would favor some creativity and cooperation, if that's what it
takes. But right now the man is charged with murder, and that comes
with a stiff bail. Usually a lot stiffer than this. So, that brings us to
point two: I haven't got an opening in my trial docket for five months,

not even for a man in custody. If you plan to do any jockeying at all, any motion practice, you could be a long, long way from trial. I'm very busy these days over on the other side, so, Giselle, your guy could sit a long while, assuming he doesn't make bond. Or if you don't come to terms with Hoot."

"I'm just waiting," she said, "for the state to make us an offer."

"I offered her the sun and the moon," Meyers protested. "Offered her deals too good to reduce to writing. They're still on the table."

The judge leveled a look at them. "This case appears like it has a lot of potential for turning ridiculous. I'll remind you both that no one ever benefits when that happens. Let's see about a simple solution, shall we?"

While Giselle Meany and Hoot Meyers were with the judge in his musky chambers—a very long and hollow period it seemed to them—the old jailer led Henry Brusett into the courtroom and had him sit in its foremost bench, and he planted himself at parade rest nearby; Karen Brusett came in at another door to sit near the aisle on the very back bench and finger her seamless pearls like prayer beads. Timidly and unsuccessfully, she tried to get her husband's attention; Henry was careful never to look her way. A farmer and his lawyer, both in antique leisure suits, were there to quiet title to a piece of the farmer's pasture; a girl awaited her first divorce, two toddlers on her knees requiring constant jollying; Valley Bank's attorney had come to seek a small herd of llamas in satisfaction of a loan. Meanwhile in chambers, the judge carried on with another highly detailed story from his hallowed tour of duty with the judge advocate general's office in Turkey. The judge talked, and as he talked, the court reporter and the clerk of court stationed themselves in the courtroom, beside and below the bench; the reporter from the *River Register* wrote impressions of Henry Brusett into a notepad: lopsided, subdued, haggard. Kook?

At last Judge Samara said, "So east is east, and west is west, and, as we used to say in Ankara, the Middle East is neither here nor there."

They got free of him just four minutes before Judge Samara would take the bench. Giselle Meany, who had a cold, made a pass through the women's room to blow her nose and pee, and as she was washing her hands, her briefcase, which had cost little more than a cheeseburger and was of Chinese origin, tumbled from the edge of the sink and burst on the floor, and files slithered onto the sticky tile. She reassembled it all, but the latch was ruined, and so she held it as a schoolgirl holds her books, pressed to her chest, and she strode out into the hall, and down it, and came to the front stairwell of the courthouse and encountered there one of her clients, Sean Mobius, who happened to be groping the supple flank of Cindy Holter as he sought her minty gum with his tongue. This was the very girl, the very violation, who kept sending him to jail.

"Sean, get a move on. You're late for court. She should stay outside. In fact you should go. Fast as possible. Go. Please." Giselle Meany, hoping to instill some different and more appropriate urgency in her client, stamped up the final few stairs, and as she gained the landing outside the courtroom, her modest heel collapsed under her right shoe, and she twisted her ankle. She dropped the briefcase, which exploded again. She sat on the horrible carpet and determined for certain that she could not restore the heel to her shoe, and that, if she were to shed a single tear just now, her life, her professional life at least, would not be worth living. The lovers looked upon her plight but never released each other. She collected herself again, heel in the pocket of her blazer, files scraped up and back into the sprung case, and very emphatically she stood. "Sean. Come *on* now." He was like the pet one wishes to return to the Humane Society, even if it is to be euthanized there.

She pushed through tall, heavy doors and into the courtroom, and she banished the rebuke then forming in Judge Samara's mouth by manfully limping down the aisle. The first case was called, and she was late for it; Henry Brusett and the jailer were already standing at counsel table awaiting her. Karen Brusett rose up as she flew by, seeming to want a moment, just a moment, just a word. But Giselle flew by.

"Giselle Meany, Your Honor, for the defendant."

"Catch your breath, counselor. Do you need a moment?"

"If I might just . . . I'm having a little trouble finding the correct, uhm, file. Oh, okay. Here it is. It's more or less. Yes, here it is. No, Your Honor, I'm fine."

"You've seen a copy of the information, Mr. Brusett?" asked the judge. "They spelled your name right?"

"Yes."

Giselle Meany sensed that her client intended to face someone's music today, and she didn't think he could afford such a disaster. Seamed and beaten, he sat beside her, the good boy resigned to his medicine.

"I have before me an advice-of-rights form with what appears to be your signature at the bottom. Is that signature yours, Mr. Brusett?"

"Yes."

"You understand that you're charged with deliberate homicide?"

"Yes."

"You know the maximum and minimum penalties for that crime?"

"Yes."

"Ms. Meany has entered an appearance, so you are represented by counsel."

"Yes," said Henry.

He seemed to like this easy answer. Eventually, though, if he kept giving it, he might corner himself with it.

"Then you know what you can do about it? You've talked about that?"

"Your Honor," Giselle interceded at last, "I'm afraid that—could the court please rephrase the question?"

"You've got three options now, Mr. Brusett. You can plead guilty, or not guilty, or, if I consent to it, nolo contendere, or no contest. You've talked about all this with your attorney, Mr. Brusett? She's advised you of this?"

"Yes."

"She's explained all the terminology?"

"She did."

"Possible consequences?"

"Yes."

"Then you should also know that you can defer entering your plea if necessary."

"No," said Henry. "Now is fine."

Giselle Meany's stomach soured and dropped. She found Mr. Brusett's ankle with her toe. She had failed him. "May I have a moment to confer with my client, Your Honor?"

"You're supposed to do that on your own time, counsel, not on the court's."

"The unexpected comes up, Your Honor."

"Not for the well prepared. Confer. Briefly."

She made a small megaphone of her hands and pressed the belled end to Henry Brusett's ear, and hissed into it, "Not guilty. Not guilty. Not guilty. Please. You can always change it later." She pulled away to see Henry's answer, as he would not speak it. His face was full of apology. For what?

"Ms. Meany, may we please get on with it now?"

"Not . . . " she said. "Your Honor, my client will be entering a plea of . . . " She glanced at Henry for any encouragement, and Henry was having none of it. "Not guilty," she said.

"Is that your plea, Mr. Brusett?"

Giselle pressed steadily down on the arch of his foot, and under a pretended attack of sniffles breathed, "Nooh . . . no."

"Oh, I . . . no," said Henry.

"This is not going well. What *is* your plea, Mr. Brusett?"

"I'd have to say I'm . . . "

"Judge," said Hoot Meyers, rising to it, "the defendant appears to be very heavily medicated this morning. The state wonders at the enduring validity of any plea he might make in this condition."

"If he's too goofed up, Mr. County Attorney, to even enter a plea, how do you propose to prosecute him? Mr. Brusett, do you understand me? We got a little sidetracked, but in the course of these things, I usually ask the defendant if he's taking any medications. Are you taking medications, Mr. Brusett?"

"Yes."

"Do they affect your ability to know what's going on? Do you know what's going on here?"

"I've got an idea."

"Do you know why you're here today?"

"Here to say I'm guilty?"

Giselle Meany felt her legs inflate, her bowels melt entirely. She was letting him dig himself a hole in the record. "Just because he says . . . someone who's impaired is, by definition, not the best judge of their impairment, or of . . . "

"If you had concerns like that, counsel, you should have made a motion to that effect—that you wanted him assessed. Is that your motion, Ms. Meany?"

"Yes," she grasped at it. "Defense moves for an order for the defendant to be evaluated for fitness to proceed and suspending all other matters pending that determination."

"Prepare the order for my signature."

Having survived the bad detour, Giselle Meany pressed her luck. "In the meantime, Your Honor, about the bail . . . The state is not opposed, and now that the court has actually seen Mr. Brusett's, uhm, situation, Your Honor . . . "

"Counselor, if your client is found unfit to proceed, then I'm probably required to have him locked up somewhere until he regains fitness. So, with that in mind, you're asking in practically the same breath for a mental evaluation and a reduction in bail? Is that what you're leading up to?"

From the corner of her eye, Giselle Meany saw Karen Brusett raise her hand to ask permission of the judge to speak.

"Miss? You have something to add to this discussion?"

"He'd do a lot better at home, sir."

"You're his daughter?"

"No," she said.

"We'll take your remarks under advisement, miss. Giselle, do you have anything more?"

Henry's hands made a canceling motion just above counsel table.

"Nothing," she said. "We have nothing more at this time."

· 21 ·

PRISONER MIGHT SLEEP through a short incarceration, but
not a long one. Jail sleep soon became, like jail food, a pale
imitation of any real sustenance—there was no point in it,
and little by little, the formerly hard-sleeping Henry Brusett was losing
the knack of slumber. Even the drugs were of small service. At night
he lay in a posture he had perfected that allowed no part of his flesh
to touch the plastic mattress, and Nat and Leonard, who almost never
retired to their bunks, were to the night what the television was to the
day, a tireless source of low-grade fascination. He listened because,
unless he wished to push his fingers deep into his ears, he had no
choice.

"No debtors' prison in America?" Nat saw hypocrisy in everything, in every safe assumption. "That's all I am. At worst what I am
is a debtor. And here I sit. Oh yes, oh yes, there's a debtors' prison, all
right."

"What do you owe?"

"A little product," the cheat conceded. "I owe a few ladies . . .
well, several, maybe, an apology. You know, that's a very good idea.
In fact, I meant to do it all along. Sure, I'd just really sincerely apologize, and then maybe we could finally get this whole thing . . . And see,
that's the thing, that's why I'm not a criminal. I never meant anyone
any harm. Not even, like, economic."

"You feel pretty bad, do you?"

"Not that bad, actually. It's not like anyone was really, I mean, what did I do *wrong*, really?"

"Why apologize then?"

"You have a point. Sure."

"But you could," suggested Leonard, "apologize for who you are."

"How do you mean? Who I *am*?"

"You're a form of pollution, don't you think?"

"Oh, come on. That's a little . . . no, that's *very* harsh."

"You smell very funny, prisoner, to any right-thinking citizen. You are the fish in their refrigerator."

"No, I am not. I am a, quite a cordial kind of guy. You say these things because no one ever says them about you—mean things. You don't know how it feels. Because, if people didn't like me, I couldn't begin to . . . How do you think you have the right to call *anyone any-thing*? You? And, yes, I do hate it. I *do* think I'm too good for it. In here. I'd hate it if I was here a thousand years. I'd never get used to it. It is just so, so unfair. How is this even fair?"

"Do you know how many kittens are slaughtered every year? You sit here fat, dumb, and happy while they're being gassed and drowned and so forth—and you have the raw nerve to complain? To talk about innocence? You've just got to get beyond good and evil now; those categories have served their purpose, you can't get too involved with that in here."

"Amen. But—oh—I don't know about that. I don't know if I could go quite that far. If I ever thought . . . There's evil, I know for sure. You're . . . "

"No. I'm beyond it," said Leonard. "The universe does not trouble itself about my conduct. The problem, really, is boredom. Why isn't that ever criminalized? These fuckers can bore you, and bore you, and bore you just mercilessly, and the authorities have no way to intervene.

You have to develop your own amusements, your own code. It can be hard, but we rise to it."

Nat was in a mood to challenge the prevailing philosophy and, of course, his fate. "You know what's wrong with this? I'll tell you what—I am the grease. Society's grease. Because I go out there, and I sell, and sometimes I don't necessarily sell product that I actually have. Actual product may not move that well. I like to think that I sell dreams—but in the end, it's always back to the unholy dollar, isn't it? In the end, your clients never seem to remember how good you made them feel when you were closing. All I know is, every time I try to be a little bit more ambitious, try to really make something of myself, something bad happens. And it just keeps getting worse. I'm a young man, but I sure don't feel young anymore. Business is starting to take quite a toll on me, I'd have to say. It's getting to where I often wish I *wasn't* such a self-starter."

"Sometimes in the joint," said Leonard, "you'll run into an accountant, or some fingers-in-the-cookie-jar little turd, and they'll be the most miserable people in population. Even in some low-security, rinky-dink cakewalk they're miserable; poor fucks aren't on the road to enlightenment. Accountants. You only have to talk about a shiv, and you bleed 'em white. They're uncomfortable all the time. Greed does that to you."

"Well, that's not me," said Nat. "I don't want that much. I'm not asking for more than anyone else—a place I can call my own, an attractive wife. I've always wanted a collie. Wanted an insurance agency at one time, but I doubt that I could be bonded now. It would be very hard to get into law school, probably."

"How old are you?" Leonard asked, incredulous, disgusted.

"Twenty-five."

"What a quivering square. Why don't you just accept it? You can't get in that club. They'll never let you in. It's root hog or die for you, Cindy Lou. You're a criminal now. A junior criminal. Spicy."

"You don't know me," said Nat, hopefully. "How could you know me at all?" There followed the long, hiccupping sighs that meant he was preparing to weep again. He would empty himself of salt.

"You better stop that whimpering, Pam. You know that turns me on."

"Why can't you call me by my real name? That is not too much to ask. Do you think this is in any way fun for me, or pleasant?"

"I would hope you were entertained. I know I am."

"I get it. I get it. I know you have needs, and I imagine they have to be taken care of somehow. I understand that. We've been all through that. If I have to help, if I have to help you with that then I will, but . . . " A sound burst up through Nat's nose; his terror at a tipping point, it rang in him as he considered his fix. The bleat of a wounded doe, it was the only expression he ever tried to suppress.

"I told you," said Leonard. "Didn't I tell you that you better not keep that up. Oh-oh, it's that glow again. I get that glow for you when you do that."

"I said I'd help. You don't have to—oh please. Wait. Nohb."

Meat banged metal. The prisoner at Henry Brusett's feet snorted awake; Jamie, no doubt wide-awake now. They heard Nat being dragged across concrete floor, slippers slapping in a furious resistance that saved him nothing.

Henry Brusett loathed his fascination for this but he could not quit it.

"Wait . . . *Pleease* . . . "

"What else is there for me? You know what I like."

"Anh. Anh. Auhngg nuuhgh."

Afterward, for a little while at least, they would lie down, Leonard contentedly, Nat cocooned in his hard-won, temporary safety—and they would sleep. For his part of the routine, Henry Brusett would get up then, sit at the picnic table, and enjoy the voluptuous quiet. He had a bundle of letters from his wife that he kept in a paper sack with his reading glasses, and these came out when he could be alone with them. The envelopes were marked in soft pencil with the date and time of their sealing, and some of them were quite fat. It seemed she was in the habit of making notes to him throughout her day. He'd read them in order, first to last, and it was while reading these letters that he'd first discovered the little tremor developing in his right thumb. Wide, gray strokes on oatmeal paper, a child's writing tablet. Her pencil was a thick instrument, and she could fit very few words per page. She wrote to say she had picked the corn. The nannies loved the husks and tassels, and now their milk was worth drinking again. Chokecherries were starting to look like they'd come in thick this year. The truck was leaking oil from the transfer case. She could deliver him books, but then he would have to leave the books in the jail. The jail had a policy about every single thing. If he wasn't too mad, she wondered, would he please see her? Wouldn't he see her so she could say how sorry she was? She'd been meaning to do that even before they took him away.

She wrote to say she'd fixed the truck, she thought, with something she'd found at the auto parts store called Liquid Steel. Was this a repair she could rely on? She wrote to apologize and apologize and apologize, though she never specified her wrongs. She wrote to say that, though she was doing all the things she usually did, she seemed to have so much extra time on her hands. Did he feel like he had extra time on his hands? Sorry—stupid question. She wrote to say she'd started to prepare the trailer for winter, cleaned the stovepipe, and she'd already begun to bed the garden; there were a few good radishes left in the ground. Now, she wrote, she had realized she'd been letting him take care of too many of the details, the bills and all, and she thought the responsibility of it had maybe got him down a little bit, but she was doing a needlepoint, she said, with a bluebird on a cherry tree, and she'd send it to him when she was done. If he wasn't already home by then. She included a sketch of the pattern, the finished bird. Karen recounted how her father had been around to say she'd better come back and live with the folks again, she'd better get a divorce, she'd better try real hard to get right with her Lord. He'd offered her the use of her old room, and she wouldn't even repeat what she'd said to that, but she'd answered him so that she doubted they'd ever speak again. Not if she could help it. "GOOD RIDDENS!!!" she wrote.

She wrote to promote a plan in which they would move to Elisis when he got out of jail, and he would take the healing waters every day, and she might find some work at the big hotel or maybe at the pole yard. She needed steady work, she thought. People came to Elisis from all over the world to heal, and here it was just a little ways down the road from them. They should think about moving.

She wrote to say she'd talked with the lawyer and she knew just what she should do. She said she missed him, but knew that everything would turn out fine. It had to. She loved him, same as always, and she could hardly wait until he felt better again. They needed to get back to eating their meals together when he got home, doing things together again, and just being together. It was time to stay positive, she wrote. "*Positive, Positive, Positive*," was the whole of one letter. "*You are not bad!!!*" read another.

She wrote to say that their luck was due to change and it almost had to change for the better. She wrote and mentioned the current temperature on Fitchet Creek. She wrote to say that sometimes, when she missed him too much, she got out the hammers and played *Mattie Groves*. Everything would be fine in the end, she said. There had been a moose around lately, a cow that had moved into the head of the marsh on Road 262.

Henry Brusett broke open that morning's letter, and it began with a declaration: She'd been depending on him too much, and she knew it, but now he could depend on her because she would never let him down. Not anymore. She would not let him down. There had been another reversal with the goats; she didn't know what the girls had gotten into, but their milk tasted skunky again. And, "I keep coming in every visitor day and they say you didn't put me on the list yet, but I will keep coming because I know you will be ready to see me some day and some things you have to say face to face. You may think this is very bad and your right but we have to stick together. This experience really shows you how much it is important. Those turkeys are back around. I got some corn for them so they will stay this time."

Henry Brusett read it all in order, and returned each scrap of paper to each envelope as he finished with it. He restored each envelope sequentially to its place in the bundle, and when he'd finished a night's reading, he'd rebind them all with a twine that he'd twisted up out of threads pulled from his jumper. This packet gave him Fitchet Creek as it had been when she'd first joined him there, a paradise with a short half-life, ten acres where they offended no one and where kindness, of all things, was the prevailing order. Fruit of an abandoned orchard. He bundled the letters and put them back under his mattress, and then, dread quietly accumulating, he awaited the rest of the day. Leonard woke, and urinated, and reclaimed his usual post at the picnic table, mopping his face and neck with a bare hand as if to spread the rictus of boredom across his features. "Why the fuck don't you ever say anything? You and your Gary Cooper thing, who needs that shit with a headache going on? With his usual fucking headache. Who appointed you the fucking riddle of the Sphinx? Say something for once. What's on your mind?"

"I can't think of anything."

"Come on, you can do better than that. You've heard many chapters from my tale of woe, so, come on, you better try a little harder than that. It's your turn. It's the middle of the morning-night, whatever. Tell me something. Anyfuckingthing."

"There's digestion. That's what I think about quite a bit. I usually got stool like concrete, so that'll occupy your mind. What do you want to hear about it?"

"Fuck you and your fucking bowels. You've been alive, tell me something. You ever been to war? Ever steal anything interesting? Ever loved your neighbor as you loved yourself?"

"I never had many neighbors. Probably why I don't have many stories. Never knew I'd be called on to entertain."

"You're a hard-ass, aren't you?"

"No," said Henry Brusett, "and I never even thought I was."

"Yeah? Well, that's all I am. Little bit limited. I've got what they're calling a small skill set. You know what the cancer rate is among recidivists? The average life span? You'd prefer to die with your boots on, or, in our case, your shower slippers. Aaah. Who's ever worth shaking down in here? I mean, ever. These penniless fools. If we could ever just get a couple hundred or so together, I bet your cousin Tubby could come up with all kinds of goodies, couldn't he? I'd like to get my head up in the ventilator shaft with a spliff. Anything. Except meth—I just cannot tolerate that odor. What do you like?"

"I'm good the way I am."

"Yeah, you would be. You get yours delivered, don't you? Percocet? That may be my all-time favorite. Got over my fear of needles just so I could jam Percocet in my arm. Ever try that in a vein?"

"No."

"It's delicious. You should get your hands on a works."

"I don't get high on it," said Henry Brusett. "It gets me just about normal."

"Much as you're taking? Oh, that's a shame. That'd put me in a low, slow orbit around the moon."

"You think you'd like that?"

"I'd like," said Leonard, "a spike through my eye, if it meant a moment's diversion. It's the tedium, baby. That's the enemy."

"Well," said Henry, "I've noticed Fess and Tubby, they don't watch me swallow. You want to make a deal?"

"Deal?" said Leonard into a suddenly overburdened friendship. "I don't make deals in here, prisoner. I take what I want, and *that's* the deal. I don't want to get started on any other precedent. You better give me some fuckin' pills if you've got 'em to give."

"It'd be everything I can do," said Henry Brusett, "not to swallow those once they're in my mouth. So, no, if you get the pills, I get something."

"Or I could just take 'em from you. I do hate this dealing. It's unnatural to me."

"Or I could just swallow, like I usually do. Like I'm supposed to do. So, what then? You gonna work me over? Wouldn't get you any drugs. You want these, you're gonna need my cooperation. I'll give you all but the one, the anti-anxiety. That wouldn't do you any good."

"Oh, I've got anxiety," said Leonard. "I'm the poster child. So what do you want? Out of this *deal?*"

"Want you to lay off that kid."

"Why? Got a little crush, have we? Why didn't you just say so. Not that I'd share. Is that all?"

"Him and the other one. And everybody. Leave 'em alone."

"What are you, a prude?"

"Little bit, yeah. You might call it that."

"Got any idea how wasted your sympathies are? But, all right. I'll go for it. Give me all my lovelies, and that's your guarantee. I get a load on like that, and I'm pretty Zen. My appetites would tend to zero out, which is the whole idea of downers, isn't it? But I've seen how you jones without these, man, so here's another part of the deal—no dying, okay? Don't you curl up and die now, because, personally, I don't care to be haunted in here. That would be the last straw."

WHEN
YOU
ARE FREE

·22·

SHE WAITED THEN in dismay, but no one came, and before long Karen Brusett was longing to be harangued, or made to feel guilty, or for any human exchange, but no one ever came. She canned applesauce and corn, more provision than she could easily store. She finished the embroidery for Henry, a plump bird among plump fruits, a pattern built of intricate stitching. Though faithful to her daily correspondence, she came to regard it as self-indulgence; Henry must not read her letters because he never gave in to her many pleas to let her come and see him. Her letters, she imagined, were only a journal and served only to reveal how she became, without at least a little company for direction or for distraction, mortally bored and boring. She was not nearly so self-sufficient as she had thought herself at Henry's arrest, and she feared a winter in this purer solitude might freeze her solid.

Karen had been hoarding more firewood than she could ever reasonably hope to sell or burn, and drinking beer at all hours, and one morning out on Rugged Cross Road, with her load lopsided on the truck and with High Life on her breath, she was startled if not surprised to see an urgent light display in her rearview mirror. The officer behind her made his siren yip, and she looked for a wide spot in the road. She'd been courting trouble, she knew—no insurance, no current wood permit, no decent jack or jumper cables; her deficiencies were legion. She owned a driver's license that she didn't even bother to carry, and she was a disaster, and she had gone out of her way to bring it to someone's attention. Now that attention had arrived in the form of a deputy making his way to her side with his hand on the grip of his pistol, and she found she didn't necessarily want it.

"Ma'am."

"Hi," she said without exhaling.

"Remember me?"

"You're . . . ?" Was he flirting with her? "From . . . ?"

"Deputy Sisson," he said. "I was there that night you . . . "

"Oh," again with an inhalation. The deputy had been different at night, more boyish among the other officers. She remembered him as pale in someone's headlights. "That's right. Sure, now I do. How are you?"

"How am I? Fine, I guess. You know why I stopped you?"

"No," she said somewhat truthfully—there were so many possible reasons.

"The way you've got your dog up there, that's against the law. What keeps it from flying off every time you stop or make a turn? All it's got is a lumpy little spot to stand on, and that's . . . You didn't know that was a bad way to go?"

"I did, but she won't ride in the cab. She just barks and barks if you put her in the cab. It's, it's horrible. But I do not like to break the law."

"That isn't the real reason I stopped you," said the deputy. Karen Brusett felt her troubles multiplying. What else? Would she have to walk a line on the highway for him? Say the alphabet without singing? She could not be very drunk, she thought, and still be this embarrassed. She could hardly afford to pay any amount of fine. But maybe this officer would take her to jail. This might be her best chance of seeing Henry.

"I've got a subpoena for you," he said. "Sign right here."

"What's this?"

"Just what it says. You're to appear as a witness for the state."

"State of Montana and Henry Brusett? Well, this would be—Henry's trial? Wouldn't it? I thought they weren't gonna have that, not for a long time yet. They must've got satisfied he's not crazy, which I could've told 'em for free. But, already? This is so soon."

"Says October 15," the deputy noted. "Ten in the AM. So be there, or be square. Or be arrested, actually. Sorry, didn't mean to be unprofessional. They've got us on these thirteen-hour shifts. You get goofy after a while."

"But—against my own husband I'm supposed to testify? Against my own husband?"

"I guess so. You might want to go home, ma'am, and brush your teeth before you do too much more driving around. And get the dog off the top of that woodpile, too, would you?"

Karen Brusett did not drive home. She drove in that direction until the deputy was out of sight, and then she turned around in the road and made straight for the county seat, where she might expect to encounter even more police. Nosy police. Hard by Karen's side Clementine barked without pause, tireless and intentional, and much closer than she knew to being abandoned at the roadside. In town, the mushroom burger deluxe had become the special at the drive-in, and two demolition derby cars were on display in an abandoned lot. Greg's bakery had gone out of business.

Karen feared to leave Clementine in or on, or tied to the truck, so she led her by her collar, a clumsy undertaking—up the stairs, and through the hall, and she opened the lawyer's door and leaned in. Eleven in the morning, and no receptionist in the outer office, and that girl, who was supposed to be Ms. Meany's something-or-other, her assistant, was completely useless, and Karen thought that she'd make a far better helper if she could ever worm her way into the regular workforce. What could possibly be wrong with a steady paycheck and doing the kind of work that is done in tidy clothes? Why not? Sometimes she thought she must be getting old already because she had come to want lighter, prettier shoes. People had regular jobs. It was nothing impossible. "Hello?"

"Come in," the lawyer appeared between the dividers. "Sorry, it's been, oh, Karen. Hi. Well, come on in."

"I've got my dog."

"Oh, good. The more the merrier. Come on in."

"No, she'd get wild in there. She barks like that when she's cooped up. Could we go outside for a minute?"

"Outside?" The lawyer had an apparatus in her ears. She took it out.

"So we can talk. So she'll let us have some quiet."

Ms. Meany locked her door behind her, and as a troop they went back through the halls, down the clanging stair, and across the street to the grim park where Clementine put her nose to the ground, breathed up its history, and peed on its vertical parts. They sat in the swings, on brittle rubber straps, and like girls on any playground they rocked in them, under the soothing creak of the chains.

"I got a thing that says I have to testify. This is about the worst I've felt since this all started. I thought I was scared before. Geez, what next?"

"I told you it was possible. Anything else? Have you had anyone coming around? The sheriff's people? Meyers? Anybody wanting to talk again?"

"No. But I do have this thing. Already. I mean, isn't there any way around it?"

They swung to and fro, synchronized. The lawyer was very lucky to be smart, because without her intelligence, she'd have been a mash-mouthed, painful sight. Her complexion did not improve for being seen in the great outdoors. "Karen," she said at last, "I can't give you any advice. I really can't. You're a witness, and it's a very big no-no for me to try and influence your testimony in any way. I told you that you have certain rights. Just like everyone else has been telling you. But I told you nothing more than that. You understand?"

"Sure, I do. I guess. But what should I say?"

"I can't tell you. That's exactly—well, that would be the very last thing I should tell you. No one can. Or should. That will be up to you now. Entirely up to you. You'll say what you think you should say."

"Oh? Well, thanks so much for that. At first everybody kept tellin' me, 'Don't say anything.' Or I thought that was what they were tellin' me. Did they mean that? Did you?"

"That is one of your rights," said the lawyer, "under certain circumstances."

"Why doesn't anybody ever say anything straight out? It is—or it isn't. You are—or you aren't. Why not like that?"

"I don't mean to be unclear. But it is complicated." Ms. Meany's tone suggested that she regretted these complications more than anyone. She seemed a good sport, and too much put upon, and Karen Brusett was touched that a professional person would get her good shoes dirty and indulge the whims of a disturbed dog just to talk this way. Karen was ashamed to keep fishing for better news when the woman had been clear from the beginning that she wasn't prepared to offer much. The news might never be more than mediocre.

"Weren't we supposed to have kind of a long wait? Before they had that trial? I was gettin' ready for a long wait, and, you know, I thought we'd just wait 'er out and hope for the best. That works sometimes, doesn't it? Wait till they're not so mad about everything." She had hated the waiting very much, but the alternative, now that it was upon them, was worse. "I mean, this is just right around the corner. This is next week."

"I don't know if Henry can stand to be in there much longer. He's not doing too well. Seemed to me he was going downhill a little every time I saw him. I don't know what's going on. They absolutely swear to me he's getting all his meds and eating, but he doesn't seem to be doing too well at all."

"Remember before? When I said I'd do anything? You know, those jailers, they never said a word to me, not one word. Never mentioned it—not even Tubby—you'd think they could've at least told me he wasn't up to snuff, or . . . not like I could do anything about it, but, ever, and he still hasn't put me on that list, either. His guest list? He just won't let me see him at all. Yeah, we'd better get it over with. Anything. That's what I said I'd do, and that's what I'll do. To get it over with."

"I'm sure you would."

"Well . . . ? Tell me what it takes. From me? To get this whole deal out of everybody's hair. And over with, that would be the main thing."

"Again, I can't advise you on that. Except, I suppose I might just offer some friendly advice, some very general advice—don't do anything dumb." At various times and in various ways, the lawyer attempted to smile; she had never in Karen's presence succeeded.

"The one thing I won't do is go to Henry's trial and testify against him."

"You'd have to take the stand at least. They can throw you in jail until you do."

"Okay. Then how would you, like, stop the trial?" Karen wanted to sound smarter, or truer, or more decisive. She always sounded so much better when she was talking to herself.

"That's not in our hands. Meyers could dismiss it, but I've put it to him, you know, and he tells me he'd dismiss if Henry wanted to say he was defending himself—or you. Defending you. Henry doesn't seem to want to say that."

"Still won't? He was in a fog; I doubt he even knows what to say."

"He doesn't want to say anything now. Nothing. Last time I spoke to Henry, he'd decided that he'd waited too long. He's decided anything he might say now would be a lie, and so now, even though they're really kind of bending over backward to give him an easy way out of this, he won't take it."

"Yeah, but weren't you sayin', 'Be quiet'? You told him that, I bet. I bet you told him more than once."

"I did, and it was the right advice at the time."

"*Every*body. They were all pretty much sayin', I thought, you don't have to talk, or you shouldn't talk, or it was kinda like that. So now he won't talk. See?"

"Right. But now there's another way to go. It would be a lot more of a sure thing. He could even say he doesn't remember what happened, and I'm pretty sure we could get him out of jail. Something could be arranged. But he won't. He won't say anything now. And you hate to browbeat the poor guy because he does seem to be kind of fading, but at the same time, you want him out. I did tell him to not talk, and I did really emphasize it. But now we should be considering just anything that would get him out of there, so what was good advice when I gave it, is now—we have other options."

"But if he doesn't, then that leaves you with a trial, huh? Gotta do it?"

"Right. That and the fact that there's been an opening in the judge's calendar. We might as well take it while we can."

"But you could lose?"

"Yes. It's always possible. In fact, to tell you the truth, I usually lose."

"And it would be murder then? They could call it murder if you lost?"

"Deliberate homicide. Yes."

"Wow. Wouldn't that be just about it for Henry? I mean, he's gone, whatatheycallit? Up the river? Or, I mean, how would that go?"

"I'm not thinking about that right now. I want to prevent it. I *should* prevent it if I do my job right. You know, our clients call the shots— whether we go to trial or not, that's their call to make, and our clients aren't necessarily too smart about it, or use very good judgment, so we go in on a lot of unwinnable cases, lost causes. PDs do. We lose a lot at trial. But the case that really scares you is the one you know you should win, and this is . . . I probably shouldn't be telling you all this. Really, Henry could say almost anything, I think—even confess—and we'd have him out of there for good in just a couple of days. And he's, well he's in pretty tough shape, Karen. So I've advised him that he's got a way out. Several ways. But they'd all require him to say a little something."

"I could," she offered. "I'd say whatever they wanted me to say. Hell, let's get doin' it."

"It wouldn't be enough. Any self-defense kind of claim, they'd have to hear it from Henry himself. He'd have to say why he thought he needed to . . . They'd kind of have to know what he was thinking. But he doesn't want to talk. Plain and simple—he's done talking, and for all I know that could still be the best idea, the best approach. Almost always is."

"The trouble with Henry—he'll get an idea, he gets some idea in his head and then he chews himself up with it. He gets these crazy standards for himself. You leave him with his thoughts, or whatever those are, and this is what can happen. No time at all, and he's got himself to where you can't even help him very much. You know what? I think what I better do is just go ahead and tell 'em it was me. I think I better tell 'em I . . . "

"Whooah, no," said the lawyer. "Don't. Not if it's not true. Once again—you have the right to remain silent—but you don't have the right to lie."

"Well, that's not too convenient, is it? How do you know I'd be lying? How do you even know what I was gonna say?"

"I don't. What I'd really like to do is just continue to bask in my ignorance, okay? This is a strange, strange . . . Henry is a very unusual . . . and you . . . I just have a hard time imagining that either one of you would do anything too awful. I like you both quite a bit, and I'm not too sure I haven't let it cloud my judgment a little bit, but I just don't see how they can prove a crime. Against anyone. I'm talking about the way I see things—as they are now—with what we all know now." The lawyer checked her swing, hung with her hands high on the chains and, much weighted, she appeared to stare down some new thought. Karen also stopped, never wishing to interfere; in the absence of the necessary miracle, she still held out hope for a better plan, and she watched what she took to be the clouds of a forming strategy skid across the lawyer's face. But it was soon clear that the lawyer was only entertaining second thoughts, and to no good purpose, and it made Karen a little angry.

"So what about that sanity thing? What was all that about?"

"I was buying time."

"You didn't think he was . . . he didn't understand?"

"No. I never thought that at all. I was just buying time."

"Time for what?"

"For nothing, as it turns out. Turns out the best thing to do is just get on with it. Hope we get an acquittal. He's put us in quite a must-win situation here. And then, on top of all that—and maybe this'll make you feel a little better—he won't see me anymore. This last week he's just . . . He won't talk to me, won't talk to anybody. Apparently he's got all he can do just to tolerate it in there. I don't know exactly what his situation is because he won't even consent to see the physician's assistant. So, we're going through with it. Win or lose, we get him out of that county jail, and anything would be an improvement over that."

NAT HATED HER noticeably more each Friday when she made her weekly round through the jail, met with him in the holding cell, and pissed on yet another fond scheme. His hopes. This week it had been compulsion. What about compulsion? If certain mistakes forced themselves on him, what then? How could a person like that possibly be held responsible?

It was, she told him gently, no defense under Montana law. Today Giselle must be careful of disappointing him too much or too harshly, because today she needed his help. She was not, however, certain that she could even pretend patience with him for as long as it might take to gain his cooperation; Nat's wheedling never failed to strike a proud pink nerve in her. His instincts were pure and prescient, and young Nat had discovered at once that irrational corner of his lawyer's soul where she might be convinced that the jail was filled with her fumblings. He never failed to imply that if only she were to try a little harder, if only she were more imaginative, then the innocents would be free, and the gloomy authorities hereabouts might occasionally be thwarted. Nat had disremembered how, in order to avoid having reams of evidence and a small horde of enraged witnesses pass under the judge's badly offended nose, he himself had enunciated his guilt. Under oath and in open court he had offered an almost boastful admission of the holes in his enterprises; he'd acknowledged that the Ginny LaFleaur Lingerie and Fine Fragrance Company was long out of business when he'd acted as its agent. Thermo Nuclonic Plastics, he confessed, had never existed outside his imagination.

"It was basically a concept," he explained, "but, Your Honor, at some point, everything in trade starts out as a concept. This is economics."

Nat had told the court that the catchphrase he'd developed— Plastics for the Hottest Eternity—had been very successful, and now he hoped to pay his debt to society and then perhaps find work in the advertising field because he thought he might have a talent for it. Having said all this, he'd been sentenced, and, weekly since that sentence had been passed, he had been telling Giselle Meany that he could not and should not bear it. Whenever she met with him, he made her feel that she was the one who wished him punished, and that she had devised it, and that it was being carried out at her ongoing insistence. For Nat, there was no connection between anything he might have done or failed to do and his current residence, and after long exposure to it, it was very hard for Giselle not to openly loathe him, but she wanted something of him today.

"I'm losing it in here," he now claimed. "Would that make any difference? To anybody?"

"Well, I can't get you out because you don't like it. They don't *want* you to like it." Off in the laundry room, Tubby's tennis shoes were tumbling in the dryer. She spoke up. She was forever raising her voice. "That's sort of the point of the whole exercise. For them. You have to be good in here, Nat. It's quite important. Best thing I can tell you right now—you're probably a lot tougher than you think you are. It won't be pleasant, I'm sure, but you'll make it. You know you will."

His shoulders sagged another few degrees. He was just plump in his orange jumper. "I now know how tough I am. Exactly how tough. Which is something I was never all that interested in finding out."

He was a vapor never meant to be contained. He was a fart. Giselle reminded herself that the cheat would be, for his own purposes, a beating heart and striving lungs and raw confusion like anyone else. "The thing is, and I don't mean to be high-handed or anything, but the thing is, you are just not a very gifted criminal. When you get out of this, you might consider going straight. I mean, you leave such a trail." A slug's trail, that damning slick behind him. "Receipts and everything else? You go out of your way to make such a vivid first impression. I wonder, do you even really *try* to get away with it? I mean, maybe I could get the guy from mental health in here to see you. I guess I could do that, if you want."

"Yeah. Yeah, that's . . . *finally* an idea."

"He wouldn't get you out of here, though, not unless it was to send you up to Warm Springs. Indefinitely. But maybe he could prescribe something for you, if you really need it."

"No. No. Absolutely no pills. Or—wait a minute—no. No. Not for me, thank you. Psychiatrists and all those types, they've never done me any good. No one has. This is getting—I *have* to get out of here, that's the only thing that would really work for me." Even Nat, she was sure, could not fake despair so stark as this, but did he have to flog her with it?

"You're personable enough. Maybe you'd do well in the service industry. Did you ever think about something like that?"

He brightened. "What a coincidence. I have. I was *just* thinking the exact same thing. I'd start at the bottom, of course, washing dishes, whatever it took, whatever they needed me to do. I'd just pitch in and learn the business, and—sure, put me to work. Doesn't that make all the sense in the world? Start to rebuild my life? One brick at a time, as they say. What about a work furlough?"

"Do you have a job? A job offer?"

"No, but I could get one real fast."

"They won't parole you to look for work."

"Maybe you could . . . "

"No," she said. "I'm sorry. I think your deal is sealed. It is what you agreed to."

"You don't know what it's like."

"I'm sitting in it," she said. Close, reverberant, smelly—the lockup shook her every time she came into it, and even with that, she could leave. In fact, she arranged her regular visits to the jail for this hour of the day just so that she might go straight home afterward and shower. She made a point of shaking her clients' hands. "No, I don't know what it's like. Doesn't mean I don't sympathize with your situation. There's just nothing I can do about it. I'd guess this is probably not the best time to ask you for a favor, but I really need you to do something for me."

Nat was alert again. To have any currency in this market would improve his current standing, and he'd seen the generous impulse enough to know what it looked like. "Happy to do whatever I can. Which isn't very much, while I'm in here. But if there's any way I can be of service, you just name it." He pulled at the neck of his jumper and stroked his face with a wobbly hand.

"I need you to talk to Henry Brusett for me. I need you to go back there right now and convince him he has to come and see me. Now. As he may have told you—or I may have mentioned it—his trial is set for Monday. This coming Monday."

"What would happen," Nat wondered, "if you won?"

"What would happen?"

"I mean, they'd just let Henry right out of here, wouldn't they?"

"Well, yes."

"Immediately?"

"The judge orders it upon the verdict. The right verdict, and off he goes." She spoke as if she were well acquainted with the ritual. "He walks out of court a free man."

"*I*," said Nat. "*I* need to get out of here. Before anybody else. Me. Me first. Trust me, it's that important." But no one Nat had ever known for more than three days would squander a moment's trust on him, and, pitiably, he knew this. Whatever he said was qualified.

"I thought we'd already covered that pretty thoroughly. Nat, can you talk to him for me? Would you? Please?"

"What do you want me to say?"

"Today," she said, "I mean, as soon as you go back there, I want you to tell him he has to talk to me. Right now."

"He's probably asleep. He stays in his cube. We all do."

"You can wake him up. It's important."

"Yeah? *He's* important."

"Oh, come off it now, don't tell me you can find anything to envy in Henry Brusett. Come on. Listen to yourself."

"What if he loses? What happens then?"

"He's not losing." Her rare, slow, flat bravado. She was far too smart to ever be entirely confident. "He doesn't have to lose. Especially if you can get him back here to me. He really doesn't need to run the risk of losing. I don't know, maybe he's doing better now, but he wasn't looking very good, or sounding very good, and a trial's quite an ordeal. There's really no reason to go through it now. The message—and I tried to tell Tubby all this already, but Tubby got it garbled up—is this: I can get him out today. No trial. Will you tell him that? The closer we get, the more they're offering. I can get him out. He doesn't even have to say anything at all. They'll let me speak for him."

"Is that good? You speaking for him? He's *what*? Getting out?"

"If you can convince him to talk to me. But it's got to be today. We've got until the end of the day. Let him know he can be out of here before supper if he'll just talk to me."

"Him?"

"I spring who I can, Nat. Anybody that I can get out of here, I get out of here. I do what I can do. For everybody. *He's* got a break, and we really need to grab it. I mean, it would be negligent endangerment, no felony even. Time served. No probation, nothing. Just get him to come in here and give me the okay, and he's out."

"Yeah," Nat, speaking as the co-conspirator now. "I'll let him know. I'll see if I can pass it along. Still, I have to wonder, I do wonder a little bit—I sure wish somebody could help *me*, that's what I wish."

SHE COULD NEVER quite get the hang of wearing casual clothes; any sort of trouser seemed to emphasize Giselle Meany's strangely made hips, but trousers were necessary if she wished to sit with due modesty in the plastic stands of the high school's gymnasium, seating made for midgets. As an oddity among the others here, she knew her presence made them self-conscious, but so long as she lived with Sheila, she could expect that most of her Saturdays would be claimed by team sports, the wholesome rigor of sitting in someone's punishing stands. Season by season, Giselle found her daughter's many games obscure. Even volleyball's mild rituals had never really explained themselves to her, and she had at times further estranged herself from the home crowd by cheering at wrong moments; she often failed to grasp the import of a play, a ruling at the net.

Everyone here, it seemed, had grown up steeped in these games and had from infancy known everything about them, and Giselle heard profound discussions of the rules, of players' strengths and weaknesses, of coaching blunders. She deplored and envied the common ability to heap abuse on the officials, and she was often touched at how people in this famously small state knew the parents of competitors from other towns. These competitions were generational, essential she supposed, and there in the middle of it all, two or three times a week for the last several years, sat Giselle Meany, oddly happy, her enthusiasm somewhat in check, her hams aching. With a special gift for remaining the stranger, she sat with women of apparent and imposing competence—matrons of all ages—and there were women who tanned to improbable tones under sun lamps and went draped in gold to every bake sale, and women who, in studied self-abasement, wore their sweat clothes and ten-dollar tennis shoes. Giselle did not like to believe that she was superficial, but she could not believe that she belonged. Girls talked of girls. Boys talked of girls and feats of petty dominance. She overheard them. Women talked of food and children, men of machinery and reverently of rain and contemptuously of the government. She sat among them. In theory they had the game in common, a desire to see their children publicly succeed, but Giselle Meany usually found herself at a slightly different event. "Go, girls," was her cry. "Go."

She had come early and claimed a seat along the top bench so that she might have the wall behind her for a backrest. Her Sheila had never, not even as a freshman, played with the junior varsity, but Giselle was bullied by the egalitarian impulse to come and see the lesser team play, though it meant more hours on the benches. It was touching to watch these younger girls—the uncoordinated and the lumpish girls, their every move full of apology and hesitation, who tried so hard, so ineffectually. Their ball was on the floor as much as in the air, and the junior varsity squads played a surreal and heartbreaking game resembling soccer as much as anything, and these games could be very long. Giselle watched, however, to offer her most sincere encouragement, "Okay, girls. Go."

Meanwhile, Sheila was somewhere in the building, somewhere well out of sight, awaiting her turn.

Sheila was, biologically, the daughter of an assistant professor of phenomenology whose specialty was chaos theory and who dutifully and distantly sent support payments from wherever he then happened to be chain-smoking unfiltered cigarettes in the European manner; Sheila's mother, of course, was the improbable Giselle Meany, which must be so awkward for the poor girl. There'd been nothing in her daughter's breeding to predict this glorious beast, and Sheila was so obviously a self-invented creature, five and a half feet of vindication and accelerated evolution who made an invariable pre-game meal of oatmeal and toast four hours before she expected to play. Sheila liked her predictable surge of energy, and as she took on fuel, she would describe for Giselle what and whom to look for in that evening's opponent. "Candy. Candy *Cain*? I am so, so glad you stuck me with just a regular name.

280

But she *is* six feet tall. She's strong as a guy, too, so if she gets a decent set—*boom*—and you don't want to be under that when—*boom*—she'll come right down with it." In the car, she would talk a bit faster and more randomly, and then as they neared the gym, she would pull her game face on and cease to talk at all, and then at the gym they parted company, and Giselle would not see her girl again until she led the varsity onto the floor, circling it with her long, pointed stride and with a volleyball tucked under her arm like the head of some earlier adversary, and her jaw working, and she'd run them in a grand circle round the gym, gather them into a smaller one where the team joined arms and leaned in at each other, and, their hips swaying, they would come to resemble the floating, sucking organism glimpsed in a microscope. *Oooh-aaah, Oooh-aaah.* Theirs was a masculine cry, but more piercing.

High above, Giselle stood near a speaker through which Aretha Franklin demanded respect, and Giselle was sore pressed to contain her pleasure, but Sheila had pleaded with her never to clap for them again during warm-ups. "Never, *ever*—okay, Mom? It just isn't done." Now that the evening's proven athletes were on display, aficionados had begun coming into the stands, and Giselle began to hear her daughter's name on their lips. "You get down and see that Weeksville game? That little Meany is gettin' to be a killer, just a killer for 'em. She gets better all the time."

To hear these praises made Giselle happy, then nervous—they expected so much of her girl—it was nerve-racking to have a transcendent daughter, and so, to pass the time until "The Star Spangled Banner" was sung, Giselle made her way to the lobby against an inflow of fans, and she fell into one of several long lines working slowly toward a concession stand manned by densely pimpled pep clubbers. These teens invested every transaction with layers of confusion, and Giselle pretended patience for it and slowly shuffled forward. She wanted bottled water, something to occupy her hands, something to wet her mouth.

Of those faces familiar to her in the surrounding crowd, nearly all belonged to men. Cops and former clients. Overwhelmingly she knew men, men who might, if they were caught glancing in her direction, offer her a curt nod. Giselle, for her part, gave everyone alike the glazed look of a bank teller. Deputy Totter was there, out of uniform, and just behind him Jack Harney, a criminally hard husband, who had fallen into one of the lines, to all appearances ravenous for his hot dog, and Harney stared steadily ahead to where he was to receive it, and he would look at nothing else. One may not smile upon such acquaintances. Such acquaintances were about all she had.

Giselle Meany was just enough disfigured that she was not accustomed to be stared at in polite company, and so at first she found it hard to credit her sense that someone's frank gaze had fixed on the side of her head. Used to the privacy of ugliness, she needed an effort of will to turn and confront the interested party.

She didn't know him. His was a face she would have remembered, and she knew she'd never seen him before. He did not turn away. Between them a pair of schoolgirls, eight or nine, and blond, and each with a paper dollar in her fist, debated the merits of Lemonheads. Giselle didn't know this man, but he didn't look away, and she guessed that he was interested, that he was emboldened because he'd been born, probably, with roughly the same defect that she'd acquired at work, an upper lip with a leonine partition, a lip stretched and divided and flattened until the only expression left to its owner was one of constant chagrin. They exchanged this look. He was a man otherwise well made and of about her own age. His left hand was out of view. She'd never seen him before, and wasn't likely to see him again, and she was thinking hard for something sane to say to him when the man spoke to her.

"You're that lawyer, aren't you?" He formed his words well down in his throat, and they were compressed for passing through immobile lips. The girls' wheaten heads turned up at him and their chatter ceased.

"I am," she said. Giselle almost regretted that her own speech had been left unimpaired, and she certainly regretted her local celebrity. Conrad County's criminals were numerous and poor, and her efforts on their behalf were much in the papers, and her work and unfavorable reputation dogged her everywhere. "Yes," she said. "I'm probably the one you're thinking of."

"You're the one who does the trials." Emphatically not a question.

"Most of the criminal trials. I'm the public defender."

"This one they've got coming up on Monday, is that yours?" A tidy fellow possessed of a few terrifying certainties, he was, from the nose up and the chin down, no doubt handsome. Groomed and ruddy, and if only he hadn't also been so angry, and if only his eyes had been any other shade of blue.

"It's mine," she said. "I'm involved in that one."

"Yeah? I got a jury summons. Now the clerk tells me I have to come. They can actually haul my ass to jail if I don't."

"Sorry, I know it's . . . Sorry. I don't know what to tell you. But the way things look right now, we will be sitting a jury. Who knows, maybe you'll find it interesting." She might have assured him that he would never sit on any jury trying any client of hers, but she didn't.

"Twenty-five dollars a day," said the man, "and gas to and from. You do realize a guy can't pay his bills that way? Don't you? These things, if you ask me, are a waste of time and taxpayer dollars. These trials you people do."

"I have never done a single one I could get out of doing," Giselle claimed. "So . . . "

This was true. She was not especially good at trial; she worried too much and too obviously, and she was too often caught staring into the headlights. There was no game, she thought, no game of any kind that she'd ever play with anything like her daughter's confidence. " . . . so, be seeing you Monday morning. Bright and early, huh?" She had come to wish a maximum of inconvenience for this other high-strung harelip.

HENRY BRUSETT WAS stronger than he'd been in some time. Having passed through the worst of withdrawal, and for lack of any better occupation, he had devised some anodyne exercises; he stood astraddle of the drain in the floor with his feet at shoulder width, and with both hands he reached as high as he could reach, and in the chromed mirror above the sink he made for an interesting ruin. He knew he'd look even worse if he were distinct in it, but Henry, on his own side of the bad reflection, was reclaiming parts of himself he thought had suffocated. He had learned how to turn down certain side streets in himself for hours at a time, go to places where the pain was not so strong, and, as with every other thing of importance he'd ever learned, he had learned this in the hardest possible way and too late. He'd learned to breathe well at last, to become tall.

"You're going in that courtroom," Nat predicted, "and they'll take one look at you, and they'll—never in a million years, my friend. You just don't look the part. You're gone, and I'm, oh, but, don't get me wrong—I really appreciate what you've done for me so far. It's been above and beyond. Very slick, though. To look so rough. I mean, they'll just never buy that you could even . . . even if you wanted to. Appearances mean so much, don't they?"

"If I do get out, I'll tell Tubby what's been going on. He should be able to come up with something for you. To help. Maybe they'd get him out of here. They must have transfers."

"Tubby? No. I already told you, no. Didn't I? If Tubby, or if *any*-body else knew, that is the only possible way this could get any worse.

Our little secret, okay? We all know some of the things that will happen to us some day, but does that mean we have to talk about them all the time? That's unhealthy, Henry, but, oh, just when I was starting to heal down there. What you have to do, though, you just have to enjoy the moment. We have to. I'll tell you what we should talk about, we should be talking about your plans for when they let you go. What you need to do, my friend, is get out there and really seize the old bull by the horns; get out there and make yourself healthy again, and just get with it again. You just can't know how much it would please me to think that *somebody* is getting ahead in this world."

"*Anda*," said Leonard from his bunk, from out of several weeks of stupor. "*Rápido.*"

Nat regarded him with unslaked rage. "Having to listen to him, having to listen to him all the time, that'll be almost as bad as . . . It's that poison he's always talking. I hate that so much. That really takes the wind out of my sails."

SUNDAY AFTER SUPPER, Tubby brought round a Salvation Army suit, a houndstooth the lawyer was insisting Henry wear in the morning, along with a white shirt and black socks, and a pair of black shoes two sizes too large for his feet. It was all dead man's wear. He also received a brand new change of skivvies and a Bible with silk ribbon tucked into the book of Job. The latest of Karen's letters came as well, and these were from a series she was writing on grocery sacks that she tore along their sides to make of them a single long sheet that came to him rolled as a scroll and sealed, barely, with Scotch tape. She'd told him she thought it bad luck to buy any new writing paper now; she'd tried to spell superstitious. Under jail light, her soft pencil was hard to decipher on the wrinkled brown paper, and her scrawl became quite wild upon such broad and unlined surfaces. He had from these letters, because they were a little hard to read, the small additional pleasure of solving an easy puzzle.

Remember that bob cat kitten I told you I found. I let him come into the house. He moved in but goes outside to do his stuff, but then he bites right thru my hand. That part by my thumb. That is sore. When you see me that is why I will have a bandage on. I should be glad it was just my hand. But I am not. I did not want to look this way when I was in the court.

To think that anyone, having seen her face, would take much notice of a bandage—that modesty was one of many ways she wrung his heart.

I am worried but I am not worried and I know that doesn't make good sense. You know how bad I am at explaining so I won't even try. I do believe in you for one thing. I have been thinking a lot but I don't get any new ideas except I know what I did wrong. Which was very wrong. And you are the only one I can believe in or understand so I wish I knew what to do. But I do know really what I will do. I think they told me. You should not have to worry. Also you should not have to be in jail. Maybe there are some things I can do to take care of you when you are free. I should take care of you and I know you don't like that but I should anyway. Only if you need it but I think you need it. It has been hard. We had hard frost last night. Is that early? My hand is so big but it is not any new colors or bad yet. I am sorry if this is bad writing. I really like that word penmanship. It is Saturday nite honey and the only reason I even know is because you're trial is coming up so fast. I keep track a little bit because of that (of time).

Time and distance, and not too much of that—a little separation, and she was running out of things to say to him. Her last letter had been written very early that very morning.

I know who is good.

You are. Very good.

You know.

You can trust me. I am always on your side and did not forget who is good.

I love my good husband. Wait and see. You will see what I mean.

I don't have to say it. I can be quiet and you will know. When I'm quiet no matter what.

I think you don't read these but you will know what I mean soon.

I hope it isn't mean if I tell you that boy was a good boy. Or maybe he was a man. He was nice in a nice way and this is hard for us but what can we do. Bad people would not care but I am the kind of person who sees him all the time when I close my eyes. That boy was way nicer than I am and that is one of the things wrong and I have been wondering if you read my letters or if they read these letters, if the cops do. What do I ever say? Do they get a thrill when I say I love you? When you get home I will put so many eggs in your cake you won't believe it. I know how much you like it rich. No matter how hard I work I cannot sleep now. I get tired but cannot sleep. It is the middle of the night again. What can I say? For sure I will say good luck because I am out of room on this sack.

Forever yours,

Mrs. Henry Brusett (also known as Karen)

MEYERS LIVED IN the house he'd bought his wife as her reward for surviving her illness, and he kept her ashes in a pot. He'd managed to give Claudia less than two months of her darling Craftsman-style home down by the river, and now he was already rounding into his second decade here. His son Robert had made Claudia's urn, and it was displayed with several other Robert Meyers ceramics in a Plexiglas case above the mantel, pots on sculpted sand, on reed matting, pots as kinetic and pregnant as seeds, and proceeding from out of a serenity that Hoot Meyers envied, even begrudged, even of his son. For his part, in his generation, he could appreciate elegance as it occurred, but it would never be the dominant theme of a house he'd densely furnished as a museum. Meyers owned a McClellan saddle, if he no longer owned a horse. By his bed stood a treadle-driven grindstone, a Swede saw, an ice auger; similar devices were all through the house, standing idle now, but ready to serve, to bore, to crush long after the men who'd made them were no longer even afterthoughts. From every parcel of land he had ever owned he'd gathered up at least one of these indestructible tools, equipment that, like Hoot Meyers himself, had its proper historical place somewhere near the end of the Iron Age, and his clutter could make getting up to pee in the night an iffy proposition; Meyers had left himself just a few narrow lanes to negotiate his way through his house, and his toes were frequently some shade of red or blue. Once he'd been up for any reason, he rarely succeeded in going back to sleep.

He kept spread on the wall above and behind his refrigerator the blood orange fan she'd carried in *The Mikado*. At eye level, at every snack and meal, Claudia's permanently rising sun, the only artifact in the house that he dusted with any diligence. Well acquainted with 3 AM, Hoot Meyers made coffee and scrambled some eggs. He stood, breakfast in hand, at the picture window overlooking the river. There was a tower on the far shore with lights and cable rising to it from the near shore. Closer at hand, two tall poles bore crowns of osprey nest that were sometimes active all night. There had been a drawdown at the dam earlier that week, and wide, green mudflats had been revealed along both banks of the river; all through dusk a hatch of some newly prolific bug had been shimmering just above the water. Now the water was black except where the cable lights and a waning moon were reflected in it.

A cider press, a cracked bellows.

He showered, shaved, trimmed the hairs in his nose, and he pitched a change of underwear, a can of Right Guard, some gum, and a lightly used notepad into a war bag, and he walked to the courthouse with a suit and a shirt still in the drycleaner's plastic sack. For as long as he'd been a town dweller, he still found it novel and nice to walk to work, a brief walk on pavement, and to arrive there with his boots unmuddied. Meyers let himself in with his key and climbed up through the dark of the back stairwell. He did not need or use the lights; he preferred that it not be known how early, how sometimes absurdly early, he came in to prepare. His job wanted silence and seclusion, from which he might sometimes impose a moment's order. Only by winning what he thought he should win could Meyers endure or take much warm interest in himself anymore, and he liked to leave the impression that he won by luck or brilliance, or that he won because he was in the right, but his luck was manufactured here in this half-lit building. He suffered to completely prepare, and so, in most things, his judgment seemed to prevail, as was only proper.

But the routine for throwing a trial, if there could be such a thing, simply would not occur to him, and he was very much afraid he'd given himself six hours to dress for court—and to brood on it—a hundred times the time he'd require.

·23·

HE HAD ALWAYS wanted to say he'd hit the boy, but he knew that from the moment he might confess, that from then on and thereafter, he'd be hounded for his reasons, and it was his reasons he could not bring himself to speak. What would be left of a man who had admitted, who had accepted in himself, that he'd been so wrong-hearted and mean as to kill some poor kid? So he did not confess, and he would not lie, and the fruit of this principled coward-ice was a hundred citizens congregating to make Henry Brusett their constant study. Now, no matter what came to pass, they would never devise a more perfect hell for him than this trial.

It was a churchy room with its ranks of pews, the judge's bench for an altar. Behind the bench a portrait of Wilbur Farrand Conrad, mournful in his vigilante's tweeds, stared down at everyone. Having given his bloodied name to this courthouse, this county, he was now quite as dead as any dangling road agent.

With much fussing, the bailiff arranged sixty-two citizens accord-ing to the plastic placards on their chests; he seated them fifteen abreast on the pews, and from the prosecutor's table, Hoot Meyers looked them over and made notes. In the gallery were reporters, and a high school civics class come to see the workings of justice, and there were loiterers and ghouls, and, off in the corner farthest from the accused,

Mr. and Mrs. Wesley Teague had joined hands with each other and with a local man of the cloth; they were unremitting in their prayers. Henry Brusett knew them at once for the young man's parents and thought that they were among the mildest people he'd ever seen. They were dressed in pastels, as for a garden party. Still, he could hardly suppose that they were there to wish him well.

There was no part of the room to which he might comfortably turn, but Henry thought it would seem artificial of him to stare a hole in the defense table or into his own folded hands, and, as was usual for him in any crowded place, he didn't know what to do with his eyes. "Coast to coast," he thought he heard Ms. Meany say. "A farmer in every poem and kitchen." She spoke to him in fast and low outrushes of breath, and she knew she was hard to understand. She had set out a legal pad before him and provided him with two sharp pencils; with one of these she slashed a clearer message:

HELP ME
GIVE ME GOOD JURORS, BAD JURORS
G FOR GOOD   B FOR BAD
MARK BY NUMBERS WHAT YOU THINK
SEE LIST NEED YOUR OPINION AND
YOUR HELP PLEASE REAL IMPORTANT

He read his lawyer's note and was too ashamed and too embarrassed to do more than shrug.

Fine, she thought, because she did not think she would require his active cooperation. For once she might be getting all she needed of a man. Giselle Meany was set up at last in the right case, with the right cause and the right client, and she had assured herself in the middle of the previous night that this time she'd be the right advocate. In her mind, she welcomed Mr. Brusett to be as indifferent as he wanted; they were still going to win. He could be as mulish and mute as ever he might wish, and so much the better, because his reticence was the meat of their defense; he simply seemed too shy to do much evil. Giselle thought she'd done well by him in the way of wardrobe, too—brilliantly, miserably turned out it in the Salvation Army sports jacket with its tiny, twisted checks and with its cantilevered shoulders, he did not look the wino as she'd feared he might, but a Cuban band leader, pre-Castro, and too ridiculous and secondhand to fit anyone's notion of a killer.

Giselle thought that as soon as she brought her occasional tremors and her heartburn under control, she might begin to brim with confidence this morning, and what a lovely fall morning it had been. She'd had a brisk walk before dawn and told herself how she must try this case in a confident mood, and to that end she was already permitting herself some pleasure in the victory she so fiercely intended, and even with the foofaraw of the judge coming into court, even with the rising and being bidden to sit again, even the sight of the judge's faceted skull and his preening, soaring self-regard—none of it slowed her heart rate or polluted her resolve. Judge Samara made an address containing the words "grave," and "gravity," and "*graveman*," and, though she despised him no less for it, Giselle Meany was exalted when he intoned the lyrical old legalisms. "The state," the judge finally said, "can commence with its voir dire."

Hoot Meyer's bearing was that of the quickest chicken at the cockfight, but he had taught himself a passably friendly manner, and, adopting this, he stood and introduced himself to the jury pool as the county attorney. He mentioned the judge's name again and the length of the man's storied career, and then to take full possession of the room, and out of a standard courtesy, he introduced Giselle Meany and her client. He referred to Henry Brusett as the defendant, another customary designation, but one that in this case did not come handily into his mouth.

Hoot Meyers would never in his life look upon or think upon Henry Brusett without seeing the big-eyed boy forever running the perimeter of Mrs. Callahan's playground, a faint and hopeful smile for his schoolmates, the kid who could not quite make himself join in. Henry was as timid as ever, and ravaged, and draped in some kind of fat man's clown suit they'd got him to wear, but here he was, against all odds and as luck would have it the only citizen in the county to whom Meyers owed any specific loyalty. Meyers had signed onto many mortgages in his time but was rarely otherwise burdened. He had conducted himself with a bright zeal about owing no favors, and the last thing he had expected so late in an essentially honorable career was to find himself caught out this way, indebted, compromised. He was so far from knowing what he was about that on the thinnest of evidence he'd charged a man—a man whom he knew to be gentle—for murder, and the defendant stood accused primarily by his silence, a silence Meyers himself had recommended and upon which he continued to rely.

Hoot Meyers had long wished to let more light and air into his being—instead of this bramble of subtleties.

"We have to ask you some questions," he threatened, "because we have to make sure we seat twelve fair-minded people in that jury box. Completely fair-minded. So I'll need to ask you some things, and some of them may get a little personal—information that usually wouldn't be any of my business." Meyers knew at this moment that the fix was in, he found himself doing it—there was no poorer trial craft than to scare your jury with the first words from your mouth. With questions blunt and numerous, he'd have many chances to make them uneasy about him even before he'd even started to argue his weedy little case, and with startling and disappointing ease, the winning tricks and instincts could be reversed; he'd been naive to worry that he couldn't botch a prosecution as necessary. Nervous jurors. They sat very erect on the benches, their chins traveled up, their chins traveled down, all with equal misgiving.

"So, to start—do any of you know Mr. Brusett here, or know about him? I only want a show of hands."

Jurors fourteen and forty-four raised their hands, Muriel Crown and Brick McQuiston.

"And how is it you happen to know him, Ms. Crown?"

"You know how. Same way I know you. Same way I know about everybody." For many years now she had worked the counter during supper shift at Auntie Belle's Family Diner. She wore an amethyst choker, cut the widest wedges of pie, and tenderly called every male she served "mister."

"I know," said Meyers, "but why don't you go ahead and let everybody else in on it, too."

"Well, I mean, I didn't know him *that* good. I'm a waitress. He was a customer, or used to be. Not lately. It's been a while back since he came in."

"Anything about that, what you do know of him, that would prevent you from looking at the evidence impartially?"

Ms. Crown, accustomed to coo at distracted diners, had little experience of having her opinions, her wisdom sought this way, and it was something exhilarating. "He was a quiet guy," she considered. "Real quiet. And he never left me less than fifteen percent. That's all I could say for sure."

"He's not charged with being cheap." Meyers, with his desire to fail, was liberated from all but the most formal courtesies; surely he'd get his jury chosen by noon. It was good to finally be on his feet, working. "Is there anything you know about Mr. Brusett that would prevent you from looking at the evidence and hearing this testimony impartially? Can you be fair? Fair to both sides? That's all we need to know."

Ms. Crown desired very much to do her duty. "I think I'd be real fair. Only thing I got is my common sense, but I've got that. Might as well try and put it to good use for once."

Meyers only looked at Mr. McQuiston, a man of middle age with a dewlap and slight, oddly square shoulders, and McQuiston volunteered all in a rush that he was a millwright, or had been until recently, and that he knew Henry Brusett from "around," and that as far as he was concerned, the whole damned thing was a scam. Meyers cut him off before he could explain his theory, and asked that he be excused for cause. The jury pool was reduced to sixty-one.

For an hour then he was at them, probing every sinkhole of their memories for traces of unacknowledged bias, unmentioned debility, and in the name of thoroughness, Meyers was at them until he was very sure he saw their faces calcify in resentment. Some admitted to prior acquaintance with certain officers of the court, some of them also admitted to having strong feelings on account of it. Some admitted to intolerance for the law itself, an abiding mistrust. A felon was excused from duty, a nursing mother, a gentleman with a bad back, a gentleman with bad hearing. There were the usual clever ones who thought to cite some arcane or invented prejudice to get themselves released back to their own business. " . . . and she was my little cousin, and they never caught the guy, so now, I think it would be just about impossible for me to let somebody off on a deal like this. I just wouldn't risk it. Somebody getting away."

When at last Meyers sat down, there were forty-eight jurors left in the pool, and Judge Samara mercifully called the trial's first recess, after which Giselle Meany went to work on them, and where it had been restless before, the jury pool nearly revolted under her new line of questioning which was couched, as near as anyone could tell, in algebraic terms. "Now as we examine . . . you are Mr. . . . . Hellbron? Well, Mr. Hellbron, have you ever stopped to think why it is that innocence must come before guilt in our system of justice? And, more than that, do you think that guilt can ever be any kind of absolute?"

"Have I? Probably . . . what was that again?"

Even Ms. Meany knew that she wasn't going over well, and that she'd not be learning anything more about them nor teaching them anything more of Anglo-American jurisprudence, and so she soon let them alone, and then there was the ceremony of passing the jury pool for cause by which it was agreed that those left had not exhibited or admitted any unacceptable taint. Then there was a longer rite, a more secretive and medieval shuffling of notes from attorneys through the bailiff to the judge, and back again, and a dozen more jurors were excused, two by two, on peremptory challenges, excused on lawyer's whims or for no reason at all, most often to their great relief, but finally twelve had been selected, and an alternate, and when they'd taken their places in the jury box and had their half hour of Judge Samara's preliminary jury instructions, every one of them regretted to be among the chosen.

Henry Brusett, five weeks without the pills, was finding it nearly impossible to sit so long in one posture, in a hardback chair, and he was mortified to be the wretch who was putting everyone to so much bother, and the routine they so elaborately followed for his protection was often inscrutable, always tedious to him, and so he concentrated on holding himself together as some semblance of a man. When at one o'clock the judge finally called for a forty-five minute lunch, Henry was returned to the barracks cell, and there he passed the time writhing, stretching, breathing deep. His mind was very clear—no consolation. Nat told him he looked sharp, that a fresh shave really went a long way toward sprucing him up. The bars were painted that baby blue, as they had always been.

Giselle Meany sat in her idling Subaru with the world news from the BBC and a tuna fish sandwich that was not half as much as she found she wanted to eat, and she told herself in various ways that things were going well for the defense. That was a jury, she thought, with a strain of sweet rationality running through it. Simplicity, she reminded herself, was the soul of elegance, and elegance a function of truth. She must somehow keep things simple.

The county attorney, who could not afford to let other crises stack up while he was at trial, took some calls. There was a conflict of police authority in Elisis with a tribal cop, a city cop, and a sheriff's deputy who had somehow convinced one another that a certain Canadian had immunity to fistfight on Main Street. No one could see where they had clear jurisdiction to interfere. There was a conference call. "If he hurts somebody," Meyers told them, "arrest him. What do you think, it's an international incident? If he's outta hand, run him in. How many different ways can you guys dream up to not do your damn job? Same goes for a Mexican or a Mongolian or Hmong, or whathaveyou. When they're here, they're under our law."

There was also a dog bite in the western end.

"You do not mess with somebody's Achilles tendon," the victim was saying. "Doc says the vicious bitch could've crippled me. Then what, huh? And these people, these Billingsleys, they seem to have her throw a new litter every six months or so, and now it's got to where it's just about intolerable around here anymore." Perhaps. Meyers sucked on oat and molasses pellets originally rolled as horse feed; he made only such sounds as he needed to make into the phone.

At last he allowed himself five quiet minutes of green tea in a translucent cup, and he calculated that his old friend Henry Brusett, his very old conscience, should not be more than two days from freedom, or from as much of it as any man with a past can enjoy. The day's central chore was done for Meyers—he'd got the right jury for his purpose.

There were at least two of them in the box, he thought, who could be counted on to vote down almost any proposition the county

attorney might care to advance. Mrs. Larson, for all Meyers's probing, had never mentioned how he'd kept her son on probation for five
years, and how poor Jimmy had been in constant trouble with so much
official intrusion into his life. Meyers remembered seeing her at nearly
all the boy's hearings. The woman would surely loathe him for pros-
ecuting her boy—he knew a mother's heart, a certain kind of mother,
and she'd avenge herself the moment God showed her how. There was
also Connor Shrenk, now juror number six, who had just a year earlier lost a right-of-way and with it some business in a dispute with the
county commissioners. This trouble had a face for Shrenk, and that
face was Meyers's. "No," he'd said when asked, "no, I mean, I do
know you from before, from another thing, but that wouldn't have
anything to do with this. Would it? It really couldn't have, could it?"

One of these two, or at least someone of the twelve, must certainly
see that he had no case. That was the saving thing, the particularly odd
thing about it: He had no case. Hoot Meyers came into court just thirty
seconds before Judge Samara gaveled them into session, and the county
attorney began the afternoon by waiving his opening statement.

"Ms. Meany? Do you wish to waive also?"

"I . . . *no.*" She was not in rhythm. It was the county attorney's
style to punch and punch, and it was unprecedented for him to forgo
the first punch. Giselle's own opening was scripted, but she'd written
it to refute what she'd expected Meyers to say. It would sound ridiculous now that he'd said nothing. She made her way before the jury,
suddenly ponderous, an old-time, orotund orator, buying that extra
moment to improvise. "This," she ultimately said, "is the part of the
trial, ladies and gentlemen, where both sides summarize the evidence
as they see it." Why did her voice always quake? A mangled face and
stage fright, what was she doing in a public line of work? "Either
way, on either side, as you'll see, there's not much evidence to talk
about in this case. The evidence the state will show you in support of

this very, very serious charge is a stained pair of dungarees. And that is all. And . . . I believe they're called 'dungarees.' But, that's it. That's all, and I am very confident that in my closing statement I'll be able to talk to you again, and marvel with you at how anyone would ever be so . . . carried away, so carried away that they'd ask you to make such a terrible assumption based on about a scintilla of evidence." She saw their eyes glazing. Keep far, she told herself, far from the conceptual, and she sat down.

Hoot Meyers called young Deputy Lovell as his first witness, and from the moment he took his oath, Lovell was unable to tear his vigilant eyes from that part of the gallery containing the press corps. He'd worn his body armor for the occasion, a very brown tie, and his hair and scalp glistened with gel. Meyers had coached him on his performance to the extent of telling him to keep his answers short and direct, but Lovell had some trouble with this as he came to the juicier parts of his testimony.

"I knew the subject was deceased the minute I saw him, but just to be sure I checked for a pulse, and there wasn't any, and you could see he was nonresponsive, completely nonresponsive, and that's what you're trained to look for, the eyes don't respond to light, so we knew he was dead."

"Deputy Lovell, let's just take it one thing at a time."

Taken one thing at time, there wasn't much to relate. His time of arrival. Who he'd found, where he'd found them, what their condition had been. The blood, its amount, its location. What, if anything, they'd said to him. Meyers had got as much as he wanted from Deputy Lovell in under twenty minutes. Already disappointed, the deputy was crushed when the public defender said she did not wish to cross-examine him at this time. The county attorney hadn't asked a single question about the separate investigation he'd done, his discovery of the victim's car, his early discovery of the kid's identity. *Why*, Lovell wondered, *wouldn't they be interested in that? Why was recognition always slinking around the corner whenever he approached?* Though he'd been on the stand very briefly, Lovell's hair gel had begun to slide down all points of the compass, trickling down his head, and even if the dignity and hope he'd brought into the courtroom with him were gone, he sat at attention until the very end of his testimony.

Meyers then called Detective Flaherty, who came to the stand with an unauthorized campaign hat tucked under his arm, the regulation Kevlar and nylon ensemble, and he wore on his chest a good-conduct ribbon, also unauthorized. Meyers walked him through his name, his job description, his length of service with the sheriff's office, and he then referred him back to a certain night in August.

"Were you on duty that night, Detective Flaherty?"

"They paged me."

"At what time did you make it to the Brusetts' place?"

"Twenty-three thirty-nine hours."

"Civilian time," Meyers suggested.

"Eleven thirty-nine PM."

"Who else was there when you arrived?"

"The subject," said Flaherty. "There, we had the subject, and . . . "

"The subject of what?"

"I mean the victim. He was there. Obviously. Then Mr. Brusett. Deputy Lovell, Deputy Sisson, Mrs. Brusett. The medical people, the EMTs, I guess there were three of them, with the driver."

"Who, if anyone, did you speak with when you got there?"

"Well, the deputies. One of the ambulance people. I think he was the one who looked Mr. Brusett over. The way he was acting, because of the blood on him we didn't know. It was hard at first to see who was hurt. But he wasn't. We finally figured out he was fine. Mr. Brusett. But he was still acting funny."

"Tell the jury what you mean by 'funny.'"

"Well, he just wouldn't, he was kind of staring off into . . . Maybe it wasn't so . . . because it was a little bit like now. How he looks now. Sorry, Mr. Brusett, but . . . "

"He looked like this?"

"But worse," said the detective. "I'd say he looked quite a bit worse than this. In some ways. But there was nothing wrong with him. That EMT really did a nice job of looking him over, and there wasn't anything wrong with him. Getting that sorted out was, well, we prioritized that so it was our first thing we did."

Flaherty spoke of examining the body of the victim as well, and this he'd done personally but not for very long. The light and the environment were so poor, and the cause of death so obvious.

"What did you do after you'd looked the victim over?"

"That's when I first tried talking to Mr. and Mrs. Brusett."

"What, if anything, did you learn from them at that time?"

"Their names. I think that was about it. Out there, that's all they told us. I think she mentioned they were married. That was it, though. Mr. Brusett didn't say a word one way or the other about anything."

Meyers showed the detective a pair of Can't Bust 'Em overalls bundled in a plastic bag, within a grocery sack. He showed him the evidence tag. "Identify this item, please, Detective Flaherty."

"That's his coveralls. Mr. Brusett's coveralls that he was wearing that night. We got a good chain of custody on that. Hasn't been out of the bag except one time since I put it in there, but you can see right there on the log where I signed it over to the lab, and the lab signed it back to me. Because we had it checked to make sure it was the victim's blood, even though it was. Well, that was pretty obvious, too."

Meyers had the coveralls admitted into evidence, and then he removed them from the paper and the plastic bags, and he held them up so that Flaherty and the jury could see the chocolaty stain on the bib and in the lap of them. "Is this what it looked like before Mr. Brusett took it off?"

"Yeah, that stain was a lighter color then, but otherwise, yeah, the same. His shirt was bloody, too, and we had that, but it got misplaced." As a result of uncorrected eyesight, the detective's neck was crooked as a turtle's.

"What, if anything, did you find by way of physical evidence that might have explained what had happened to Mr. Teague?"

"Well, we didn't know he was Mr. Teague yet."

"All right. Did you find anything that might explain how the victim became a victim?"

"Objection," said counsel for the defense. Giselle had been so long without speaking that her voice broke as she raised it. "Counsel keeps referring to a victim, when the state has done nothing to establish that Mr. Teague was in fact a victim. Facts not in evidence."

"Withdrawn," Meyers volunteered. "I'll rephrase the question. I'll rephrase it so *everyone* is happy. Detective, was there on or about the person of the deceased anything that might suggest how the deceased became deceased?"

"You mean physical evidence?"

"That's what I mean."

"No. There wasn't any."

"No?" Meyers needed convincing.

"Well, they were both wet. Mr. Brusett and the, uh . . . young man. Water and blood. More water on the body, more blood on Mr. Brusett, even though, you know, it wasn't him who'd been bleeding. We found 'em wet and bloody, I can tell you. Tell you that much." Detective Flaherty had been Meyers's witness nearly a hundred times, and he hadn't learned a thing by it, and getting anything out of him by direct examination was very much harder than it should have been.

But Meyers didn't want much from him today. Today the dull detective was a jewel for his purposes.

"What, if anything, did you do after you completed your investigation at the Brusetts'?"

"We transported the suspects to town. The Law and Order Complex. Gave 'em a chance to relax a little, see if they'd open up to us. But they didn't." Flaherty wore a hat of some kind everywhere except for church and for these unfulfilling trips to the witness stand; he longed to have his hat on his head.

"Are you telling the court you questioned them?"

"You could call it that," said Flaherty.

"What would you call it?"

"Where you ask questions but the people don't answer. We thought they wanted to cooperate at first. They didn't. We had some one-sided conversations, put it that way. They didn't want to say anything."

"What did you do next?"

"Next?"

"The next step of your investigation."

"Oh, uhm, well, we found out who he was. The deceased person. Got a positive identification on him. Calvin Teague. Found out he was from Iowa."

"What else?"

"Objection," croaked the public defender. "Leading."

"Ms. Meany," said the judge, "I'm inclined to give some latitude on this, otherwise we'll never get through it."

"We're through it now," said Meyers. "Or my part of it. I've got nothing more for this witness at this time. Pass to the defense."

She had written her sequence of questions for Deputy Flaherty on a short stack of recipe cards that she now chose not to use. Giselle cleared her throat, rose, and she felt wonderfully exposed, standing where she stood. Counsel for the defense. "Detective Flaherty, how many shoes was the body wearing when you first examined it?"

"One."

"One shoe? To your knowledge, was the other shoe ever located?"

"Not that I know of. That would be a low priority."

"Would it? You say the young man was wet, you mentioned water. Do you know how he got wet?"

"Not for absolute sure, but they were just outside this shower stall they had rigged up, an outdoor shower. Just outside the door of that. His clothes were wet."

"Were the clothes drenched? Soaking wet? How wet were they?"

"Does it . . . I don't remember exactly. Not real wet. Damp?"

"Where were you able to locate blood?"

"Fair amount of it on Mr. Brusett, like I said, and some of it on the vic . . . just there on the back of the deceased person's head."

"Was there a lot of it?"

"Depends on what you mean by 'a lot.' There was enough, I guess."

"Any blood on the ground?"

"Not that I could see in the dark."

"Any blood in the shower house?"

"It would have got washed away if there was."

"Any blood splatter anywhere?"

"I didn't find any, but . . . okay, you could say there was not a lot of blood. Just what was on those two guys. But, you know, he didn't bleed to death, I don't think."

"Now, in your investigation you must have looked for signs of a struggle."

"Sure."

"And according to your report . . . "

"I didn't find any."

"Did you look for a weapon?"

"We did. But you have to understand, they're up there in the middle of a forest. Weapon's pretty easy to hide up there; you could hide a tank."

"You looked for a weapon?"

"Yes."

"Did you find one?"

"No."

"You took statements?"

"I tried to. Didn't get any. That's not my . . . "

"No statements were given?"

"No."

"So, based on your investigation, you arrested Mr. Brusett at the scene on the charge of deliberate homicide?"

"No, I didn't. But I did transport him down to Law and Order."

"Where you arrested him on the charge of deliberate homicide?"

"No. I called the sheriff. He thought we should . . . complete the investigation first. Before we filed."

"So you completed the investigation?"

"Yeah. Yes."

"And in your ongoing investigation, what more did you learn about the case that you didn't know that night?"

"What do you mean?"

"You let Mr. Brusett go that night with no charges. Correct?"

"Correct."

"You continued your investigation?"

"Correct."

"What more did you find out?"

"Who the young man was. We got his identity figured out."

"And now that you had the name of the deceased, you thought you had enough evidence to go forward with a charge against my client?"

"That wasn't my decision," said Flaherty. There was a flesh tab on his nose about where he might have pierced it had he been a girl.

"You could have charged him with deliberate homicide at the scene. That's within your authority, isn't it?"

"It is. But there are times when you don't work it that way."

"You could have charged him with deliberate homicide at the Law and Order Complex, if you had chosen to do so?"

"I talked to the sheriff."

"And the sheriff told you not to charge him?"

"Not charge him at that time. I wasn't supposed to charge him yet."

"Why?"

"As I said, ma'am, to complete the investigation."

"Then, because the body was identified, you felt you had enough evidence to charge Mr. Brusett with a crime?"

"I didn't. As I say, they took that decision out of my hands real early."

"You were the lead investigator on this case, Deputy Flaherty?"

"I was. I always am if it's anything very serious around here."

"And, as the lead investigator, you did not at any point choose to charge Henry Brusett with any crime?"

"No," he said.

It had been too easy, gone too well. She told herself to stop now. "Defense has no further questions for the officer at this time."

Hoot Meyers declined to redirect.

There was a small chance, a wild hope that he might present the whole of the state's case before five o'clock. Meyers called the medical examiner to the stand, elicited Dr. Fitzroy's credentials and a brief description of his arrangement with Conrad County, a county whose curious deaths were not yet sufficient in number to warrant a full time ME. He was summoned as necessary from Kalispell. And, yes, following the aforementioned night in August, he'd examined the decedent.

"Dr. Fitzroy, in the simplest possible terms, what caused Calvin Teague to die?"

"Blunt force trauma to a site bordering the parietal and occipital zones, which in turn caused the brain to swell, probably quite rapidly. A severe concussion."

"Would it be accurate to describe it in layman's terms as a blow to the back of the head?"

"Yes. Not the very back, but yes, that's essentially it. The swelling starts at the site of the blow, but becomes general at times, as it did here, and when it involves the brainstem even peripherally, then autonomic function ceases and mortality occurs very quickly."

"Is it at all possible that this young man bled to death?"

"No. A scalp laceration can bleed quite a lot, but here the injury occurred in . . . The blow occurred where the young man's hair was quite thick, and the injury to his flesh was minimal, a fairly slight lesion. Then, too, the heart would have ceased pumping very soon after the blow was delivered. It was probably more like a steady leak than any serious bleeding."

Mrs. Teague moaned and buried her face in her husband's chest.

"How much force," Meyers asked, "does it take to cause the kind of concussion you observed in Mr. Teague?"

"The force of the actual blow is just one factor. But you find it doesn't take a lot in some cases. The brain can be a very willful organ, and very fragile; it survives impossible injuries at times, and at times succumbs to fairly slight ones."

"In short, though, a blow caused this death? A blow to the back of this young man's head?"

"Yes."

"The state has nothing more at this time."

Giselle Meany's whole urinary tract felt heavy and hot. She'd been trying to keep her voice lubricated by drinking water. She'd devised her line of interrogation for the doctor just two nights before, and her notes were essential; notes spread in front of her on the counsel table, a client indifferent at her side. "Dr. Fitzroy, how many head injuries would you estimate you've seen as a medical examiner and as a practicing physician?"

"There are probably ways I could assemble those numbers, but . . . a thousand. It would be very safe to say I've seen a thousand such injuries. More of them in my living patients, of course, but it's quite a common cause of death in forensic practice as well."

"Were these all homicides or attempted homicides, these head injuries you've seen?"

"No," said Fitzroy dismissively.

"What percent of these injuries, then, were from blows inflicted by other people?"

"Percent? I couldn't begin to estimate without an extensive review of my records."

"Is it more than half?" she asked.

"No. By no means."

"People injure their heads falling down?"

"Yes."

"Things fall on their heads? They're thrown from moving vehicles and animals?"

"Yes, and . . . yes. It's a vulnerable part of the anatomy, of course."

"There are many possible sources of blunt force trauma, aren't there, Dr. Fitzroy?"

"Yes."

"Would it be fair to say that the thousand head injuries you've seen have occurred in at least a hundred different ways?"

"Again, you're asking me to . . . "

"Merely asking you to summarize your experience."

"Heads are vulnerable. They are damaged in any number of ways, as is true of all physical injury to any part of the body."

"Anything can happen?"

"It often seems that way."

"Now, around the wound, such as it was, this small lesion you mentioned, what did you find? Was there any residue of any kind?"

"A certain amount of dried blood. I found no traces of anything extraneous, but there had been bleeding, which tends to flush away debris, and you have to understand that our budget is very . . . "

"No residue?"

"None that I could see."

"Nothing to tell you exactly what came into contact with this young man's head?"

"No. As was made clear in my report, I had no idea about that. Perhaps with better . . . "

"Dr. Fitzroy, apart from the fatal injury, what was the condition of the body?"

"There were some first-degree burns, sunburn undoubtedly, on his nose and the tops of his ears, very common among pale-complected people. Extensive anterior bruising. Bruises on his back, the backs of his legs, his buttocks, one heel. The state of lividity of these injuries would indicate they came about at some point preceding his time of death."

"What would have caused all these bruises?"

"As you yourself have established," Dr. Fitzroy exulted, "it may have been anything."

"But you don't know what caused the bruises?"

"No."

"You cannot determine exactly what caused any of the injuries you observed on the deceased?"

"No. But the most probable . . . "

"Thank you," said Giselle, "but we can't indulge in speculation here, doctor." She could not remember having been happier. "Nothing further at this time, Your Honor."

Hoot Meyers once again declined to redirect. He was attempting to have the bailiff call the state's final witness when Judge Samara intervened, "The court hasn't given you leave, Mr. Meyers, to call that witness, and the court does not intend to. Not today." The judge then continued, silently, to look upon Meyers, and he looked upon him long enough for nearly everyone to guess there must be some significance in it, and then he addressed the jury. "I'm going to call it a day for you folks. You'll not be sequestered, which means I'm trusting you to go home tonight and not talk about what you've seen and heard here today with anyone, not even among yourselves. We've got the television people and the newspaper people here, and you'll have to leave it up to them to do the reporting. If you were to have any improper contact with someone, anyone, before we reach a verdict, then you could scotch the whole thing, and we'd have to start all over again. I'll warn you now, that's expensive, and you can be required to pay for it if I find that it was your fault. It does not appear that this is going to be a very long trial, and the court expects that the case will be in your hands some time tomorrow. In the meantime, go home, have a barbecue if it isn't too chilly, or do something that takes your minds off it, so you can start fresh tomorrow. We'll need you back here not a second later than nine o'clock tomorrow morning."

The jury filed out, but before Judge Samara closed session he said, "Ms. Meany, I'll see you and your client and the county attorney in my chambers."

This was the pinhole, Giselle feared. Now something was happening to her seamless defense. She knew it had gone too well. While she'd been enjoying herself so much, something had gotten by her. What had put the judge in his snit?

In half the judge's chambers, a room fit for storage, sat Judge Samara behind his completely empty desk, and into the other half of it were squeezed the clerk of court, the court reporter, Henry Brusett and Tubby Ginnings, and Hoot Meyers and Giselle, and a climate developed at once among them as on the airless floor of a rain forest. Things had been going far too well, Giselle thought. Judge Samara's self-regard was such a large and unchartable territory that it was impossible to anticipate how and where he might take offense, and he was pursing his lips, waiting for the court reporter to set up again, and Giselle awaited trouble.

"This is District Judge Carbon Samara," he said when the court reporter gave him the nod, "in closed session, and stating: On September 2 of this year, I gave the Conrad county attorney leave to file an Information in the instant case, the State of Montana versus Henry Brusett. In so doing, I found and affirmed that there was probable cause to go forward with a charge of deliberate homicide against Mr. Brusett, a homicide alleged to have been committed on the person of one Calvin Teague. The court wishes to make a distinction at this time. The court may, when considering whether probable cause has been established, take into account the suspect's silence. When I permitted the county attorney to file these charges, it was my understanding that he would be supplementing his case in some way sufficient so that he might reasonably hope to prevail at trial where Mr. Brusett's silence could not be used against him. I placed my trust, perhaps unwisely, in the county attorney's experience and judgment to build a case he could conscientiously bring to trial."

He nodded to the court reporter, who raised her eyebrows and let her machine stand idle as she left the judge's chambers, followed by the clerk of court.

"Hoot," said Judge Samara when they had gone, "I know what you're doing in there. You arranged all this just to publicly humiliate your sheriff's department? Maybe they deserve it, it's not exactly a crack unit, I'll agree. But this is not the place for it. You don't educate these clodhoppers in my courtroom. It seems to me you're trying to descend to their level. This is just so half-assed it's embarrassing. I'm embarrassed."

"It happens," said Meyers. "Embarrassment. Probably good for the soul."

"What?"

"Humility, huh?"

"No," said the judge. "No thanks. I drive a hundred miles each way, every day you drag me down to this . . . On or off the record, Mr. County Attorney, you're still subject to contempt of court. I'm letting you know something right now—if you don't get something very solid out of the one witness you've got left tomorrow, then there's a good chance that I'd rule favorably on a motion by Giselle for a directed verdict. You haven't established a prima facie case so far, and from where I'm sitting, it doesn't appear that you even tried. If I make such a ruling, Hoot, I'm considering sanctions against your office. I may just have you pay for this little boondoggle out of your budget. If this proves to be a complete waste of time, the county attorney's office may be paying for it."

"You'd be a long time collecting," said Meyers. "I guess you could get it out of my salary. Unless I quit."

"Before you get yourself into some kind of contempt that causes a mistrial here, Mr. Meyers, I'm going to wrap this up. I will grant you this much: We must be going at some kind of record pace for a murder trail—but it's embarrassing. This has been, and I'll say it in Mr. Brusett's presence, a damn poor showing. Just a friendly word of advice to a fellow member of the bar, Hoot: Get some counseling if you need it. You're not yourself."

"Well, let's hope not."

·24·

SHE WAS FINALLY able to meet with her client again. They'd been given ten minutes alone together in the jury room, the room where she'd first talked to him and where she'd stumbled into her unshakable faith. This time, though, they stood near the windowed wall, and this time the larch were turning on the mountains. In all the year, this was the hour, the day, the month when the light would be most filled with longing, and she meant to hold on to this moment for a very long time. "Well, you mule-headed old . . . guy. This looks like it might be turning out pretty well, after all. Doesn't it? Don't get me wrong, it's been a very precarious ride, but one thing about it, if you win one, really win one, then it's over. Your guy just walks away, and it's over. But I'd have a win. Man, you cannot know what this means. How do you feel, Henry? Did you understand that in there? Know what the judge was saying?"

"Fine," said Henry, distracted. His wife was down on the tawny grass, strolling the courthouse lawn.

"Henry, Henry, I think we may have this thing just about won. It'll come down to Karen now, and she tells me she's not giving them anything. She's always given me the impression that she doesn't intend to help them. And they need a lot of help. Ooh, Henry, if I'm not very much mistaken, I think you're good to go. Almost. Acquitted. What would you think about that?"

"I'm glad you're happy. So what would she have to do, just sit there?"

"About that, yeah, and unless I'm mistaken, that's exactly what she intends to do."

"Can she get in trouble doing that?"

"Conceivably, but I don't think so. I really don't think she will. There's a few charges they could threaten, but that wouldn't get anything out of her. Come on, Henry, you should be happy too, the judge as good as told us. I think by lunch tomorrow . . . You may owe me lunch, buddy. I may even let you buy me a drink. What do you say?"

"You did real good in there. But I wouldn't put too much stock in anything that judge says. He talks, but he hardly says anything if he can help it."

"Sure, he's an asshole, but he's our asshole now." Giselle was dancing—she thought it might be the twist or the pony. "If he wants to be on my side for once, let him. Whoop-ee." And Giselle had a long moment where she forgot she was inadequate. Mrs. Brusett walked below with her hands at the small of her back, pacing a tight circuit on the broad grounds, her head bent. "Shit," said Giselle. "Shit, shit, shit. She wanted me to tell you that she'd been excluded from the courtroom. Which was actually my doing. I made a motion to exclude, which is standard, and I hadn't even thought about it, but it kept her out of court until after she'd testified, and since she's testifying last— she told me to explain why she wasn't there, and I forgot. She told me to be sure, and I forgot. I just got so wrapped up in everything else, doing everything else, I'm so sorry. I hope you didn't think she'd . . . I usually get so flustered, but for the most part, not so much today. Today I was pretty good, I think."

"You were good," he said.

"You don't have to keep saying it."

"No, you were real good. Couldn't have asked for better. Thanks. But we better not make Tubby late for his supper; there'd be your crime against nature. Sure, you did great."

"You've been worth it, Henry. I know you are."

With a flourish she turned him over to his cousin waiting outside the jury room door, and Tubby hustled him down the stairs and out the door of the courthouse, where Karen saw them and began to jog across the lawn toward them.

"Whoa," Tubby called to her, "hey, whoa there. Things are goin' good. Better not screw it up now. It's still not over, and you're still a witness. I just do not want to screw things up for you guys, so you better not try talkin' to him. Tomorrow. Tomorrow he's all yours again, I bet. Tomorrow he'll be home."

She stood on the lawn in her slacks, and in a tailored jacket with quaking fringe, something new and sporty she'd got, and she watched Henry Brusett make his short passage to the jail; she put her right fist on her heart and lay her other hand over that, and she mouthed, "I love you," and for once he understood her.

"You got somethin' goin' with women," said Tubby when they were safely inside. "Boy, I'd sure like to have your secret, cuz. What is it? Is it 'cause you're such an outlaw? I've never got anywhere near that kinda loyalty out of 'em. You can just wear this same outfit tonight, Henry. How was I supposed to get around to washing your jumpsuit? You'd just have to change into it for court tomorrow, anyway. Now I'm here all night, you know that? Again. I never, never get a break anymore, I might as well commit a crime myself, much as I'm here. Tomorrow you walk, and I'll be . . . at work, man. Goddamn, win the ladies over, that's how it's done, huh? That's how you get over. Oh, no. No, no, no. You smell that? It's that make-believe meatloaf again. Man, I am tired. Tired. Oh, you better give me that pencil before we go back."

"There's a half-dozen pencils back there, Tubby."

"Yeah, but they're all those carpenter's pencils, those stubby little deals. Can't be used for weapons. This number two you got, you could really poke somebody with that thing. I'm not sayin' you, but once it's back there, there's no tellin'. No weapons, that's my jail. Not if I can help it. See my point? My point. Ha. Ha. Ha. Henry, you got one more day left, and then maybe you'll get out there and run into somebody with a real sense of humor. But that meatloaf, man, how could I even be funny? Knowing? How'm I supposed to?"

Henry Brusett was no more enthusiastic for the meal than anyone else, but he felt he had to have it. For strength.

At dinner, Tubby passed word of Henry's almost-certain good fortune and his imminent release, and upon hearing the news, Leonard said that he was tired, at any rate, of being limp and wasted, and he grinned in his limp and wasted way at Nat, a grin to signal the coming end of the moratorium, to say that they had months before them to share with no further interference. That special intimacy. Nat wept.

Leonard napped again after supper; he'd been napping twenty hours a day, stupefied for the remaining four, and even when Tubby had finally understood what was going on, he'd never thought to challenge it. Life had for these few weeks been so much easier with the big man well drugged. The barracks cell was no more volatile than a hospital room while Leonard was napping, and Tubby had agreed with himself to take whatever help, whatever peace came his way. He was so shorthanded. Tubby cleared the supper dishes and took them into the kitchen and washed them, and then he threw a spare mattress on the floor of the laundry room and went to sleep on it. If he dreamed, he would not later remember those dreams.

There were just the three prisoners in the barracks cell that night.

Leonard napped on a top bunk. Nat watched television, a game show, and the cheat devised a routine where he spoke the answer even as the host was speaking it, so that he could pretend he'd thought of it just in time. Nat briefly forgot his troubles. He said he'd be winning tens, maybe hundreds of thousands if he ever got on that show, and the first thing he'd do was try and get his mother's car out of the impound lot. He'd buy some insurance and some savings bonds, and he'd start being a lot more cautious about the company he kept. He had some ideas about turning things around. The excitement of the game show seemed to put these ideas within reach. The South American country named for an Italian? "Ur-uhhh . . . Co-lombia." Nat could almost feel the host placing the key to the next door in the palm of his slightly sweaty hand. *This* would be a good night for him, a pleasant little night tonight. Tomorrow . . . He'd think about tomorrow tomorrow, if then.

Henry Brusett had accumulated so much correspondence from his wife that at some point it was no longer convenient to keep the bundle under his mattress. A grocery sack stood half full at the head of his bunk, and this too was defeating all practicality. She'd put her best and bravest thoughts on many kinds of paper for him—and the letters had piled up. But how deep would be the pile of her misgivings, the thoughts she hadn't sent? He had never supposed he deserved her. There were particular letters that he kept apart in a separate packet, and these he continued to read every night, long after they'd laid claim to his memory.

Dear Henry,

There is a little clearing not far up the hill from our place. I have been in it before a few times but not at night. At night and I don't know why this would be so you can see the stars a lot better from there.

and

Dear Henry,

Remember when you told me that Triumph would always be trouble. It has been a great car and it still is a great car. This is a great car even if it won't go very fast. It has always got me everywhere I wanted to go.

and

Dear Henry,

You were the nicest man when I met you. You were always such a nice surprise to me through the years.

Henry read these and returned them to the sack with the others. He rolled the sack closed at the top, and he propped it at the foot of his bunk. With his blankets he closed himself off for a time and listened to Nat listening to the television and to Leonard's mumbling progress through his long, troubled, artificial sleep. Henry Brusett tried to make his way in his mind up a mountainside, to the side of a bursting creek; he tried to think of himself with any kind of tool in hand, tried to recall the scent of dawn, but he could not for all his wanting it, needing it, bring any of that back. Once he'd had a purpose, and he'd fit that purpose, and that had been his luck. His memory worked best, though, when he was remembering where he'd been wrong. Henry opened the sack with the letters again, but withdrew from it only his glasses. He rolled the sack very tightly then and set it again at the head of his bunk. He popped the lenses out of the glasses. It was a long while since he'd asked much of his thumbs, and it pleased him to see they were still strong. Having decided the lenses were not worth trying to sharpen, he slipped them in his pocket.

There was a camera aimed at the picnic table, and a camera for every corner of the barracks cell, and one for every other cell in the jail, but prisoners here came to know very quickly that these were blind, that no one was watching. There had been a budget shortfall many years earlier, and since then no one had been watching, and though the eternally-lit jail had originally come about because of the cameras, when the cameras blinked out, the lights stayed on. A policy had been established. Prisoners here would live under forty-watt bulbs, and if they wanted the comfort of darkness, they could get it behind their blankets, or they could close their eyes.

Henry Brusett placed his glasses on the floor and crushed the heavy wire frame beneath his heel. He rolled the resulting tangle ninety degrees on the floor, and he crushed it again. He twisted the earpieces away from the mangled frame, and then twisted them back onto it, reinforcing the weak center, the nose piece. There was a badly welded gusset plate in the picnic table, and a gap forming a small V, and using this as a vice, Henry twisted tight his crudely braided wire and brought the whole assembly to a sharp, barbed point. He'd made himself a dirk, but a short one.

"Remember her?" Nat said, talking equally to Henry Brusett and to the television. "Remember that girl? She always plays the ditz."

"Why don't you go lay down?" Henry told him.

"Lie down?"

"Yeah, if you don't mind."

"I'm . . . what is . . . what's that?"

"These things can cost up to twelve bucks apiece," Henry said, "even a half-decent pair. I had 'em laying around all over my house. But, yeah, you better lay down. Just for a little bit."

"I . . . well, whatever you say, Henry. You're the man tonight. But I thought maybe we'd stay up and, I don't know, 'reminisce' wouldn't be the right word, but . . . shoot the shit. I know you're not too social, but tonight of all nights, I'd like to share. How you must feel. You must feel like a million dollars. Like you've won everything back. Your good name, your freedom. Wow. Don't blame me if I envy you, man, especially under the, under the circumstances. I promise—no more crying, either. Not until you leave. Why bum you out?"

"Why don't you lay down? Get back in your bunk and lay down."

Nat could not recall him previously asking anyone for anything. "Sure, Henry, I guess I can . . . oh sure, if I turn like . . . I can watch about as well from right here. Quite comfortable. Chat with you, too. This is not too bad at . . . Henry," he said, "Henry," he said. "No."

Just over two inches of tangled wire came out of Henry Brusett's fist, all the blade he could make of it, and there were only just the few places where his tool might suffice. He struck at Leonard's neck, hoping for the big artery, but Leonard, sensitive above all things to the coming blow, turned from it as it fell, and the dirk lodged in a crease between two heavy sheaves of muscle, and then an adrenal gland like a rotten, bursting melon brought Leonard up off his bed and out of his long funk, and a single thrust of his heel broke three of Henry's ribs and drove him to the far wall where Leonard caught him, pinned him, pinned his arms to his sides and lifted him off his feet. "Hey wait a minute," said Nat from where he still lay. "Come on. Come on, you guys."

Leonard squeezed, and as he squeezed he rammed Henry's nose with his forehead, and Henry's nose became granular and soft and wet. He swallowed very fast so that he wouldn't drown in his own blood and snot. Leonard rammed him again, and Henry tasted his chalky teeth. He saw blood beginning to well around the mangled metal still jammed in Leonard's neck and, just when Henry Brusett's legs were at long last numb, he saw that Leonard was gathering himself for another effort, and so he seized the hideous dirk in his broken teeth, and he twisted and he pushed at it until a thrilling new pain shot through his teeth and a wet warmth surged onto him. Leonard shuddered.

They were on the floor. Leonard had dropped him.

Henry Brusett heard the rattling gasps and could not distinguish his own from Leonard's. He could not be very happy about it, but he no longer felt any pain at all.

Later, Nat would tell them that he had screamed and screamed and no one had come. Later, Nat would ask them to consider that if the county couldn't do a little more to ensure inmate safety, should the county be holding prisoners at all? He was sure he'd been yelling almost the whole time it was happening. It seemed like it had taken hours for them to go down, and he was pretty certain he must have yelled at hearing bone break, really loud, but no one came to help. Nat said that when they fell, they fell on their backs and lay parallel on the floor. He'd gotten off his bunk then and gone to them to see if anything might be done, and as he stood over them he felt Leonard's blood lap his naked toe, and he screamed, he knew for sure he'd screamed then, and still no one came, and that's when he understood he'd be watching them die, and that's when he felt he must owe each of them a little something for their dying. Any obligation was strange to the cheat, but they were leaving now, and it had fallen to him to watch them go. They lay face to face, not two feet apart, and he could see that they wished to speak to each other, their eyes were full of that intention, but their mouths could shape only gurgling blood and pink bubbles. Nat, for once in his life, was not dying, and he felt he owed these men something for it, and he wished he might translate for them so that at least they could tell each other whatever needed to be said. But what could that possibly be?